# THROUGH THE LOOKING-GLASS ... DARKLY

As we approached the turnoff for Wonderland, I had the oddest sensation in my head, unlike anything I could remember. It was—*alien*. It wasn't scary, it was just absolutely indescribable. Riki gasped, obviously sharing the sensation, but said nothing. It seemed to be coming from more than one source.

I pulled off the road and into the parking lot of a Dunkin' Donuts, and at that very moment I had a vision. Not a dream, since I was wide awake, but a vision as clear as day. Riki saw it, too, and her jaw dropped.

There were shapes like men in armor, standing in formation behind my old boss Walt. In front of them was a terrified farm family—two men, three women, and a bunch of children. Good old Walt. Kindly Walt, my old partner and someone I thought I knew as well as anyone in the world.

And right there in the donut-shop parking lot, good old Walt took out a semiautomatic rifle of some kind and blew them all away without a trace of emotion, not even when he hit the children ...

By Jack L. Chalker
*Published by Ballantine Books*

AND THE DEVIL WILL DRAG YOU UNDER
DANCE BAND ON THE TITANIC
DANCERS IN THE AFTERGLOW
A JUNGLE OF STARS
THE WEB OF THE CHOZEN

THE SAGA OF THE WELL WORLD
Volume 1: *Midnight at the Well of Souls*
Volume 2: *Exiles at the Well of Souls*
Volume 3: *Quest for the Well of Souls*
Volume 4: *The Return of Nathan Brazil*
Volume 5: *Twilight at the Well of Souls: The Legacy of Nathan Brazil*

THE FOUR LORDS OF THE DIAMOND
Book One: *Lilith: A Snake in the Grass*
Book Two: *Cerberus: A Wolf in the Fold*
Book Three: *Charon: A Dragon at the Gate*
Book Four: *Medusa: A Tiger by the Tail*

THE DANCING GODS
Book One: *The River of the Dancing Gods*
Book Two: *Demons of the Dancing Gods*
Book Three: *Vengeance of the Dancing Gods*
Book Four: *Songs of the Dancing Gods*

THE RINGS OF THE MASTER
Book One: *Lords of the Middle Dark*
Book Two: *Pirates of the Thunder*
Book Three: *Warriors of the Storm*
Book Four: *Masks of the Martyrs*

THE WATCHERS AT THE WELL
Book One: *Echoes of the Well of Souls*
Book Two: *Shadow of the Well of Souls*
Book Three: *Gods of the Well of Souls*

THE WONDERLAND GAMBIT
Book One: *The Cybernetic Walrus*

# THE CYBERNETIC WALRUS

BOOK ONE

OF

THE WONDERLAND GAMBIT

JACK CHALKER

A DEL REY® BOOK
BALLANTINE BOOKS • NEW YORK

*A Del Rey® Book*
*Published by Ballantine Books*

*Copyright © 1995 by Jack L. Chalker*

*All rights reserved*
*under International and Pan-American Copyright Conventions.*
*Published in the United States by Ballantine Books,*
*a division of Random House, Inc., New York,*
*and simultaneously in Canada*
*by Random House of Canada Limited, Toronto.*

*Library of Congress Catalog Card Number: 95-094843*

*ISBN: 0-345-38690-6*

*Text design by Ruth Kolbert*
*Cover design by Kayley LeFaiver*
*Cover art by Paul Youll*

*Manufactured in the United States of America*

*First Edition: November 1995*

*10  9  8  7  6  5  4  3  2  1*

*To the late Philip K. Dick,*
*two of whose early works inspired this madness,*
*but didn't, to my mind,*
*face all the implications of the concept*
*in any of them.*

# AN INTRODUCTION
# AND EXPLANATION

This book and two others to follow will make up the saga known as *The Wonderland Gambit*. Unlike most of my books, the very nature of this allows people to read this book and get some resolution, although all the questions and a lot of the real fun is yet to come.

I've come across discussions on such diverse platforms as conventions, fanzines, and the Internet where people argue whether I write fantasy novels or science-fiction novels. Most people think I write predominantly fantasy, and in this they are wrong. What I do not write are *engineering* stories—hey, gang, let's build a space station! Hey, let's terraform Mars! Those are all well and good, and some folks do them well, but they are very much in the tradition of *Astounding* in the Campbell era, a magazine I am not going to ever denigrate but which, I think, told as many variations of engineering stories as I ever want to read.

Those kind of stories also pretend that they are predictive. Ah, yes—I well remember George O. Smith's one-hundred-foot-tall vacuum tubes, the giant state-sized computers, the total lack of portable computers and desktop power (you'd think at least one writer would have predicted the word processor, wouldn't you?). Stories with such wondrous vision—why, once we put a man on the moon, there will be space stations in ten years and moon colonies in twenty and missions to Mars and beyond! Uh-huh.

My late father was born two months before the Wright brothers flew their first plane at Kitty Hawk. He died twenty years after the last man walked on the moon, the last one that's likely to walk on the moon or beyond in my lifetime. I pray not in my children's lifetimes, but we are a world and a nation who seem to have lost our dreams and are spiritually dying for it. We can see that in the current generation (they hate the label "Generation X" but "war babies" and "baby boomers" hated their labels, too). It's not a dumb generation, it's not a generation wrapped up in fantasy like the late sixties, it's not "lost" like the generation of the twenties. It's just one without faith in institutions and an unshakable belief that things are going to get worse.

These are the folks who read cyberpunk; it's the boomers who read the engineering stories and dreamed of terraforming Mars.

Me, I look in different places. I look in books and articles on the "new physics," in arcane studies in biology, chemistry, and other subjects, and I keep bumping up against visions of the future that are often not terribly nice but hard to ignore. It doesn't matter if some of my readers think it's far-out fantasy (or some psychological hangup); nothing pleases somebody in my business more than getting equal fan letters from those who like epic adventures or complex sociopolitical works and from university physics and mathematics departments and the like. The only downer is increasing evidence as I get older that my own playing around with the human mind and form seem increasingly more likely than terraforming Mars.

And now I come to computers. Not today's, of course, or maybe not tomorrow's, but for all the wonders of cyberspace it still looks like cyberspace. Why should it? How good can it *really* get? Those who have run into me online know that I'm not a novice in this area and that I got my Junior Pournelle Merit Badge long ago. Nothing at the *heart* of the premise here isn't being discussed and worked on right now. I think you should worry a little about it.

The basics come from a lesser-known and minor book by Philip K. Dick that I read probably thirty or more years ago and which had been written a decade before that. I've always felt an affinity for Phil Dick; after the four millionth question of "Why do you always do all that body switching?" I used to get upset and scream "Did hordes of people ever ask Phil Dick when he was going to stop writing 'What is reality' stories?" Well, I only knew Dick slightly, but I happened to mouth off this question at an SF convention within earshot of a number of people who'd known him well.

It turns out, yeah, they did.

Well, writers write certain kinds of tales. We're best when doing so. It's nice there are so many to choose from. Comfortable and basically optimistic old-fashioned SF of the terraforming-Mars variety is still being written, and if you're of the "future is bleak" school we have cyberpunk as popularized by Max Headroom and perfected by William Gibson, and everything in between. I *do* write nontransformation tales, but while all these people who are made uneasy by what I do to folks say they want them, they don't buy them.

Which brings us to the current project. Please be warned that absolutely *everything* is up for revision in *The Wonderland Gambit*, and I do mean *everything*. By the time we're through, I hope we'll make some people think, others will be offended, and we'll be going places like we've never been before. Not in *this* book, though. This book simply establishes the premise, gives the background and some of our very large cast, murders a few people (but not necessarily permanently), screws around with identity and ego, contains a hookah-smoking caterpillar, a pipe-smoking dodo, an all-female biker gang and drug cartel, a cigar-smoking Native American woman who says she goes into a parallel universe via the trees, the Roswell saucer, at least two possibly alien races, a *little* antigovernment paranoia, a bunch of two-faced villains, and a lot of mind control.

We won't get complicated until the next book.

Jack L. Chalker
Uniontown, Maryland
Summer, 1994

# PROLOGUE

# RABBIT HOLE NUMBER SIX

*I wonder how many of us would still have gotten into the god business if we'd read the fine print and studied the job description more carefully?*

*I once knew somebody who said that the only rational definition of insanity was when you saw a different world run by different rules than anyone else, and that your alternate reality, whether pretty or ugly, good or evil, was therefore false because it was yours alone. When most everyone else saw the same things you saw, felt the same things you felt, and believed what you believed, then the one who didn't was the insane one.*

*It was a scary, and eerily prophetic, definition of reality.*

A sudden brilliant yellow-white light exploded into a hundred tiny beams, spreading out as they headed straight for me. I was ready for it; I ducked, rolled, and went down one level on the grid, coming up and firing back at the point of light as close to its firing at me as I could. Neither of us scored a hit, but I could see mine strike a bar and flare up, momentarily illuminating the area in a dull orange glow and revealing the three dark figures that were moving, almost like monkeys, along the grid.

They had the advantage of field of fire with those wide-spread needlers that were absorbed by inert matter and fried only living flesh. No afterglow. My single needler wouldn't get more than one of them, and maybe not kill even that one, but it sure showed me the targets. I fired four shots in rapid succession and jumped back up to the higher level where I'd just been.

I heard a scream that seemed to go down and down until it finally got swallowed up in some infinite pit below. There was no faking that sort of thing convincingly; at least one of them had bought it. I hoped it was enough to take him completely out, but deep down I knew that I'd see these bastards yet again. This wasn't like in the Worlds; the rabbit holes were less permanent if no less painful or difficult.

At least these forms were made for the holes. Perfect mobility in all sectors, a full three-sixty ability, balance like a cat or monkey—too bad *they* had exactly the same capabilities!

> *Or would you like to swing on a star . . . ?*

Oh, lord! No! Get *that* out of my head. All I needed was to wake up as some singing priest in a bad Hollywood version of forties Chicago!

Not that it would be that simple. Not now. Not after all these transitions. They were getting harder, more sophisticated, and more alien each time. I bet I wasn't the only one who thought we were a pretty sick bunch.

> *Oh, where have you been, Ragle Gumm? Ragle Gumm?*
> *Oh, where have you been, Darlin' Ragle?*

Down two levels and to the left a bit. I knew somebody was there, but I also figured that they'd split up: the one I didn't take would zero in on my flash. Damn! What the hell did the others owe Stark, anyway, or whoever or whatever he or she or it was, this incarnation? Might attracted the weak and disaffected, I suppose. It didn't take much effort for the True Believer types to latch onto some extreme. Stark certainly offered that, a sense of strength and dedication to purpose. He was nuttier than a fruitcake, of course, but what did *that* matter?

If we only knew whether or not the universes kept on after we all got booted out of them! On the other hand, which one of us dared go back and find out, and leave the Ahead to the others? You'd never catch up, not if time had any correlation at all between inside and out.

I listened closely, trying to make out movement or breathing in the dark, and within a minute or two had the one I'd spotted before, a darker shadow against the overall blackness, still not too far below me. The other one—I was certain it would be dear Al—was completely still, somewhere out ahead and probably a little above, waiting.

I wasn't about to wait forever. Two against one was still two against one, and I had no more hope that added enemies wouldn't show up than I had hope that a horde of friends and allies would also appear. It was possible—hell, *anything* was possible, and at no time in creation had that been a truer statement than now—but not bloody likely.

But if I could move over, very slowly, very quietly, ever closer, closer, bit by bit, to that one near me, I might have a chance to even things up. Of course, if this one was Al Stark, then I was dead meat, but somehow I just couldn't see him being this noisy or making himself this clear a target when it would benefit somebody else.

The problem in this particular hole was that we had only the rafters, a sort of glorified jungle gym going in all directions for probably infinite distance. The weapons were ones that we picked up along the way. No real illumination. By this point, however, I'd been able to pretty roughly calculate the distance between bars and levels and had found a nice little arithmatic progression. At this point, I was maybe one and a half meters from the next one in back of me and about two meters down. This distance would open a bit if I got closer to the target below me, but there was one "rail" that would stay almost perfectly parallel to the bar one below me. Moving down to that bar, then back to the next one behind me, was tricky without making noise, but I'd been in here long enough now that I had it pretty well down—or so I hoped.

Not so the target, who was clearly getting impatient and nervous, which was just where I wanted him to be. Now I needed to ease over, carefully, very carefully, until. . . . Yeah. One up from the target and so close I could hear the breathing and almost smell bad breath. Now the trick was to twist my body so that both feet and my left hand were steady on the rails but my gun hand could go down, right behind the target, just so. . . .

I fired up and to the right, getting a brief glimpse of a dark figure three levels up from me. He, however, had only a bright flash and he was ready, firing a full-spread volley right at the source of that flash.

The poor target, around whom I'd shot, never even had a chance to react, still turning toward me and raising his or her own pistol to fire when the partner, the stalker above, raked through the target body with all those little finely focused beams.

The target cried out—a woman's voice!—as her body was almost split in two, and she tumbled and fell down, down into the endless oblivion below.

I, on the other hand, was wasting no time at all, heading across on the parallel beam toward the shooter but away from the former target, not as concerned about noise now as taking advantage of the accidental kill.

"That's got to be you, Cory," the shooter commented, the voice eerie and somewhat electronic-sounding, yet damped, with no echo. If this hole had walls they were much too far away to interact with us. "You and your video games again, I suspect."

He was trying to entice me into firing, giving me in effect a free shot so that I would betray my position. No go, Stark. Not this time.

"I'll win, you know. In the end," he taunted, the cold and unpleasant natural intonations of the Al Stark voice coming through even the strange distortion of the hole environment. "You're better at playing this, but I'm better at doing this for real," he continued. "It's different when it's for real, even if, inside here, we know we won't *really* die. There's always that hesitation, that unwillingness to bet it all, that you've inherited from your own background. I cured it in myself. It was a weakness I could not afford. I cured it not only *here*, but long before I ever knew that there *was* a 'here.' Come on—take a shot. I'll take one, if you like. I'm not trying to hide from you, because I know how little difference it makes. Are we in fact the first? The tenth? The twentieth? Do we know? Do you care? I don't. I exist until I control again. That's not difficult."

I could see a spot in the darkness where I knew he must be, but the odds of me actually taking this looney out were no more than fifty-fifty, if even that with the single-beam pistol, while his wide needler had much better odds. I needed to get a *lot* closer to him before I could take him on with confidence.

"That was a nice move back there," Stark commented, sounding like he really meant it. "Very neat. You've been improving consistently, I must admit. You know, this is getting kind of boring, though. Why not just have it out and then translate to the next plane?" He began to walk along the rail, but I began to detect a worried tone in his voice that hadn't been there before.

"Cory? You *are* still here, I presume? Not trying to make a hasty exit below, I trust?" He listened a moment, then relaxed. "No, you wouldn't. It isn't like you. Hmmm. . . . Let me see. . . . Considering how much you've improved at this sort of thing, what would you be doing right now? Too far from me to be sure, and you want a sure shot, don't you? That trick won't work twice. Over two meters below me here, so that's inconvenient for grabbing. That means you'll try it on my beam, or on the beam above."

*Wrong, you fascist bastard! Right behind you!* I lunged forward, striking his back with enough force to knock him over. The rail widened in an instant, and I was upon him without even thinking about it. I had forgotten just how strong he was, but I was too mad to care at this point. I wanted him, wanted him dead and out of there. Even more, I wanted him dead for real, but that didn't seem to be possible in the rabbit holes. Only pain was possible, and lots of it.

He twisted around, and his knee caught me in the groin. The blow wasn't as effective as it should have been, all things considered, but it still hurt and had considerable power behind it, making me slacken my own grip on him. He used this to twist in one neat motion, turning to face me while also bringing up his needler. I couldn't see it but I could feel the twist and knew what he held in his hand. I saw no choice but to kick away and hope I hit the arm with the gun.

Instead, I kicked hard into empty air and lost my grips, my legs shooting out from under me and my ass landing right on his face.

The moment he realized what had happened, he bit it.

I slid back quickly onto his chest, and he surprised me by managing to actually sit up, while bringing up his legs to catch me in a kind of wrestling hold. I clamped my legs around him and held on, bringing up my own pistol and shoving it into his face.

He froze, then sighed.

"We're going over together, Stark," I told him. "You and me into the void."

He chuckled. "I'm almost tempted, but not in these circumstances. That's the difference between you and me, Cory. You have to win every time. I'm patient. I can wait until the perfect situation comes along. I bounce back quicker than most, you know. See you in the next Hell, sucker!"

Before I could do anything, he dropped back on his back and one hand came up, grabbed my gun hand, and deliberately pressed the trigger stud which was still aimed at his head. There was a flash of light, and what it showed, I would have preferred not to see.

I felt his body convulse, and I backed off him, having no doubts that he was dead. Although I should have felt triumphant, the fact was that I felt sick and depressed instead. Not only at the thought of yet another round, another Land, but also understanding full well that Al Stark had been right: there was no way I'd have the nerve to do what he did, even here. "The cowardly dictator" was a cliché; some Nazis had real guts.

So far the pattern had held true. We'd tended to come out in each Land as at least social counterparts of what had gone in, whatever that was at this stage. That meant that we'd meet again, and if one of us spotted the other first, *there*, out in the "open" as it were, then for one of us this might well be the end. At least if the Land was one of our own; God could not be denied, even subconsciously.

Then, again, it would help to know just how many others were actually along for this ride with us. I knew of seven so far, including Stark and myself, but at least one Land hadn't fitted any of the obvious rules. How big a playing field we were actually on, how many "real" people there actually were in this, there was no way of saying. How could we know, when we didn't really know about our own selves? Were we who and what we thought, or did we echo one of the Lands? Were we instead something else entirely, some sleeping dreamers of unknown alien origins? All the data of the Lands had to come from *somewhere*; if it came from any of us directly, it came at least partially from experience even if long forgotten. If it came from programs, even algorithms, somebody or something had to get that information down to that incredible detail and put it all in. Somewhere out there was a strong reality, where things were always just so and we were "real" as well. How did we get what we needed while our consciousnesses were elsewhere? Who fed us, turned us, cleaned us, cared for us? Or was it all automated?

The worst part was, I'd never been certain we'd recognize it if we saw it. Any of us. What *was* reality, anyway? Something firm and concrete? Hadn't we all once lived in a personal reality we believed was just that? Was reality what the senses brought you? Hell, even in my last static persona we'd gone a good deal beyond that, to fooling the eye, the ear, the nose, all the senses. A simple flight simulator could convince you that you were plummeting ten stories to the ground when you were really falling only a few meters. Even a giant wrap-around screen that filled the field of vision could give your sense of balance a run for its money. Cinerama, IMAX, those kind of things had been designed on exactly that principle. Then there were virtual-reality helmets and gloves, and—but, of course, that's jumping ahead of and around the story.

I had to make this maze, traveling down, and see if I made it before anybody else. If I did, maybe, just maybe, I could end this thing if I could face my own mental quirks and demons. Maybe.

There had to be an ending, just like, sometime long ago, there had to be a beginning. Or was it long ago? Wasn't time in many ways a sense as well? Was all this happening in the blink of an eye? My God—

*Down and down I go, 'round and 'round I go. . . .*

I still had to be carefu!. I hadn't kept track of all of them, of course, and it was more than possible that some got past me.

There was a sudden, inhuman screech below and just ahead of me, and I began to smell a dank, dead flesh odor that grew more and more powerful.

There were Snarks down there ahead of me, too. There were always Snarks. That was why I might still be first in this new branch. These sounded furry, vicious, and full of rending teeth. I couldn't tell their number.

Beyond them could be Boojums and even an ambush. I might still not make it. Probably wouldn't, although at least I knew this time Stark wouldn't have any more advantage over me if they *did* kill me. Not in the next incarnation.

I took some deep breaths, checked my weapons, and went forward. I was a god, not an oyster, and, like all gods, I, too, was insane.

# I

# THE
# CATERPILLAR'S QUESTION

I don't know what single factor had concentrated so much of the computer industry in Washington State, but most of the time I was glad of it. Winters could be a little unpleasant, but they were never grim, at least on the western side of the mountains where I lived, and while you could see the deep snow on the Cascades to the east and the Olympics to the west and particularly on the vision of Mount Rainier that always hovered like some strange home of the gods over the southeastern sky, it was usually above freezing in Seattle and the towns along Puget Sound to the north up beyond Anacortes.

As somebody who'd been born and raised in the northeast, I always got a kick out of Seattle-area people when it *did* snow or ice over just a bit. They hunkered down and bunkered down as if it were some horror like the winters of Duluth or Nome and waited it out, rarely venturing outside the confines of their metro area until it melted in a day or two and always driving through that one to two inches of slush as if it were forty feet of quicksand.

I'd been in the area about ten years, and if I hadn't quite

achieved my ambition to live on a luxurious houseboat moored in the lakes or canals like the rich yuppies did, I nonetheless had a pretty large house on a decent lot over-looking an arm of the sound over on the Bremerton side, and I was one of those contented commuters who went down to the ferry in the morning, read the paper and ate breakfast while it slowly crossed to the city, then hopped a trackless trolley north to my old offices. They had once put "super fer-ries" on the run, reducing the crossing from an hour to only thirty-five minutes, but we'd boycotted and protested and marched until we got those monsters slowed down to the old schedule. You couldn't have breakfast and read even the lead-ing stories in the paper in a mere thirty-five minutes!

I was a whiz kid in my grad-school days, sought by all sorts. I was recruited by IBM and DEC, all the biggies, but I always felt that I wasn't cut out to work for one of those big monoliths. Nice companies, decent security and benefits, but suit-and-tie types all the way; bureaucracies so big that it was said that had the companies been oil tankers they couldn't have turned in the middle of the ocean without going aground waiting for all the captains to make up their minds and sign off on the idea. Even Apple seemed to be losing its old image and going corporate then. No, I wanted in on a ground-floor operation, find and perfect some suite of utilities or some neat program that would knock their socks off and eventually cause one of the big boys to buy me out for a few million, af-ter which I'd build my dream house, put in my dream com-puter, and spend my days doing nothing in particular unless I wanted to. I think they called it being an "independent consultant."

I even got a job offer from the NSA and that had really surprised me. I mean, the National Security Agency had only been admitting it existed at all for maybe a couple of years back then, although anybody who was in any way involved in computers knew all about them. It was the most super-secret electronic spy agency the government had, or at least if there was one even more secret, then it was *really* good. You had to have super security clearances to even be looked at by them, and it'd be years before you got cleared enough to get where you really wanted to be. Also, the money was the usual GS government grade stuff, hardly what anybody good enough for them to want would consider a decent wage.

That said, you might wonder why in hell anybody would want to go to work for them. The answer is simple: they had a "black" budget, a budget that was totally buried in everybody else's budget so nobody could tell how big it was, and it was never itemized. That meant they spent like drunken sailors on R&D, and that meant that they ran, developed, created, and subsidized the greatest, fastest supercomputers in the known universe. They were almost certainly years, maybe decades, beyond where anybody else was, and everybody in the commercial sector knew that they were playing with years-old NSA technological hand-me-downs.

It was said that by the early eighties they had achieved the Ultimate Paranoia—they could intercept and decrypt literally any message sent electrically anywhere in the world and they did. Think if it: every phone call, every digital transmission, satellite transmission, radio, TV, all bands, all waves, you name it. Countless billions and billions of them every day, any day, constantly coming in and constantly growing.

Of course, you already see what happened, right? Big Brother had all the answers George Orwell never dreamed of, but it never could figure out the questions. The government was drowning in an unstoppable and monstrous tidal wave of information that never ended and it *still* needed ESP to find anything. A sort of infinite, quantum version of my own office. That was why *I* had computers, even though they were a lot smaller and fit on desks. The computers were the only places I could stick information and actually *find* it again.

Provided, of course, I could wade through the junk and find the computer. I knew there were three or four in my office at any one time, but I never was able to find more than two at a particular moment. The junk just kept piling up, and after we got that wireless LAN. . . .

Okay, okay, enough shop talk. It doesn't matter anyway, particularly not now. In fact, it seems lifetimes ago, but it still forms a part of what I've come to think of as my "core" self, and that's all the reality I've really got left to hang onto.

Anyway, I went with this little startup in Seattle because I liked the area, liked the culture and the scenery. It was also a damned sight cheaper and cleaner than Silicon Valley, didn't make me feel like I was undressed in somebody else's church like central Utah, didn't have New England winters or south Florida's crime rate, and wasn't the government.

We'd gone into a cooperative venture with a Canadian company to develop a really good, solid, fast wireless LAN and it was beginning to look like it was going to pay off. A LAN is a local area network, which is simply a fancy way of saying you want to string a bunch of small computers together to make one big one from which any data you want on any of them can be retrieved by any machine, just like mainframes. Networks were the big thing, of course, but running those miles of fiber-optic wires, installing hubs, drilling through walls or putting in movable panels just to shift machines, was a pain for small businesses. There'd been a lot of wireless schemes out there, but they tended to be too slow, too restrictive, or too liable to get garbled to bet your business on them, and it seemed like every time you licked one problem it raised the problems in the other areas. Kind of like the old arcade game of Whack A Mole—every time you hit one of the critters on the head with a mallet another one popped up somewhere else.

Not that we weren't selling product—our Canadian subsidiary was doing well putting LANs into local and provincial government operations, and we'd done several major corporate installations in Washington, Idaho, and Oregon, but not a lot further than that. The problem was that we were too small and in too competitive an area to get the big-buck investors that would allow us to put a trained sales force all over North America and really push this system. We had a few thousand individual customers but not the big score. In fact, a lot of folks just hadn't heard of us in spite of our becoming a corporation with more than forty million coming in.

Alas, all that wasn't profit. In fact, most of it went to pay off old expenses and loans and to keep manufacturing going. It was a sober lesson in capitalism for somebody who'd slept through those classes in college. Gross versus net. It was frustrating. Here we had the best product on the damned market and we couldn't get the word out!

Walt Slidecker, the man who'd recruited me, was one hell of an organizer, but he seemed to lack that supersalesman's spark you saw in a Bill Gates or Steve Jobs or any highly successful business head. When I'd first met him, a few years back, he was only trying to build this business while running a Netware installation and consultancy business, and I remember he had this big sign in back of his desk then that I always thought said it all about a service business:

QUALITY! SERVICE! PRICE!
PICK ANY TWO.

Honest words to live by, but not necessarily words to sell with.

At any rate, it was in mid-spring, when nobody wants to do anything but go home and enjoy or maybe just sleep in, when Walt called me into his office.

"Cory, I'm afraid we got cash problems, period," he told me, knowing it wasn't exactly news. The next was, though.

"Sangkung has made an offer for our patents, stock, and copyrights," he continued. "All debts covered, an infusion of fifty million in capital, and the guaranteed retention of our programming staff for at least one year. Sales gets a comfortable separation. *Very* comfortable on my personal end—five million cash and no restrictions on the future except that I'll do no work in networking for five years after they buy. All manufacturing, of course, moves east. Thailand, I think."

Even though I'd been afraid of it, had been waiting for it, I still felt shock. "Walt, you can't do it! You know what that offer really means. They get all the creative stuff forever, send me their bright boys to explain the system and to Rob to learn the communications clearances and legal stuff, and then it's bye-bye everything but a storefront."

He nodded. "I know, but there doesn't seem to be much choice here. The last gasp would be to land a really good GSA-type contract but that means hiring a Beltway Bandit back east and really putting resources and money into sales. We fail at that and they won't have to guarantee us anything or pay us a dime—we'd be flat broke and picked up at auction. And several folks like Sangkung who do work with the feds even now will find it very much in their interest to keep us from being a success. You see where this puts me? Rock, meet hard place."

I could sympathize with him and even see the logic of it, but emotionally I just couldn't accept this. "Damn it! I mean, I've always thought of myself as liberal and all that, but a country that exports its raw materials and even its ideas and patents and imports tons of finished goods is a third-world and soon third-rate country."

"You know the hardware comes from a half-dozen Asian countries and is assembled in Mexico for sale in the U.S. and Canada," Walt pointed out not without justification. "Hell, all *we* do is make the software disks and seal them in the envelopes and do the alpha, beta, and general bug testing. The most American-made thing in this company is the manual."

"Yeah, yeah, but that's not the point. The business is *ours*. Right now, *we* created it and *we* control it. After this, it'll be *theirs* and it won't come back."

"Would it make you feel better if the same offer had come from New York? Or Québec city? Or maybe London?"

"No, no, you know what I mean."

He paused for a moment, letting me calm down, then said, "I think I do, yes. But, Cory, it's not *ours*. *We* don't control it. It's *mine*. I admit it's mine mostly because we had to cancel the stock offering after the terms looked like they would kill us, but it's still mine. I have half. You have ten percent. I realize that programming can sometimes cause weird things to happen to the basic abilities, but surely you can still figure out that if you could get every living soul with a share you'd only tie. No, Cory, I'm sorry, but the ball's entirely in my court. Always has been."

I breathed hard. "I see. Sounds like you're not telling me about an offer but about something already decided."

"No, not yet, but I've been running things through the accounting people and it keeps coming up the same or worse."

I looked at him. "What could possibly be worse?"

"*Much* worse. At least two offers came in bigger than this one, and both of *them* were pretty much domestic—at least, as domestic as *we* are. Want to guess from who?"

I didn't have to. Which domestic companies with stakes in local area networks would love to buy us and just put us out of business because our product was eating into their inferior but far more profitable competitive products? Betamax was always the superior format in every way, but VHS had won the marketing war.

I wasn't quite ready to accept it, though. "Damn it, Walt, the whole idea of this sort of thing, the idea behind our whole damned culture, is that if you build a better mousetrap you make a million bucks. Well, we *did* that. The Subspace LAN is the best damned technology on the market! *Years*, maybe two or three, beyond anything the competition has. And while we aren't setting the world on fire yet, it's in sight! Broaden the market, get a few Fortune 1000 companies and government installations, and we'll bring costs down and eat the rest alive! And now you're telling me that we've got to sell out? For *peanuts*?"

He shrugged. "As much money seems to be coming in, the

bottom line, the net after all else, is pretty puny," he reminded me. "One good nuisance lawsuit and we're dead meat. Grow up, Cory. It's never been that *Young Tom Edison* crap Hollywood sells us. Or, at least, it very rarely has. They sued Bell almost to ruin to steal the telephone from him, and he won as much from sheer luck and a fluke as anything. Edison invented a bunch of handy things that didn't seem like much but built up a big nest egg so he was almost unassailable. Then Bell and Edison could go around suing other small inventors, right? I mean, there's nothing in the Apple Macintosh that didn't come out of Xerox's Palo Alto Research Center in the early to mid seventies. Poor old Xerox. Let the copier market get away, never thought that the laser printer was a consumer item—brightest R&D and dumbest sales staff in the world. So what happens when somebody else clones the Mac? Apple sues, of course. Company founded by two guys who put in their own autobiographies how they came up with a black box to cheat the phone company that now sues somebody who puts a little trash can on their computer desktop. You tell me what's right. You find me those Fortune 1000 customers. You find me some government contracts in the next thirty days, and I'm with you all the way. I'll even increase your stake in the company and give you a better percentage. Hey—you think I *want* to do this? I *started* this, remember? I recruited you and most of the others here. We all worked like hell and we made something here. Now we've hit the wall."

I sighed and got up to leave. "I know, I know. Well, I'll look around and see what's what."

"Where are you going?"

"Out. Home, maybe. I've got some time coming, and there's no tomorrow, so fire me." And, with that, I left his office.

I knew I wasn't being fair to him, that this probably hurt him as much as it did me, although his millions would ease the pain and my ten percent of what was left after the settlement would maybe pay the mortgage and food bills for the year if I ate sparingly. I knew the kind of accounting these things went through and who wound up with the pie.

Rob Garnett, our sales manager, saw me heading out and came out of his own office to intercept me. I knew the Sangkung people and so did he; those fresh-faced suit-and-tie conservative businessmen from the New Asia wouldn't waste ten seconds laying off the co-chair of Seattle's Gay Pride Parade. Rob's sexual orientation had never given any of the rest of us a second thought, but those boys were famous for "image," and if they closed down the whole place who could scream discrimination?

Rob wasn't a born salesman, either, but he was a schmoozer, the kind of guy who could sit around a bar just talking to people and wind up with all of them picking up his tab, never quite figuring out why they did it. He was just a likable sort, and not one of those up-front queens. He was just another businessman facing middle age who'd just slipped on a rug he hadn't known was there. Still, in a bigger setting with better capital and a larger sales force he might do wonders. He'd actually been headhunted by Novell, the big boy in networks, but he'd turned it down because it meant moving to Utah. He was quite comfortable most places but somehow he didn't think there was a closet big enough for him in Utah; life was too short. That's not to knock Utah or its people or its religion, but, face it, if Utah were a tuxedo Rob would be a pair of brown shoes.

"You just got the word, I take it?" he asked me.

I nodded. "Guess it's time to check the want ads and the Good Old Boys, huh?"

He shrugged. "I smelled it. Smelled it the moment the patent passed muster. We came up with something everybody wanted and we couldn't exploit. It doesn't take a genius to figure out we were a target. I just thought it would take a little longer. I *still* think Walt's paranoid with this lawsuit business; he should give 'em a few months, let us take a whack at Uncle Sam or maybe an OEM deal with HP or Compaq, get the price up real good and make it essential we get jobs or big payoffs. I wouldn't mind so much if I got a big settlement and could loaf, or was younger and could pick up an equal or better position, but this is just the pits."

"Yeah, well, I'm going home to open a beer or three and contemplate the sunset," I told him. "Anybody runs into a software problem or starts getting Voice of America broadcasts on their LANs, tell 'em to see Sangkung."

"You gonna stay on with 'em? They'll get rid of *me* pretty fast for several reasons, including the fact that they hardly need a sales force, but they'll need somebody to teach their clever programmers the ins and outs of that code. It's a company patent, but most of it has your name all over it."

"I don't know," I told him honestly. "Not enough contemplating yet. They want to come up with maybe a quarter mill for my services as teacher, adviser, consultant, and guru, fine. Not at what they're paying me now, though, and even at that price only until I can get something better." I looked around. "Hey, I'm gonna get and fast, Rob, before everybody else in the company comes up and we have this depressing conversation a hundred more times. You may as well, too."

He shook his head. "No, I'm staying until the ink's on the paper. I've got a lead on a Beltway Bandit back east and he's got a couple of folks on a very nice hook, including the Defense Department."

"I thought we weren't doing military, period. That was from the start," I reminded him. Jeez, we were left-wing nuts sometimes. No wonder the generation behind us was so far to the right!

"Cory, a solid, secure wireless system that's so portable it can be fitted into any computer and compact enough so that data enough for an army can be carried in a suitcase—that's our SS-220A. We're talking about selling *thousands* of units to the customer who never asks about costs. Are you gonna say we don't sell there when we can and maybe save the company? Go down on principle, then Sangkung comes in, picks it up, and wholesales it to everybody from our own military to the Iraqis, Libyans, Colombian drug cartels, you name it." He paused a moment and eyed me steadily. "We're too old for this, Cory. *Hair* is a bore."

I shrugged. "Do what you have to, Rob. I'm going home." And, with that, I left him there, heading down to the street and crossing to the bus stop to take me down to the ferry terminal.

The fact was, I was just paying lip service to the old principles anyway and I knew it. I hadn't had a political thought as such in years, I drove a Porsche, actually owned a handgun—"for protection," of course—and last time I voted Republican. It was just ... well, so much of my youth and ideals had gone without a whimper, without me even noticing, it was next to impossible to drop this one without at least a token protest.

I needed something stronger than coffee but didn't really feel like a lot of company, so I settled for some brew anyway, bought at the ferry's cafeteria, and wandered out onto the deck. It was a nice afternoon, weather-wise at least, and while you needed a coat, the stiff winds that blew into you on deck much of the time were almost absent or at least comfortably bearable. As we left the skyline of Seattle, I took a look at it almost as if I'd never seen it before. We don't generally look at where we live in the same way as a visitor might, for all that we love the place. The New Yorker who's been to the top of the Empire State Building is still looked upon with awe and wonder; so is the San Franciscan who wouldn't ride a cable car on a bet because it's so full of tourists. It's another thing when that comfortable familiarity is suddenly jerked out from under you, and the feeling of security shatters.

The truth was, I had a ton of debts, a massive mortgage, and I'd saved almost nothing. I could probably cover things with what I'd get from the sale of the company for many months, maybe up to a year, but I doubted if I could really cover everything I owed down the line. Plenty of time to get another job, but not one as comfortable a fit as this one, and almost certainly not in this neighborhood. In fact, it would be a lot tougher than most people would think, since my expertise was in networks, and if I took a job with a networking company, Sangkung would almost certainly sue me and the new employer for trade-secret violations, whether I committed any or not. They weren't the only ones well known for doing just that, and they had their big-shot lawyers on fat retainers so the cost wasn't through the roof for them to do it. If I went to work for a big fish, that wouldn't be a major deal, but I just couldn't see myself in that kind of environment, no matter how good the company really was. It just wasn't my style.

Looking over the waterfront from the Space Needle north, I felt almost like I was looking at an old lover for the last time, one where the romance had just faded but not the memories.

I guess that's why I hadn't noticed her, although she was eminently noticeable. She was on the opposite side, sort of looking at the sights, but also, I had the strangest feeling, looking at me. Why I'd think that, I didn't know. I mean, I was the average egomaniac in my comfortable areas—I basked in the *genius* label and I also thought I was a decent sort of guy and a good conversationalist, but I never fancied myself as the kind of man a woman who looked like *that* would be attracted to on sight. Forty-four, going bald and gray all at once, with a potbelly that indicated more sitting than exercising, I wasn't exactly what I would think of as a prime catch. The same couldn't be said for *her*, though.

She was maybe in her twenties, although which end it was impossible to say. She had a face out of an old Bardot movie, figure courtesy of *Playboy* centerfolds, strawberry blond hair in a kind of short Tinker Bell cut that went great with that face and form, all dressed in designer jeans that had to be sprayed on, high-top brown leather boots, fancy sweater about a size too small, and a fake silver fur wrap. I had to imagine the big eyes in back of the designer shades, but what I saw was more than enough. To say that she was the object of everybody else's glance within range would be understating it; to say that she obviously enjoyed it might be equally true. In fact, the only turnoff about her was that she was smoking a rather fat cigar, standing just inside the windbreak on the back next to the remaining ash tray aboard these vessels. On the other hand, the way she handled that cigar was suggestive enough that no man would have even bothered to run out for mouthwash.

Rather incredibly, she seemed to be by herself, although she might just have stepped out to have that cigar and have someone waiting inside. Still, no, nobody *I* knew would leave her alone in wolf country.

Okay, I admit it, I was tempted to go over and introduce myself to her, but I also had a sense of reality about me and no desire to suddenly confront her boyfriend if such a person existed. He might not, but he somehow would materialize fully formed, I knew, if I made any moves in her direction.

Still, we made some sort of eye contact, as it were, the kind you feel rather than see, and then she smiled at me behind her dark glasses and turned and walked back around the corner of the boat. I looked back in the glass to see if and when she came in, but she didn't, so I slowly walked over to her side and looked down the full length of the rail toward the current bow of the double-ender.

She wasn't there.

Probably just went inside further on, I told myself, and went back inside. The chill and the massed smoke from the desperate few smokers around was getting to me.

When we pulled in at Bremerton, I looked around to see if she got off with the pedestrians, but she didn't. Probably in one of those vehicles below now roaring off the vast deck and out into the real world. Ships that pass and all that. It didn't really matter anyway. Any future with a girl like that was strictly male fantasyland anyway, and I had a comfortable and more realistic relationship going that was better for me all around anyway.

In fact, that woman probably was as much of an airhead as the stereotype, but it didn't stop me from thinking of Riki's persona inside that bombshell body. Nice combination, but then I'd have to arrange to be in the body of one of the Chippendales or at least a young Cary Grant—she always liked Cary Grant—to even it out, and then we'd both be too perfect for the world.

I expected she'd be home today, and pretty surprised when I walked in. We'd lived together for three years now and were pretty used to one another, and I never, *never* came home in the middle of a weekday, usually not even if I had time off, unless it was some kind of emergency. I realized now I probably should have called ahead, but by this point I was close enough to home to make it a moot point.

She'd been born Erika Francesca Wrzkowski—"Warchevsky," she claimed it was pronounced—and she was proud of her half-Silesian ancestry, but she hadn't gotten along well with her family in years and had long ago tired of having to spell or expect others to spell and pronounce that name. She'd started painting as Riki Fresca, and after her father died she legally changed her name to match. I thought it sounded too much like a soft drink, and maybe she'd agreed over time, but by then she was building a reputation and the name became worth something on its own, so she couldn't change it.

Naturally, she'd always had visions of being the next Georgia O'Keeffe or a female Wyeth, but her fame came from the commercial sector, mostly—book jackets, game boxes, even movie posters and the like. She still did a lot of "pure" painting, and there was enough interest from small galleries in commercial art that she was able to bundle some of the pure stuff along with her more recognizable work, but, basically, she'd opted to live in moderate comfort rather than suffer in a garret and be discovered, maybe, after she died.

We'd run into each other on the ferry, in fact, and it was one of those things that just sort of came together over a period of weeks or months. We were both creative, though in radically different fields, and we respected each other's work and talents. Watching her take a blank canvas, put in a few pencil lines as a guide, mix paints, and then, in a series of strokes, transform what looked like a childish random paint session into a sudden dramatic scene was fascinating to watch; almost a kind of magic that came so natural to her that she was amazed that few others could do it and couldn't therefore explain it. I remember working on a part-time gig doing some video-game design during the time I was still shopping for a home employer, and how I'd had to work with this writer of the thriller the game was based on. How can you write like that? I'd asked him. Why can't you write like that, or like yourself? he'd come back.

He could teach somebody craft, just like art schools and such could teach the craft of painting so you could do one a day and sell junk at the starving-artist sales, but *art*—that which was beyond craft and into a realm of magic, *that* he couldn't teach or explain. Either you could do it or you couldn't. If you could, *then* talk to him.

I'm not sure if my own talents were similar or more totally on the craft side. On the one hand, a programmer's kind of like a mathematician, a puzzle maker, a cryptographer, and the work's often collaborative like in movies or TV. Most of it *is* pure craft, but every once in a while something comes up that's pure magic. The Russians who created *Tetris*, for example, or whoever it was who thought up *Lemmings*, strange as that person might be.

I admit, too, I was ready for something a little more permanent when we met. I was hardly a virgin myself, but the older

I got and the thinner on top and paunchier on the bottom I got, the longer the gaps between dates, let alone anything more. I don't want to make it seem like I decided on Riki out of desperation—at least not alone—but it certainly bent me more in that direction. I'm not sure what she saw in me—computer wonks are a dime a dozen around Seattle. Maybe she saw the Porsche and figured I was one of those senior vice presidents up at Microsoft with the zillions in stock or something.

No, we weren't married, and, no, it wasn't my choice, it was hers. I never quite got it straight whether it was because she was Catholic and took this seriously as a one-time thing—she sure didn't take much else the Catholic Church laid down as moral behavior very seriously—or more a matter of old feminist principles or even just nerves, but I never pushed it. If we'd thought about kids, it would have been different, but if she had a biological clock, it was running real slow. Without kids, it didn't really make much difference in practical terms, but I guess the idea that either one of us could just walk away scared me as much as it reassured her.

Well, some of the most solid relationships I ever knew, ones that went on for years, got screwed up when they finally decided to get married, so who knows? It certainly wasn't from my experience.

I walked in and headed straight for the kitchen and the first of the beers, then I walked back into the small but comfortable studio Riki had set up, figuring she was working. I could hear the TV in there blaring some talk-show stuff. I never figured out how she could work with all that, but everybody has their own quirks. I know that I'd wind up watching the vilest and stupidest stuff and never concentrate or get much done.

She saw me and immediately had the expression of somebody expecting a telegram with awful news. She punched MUTE on the remote and called out, "Cory! What's wrong?"

"Plenty, but no emergency," I told her, taking a swig of the beer. "We're gonna be sold, that's all. The company's *kaput*. A month or so from now it'll be run from Singapore and you'll need to translate into Sanskrit to instruct the workers."

"But I thought that the patent was going to do big things!"

I nodded. "It did. It made Walt and several others millions of bucks and threw maybe a hundred and fifty people here out of work. I think they'll make an offer for my services, maybe Jamie and Ben as well, since they need to have people who know what they're doing walk them through. They may even offer us permanent jobs, but at the expense of being cogs in a machine run from halfway around the world. Whatever they offer, it's going to have to be a *lot* to make *me* stay. Unless some miracle comes up, I think I'm going to have to let you support me in the manner to which I've become accustomed."

She gave a grim smile. "I get the Porsche retitled in my name, right? No—it won't work. With you around all day I'd *never* get any work done."

I gestured to the TV, where a bunch of women were screaming at an audience all in blissful silence. "I can't be any worse than *that*."

"Oh, you're *much* worse, although I got to admit that I was screaming back at that show today. 'My Boyfriend Just Discovered I'm a Transsexual.' "

"I did?"

"Don't get smart. I don't care how *anybody* looks or thinks they feel, if you never had a period you ain't all the way a woman, baby."

"I'll take your word for it."

"So what are you going to do for the rest of the day?" she asked me.

I shrugged. "I thought I'd go out in the sailboat if the weather holds up, before I have to sell it."

"Oh, come on! Things can't be *that* bad! You'll get some money out of this, and you have a *little* socked away. Besides, I'm not doing all that bad."

"Last I looked I didn't have a whole lot, and there are debts up the kazoo. We needed to make a quarter of a million a year between us just to break even, including taxes. You've been doing about a hundred and fifty grand and I've been doing the rest. We've been breaking even, babe. Take away my hundred thou a year and we got a deep hole. You can't cover it and you can't cover my debts, so that's pretty bleak."

"You'll find another job by the time that happens!"

"I'm not so sure anymore. Well, look, I don't want to think about what's still in the future right now, whether it's going off the edge of the world or bright sunshine and clover. I just want to *relax*. Let's take the boat, go out for a while, and when we're sick of it and windburned all to hell we'll go to Chapparelli's and have a really good meal with the works. What do you say? Then come back here, and if we aren't too dead tired, lose our worries in mindless sex."

She grinned. "I wasn't with you until that last. You're on. Let me get changed here and we'll be off. Or, of course, we could skip all the preliminaries."

"And go right to bed?"

"No, to Chapparelli's, you dope!"

We were in her studio, so I didn't dare throw anything at her.

While she changed, I went into my own home office and logged on to the Internet to download any email. It didn't take long—I wasn't all that popular today, it seems.

Riki decided she needed a shower because of the paint smell, so I sat down at the desk and read the messages. First one was a reply to a query I had on certain early Porsches. Second was one of those irritating plugs sent out shotgun style, this one for toner cartridges. Zap. The third one, though—it almost brought me up short.

*"Cheer up,"* it said. *"Everything you think you know is wrong, anyway."*

I frowned. No signature, but there was always an electronic one. Just a number—anonymous, and probably hidden. Some jokers used this to bug people they didn't like, and I didn't like it much, either. Still, this *had* to be somebody who knew me, and, by inference, already knew what would be a small paragraph in next week's *Infoworld* that we were being eaten. Kind of insulting, though. If everything I knew was wrong, why was it worth these kind of bucks to Sangkung?

Still, it bugged me, and I wanted to discover who the hell was into knife twisting. There was always an electronic trail, somewhere, when you sent this anonymous kind of email message, no matter how clever you were. It had to get here somehow.

I had a little program that might do the trick. I'd had pranks played on me before, and this was what I'd come up with: a program that was invisible if you just did things the usual way, but if you didn't include a return address header so the sender could be identified, it stuck a little message to the sender that said that anonymous messages were refused and blocked them. It wasn't any big deal; not nearly as tough or as much fun as the one I had cooked up after I got inundated with junk email, a program that tagged the senders and sent them their own message, backward, *fifty* times for every time they sent it to me. Talk about overloading a gateway. . . .

"What's wrong?" Riki asked, coming into the room. I turned and saw that she was as close to ready as I could reasonably expect.

"Somebody being cute, probably from the office," I told her. "No big deal. I'll catch 'em sooner or later. In the meantime, this will keep them from doing it any more. Come on— let's go. Your hair, complexion, and clothes are going to all be ruined anyway, so what's the big deal."

She grinned. "Just the way you are, huh?"

"Well, don't sweat it, anyway."

It felt good being out there, just the two of us—and about a hundred other boaters, of course—on the sound enjoying a nice breeze and a warm summer sun. It wasn't much of a boat—a glorified skiff with just enough sail for one to handle if need be—but it was mine, at least as long as I could continue to make the payments. It was kind of peaceful to just be out there with Riki, the wind, the salt breezes, and the birds, cut off from the real world and its worries.

And we *were* cut off. Although I had a battery-powered marine-band walkie-talkie in case we got in trouble, I was otherwise completely out to all callers. I'd never even joined the cellular revolution, because places like the boat and the car were *supposed* to be for peace and quiet. It was like the picturephone. They had that perfected *decades* ago, but it never caught on except as a business teleconferencing tool. The phone folks never figured out that the *last* thing people wanted was to have to be all dressed and presentable just to answer the damned phone. Likewise, in spite of the fact that everybody and his mother seemed to have a cell phone for everything, I didn't. When I didn't want to be found, I didn't want to be found, damn it.

Riki and I didn't even talk much to each other while we were out together on the boat. We'd occasionally lie down next to each other and lazily drift on calm days, but it wasn't a talk kind of thing. The rest of the time, she'd take the helm for a while, then me; sometimes we'd just let it go if there wasn't any danger in the area. It was what I, at least, worked for—moments like that.

Finally, though, bodily needs took over. For one thing, the boat wasn't big enough to have a bathroom aboard, so you never got too far from where you knew one was, and, for another, it was getting to be dinnertime.

We headed to the marina and Chaparelli's Restaurant.

Chaparelli's wasn't high cuisine; rather, it was one of those typical dockside places with the chintzy decor and Formica tables and even a row of diner-like stools at one end. It wasn't even Italian; the name was an old one that sort of came with the liquor license. It was Greek, actually. The fake Italian

Greek, if you know what I mean. It served good, solid meals at reasonable prices mostly to locals and marina types, generally fresh local seafood and pasta. Not four stars in the Michelin guide, no, but it wasn't McDonald's or Denny's, either.

Somebody'd put in a bunch of quarters in the jukebox before we'd arrived, and I groaned. "All Elvis all the time! That's all I need!"

Riki laughed. "Cheer up. It's not so loud in the back room, and you can stand it. You're macho. You're tough."

"Nobody is up to the entire page of Elvis on that jukebox," I pouted, but we got seats and managed to somehow relegate the King to the background. I used to like Elvis when he was alive and I was young, although I always thought of him as more a country singer than a rock and roller. But after he died and they built the Worldwide Church of the Risen Elvis I just revolted. Maybe I'd have more appreciation if I was an ex of Lisa Marie or Presley had given me a Cadillac or something, but I never could see making gods out of famous people, alive or dead.

I still managed to get my seafood platter with a side of linguine almost all down when I suddenly noticed that Elvis wasn't playing anymore. It wasn't so much that I was listening, it was just the same sort of thing as noticing quiet after a session of loud background noises. Then another song started, and I barely noticed the group singing the rather mundane tune, but something caught in my ear and I suddenly stopped, fork halfway to my lips.

> "... Ask not why we sing this song,
> 'cause ev'ry thing you think you know is wrong ..."

"What the hell?" I said, putting down the fork.

"Huh? What's the matter?" Riki hadn't noticed the tune.

"That song. I'd swear it said ..." But by this point the song was over, and they were playing some good Seattle band music.

"What are you talking about?" she asked, looking very worried.

I was worried myself. "Just humor me. I'll be back in a minute." I got up, walked back to the jukebox, and looked through all the selections. Nothing looked odd, unusual, inappropriate, or even particularly new.

I walked back to the table, wondering if I was suddenly losing my mind.

"Find what you were looking for?" she asked, knowing the answer.

"Uh-uh. I guess it's just been in the back of my mind or something and I heard a word and put the rest together. Either that or it's like the guy in *Harvey* who looks up what a Pooka is and the dictionary defines it and then asks, 'How are you, Mr. Wilson?' " Riki shared my fondness for old movies, and that was one of the great ones. I just never expected to feel like I was falling into the plot of it, which concerns, as you might know, a kindly little man and his friend, a six-foot invisible bunny rabbit.

Well, at least we got to finish without any more incidents more irritating or mysterious than a new round of all-Elvis selections, but I didn't feel like staying. It was beginning to bug me, not only that I'd gotten that message, but that it had tickled the back of my mind so much that I was now hearing things.

"I'm afraid I'm not the world's best date tonight," I told Riki apologetically as we left.

She squeezed my hand. "Don't worry about it. Let's just walk back up to the house and take it easy like we planned, huh? So long as we stick to the script things can't go *too* wrong."

"Not unless I'm having a breakdown. It's been a hell of a day."

"Why do you let this get to you, anyway?" she asked me. "I mean, what's the meaning here? 'Everything you think you know is wrong.' That's pretty stupid, but it doesn't sound all that threatening. It's not like 'You will be dead at midnight' or something like that. Sort of stupid, really. Covers a lot of territory, though, I have to admit."

I chuckled. "I guess you're right. *Everything*, huh? There goes all those years of school and college, I guess, and all the rest. You're all a delusion, the whole town, the whole country, the whole world, the whole *universe*! I dunno—it just kinda feeds into my natural paranoia at a time when I'm down, I guess."

"I had an aunt who believed that, you know."

"Huh? You did?"

"Yeah. She was a Christian Scientist. Thought the whole universe was an illusion, and all pain and misery and even death were fakes, too."

"Did it work?"

She shrugged. "I dunno, but I always had this funny feeling when I saw their reading room. It was always filled with real old people, so maybe there *was* at least *something* to it."

I laughed. "Or Darwin was right and they've bred themselves into a high state of immunity! Heck, I'd still figure you would find that one attractive."

"How's that?"

"Only major denomination I can think of founded by a woman. Only major one of *anything* in that area, at least the respectable religions, anyway."

"Yeah, well, in my misspent youth I hung out for a time in an Arizona commune that used peyote and all sorts of other Native American herbs and drugs."

"You took it?"

"In those days I'd take anything. But I only took that Holy Circle Communion once, a mixture of a bunch of stuff like that. It was kinda scary. Weird visions, weird creatures, and then, at the end, the whole world sort of disappeared. There was just this grayness all over, and a lot of flashing like lightning or something, only in regular patterns. Scared the hell out of me. I still can't say why. I left them and that whole life shortly after. Haven't even been *drunk* since. Hell, I even gave up smoking and took up jogging. Talk about scared straight!"

I put my arm around her and squeezed. It was odd—all this time, and she'd never mentioned that. The commune, yeah, and all the experimentations, but not what had jolted her out of it. Until now I'd figured that all the "pure" art she'd done that was so dark and cold had been from the drug experiences. Now I understood a little more about her, but in spite of that it didn't comfort me. Hell, I'd always been a straight arrow. Okay, I smoked cigarettes for a few years, and I was still known to have an occasional good cigar, but beyond that I was pretty boring in the sin department. The worst thing I'd done was that I'd cheated on my German exam in tenth grade.

And I'd had the same kind of lonely, gray dreams as she was describing now.

Was it our similar sense of paranoia, recognized on some subconscious level, that drew us together and kept us pretty well together, or what? I began to wonder.

"Why do I have a feeling this ain't gonna be one of those warm romantic evenings?" I grumbled. "For either of us?"

"I know what you mean. I think you're communicable," she responded, not at all playfully. "I'm getting as dark and depressed a mood as you had coming home and haven't licked."

We made it home anyway, just as full darkness enshrouded the whole area. I was determined to at least make a go of it, and I figured she would go along and maybe try and lick this thing, too, but as I walked past my office I saw that the light on the answering machine was blinking. Riki had gone to the bathroom, so I went in and pushed the button to see who it might be.

*"Number of messages received, two,"* said the mechanical voice chip. *"Thursday, five fifty-two pm.* Beep!"

"Cory, this is Rob," came a familiar voice. "I may have

some good news/bad news type stuff. Won't be able to tell until tomorrow, but here goes. My guy in D.C. says that there's a fellow there who's more interested in *us* than he is in saving the company. I know you don't like the feds, and I like 'em even less, but it's something to do with an old virtual reality project that was actually started by Matthew Brand, if you can believe it. The work's there, sounds interesting, and we may be taken on as contractors. It's not what we wanted but it's sure worth looking into. If you're game, just stick around the house tomorrow and I'll give you a call by, oh, noon, let's say. So, don't get too drunk, and be at your best tomorrow. At least it won't cost us anything to talk. I'm not going to be easy to catch tonight myself, so talk to you tomorrow. Bye."

What the hell? Government? Rob, too? And an old *Matthew Brand* project? God, they knew how to bait a hook, didn't they?

*"Thursday, six-thirty pm,"* announced the machine. *"One. Beep!"*

"Hi'ya, lovah!" came a sultry woman's voice in an accent so deeply southern it sounded put on. "You watch it, now! We ahn't set up to take y'awl just yet, and Al and his buddies are nothin' to sneeze at. So, you take cahre, now, and we'll try'n jog you outta this totally *borin'* little ol' existence, huh? Just don't jump at anything until we get to talk and you get a little moah of yoah mem'ry back, y'heah? And don't go to that appointment with that guv'ment man tomorrow. You'll regret it if you do! Bye foah now!"

And then she idly sang a little refrain before she hung up, one that gave me dead cold chills.

> *". . . Ask not why we sing this song,*
> *'cause ev'ry thing you think you know is wrong . . ."*

*Click!*

I immediately checked Caller ID but it said it was "out of

area," which could mean almost anywhere in the country or the world not yet wired for it. Damn! I turned, looked up, and saw Riki standing in the doorway.

"Did you hear it?" I asked her.

She nodded. "Hard to miss. An old flame?"

"The voice and particularly that accent are totally foreign to me. And I'd have remembered, believe me! But that last bit—that was exactly what I swore I heard at the restaurant. The exact refrain, only without the drawl."

She nodded again. "I figured. So somebody's really out to drive you nuts, huh? You didn't come into any inheritances lately, did you?"

"Not that I know of. And I didn't know I was missing any memories, either. I have an excellent memory, except for German."

"Cory—this is serious. Somebody's really harassing you! You should call the cops on this! You never know what somebody like this will *do*!"

I shook my head negatively. "Uh-uh. This isn't a police kind of thing, I suspect. Not right off, anyway. I don't know what the game is, but it's not just a nut. The first message was from Rob, and it promised an appointment with some government official tomorrow. He's supposed to call me at noon about setting it up."

"Yeah, so?"

"Riki—this woman, she *knew* about that appointment! She warned me not to take it! You heard her!"

That hadn't occurred to her. "Oh, my—you mean we're *bugged*?"

I looked up at her, and I was more scared than she was at this. My whole world had come to an end today, I thought, and now it was being replaced by something between a bad spy novel and the Twilight Zone. Considering what I didn't know about all this, what the hell was I also supposed to have forgotten?

# 11

# "WHO ARE YOU?"
# ASKED THE CATERPILLAR

The name Matthew Brand might mean very little to most people, but within the computer community he was something of a legend, even a demigod. He was there at the beginning of the personal computer revolution, and many of the things people take for granted came from work by him and the teams he assembled. He was always a visionary, always living way ahead of his time, almost as if what we were excitedly talking about for the "next generation" he already considered old hat. Always in the background, yet always welcome anywhere, he was with Xerox PARC when they effectively invented the personal computer as we know it—and whose executives then decided there wasn't any commercial future for it! At Bell Labs he worked on bringing UNIX to maturity as an operating system. Turn around and there he was—at Digital Research one moment, at HP, or Apple, or Microsoft the next. Money came easily to him so he tended to ignore it, following only what truly interested him at any given moment.

When he'd abandoned the big boys for a start-up company and think tank, everybody knew he was into some kind of ultra government research he couldn't get anybody else to pay for, and we all sat back, those of us who couldn't get on the inside, and waited for the next wonders to waft out of that building and small campus he'd set up just outside Yakima on the other side of Mount Rainier. Nothing did, and that in itself would have fueled a million conspiracy theories, but what *really* happened was even better for that sort of thing.

At age forty-seven, Matthew Brand, it was said, was found dead of a rare heart condition while working in his office at the campus. Nobody saw the body, it was a closed casket, and it was cremated and the ashes scattered in the Pacific as per his wishes.

But a lot of folks had been working there. Not as many as you'd expect, but maybe a hundred or so, and after being interrogated, paid off, and threatened with all sorts of dire consequences if they ever discussed their work there, they were laid off and found other prime jobs in government and industry. Key people went east to the NSA and similar installations; the rest were all over the west coast. Except for the general impression that Brand had been working on some kind of breakthrough technology in virtual reality, though, nobody ever spelled out, even anonymously, just what they were after or why the government was so interested in it that they paid a fortune to set the company up. There was no mistaking that, whatever it was, it was Brand's own concept, and that he'd sold the government on it after failing to find either private backing or adequate capital and access. Some said it wasn't even money—he wanted the government's big computers, period.

What *had* come out, and persisted since his "death," was that he didn't die the way they said and wasn't in that coffin. Sure, some folks thought he was still alive, maybe some kind of government prisoner or something, but the general word was that Brand indeed was dead, that he'd died in the building, but not in his office and not of any heart problem. Rather, it was firmly believed by most from the number of

accounts of people who were there that Brand had died in the
main lab, in the course of running an experiment, and that
this experiment had literally resulted in his disintegration.

That had been five years ago, and nobody knew what became of the work that had been done there. It had certainly
been shut down, not transferred, and all of the relevant records were still highly classified, but it was also clear that nobody knew who might possibly understand or take over the
research without Brand, and particularly if even Brand had
made such a fatal mistake.

Now, me, I'd done a fair amount of work in VR and I
knew the potential, but I couldn't imagine what you might do
that would disintegrate you on the spot. I mean, it was *virtual*
reality, not reality, after all. Almost everybody knew what it
was, and many have experienced it. In fact, if you ever went
to one of those supersized IMAX theaters where the screen
fills your whole field of vision and you felt a little dizzy or
a sense of movement when you watched, you have had a virtual reality experience. Theme parks all had the same kind of
thing paired with flight simulators to give you more of a feeling of reality, and there were even small versions that now
toured at carnivals and traveling shows. Home games now
had visors and power gloves so you could "see" what was
onscreen and move there and even pick up objects. This technology has been developed to a very sophisticated level in
simulators for the military. On the ultimate level, in a full VR
suit and strapped to a gimbal that allows movement in all directions and one could experience an even higher level of
"reality."

But it was all illusion. That was all VR was. Illusion. An
incredible, fun, and even useful way of using a computer to
fool your senses into let's-pretend games and exercises, but
"fool the senses" was the operative part. At the end, it was
just the same old you in the module or the suit or whatever.

Knowing Brand's reputation, his idea of VR was beyond

what the industry was promising us for the next decade, but it's still illusion. In the end, the body is still the body, and you might fool it in every which way, but it still had to be fed and go to the bathroom.

Still, there was nobody who had egomania to begin with in the computer business who wouldn't leap at a chance to know what Brand had thought he could do, and that's why, bugged or not, I was sure as hell going to keep any appointment concerning him.

"Do you think that might be behind this?" Riki asked me, concerned. "I mean, somebody who doesn't want this program reopened or looked at? Or maybe it's the government itself, seeing how well you'd spook."

"Could be," I agreed. "Any of that is plausible. The only way to get at what this is all about is to keep going with the flow and ignoring the rest if possible. Still, let's make sure we lock the doors and keep the alarms on, huh? If this really *is* two competing groups, I don't want to be any more of a sandwich than I have to be. Damn! I feel like I'm trapped in a bad spy movie! I'll sure be glad when we can find out exactly what's going on here."

"Maybe," she responded, a little dubious. "Half the time in the movies, when the innocent victim finds out everything they get knocked off. I think I'd just like all this to go away."

"You watch yourself," I warned her. "If they can't get me directly they can use you as leverage. I don't want to come home to an empty house."

She shivered. "Thanks a *lot*! Well, I'm not gonna get anything else done here *now*, not after *that*. The easiest way to settle this, particularly since I'm essentially unemployed at the moment, is to come with you."

Rob was as good as his word, calling just a few minutes before noon. "Sorry to be moving like this," he apologized, "but this is all coming down fast and furious. If I didn't know better I'd swear that they were just waiting for us to get canned so they could pick us up."

"Um, Rob. . . . Have you had any weird phone calls? Funny stuff happening?"

"Huh? What do you mean?"

"Does the phrase 'Everything you think you know is wrong' mean anything to you?"

"No, not particularly," he responded. "What's all this about?"

"I'll tell you when I see you. When and where?"

"How about an early dinner? Nothing dressy. Casual, maybe downtown. Tracers, maybe, at six?"

"Mind if I bring Riki? We've got a little problem here and I'd feel better with her near me."

"Now you *are* getting me curious! No, I guess there's no reason not to have her along. What on *earth* is going on with you two?"

"Um, shall we just say that, at least as of yesterday, I'd say there's a very good chance that whatever we're saying now is also being said to anonymous third parties?"

There was silence at the other end for a moment, then Rob said, "You sound worse than I do sometimes. Well, I'll mention this to—to the man I want you to talk to. Okay? See you later?"

"Good enough."

He hung up, but I waited for a couple of seconds to see if I could hear another hangup, but nothing sounded odd. I quietly touched the speakerphone and then hung up the receiver as I would normally. There was a late *pop* from the speaker but that was all. I punched it off. Bad enough to be paranoid, I thought, but when it turns out that even paranoids are the victims of real conspiracies, that makes it much, much worse.

I hadn't slept very well, and Riki probably got less than I did. Everyplace anybody lives has noises, routine noises that you filter out and ignore, and every house creaks and you barely notice, but when you're in our condition you hear *all* those noises and you imagine all sorts of dark figures lurking around. For the first time in my life, all the shades were down in the house, even on the second floor, and where it was impossible, in the glass-walled studio, Riki wouldn't set foot in there after dark and didn't even like it much in the daytime. It brought home just how very thin our sense of security and normalcy really was, and just how easily it could be shattered.

It was enough to drive us both back to smoking, political correctness, health, and public laws be damned. It was either that or drink, although right now the latter was making do. I didn't want to be drunk when meeting this guy, whoever he was, and particularly not if I was dealing with some unknown persons lurking about who had my number and monitored my conversations. Still, I needed more than I should to keep myself reasonable. When it took me two doubles to be steady, I was in pretty piss poor shape.

Matthew Brand.... It all came back to him, somehow. Somebody with an interest in that work knew that I and perhaps a few others were about to lose our jobs and that the government was going to come and speak to us about the legendary Brand work. That somebody didn't want the Brand project reopened. That was the most logical conclusion, anyway. I assumed that I was just part of a team being reassembled after five years, maybe with some of the original people and some newcomers who were available and who might be able to shed some light on Brand's work. My ego was stroked even in my otherwise nervous condition by the thought that I was in any way considered capable of following up on Brand's work. It felt like the computer industry equivalent of Saint Paul being told by Jesus, "Okay, I did the big stuff, you take it from here."

Okay, okay, I had no problems comparing myself to Paul. I *told* you this was an ego-driven business. Heck, at least I didn't promote myself even higher, but that was only because

I was familiar with some of Brand's more esoteric early work and I knew that I was good but not *that* good.

*Everything you think you know. . . .*

I guess the phrase grated so because I was at heart a mathematician—all really good programmers were. Never mind the quadratic equations and differential calculus; if two plus two equaled anything but four then I literally was ignorant as hell. The phrase just rubbed my nose in it while still not proving its own case. Any fool can assert that two plus two equals five, but could he *prove it*.

I could just see Brand now, mathematician, physicist, and engineer in one, a kind of computer-age Edison with no care for even keeping what he found, an eternal searcher for newer and more exotic toys to play with. If a man like that came up against something that literally didn't make any sense at all, that called into question all the concepts that had built our modern, comfortable civilization, and contradicted the science that always proved solid, how driven would he be to integrate it, to explain it, to *make* it conform? Enough to drive him to careless assumptions that eventually produced enough of a solid current to fry him to a crisp?

Hell, *Brand* should never have been the subject in any experiment anyway. That was a job for grad students.

The idea of potentially peeking over the shoulder at a legendary man in your field and also into the closely guarded secrets surrounding his death would have been totally irresistible no matter what.

At least for the whole day there wasn't a single taunt or weird call or fax or Internet message. It was almost as if the previous day hadn't existed, and it was beginning to fade back into those "Was it *really* that way or was it misinterpreted?" feelings. Or, it would have, had I not had that strange woman's voice on my answering machine tape.

That was my one ace in the hole and proof I wasn't going nuts and taking Riki with me. I had a spare tape, so I put that one in the machine and put the one with the recording in a case and put *that* in my pocket, at least for now.

By the time we were on the ferry going over to downtown, I'd almost forgotten it and was looking forward to this meeting and the opportunity for new and interesting work, even if it was going to be with the feds for a while. The only thing I couldn't figure out was what they might want with Rob, a sales manager with a social life that was still definitely not on the feds' "most desirable" list.

Watching the familiar skyline grow nearer, relaxed at the rail of what was proving to be a great summer's late afternoon, my arm around Riki's waist, there seemed nothing that could spoil the trip or the rest of the day no matter how this went.

And then, over the stiff wind and all the other people talking, I heard that voice.

"Oh, yes! Ah think that the l'il ol' view is about the most *prettiest* thing ah evah did see!"

I felt Riki stiffen and knew she'd recognized it, too. I let my arm drop and said, "Go around and through the passenger salon and over to the other side. I'm going to walk around from here and we should meet in the middle. I don't want anybody vanishing on us."

She nodded, and as soon as I saw her go in the doorway I slowly moved toward the other side of the boat and that voice that made Scarlett O'Hara sound like a Yankee.

I almost knew who I expected to see, and I wasn't disappointed. This time she was wearing all leather, and tight leather at that, with a floppy leather hat and an almost impossibly long cigarette holder. She was talking to a couple of men who looked as if they were oblivious to everything but her, and she looked over at me through those sunglasses. I felt eye contact even if I couldn't see her eyeballs. We were still maybe ten or fifteen feet apart, and she gave a smile, then turned and began to walk aft, as I expected she would, her retinue of wolves following. I sped up, and she turned and opened one of the doors and headed in, the pack following. I was now just a couple of yards behind her and closing, and I reached up to slide the door open myself when I came face to face with Riki, who looked confused.

"Where is she?" I asked her.

"Huh? Beats me! I thought *you* were following her!"

"I was—but she went through this door not ten seconds ago!" I pushed past her, figuring that even if Riki somehow missed her, the pack of unwanted male admirers would be pretty obvious. Back by the cafeteria I spotted a couple of them, and they were talking to one another and shrugging. I made for them, figuring she had exited to someplace else but couldn't be *that* much of a mystery. They were right with her.

"Excuse me, mister, but did you see where that woman you were speaking to went?" I asked the first one I came across.

"Beats me, pal," he answered. "One minute she was there, the next minute, *poof!*"

"Huh? She vanished in a puff of smoke?"

"Naw. Don't be an asshole, bud. She just sorta vanished. We been tryin' to figure it out ourselves. I mean, it's not like she coulda gotten off, right? And she sure don't fade into the woodwork."

That was only partially true, because she *had* faded into the woodwork. The men weren't exactly thrilled with being given the slip and weren't very talkative, but as near as I could gather she'd gone past a post—*that* post, over there, maybe one yard square and deck to ceiling—and she hadn't come out the other side. A post right in the middle of the damned boat between the rest rooms and the cafeteria!

I went back to Riki. "You *really* didn't see her?"

She shrugged. "I saw her through the window, there. That's *some* girlfriend you got, Cory! Jesus! I even sped up to cut her off, but I swear I never saw her come in. This is getting weirder and weirder by the moment."

"What about the guys I was talking to?"

She shook her head. "If they came in, they somehow escaped my notice, and the one in the Seahawks jacket is kinda cute, too."

*Wait a minute! Think! Get hold of yourself!* Either Riki was part of the conspiracy, which I didn't believe for an instant, or she really didn't see the woman and all those guys come in, and either those men were all part of it or they watched a woman go past a post that wouldn't conceal her and not emerge on the other side.

If I thought that one of them were lying, I would have chalked it up to an elaborate trick, but I didn't believe any of them was lying. Since everybody, even Riki through the windows, saw the woman, she'd been real enough, and that left . . . what?

Hypnosis? Some kind of ESP that made you invisible? That seemed crazy, too, but it made more sense than any other explanation and would certainly explain how she could make herself so conspicuous yet vanish at will and at *very* close range. Never mind me—those guys had been practically on her rear end!

"This is suddenly becoming not only weirder, as you say, but scary, too," I told her. "Somebody so noticeable who can vanish at will. . . ."

She nodded. "I know. But she also made pretty damned sure you saw her, didn't she? Even to letting you get pretty close to her. She *wanted* to spook us! What's going *on* here, Cory? People just don't *have* powers like this!" She looked around. "She could be right here making faces at us and we'd never even know it!"

I sighed. I was scared, too, but one of our ordained social roles as men was to reassure and not show our fear if at all possible. That's one reason we die sooner. "I doubt it," I tried to assure her, although I really wasn't that confident myself. "She's dressed too conspicuously and she'd be an attention-getter even in a tee shirt and jeans. I doubt if she can just make herself invisible. No, she's done her job. Bet on her down on the car deck, maybe inside a camper or van, making herself look at least different and waiting to come off. She's played her game. Now let's do what she seems to want us not to do, huh?"

In spite of all that, I was deeply shaken. Until now, it was somebody playing pranks, or somebody bugging my phone or somesuch. Not now. Now it was voluptuous antebellum white women from Mars with strange mental powers. Now it was into the *real* Twilight Zone, a place I'd never even actually believed existed.

Either that or she missed her real calling and could have made millions in Vegas.

*Where have you been, Matthew Brand, Matthew Brand?*
*Oh, where have you been, darling Matthew?*

I was certain that all this had to do with the Brand project. What the hell *had* he gotten himself into, anyway?

Now I started having a new worry, one that would only grow as we came into the terminal and made our way off and downstairs to a taxi.

What if Brand hadn't been the victim of a bad experiment or faulty equipment or some kind of accident, freak or not?

If she could appear and disappear like this, so easily, so effortlessly, what was secure?

What if Brand had discovered something he shouldn't have and been murdered for it?

I was never so happy to see Rob Garnett in my life. The man with him was nondescript, maybe mid or late forties, short hair, dark glasses that looked worn inside or out, a ruddy complexion, and a kind of military bearing. He gave off a commanding, charismatic sense of power, but he was by no means handsome. In fact, he had a nasty scar on his left cheek.

"Hi, guys!" Rob greeted us, smiling. "Good grief! You look like you just lost your life savings, both of you! What *happened?*"

"Tell you about it later," I responded, looking at the other man.

Rob wasted no time in introductions. "Cory Maddox, Riki Fresca, this is Alan Stark. He's the government rep I told you about."

I had expected it. *"Al and his buddies ain't nothin' to sneeze at,"* she'd said on the answering machine, and now here was an Al, the very government man she warned against, and one look at him said that she was if anything understating the possible dangers here. Still, *she* was a phantom trying to freak me out and *he* was at least supposedly working for the government I paid to help support, so I had no reason to take her unsupported word over his.

I put out my hand, and Stark took it and shook it in a tight, firm manner. Military for sure, I decided. Just what branch, it wasn't possible to say.

Riki also shook his hand, then smiled and said as innocently as possible, "So you're with our government, Mr. Stark? What branch?"

"DIA attached to NSA at the moment," he responded casually, surprising even me. First time I'd ever heard anybody from Defense Intelligence Agency even say the initials, let alone acknowledge the NSA. "As I think Mr. Maddox guessed."

"You're a spy?"

He chuckled. "No, ma'am. That's the CIA and various other banks of initials. We're codebreakers. Not as glamorous but often a lot more useful. Most of the victories of World War Two were due to breaking codes as much or more than fighting. We knew where they were going to attack because of that; they didn't know we knew, and they didn't know where *we* were going to do things. It's a computer job, mostly, as you might also expect because we're here. But, hey—this was a dinner group, wasn't it? Is here all right or would you prefer somewhere else?"

"Fine with us," I told him. "On the other hand, I should warn you that somebody's been going to some pains to scare us off this meeting, and they probably tailed me here."

Stark frowned. "Sexy broad with an outrageous southern accent?"

"You know her?"

"More or less. I wouldn't worry about her. She's spooky, I'll grant you that, but she's harmless. She used to work for us until five years ago."

That was a familiar-sounding gap.

"Who's she working for now?" Riki asked nervously.

"Herself, mostly, although she may have private contacts. Come on, let's go in and eat. I'm starved myself. Maybe I can explain a lot more about this and calm your worries."

That would be more than welcome, and we followed him inside. He'd already arranged for a table well away from anybody else, although there were few in the restaurant at the moment anyway.

After we'd ordered and gotten some much-needed drinks as starters, Stark began to speak.

"The woman's name is Cynthia Matalon," he told us. "She was part of a research group the CIA had years ago. From your expressions, I think you can guess what it was about, although I can't tell you more. She has one very clever trick and she can play it on almost everybody. I think you saw it."

"Would I be wrong in guessing that the project was to see if others could be taught to do it, or at least find out how she does it?" I asked him.

"Something like that. There were a lot of such people with various tricks in the program and some of them would be really scary if they weren't almost all flakes. Sort of ironic, really. If she weren't convinced that she was the world's greatest superspy, she could probably be trained to *become* the world's greatest superspy. Fact is, they ended the project in one of those personnel and budget shakeups, and everybody was sent home with thanks, of course. Now, we had to keep track of most of them, the ones with potentially dangerous, um, tricks, so we got them jobs where we could keep track of them. In her case, we asked her to take a job spying on Brand's Zyzzx Software Factory in Yakima. Fact was, she was a secretary and we didn't need any spies, but she would never have *taken* a secretarial job, you see."

I nodded. I didn't want to believe that some folks with powers like these were around, particularly if they had loose screws, but I couldn't argue with personal experience so far.

"So what happened to her after Brand's death?" I asked him.

"Not sure, really. She got absolutely convinced that creatures from another dimension, an alternate reality she called it, had emerged somehow and faked his death and spirited him off to their own realm. Hey—I *told* you she was loopy! Said she would find him and bring him back or at least make sure nobody else was spirited away in the meantime until she could find what she called her 'rabbit hole' to their dimension or whatever. Don't take this seriously, now, but *she* does."

"Rabbit hole?" Riki repeated, frowning.

He nodded. "She still thinks she's a spy and her code name is White Rabbit. White Rabbit, Alice in Wonderland, so she's looking to go down the rabbit hole I guess. In the meantime, she's been *very* protective of the old building and campus and all of Brand's older work, even though most of it got moved out five years back."

"Most of it? You mean that place wasn't cleaned out, sold, and isn't some other company or a dry-goods headquarters or something by now?"

He chuckled. "It would make a nice base for the International Apple Growing Consortium—the eating kind, no keyboards—which is about all the conspiracy that's likely in Yakima, anyway, but we've kept it. We aren't using most of the building except for storage right now, but there were a couple of other smaller buildings there that have proved useful to one agency or another. It was mostly our money, anyway."

"But most of that's just lain vacant all these years? I thought we had a budget deficit!"

He shrugged. "The way that place was wired was crazy and potentially dangerous, so it was felt safer not to let anybody in the labs except the security people. Of course, all the equipment is in storage, but it's still impressive and a little too specialized for anybody else. We also would prefer, even five years later, that nobody see just *how* it was all hooked up, since it was tied into dedicated lines and satellite backup links to just about every computer in intelligence."

I thought he was being a bit too paranoid, even considering what I'd been going through, but, of course, *he* wasn't really the one setting policy. It was some higher-ups back in Washington who saw enemies of humanity under every bush.

I decided to see if the question could be popped in public. "Okay, if we don't need a cone of silence, can you give me a rough idea of what his project was all about? I mean, what was he trying to do?"

"Well, I can't be too specific about it, not around here, but basically it was a radically different concept of virtual reality. Back then we were moving toward what we have today, and we had some superb body suits and simulator combinations for fighter training and the like, but it was all quite limiting and all hardware based. Brand believed that he could accomplish an even more detailed VR without all that stuff," Stark responded.

"What? You mean a sort of walk-through realistic 3-D environment?" I asked, thinking of the old Ray Bradbury story about the house of the future.

"Not—exactly. Think of it more as direct input. That's about all I can tell you here, but under more controlled circumstances, you can discover a lot more."

I wasn't too sure I followed. How direct? Input into what? The nervous system itself? I wasn't any biologist, and for all Brand's genius neither was he. Of course, that might well be why he fried himself, too. I'd love to see the records, the notes, the files, but, failing that for now, there was a different direction for questions that was far more pragmatic.

"Okay, we'll leave that for now and go a different way. What is your intention regarding the old work? Is the government going to reopen the project? Is that what this is about? Am I being recruited as one of the people working on it?"

"Essentially, yes. There was strong feeling back east that what did Brand in, both literally and in the project sense, was that technology just hadn't gotten as far as he needed and he died less of an accident than of kludge fever—sort of the equivalent of plugging too many appliances into a single electrical circuit. Plug ten inputs into one outlet block and turn them all on, and you'll overload the circuit. In the past few years there have been quantum leaps of technology in just the things Brand was using. We think it's feasible now, and without killing anyone. The headquarters are still there, and, we've upgraded the hardware. Moved in the latest state-of-the-art stuff, and the new and superior links to bigger computing power, and we believe that it will be possible to reestablish the project and proceed in the way Brand would have done in this situation. We lack only one thing, and that one thing we can*not* acquire at any price."

"Matthew Brand," Riki said, sounding a little nervous.

"Exactly. So we're doing the best we can. We are assembling a team which, collectively, everything we know about them tells us is the equal of a Brand. Not as good, perhaps, but good enough, and not nearly as vulnerable to the unexpected this time around."

"And I'm one of the folks who came out of your computer? I'm flattered, but amazed," I told him. "I haven't been exactly friendly to the government or the military, let alone the spooks, over my life. I figured I had an FBI file as a radical or something, although it never bothered me enough to write and look at it."

Stark smiled, reached down, picked up his briefcase, opened it, thumbed through things for a moment, then handed me a fairly thick manila folder. I looked at it and was startled to see that it was in fact my FBI file and that it had one hell of a lot of detail about me, my life, my beliefs, my friends. Enough to make you uncomfortable, particularly with very little blacked out, unlike the officially released material.

However, the aggregate was also something of a real ego deflater. Fact was, the whole added up to very little. I wasn't much of a dangerous radical; I wasn't dangerous at all and wasn't even much of a radical beyond some rhetoric.

In point of fact, I'd been at a few events and written enough stuff for them to have kept a file, but inside I was disgustingly middle-class. Hell, the only way I could prove I was any threat to the establishment would be to turn the offer down, and I was anything but inclined to do that. The worst part was, everybody here knew it, too.

I looked over at Rob Garnett. "What's *your* role in this? If *I'm* on the borderline, then *you* must be, too."

"Pretty well, but I'm no security risk," Rob replied, sounding relaxed. "God knows there's probably more in your background for blackmail than in mine, and particularly after AIDS I've tended to be *very* faithful. Truth is, I think I'm about average in bravery, but I've buried too many friends not to be terrified. You're right—I'm not exactly gonna be popular with *this* government, but it doesn't seem to matter in this case." He gave me a familiar *talk to you later* look, which I accepted and didn't press.

"No, I didn't mean *that*. I mean, what's your role in this project?"

Rob smiled. "Because it would be like going back home."

I frowned. "You're from Yakima? I thought you were from Sioux Falls."

He laughed. "No, no. You see, I worked for Brand back then. Not directly on this, but I was one of his staff, as it were. I learned the business under him, and that's where all my sales and government contacts came from. That's how come I looked up Al, here, when we were hung out to drip-dry."

"I never knew that! You never mentioned it."

He shrugged. "I never mentioned a lot of things. But, needless to say, I worked for Matt, not for the company or the government, and my classified access was highly restricted. It's been restricted since I was in the air force. Luckily, a lot's changed now, at least in a practical sense, if not in all the ways I want."

"There will be no obvious direct government link this time," Stark told us. "The company will be private, it will have a real tax-paying corporate charter—or it *would* pay taxes if it ever made money, which, as a think tank and R&D sort of place, it won't—and will be formally affiliated with several very big corporate names in this business who are also, needless to say, very anxious to keep on the good side of the federal government."

I sighed. "What about Subspace?" Hell, I'd put several years of my life in that company and most of that patent was my work.

Rob shrugged. "What about it? Sangkung offered so much money, Walt's dreaming of his own personal Playboy Mansion, and the odds are good that nothing can really stop the sale no matter what he says. Besides, it would take months to ink a deal, and Walt wouldn't wait that long and you know it. It was kind of wishful thinking yesterday to think any other way. Let it go, Cory. There's no future there."

I sighed. "I know, I know. It's just that you two may get most of me, but my heart's still dying a little at this. You realize that."

"It is the way of the world and one of the curses of living," Stark commented. "So many times I've spent all my energies and efforts on projects only to see them collapse at the last moment and my work come to nothing. I suspect Rob feels that about the original Brand project, and probably, in her own way, Matalon feels that way, too. Being grown-up is not avoiding these things—which are worthwhile or we wouldn't attempt them—but picking yourself up after you hit one of these walls and going out and finding a new challenge and doing it over again until you get it right. I assure you, Mr. Maddox, that once you see exactly what we are dealing with here, you will go through several phases. First you'll refuse to believe that such a thing is possible; then you'll realize that it's not only possible but that, at least to an extent, it has already been done. Finally, you'll want to be the one to perfect it."

"So, when will I see this? I assume it'll take quite a while to start up again down in Yakima."

"Actually, we were well under way before you two became available. However, while it will be a headquarters and you will of necessity make many trips down there, much of the work can be done from here. You won't have to move, at least not until you yourself feel you must. In fact, we can have some folks from the naval base near you drop by with your permission and secure your home—electronically, I mean—and key in some equipment to you and no one else. You can do it from your home, without even commuting."

I was impressed, but wondered about how effective this would be. "I'm all in favor of telecommuting, but what happens when I need expertise and have to talk to others? You don't build and maintain a coordinated programming team electronically."

"Oh, but you *can*, although I see what you're getting at. Frankly, we agree it will probably be less effective, and certainly less efficient, and you will certainly meet from time to time as necessary, but, well, from a security point of view it is best that you *do* remain apart, and not know each other *too* well. That means that if we must change someone in a key spot it will not cause a complete breakdown. We had that sort of thing on the last project—that is, being forced to change someone in a close-knit workgroup. We may find that this doesn't work, but, for at least a year, until we have to go back for funding again, there's no real hurry and we'll try this my way."

"Hard to say," I told him, "considering I haven't even seen the basics of this thing yet. But there has to be a way for constant Q and A access on things I know nothing about, and a quick way to test and exchange code and files without reinventing the wheel."

"*That* you will have. I guarantee you that you've never seen a wide area network like *this* one."


By the time we'd finished dinner and drinks and all that, a deal was pretty well made, at least on my end. I didn't really like this guy Stark, more on general principles than anything else, but he was typical of the government types that stood between creative people and real breakthrough type work in this day and age. I felt that if I didn't have to see him on a day-to-day basis I might be able to forget he existed after a while.

Once he had gone off into the night, however, we stood on the street corner with Rob and felt pretty much secure once more. "So, what was it you were dying to tell me once he was away?" I asked my old sales manager.

"Well, it's just—oh, okay. You know Stark and his type. G. Gordon Liddy before he got caught but without Liddy's sense of humor. Al *likes* to have people working for him that have rather clearcut vulnerabilities. He can't always do that, since with certain specific people like Matt Brand, you took them when you could get them, sort of like Einstein in the old days I guess, but when he puts together a group, well, he generally has a way to keep you very much on his side, like him or not. Me, I'm obvious. You—well, it wouldn't be much of a big deal to add a little fiction to that folder and its associated computer files in Washington, and before long you'd wind up indicted for selling supercomputers to the IRA or something. You know what I mean."

I nodded. "I got that impression. But, on a day-to-day, is he all that intrusive?"

"Not to me. He'll have somebody on you from now on, and probably on Riki as well, but the way you were talking about this weird woman, that might not be a bad thing."

A cab was coming along and I flagged it.

"I'm not so sure," Riki told him, as the taxi came over and stopped for us to get in.

"Huh? How's that?" I responded, surprised.

"Suppose this Stark's lying about her. Suppose she's right, and he's the dangerous one? Suppose she's not who or what he said at all. I just wish she'd talk to us the way Stark did. I'd like to compare the two."

We bid good-bye to Rob, who lived in the city, and headed off in the taxi for the ferry terminal.

I turned and frowned at Riki. "What's the problem?" she asked, confused.

"Well, I'd just had enough of an explanation that maybe at least I could get some sleep, and you go and rebuild my paranoia again. Thanks a lot."

She looked at me innocently and shrugged. "Any time. All you have to do is ask."

# III

# WALTZING TO
# A NEURAL WONDERLAND

I had to say this about Stark—once his men started on the house, they were damned good and full of surprises.

The biggest surprise was a simple card that was placed inside my home office computer. I was warned not to remove it or do much of anything with it—it has self-erasing ROM. The connector on the back was also pretty bizarre, and ran virtually the entire length of the backing, and this took a specialized cable the likes of which I'd never seen before that plugged into a brand-new outlet they put in that morning. The outlet led to my roof, and a small dish, about the size of a Ku-band one-meter broadcast dish but very much two-way. I knew only from seeing it come in and never seeing it again that the connection wasn't direct—there was some kind of cube about a foot square that was somewhere in between, but I never figured out where it had gone.

It certainly wasn't going to have the speed of a dedicated line, but it would be good enough for the kind of purposes I thought I might need.

There were also no more mysterious appearances of our southern femme fatale. Most likely she knew that somebody official was watching the house now, and probably shadowing us most of the time as well, both to protect us and to nab people like her. I think Riki was particularly upset with herself because of this, though. For the first time in a couple of days, she now felt reasonably free of fear and relaxed enough to go to the store on her own, draw in the studio, and so on, and this was because one of her greatest fears as a youth was realized: the government was indeed watching her all the time!

I did, however, get a phone call from Walt Slidecker at Subspace. "When you coming back in, Cory?"

"I'm not, Walt. Consider me on sabbatical until the company's sold. I have more than enough vacation time for that. When you're out and they're in, consider me formally resigned."

"Hey! You can't *do* that!"

"Sure I can, Walt. I can do that just the same as you can tell me you sold the company out from under all of us without any warning or any real attempt to make a go of it."

"But—you were part of the deal! I mean, this is a totally new technology here and you're the only one that really understands the details of the patent!"

In that he was right. As with a lot of inventions, everything necessary for the patent was there, but not exactly how it all went together so seamlessly. It was a really brilliant little discovery if I do say so myself, and was actually pretty much along the lines of the company name. No, I don't know what "subspace" is any more than you do, but it was a completely new principle—so obvious that I was dead certain I couldn't have been the first to notice it—that allowed you to seamlessly network up to five hundred computers without stringing a single wire or adding a booster or hub, with the quiet and power of a dedicated optical line, over distances that would at least cover most of Seattle and maybe all the way down to Tacoma. If that doesn't convince you that it was worth millions at the outset, then nothing can. And if you wanted to trust more than one server in a system, you could actually daisy-chain the suckers—five hundred plus five hundred plus, well, we hadn't hit the wall when it was all over.

Simple concept, yeah, and I knew that in six months to a year or more a vast team of very bright Far Eastern MIS engineers who had just about unlimited money and resources would crack the little combinations we put in there to thwart immediate rip-offs and have it down pat, but a lot of other folks would also have the year to examine the patent. The principle was just good physics, if a bit on the esoteric side of the science; it would be damned hard to uphold a patent on it. But the procedure for harnessing and making that principle do what I said it would—aye, *there's* the rub, and the patent, and the profits. Without me, they were going to have a very bad period of going quietly nuts before they got it, with the competition doing the same. I was their leg up; I already discovered the wheel and knew how it worked. I knew it, Walt knew it, and Sangkung knew it.

"I think it's the Fourteenth Amendment, Walt," I told him with a very amused tone and a sense of wicked justice deep down.

"Huh?"

"Abolished slavery. They didn't have one for intellectual theft, but you can't force people to work for you against their will. We never did sign any contracts and you know it. We shook hands. Well, yesterday you told me that it wasn't really a partnership, not when you owned half or more of the stock, and there wasn't a damned thing I could do about it. I agreed that you were right. So, that's it. You can sell the company without even telling me or anybody else and there's nothing I can do. And I can tell you to take a flying leap off a cliff and there's nothing you can do about it, either. If I'm a partner, I have obligations. If I'm an employee, I can quit. You defined it, and now I've quit. Go to hell, Walt."

I slammed the phone down, but I knew eventually I'd have to take his calls and work out something just to keep him from calling over and over again.

In fact, I thought when the phone rang again that it was him with another plea, but it was Rob. "I'm in my former office at Subspace," he told me, sounding very, very pleased with himself. "You won't believe it. I quit, then a whole line of people quit, just like that."

"They shouldn't quit. They may need the unemployment. Let 'em get laid off." Still, I was, deep down, very pleased and touched by this. These people had all worked above and beyond the call of duty as well, from the people who wrote the manuals to the folks who oversaw shipments, they all believed they were in on something new, big, and important. That's what had made the company so good to work for, and also what made Walt's actions seem more like Caesar stabbing Brutus and the whole Senate in the back.

"They'll be okay," Rob assured me. "There's not a one that can't pick up a job in this area. If they weren't sure, they wouldn't have quit. Makes you kinda proud to be an American, doesn't it? Wonder what would have happened if car workers, TV makers, and the like would have stood this firm in the early days?"

"We'd be a third-world country," I responded snappily, even though I was kind of proud of them. "You think Walt's going to try and cancel the deal? I know Sangkung's no babe in the woods. It'll try and push down the price after this."

"Push it down, maybe, but the patent's what they're after and they'll go ahead if only to keep any possible competitor from picking it up free and clear." He paused. "Look, I'm going to Yakima for a few days and see just how well things are coming along there. Want to come down with us?"

"Not now, no. In a while, when it's all a fully going concern, *then* I'll visit the apple city, but right now I've got more than enough to play with. Still, if Walt starts calling me every hour on the hour I might change my mind."

"Suit yourself. I'll give you a report when I get back. See ya."

"Yeah, take care," I told him, and hung up. Things were

just going too fast, I told myself. My whole world had been turned upside down in a matter of days and I still wasn't all that used to the new situation.

It was time to explore this most likely very encrypted access line and see just what had killed Matthew Brand.

I have to admit, it took me the better part of three days just to figure out the directory structure, even though the search engine was the most fantastic I'd ever seen. No, it wasn't real pretty and it didn't have fuzzy icons or anything like that, but there was a graphical mode for studying a *lot* of the highest resolution photos, drawings, and such I'd ever seen on any monitor. In fact, I was soon so absorbed by the sheer technical wizardry before me, a degree of computer gee-whizzery that was almost precisely what all the computer magazines said would be coming in five or ten years, that it took a while before I got down to business.

The satellite link was far too slow for the animated diagrams and the like, but clearly I was never directly dealing with that data. Instead I appeared to have a humongous buffer of some kind that downloaded everything in huge gulps and then fed it to me in real fiber-optic time. That box I never found was the key; what medium it was using I couldn't say, but this was the most advanced memory system I'd ever seen and it didn't seem to ever run out or bog down. Must be nice when you're the government, with a "black" budget to boot; you don't bother very much about cost, because the few overseers of the money are the same ones who want your services.

Reading vast amounts of documentation on a screen had never appealed to me, though, and there was no way around that here. I did try and print some of it out, but all it did was waste paper with error messages out of the printer. This stuff was not to be put into hard copy, period.

Late in the weekend, though, and in the wee hours of the morning, I found what I was looking for, the introduction and general proposal Brand had made to the NSA several years before. It was still couched in very technical terms, but five years is a long time in the computer business and what he was dealing with then we were just starting to look at now.

*"Proposal for Direct Neural Interconnect Biotech System for Total VR Simulations,"* he'd called it, and that was startling enough. Biotech systems. . . .

It was long and complex, and I wound up having to go search for other items in the middle to follow as much as I did—and this was still *way* the hell over my head, and maybe way the hell over any living human being's head—but I was beginning to get the idea of just what he was working on and just what the aims were and why government would be very, very interested.

What is "reality"? Sight, sound, touch, taste, smell—the five senses. Standard VR tried to fool those senses in the same way that IMAX-size screens or sixty-frame-per-second films gave roller-coaster-type sensations even when you were sitting there just watching. The flight-simulator approach pared with some VR added the last touches. Body suits, gimbal devices, all that sort of thing could give you even more. The problems were manifold with this approach, however, for serious long-term work.

For one thing, whether you were fooled into thinking you were in some bizarre computer-created existence or not, your body was still real. Short sessions were all that were ever going to be practical with that approach.

And, for all the freeform abilities they'd come up with, the system was still fraught with all sorts of wires and interconnects, which meant a limit to mobility. In a sense, it was a bizarre peculiarity—one could fly easier than one could convincingly walk and move in a normal fashion, and a lot of the more elaborate stuff looked like high-quality animation but not reality. No matter how hard you tried, a virtual rose never looked, smelled, and felt like a real rose, and a virtual steak was anything but satisfying.

Brand basically called the entire VR industry a dead end,

a primitive level that would be doomed to remain that way. He wanted a perfect simulation, something that would, somehow, interact directly with the human brain and allow the human mind to access the computer information packets in the same way biological neural networks were organized to provide our real memories to us. A detachable synthesis of human and machine, a sort of symbiosis, or cyborg setup, that would provide the perfect simulation of just about anything because it would be as real as anything you actually experienced.

There were, of course, a few *minor* details to be worked out. First, did we even know enough about the brain, still the most complex structure known in the universe, to hook into it directly, convincingly or otherwise? Even if it was possible, would a single system be available that would work for everyone? And, assuming the direct connection was made, was there any computer that could feed information at or near brain speed, or hold the vast wealth of information that would be necessary to create a convincing virtual world that might even totally fool the subject?

And how, and where, would the body be maintained if the brain were hooked into this bizarre apparatus?

Incredibly, Brand believed he already had solved the algorithms to allow for computers of the sort the NSA used to actually create and maintain such a convincing reality. I couldn't follow the math, which was of a sort so strange that I felt like a New Guinea primitive looking at a complex calculus equation on a blackboard, but I could follow the logic and grant the math at those stages because clearly these had proved out or the government wouldn't have given him a dime.

Almost as dizzying but still more within my abilities to grasp were how he got and utilized this information once he had it. Like the hidden box in the satellite relay, there was an enormous fluid storage area that contained one or more of what Brand called base realities—all the history and science and math and art and culture from all the books and films ever turned online, which would of course mesh with the living mind that was somehow connected to it. A familiar base. In fact, a base indistinguishable from true reality to the subject. In a kind of tongue-in-cheek reference to it, he called this reservoir, which was a physical device, the Looking Glass, because it reflected reality.

Then, the Program. Brand labeled it ITYS, which, as it turned out, stood for "I told you so." Brand was never really political; in some ways he was the absolute one-track computer nerd. Still, he came into contact with a lot of politicians from the far left to the far right and everything in between, and, walking through an industry crammed with young urban professionals, he was more than familiar with concepts like political correctness and academic attempts to impose Orwellian-like Newspeak on whole campus populations so as to not offend anybody. He needed a setup to prove out his idea, and ITYS was it, culled from just those experiences.

With it, hooked to the subject and to the Looking Glass device, it would allow a subject, or as many as might be networked to the single Looking Glass device, to alter or create a variance or series of variances in the base reality. It became at that point a simple matter of "what ifs" if, in fact, the program understood and correctly enabled the variances. You didn't have to fill in the blanks down to the atomic level; the computer would retain as much of the base as it could and alter only what its ruthlessly logical process would have to alter.

Brand even suggested a number of possibilities, suggesting that he perhaps watched too much old television while thinking as well. The George Bailey Variance, for example—"What if X had never been born?" The Peggy Sue Variance—"What if I didn't choose the path that I did but chose a different path instead?" There were do-it-yourself alternative histories—what if Communism had won the cold war? What if the Nazis had won World War Two?

Well, you see where he went with it, and it seemed fascinating if totally impossible to ever do. Who wouldn't like to play with something like this? To actually see, feel, *live*, for a time, in a universe which was familiar but significantly different from the real world.

For government and industry it would also be irresistible long before they turned to entertainment, if such a system could ever be simplified and made inexpensive enough to allow that. Proposals, contingency plans, for the military, for the economy, for almost all the major decisions a government or policy-setting board might take—all could be examined for their consequences, including, thanks to that computer logic, all the hidden costs. Once the problem was set up and accepted, the computer would take over. You'd be stuck with what you asked for, for whatever period of time you requested, or until you exercised some key to terminate the simulation.

It was a great concept, and I even granted the unlikely idea that his programs and his computer hardware were correct, possible, perhaps even developed to some extent, although I'd hate to beta-test that program. Knowing how many bugs are in any complex piece of software, the idea of attaching my mind to a prototype wasn't thrilling.

As I say, though, I granted that the great Matthew Brand had that part all worked out.

Who compiled the knowledge base and how? And how did you connect his program and that hardware to a mind and operate at the same or at worst a negligible difference in speed between the compact and organic and the huge, mechanical, and, even if you were sitting on top of it, distant, in networking terms, device? And who would maintain the bodies and how for extended periods?

In a sense, Brand seemed too much the visionary and doomed to failure. By the time biology and understanding of the brain caught up to what his system required, his hardware and software would probably be primitive and obsolete! In any event, it just did not seem at all possible to do in reality what he dreamed of. The biophysics and biochemistry just weren't there.

Al Stark's bosses shared the Brand dream, all right, but they just couldn't let go of it. Neither could Brand. What had driven such a genius to experiment with hooking himself up as a beta subject to whatever had been worked out? I was becoming convinced that nothing less than that had led directly to his death.

Finally, I was able to sit back, even with only a bare scratching of the surface of what was there, and see what all this had been about. The question at this point was whether or not it was worth going after again. Somehow, I saw this as another wild-goose chase, a chance for some bureaucrats and politicians to spend a lot of bucks chasing an impossible dream. Going back to the Moon or to Mars would have been easier—we pretty much knew how to do that—but *this* was different. A do-it-yourself God simulator. The universe's neatest toy, but about as attainable at this stage of our knowledge as antigravity or a *Star Trek* transporter.

It didn't take long to realize that this was a total waste of my time. I began to wonder if I should have been all that nasty to Walt.

I did, however, desperately want to talk all this over with others who were even more familiar with the whole project than I was, and maybe smart enough to follow all of that Brandian math. There was no way *I* was going to be the one to score a breakthrough here; this was, as I said, out of my league. At best I could be a help with the nuts and bolts around the fringes of it.

There was just something nagging at me that I couldn't shake. Even in this era of nine-thousand-dollar coffee makers and six-thousand-dollar hammers, no single individual would have the authority to authorize the kind of expenditures restarting the project might take, nor, I suspect, would they want the sole responsibility. That meant that this had come

out of a committee, and that this committee would have con-
sulted a great many secure and trusted scientists and engineers familiar with what I was now going over.

Somebody, maybe a lot of important somebodies, thought
this could be made to work.

I still didn't believe it myself, but I was willing to be convinced, and the easiest way to do that was to come right out
and say so. Using the email facility on the new system, I shot
a note to Stark.

*"In two words: im-possible. If you really want to waste so
much of the taxpayer's money I have a lot more constructive
suggestions. More fun, too. Maddox."*

I figured that would get some kind of response.

In the meantime, Riki was dying to know as much of the
story as she could follow, and it wasn't hard to describe it.

"Jeez! You mean you kind of plug your brain into a
computer and live in a universe it builds? Wow! Sounds
neat—and dangerous."

"It's all of that," I responded. "However, it's also impossible,
so don't worry too much about it."

"Impossible? Or just not yet? What do you think? I mean,
will we be able to build something like it someday?"

I shrugged. "I don't know, but I guess you're right—it *is*
possible. It's just not possible now."

"How do you know?"

"Huh?"

"I'm serious. How do you know it *isn't* possible now?"

I thought about it. "Well, for one thing, it would mean
that we know more about the human brain we aren't admitting than we know about computers and aren't admitting. I
just don't believe we do, or that they'd have reason to hide
that kind of knowledge if we had it. No, I'm convinced that
this is still *two* ideas, and for all the incredible theoretical
work Brand did on his end, only half of it is even close to
being done."

She wasn't so sure. "I wonder. I mean, how would we know?"

"Huh?"

"Well, didn't you say that the world it created would seem so real to anybody hooked up to it that you wouldn't be able to tell the difference? That for all intents and purposes it *would* be reality?"

"Yeah, but—"

"Would it seem as real as this, here, now?"

"I suppose. . . ."

"So how would we ever *know*? Man! You could start a *cult* on the idea that this is all in the mind, or in a machine. Maybe this isn't reality at all. Jeez! Maybe *you're* really *me* and *I'm* really you! Kind of like reincarnation, huh? You don't know who you really are while you're in. Kinky and creepy at the same time."

"Don't start *that*! Reality's hard enough, I think!" I told her. "I wouldn't worry about it, though. Hell, I remember being me back to being a really little kid and I suspect you do, too. I may be slipping as I get older, but I still remember an awful lot. Much too much to believe that all this is some sort of construct. Thinking like *that*, except in fun, is a nice start toward a one-way trip to a rubber room."

"You never know," she responded, a wee bit playfully, "but it sure would explain a whole lot of the inexplicable."

*New York City and Harvard University have been dismantled. Divert him from those sectors! Move!* What was that from? Sheesh! Talk about unstoppable paranoia! I have to stop this sort of thing or *I'm* the one headed for a rubber room, I told myself. I guess in one way I was like Matt Brand—too much television, movies, and science fiction and horror books growing up. How could you always tell Future Nerds of America? None of them ever went to their senior prom, that's how.

That *did* raise some interesting minor points in the ITYS system, though. Would this "floating" knowledge base bother to construct and maintain everything all the time, or would it just do what was needed and postulate the rest? If none of the minds networked to it were anywhere near New York or Harvard and had no reason to call there, would it bother to create and maintain that many millions of individuals. Hardly. It would simply postulate what was happening there so it could create it if need be while putting what was no longer needed on hold. Saved a lot on memory that way, I guess, not to mention speed and efficiency. There wouldn't be any "dismantling," though; this virtual universe would be in many ways a very personal existence. Whatever you interacted with, whoever you interacted with, would be "real"; the rest would be left in the knowledge base until needed and constructed at near lightspeed. There would be nothing beyond any door or around any curve—until you opened that door or went around the curve. Then where you'd been but could no longer see or interact with would cease to exist.

That was kind of creepy, but made the system a lot more practical and in some cases believable, given the biological advances that were my own primary stumbling block.

Still, I couldn't let her get away with this. If *I* was going to sleep paranoid, then *she* was going to sleep paranoid.

"You didn't think it through enough," I told her. "It might be worse than the two of us actually being other people somewhere. Did you ever think that it may be that only *one* of us is real?"

I saw the playfulness go out of her eyes and be replaced with an overall expression of disgust. "Now, why'd you have to go and say *that*?"

"Because it's the answer to the jingle."

"Huh? What jingle?"

"Everything you think you know is wrong. Remember? If just one, or maybe both of us, are really somewhere else and this is some kind of alternate reality, then that would be true. *Nothing* would be real. Still, I'm not too worried about that being that case."

"Huh? Why not?"

"Because I'd hope that any virtual universe somebody might create would be at least *interesting*. This one's been kind of dull overall."

I got an answer from Stark by voice rather than secure email the next day.

"Can't say much on the phone, you know," he told me in his best conspiratorial government tones, "but I think perhaps you should come on down here for a couple of days. I think you might find some surprises of interest here."

"You're in Yakima?"

"Yes, at the old store. I must say they've done a remarkable reconstruction job on it. We'll have the last of the old equipment here and installed by midweek, I should think. Most of the new stuff is already in. Would it surprise you to know that yours wasn't the first, nor the second, nor even the fifth similar response to the materials I received?"

"Not if the people you recruited are as good as they should be in their fields," I replied. "They'd be dishonest if they didn't say that."

"Yes, indeed. In fact, it's something of a test, you might say, of professional ethics and integrity. I've decided that I was wrong to keep everyone isolated completely, and I think we ought to have at least one or two face-to-facers now and again as well as interacting by computer. I'd like you to come down here on Thursday if you can manage it. Eight in the morning, we'll supply breakfast and all that. You can come Wednesday night and we'll put you up at a motel if you like."

"You've got a deal, at least that far, but I have to tell you I'm inclined to stop right here and walk away."

"I know, I know. I respect you for it. Just come down anyway, and, before you do—got a pen or pencil handy?"

"Yes?"

"Look up a file called one-seven-seven-three-two-three-stroke-eight in the 'Contracts' section. Read it. I'm afraid it's the one thing you really will have to face to get the full story. See you Thursday, then. Email the travel office at the naval base—you have their Internet address—if you want or need good lodgings. Good-bye."

"Yeah, sure, I think," I responded, and hung up the phone. *Now* what?

The file was easy enough to find, when you had the section and number, and it was written in the usual legalese of government lawyers. Still, quite a number of things caught my eye about it, and I realized that they were expecting anybody to sign this to even get in the door on Thursday.

Tough slogging or not, I'd waded through enough of this sort of stuff in the past to make it out pretty well.

I had unintentionally lied to Walt when I said they hadn't repealed the Fourteenth Amendment. This thing sure did.

Oh, it wasn't the kind of thing that forced you to work against your will—particularly in a project like this, if you weren't doing it for sheer love then you weren't going to be able to do anything at all. It was the bit on "Personal Recognizance Category A Security Risks" that was at the heart. It basically said that I realized that I was going to have access to official secrets on a need-to-know basis in spite of my not having attained the proper clearance upon the personal responsibilities of security agencies. It wanted me to certify that, upon my own word, I was as secure as anybody who could fully pass those tests, and that if the agency or agencies allowing me access beyond my level discovered that I had, for any reason, violated that security trust, I understood that I could be arrested by said agencies and charged and held under a series of federal laws I bet weren't in the federal law libraries and would hardly ever be brought to the attention of the Supreme Court.

In other words, "We are going to trust you with secrets you don't deserve. If you let slip any of them, period, for

any reason, you will disappear and they will never even find
your body."

I kind of expected this sort of thing, but now here it was.
Did I sign it, or not? If not, that was it. I was out. All this
new equipment would vanish as quickly as it had been installed, and I would be cast out as "unclearable" into a
business that depended for a huge share of its dollars on government contracts and purchases.

Of course, it did raise the other question: If I was being
asked to sign this only now, then what I'd been given access
to so far wasn't all that classified, or at least wasn't outside
what they would have tolerated for commercial stuff. Not
that anybody would believe this stuff anyway, any more than
I did.

It even led to another, nastier question: Was this all a fake?
Did it sound impossible because it was so much science
fiction? Was I willing to sign this kind of contract now and
find out?

*You remind me of the man.*

*What man?*

*The man with the Power . . .*

There were a number of ways to make the relatively easy trip
from Seattle to Yakima, but all involved dealing with this inconvenient mountain range called the Cascades and through it
some mighty big "dormant" volcanoes. Dormant—you know,
like Mount St. Helens? Well, anyway, you could take the
freeway east and then another one south, you could take one
south and then jog east, or you could take the old, colorful
routes right through Mt. Rainier National Park—provided it
wasn't winter, anyway. In that case, the huge volcano, one of
the prettiest anywhere, got a ton of snow each year, and there
were features listed in national park guidebooks that had been
under too much snow to see since sometime in the Great De-

pression. The old park lcdge did a brisk business during the summer season, but in midwinter was buried above its roof—forty to fifty *feet* of snow wasn't all that unusual. I wasn't getting paid by the hour; what the heck, I'll always take the scenic route under those conditions, and threading those winding roads in a Porsche is one reason you buy that kind of car in the first place.

It wasn't a bad drive now, with the birds singing and the sun shining, but clearly anybody who needed the resources they were putting back into the old Yakima site would have to move down there or take helicopter lessons.

"I'm not sure why I even am in this," Riki complained unhappily. "I mean, you know my background. I couldn't get a security clearance to see next month's *Science* magazine cover, I got a Power Mac in the studio and maybe a half-dozen art programs tops, and that's all I want to know about computers. I'm an artist!"

"They were pretty insistent that you come along," I told her. "Somehow I think this went too far too fast. It's like them to do this. The moment we met with Stark we were in, period, particularly after they showed us what they say this project's about. Maybe from the point at which that southern wacko targeted me and you were there, I dunno. At any rate, we were both sucked in and that was that. If I don't sign that paper I might as well become your agent, because I'm out of doing much except maybe going to work for the Open Software Foundation, which thinks that world revolution will come when every human being speaks UNIX, or some game company."

"*Are* you gonna sign that?"

"I don't know. Would you?"

"I—I'm not in your position."

We were driving on the two-lane park road and there was a real sense of unreality to what we were talking about as the gorgeous scenery just kept coming and coming.

I sighed. "I'm afraid you are. If I sign and you don't, then they'll have a license to monitor *everything* about us, just to ensure that I don't even tell *you* about it."

"You mean they'll bug the whole house?"

"And car and probably anything else and shadow us and so on, yeah. I think that's probably already happening, although I can't prove it. The odds are real good that they're getting this conversation as easily as one we have in the office or in bed. Those guys were really good and they went through almost everything, remember. Nobody can tune out that kind of strain when you don't even know what it's for exactly. I'd vanish for days at a time, maybe weeks, and I couldn't even warn you or tell you how long or where. Eventually we'd go nuts and split. Nope, it's got to be both of us or neither of us. There's no middle ground."

"But that's not *fair*! I couldn't follow that stuff if I *tried*!"

"And I can? And I assume that's only the lowest-level stuff. But, that's the way it is. When this opens, everybody from the local papers to the computer press and industry to all sorts of unfriendly parties will want to know exactly what's going on with this new project, this resurrection of something founded by the legendary Matthew Brand. That's the bottom line, babe. Either we both sell our souls to Al Stark or we split. That's the only realistic thing we can do."

"I refuse to believe that! I *can't* accept it!" She paused. "Unless you *want* to split."

"I don't want to split. That's why I won't sign unless you do. Period. We'll pack up, put the house on the market, and move to Mexico or Costa Rica or something."

She thought it over. "You know, that woman was right! She *warned* us not to go to that appointment or have anything to do with Stark. We should have listened."

"Maybe. She also said everything we thought we knew was wrong, too, and she played a lot of stupid and childish games on me."

She gave off a long sigh. "So you've dumped this all on me, huh?"

"That *is* pretty much what it comes down to," I admitted. "Even worse, I don't know if it's worth it or not."

"But you have a feeling that they have a lot more of it done than you think, right? Otherwise why are we driving to Yakima of all places?"

I nodded. "I think they probably do have all the pieces. I never did think that they'd perfect neural implants in my life-time, but over the past few days I just figured they must have. I tried calling a bunch of folks who have been working on them for some time and found that I couldn't seem to get hold of the best ones. Wonder why?"

"Umph! Neural implants, huh? Sounds like a nice way to turn humans into machines."

"Maybe. It's always been an ethical quagmire, but it's been a safe and easy one because we just didn't know enough to really do it."

"And you think they know enough now?"

"I'm not sure, but if they're any way along at all I want to know it. I'd have nightmares about me having a plug into my cerebral cortex where they could implant memories, com-mands, attitudes, you name it, or remove undesirable mate-rial. *That's* the really scary part here. I don't think this kind of cyber reality Brand envisioned is all that practical, but false memories, now *there* is a different story. What's the difference if your present is real if your past is a fake? And that sort of thing in the hands of the CIA, the politicians, well. . . ."

"Stop it! You're making me scared again!"

"You got it. I'm scared, too, I think. We've been told this is still a few years away, but who really knows for sure? I never thought it would be as close as the futurists predicted, if only because only government could afford it and govern-ment was broke, but it's a real possibility."

"And you want to work on something like that?" she asked me.

That was the real question. *Did* I want to work on it? *Should* I? "It's cutting-edge stuff, that's for sure, but it's Manhattan Project–style revolutionary but really on the cheap compared to that sort of thing. No, I want to be reassured that I'm all wet and that they can't do this, but I also want to know if they can, and the only way to know is to work on it."

"Then we might as well sign the papers," she told me. "I mean, what difference does it make? If we didn't and put out all our speculation, almost nobody would believe us and two-thirds of your buddies in the computer business would think it was really neat if they did. And then one night we get spirited away, and after coming back from some 'vacation' we have all sorts of convincing false memories that will make us look like fools. So, we might as well. The devil you know and all that. . . ."

I blew her a kiss. "Good girl. Maybe we can at least have some tiny little voice in the debate over its use. If *we* don't do it, I'm not sure if anybody else with our fears would be there to represent the rest of us."


Yakima's always been an interesting town. As you might have guessed, its reason for existence is Washington State's most famous export, the apple, which has been grown for as far as anyone can see around the town ever since it was founded. The town itself is kind of shaped like a cross—two main streets going for miles with every conceivable commercial attraction and need filled along them, but otherwise just houses below each cross "arm" and not much else. They have some restored streetcars they run along the railroad tracks that run all over to pick up the apples, and the folks are pleasant, but it's not exactly a town most folks move to and it has few high-tech industries.

The old Zyzzx campus was at the far end of the main drag,

where you turned off just before the end of town, then went up this narrow road through thick trees and apple orchards back to a huge old mansion that at one time was owned by one of the apple barons here and which had been gutted and rebuilt inside into a lab and think tank by Brand five years earlier. In spite of a PRIVATE ROAD—DO NOT ENTER sign at the start, there was no obvious sign that this was a secured area, and it wasn't until you took the road well in and out of sight of the main highway that you met the more utilitarian gate house and armed guards and could see the extensive and very high multiple fences which enclosed the whole area, the first two chain-link style with nasty barbed stuff on top and the third solid and painted to almost blend in with the grass and trees but which had weird-looking gadgets all along it. From the looks of it, you could meet some nasty Dobermans as well as guards in between the first two, and if you made the solid one you'd find that it was electrified well up just this one side.

The guards took our thumbprints, compared them to existing cards, nodded, and one of them gave each of us a clip-on pass that already had our names and color photos on them! "Don't deviate from the road or stop until you reach the end of the tree line," the guard instructed. "Park in the lot on the left and enter the big house. Your cards are currently good only for the public areas, immediate grounds, and meeting room one. Please don't wander around without authority."

"Um, yeah, thanks, I think," I responded. And we thought our security back at Subspace Networking was complicated! I knew how the cards worked—they were getting pretty standard in the industry among the largest corporations. Once inside the perimeter here, somebody in a security shack would know exactly where we were at all times and be able to plot us. Anybody without a card wouldn't be able to open a damned door, just as we wouldn't be able to enter anywhere that the card wasn't remotely authorized to allow us to go. It was a very nice system, but it was damned expensive and only worthwhile if you really had the security jitters or a serious need to protect.

Clearing those, you turned another corner and the trees stopped and you saw the legendary haunt of Matthew Brand.

It was a monstrous Victorian-style place, a good city block square if they'd have had blocks here, and behind it were three large two-story outbuildings that looked newer and more like wings on a school, although at one time they'd probably been the location of carriage houses and such.

"Looks like the Addams Family getaway," Riki commented dryly.

There was quite a parking lot. It wasn't Disneyland, but I had to figure that several hundred people were working here at least, not counting those represented by the various commercial and drab, government-style trucks still obviously working on finishing up various things inside and out; and the big dishes in the meadow off to one side not only contained the usual types but also some like I'd never seen before.

I parked in the lot as instructed, and we walked together over to the big old house and up the wooden stairs that probably looked much like they had when the place was built except for the nonskid overlays. Whoever had done the exterior was a real lover of old architecture; the paint, the color scheme, everything had both a newness and an appropriateness to it that just seemed right. The government would never have paid any mind to that; this had to be Brand's doing, with the government just maintaining a new paint job because it was cost-effective to do so.

"The world's only computerized Victorian mansion north of Disneyland," I commented. "Bet there's more high-tech stuff in the walls and cracks of this place than anybody would dream."

"Maybe," Riki said uncertainly. "Gives me the creeps myself. I've painted places like this for horror-novel covers."

Inside, the basics of room placement had been pretty well maintained and, at least in front, some feel of the old place as well. You could already see, though, that, further back, it looked all too utilitarian and familiar.

Sitting at a huge desk just inside the door, her back to what was obviously an original sitting room now crammed with file cabinets but still showing its great woodwork and ceiling through the mess, was a Dress for Success woman I took to be in her middle thirties. She was a bit too thin and the face was a little too hard-looking for me, and the brown eyes through the thick eyeglasses seemed cold, at least when looking at me, but she was efficient. "You are twenty minutes early," she told us.

"Sorry," I responded. "I meant to be forty minutes early."

She wasn't amused. "Down the hall, up the second stairway that you pass, then the first door on your right. It will say 'Meeting One' on the door. Coffee and tea are already in there, but the food has not yet arrived."

We just nodded and walked away, following instructions but looking around. There wasn't a room we passed whose door was open that didn't seem full of computer equipment, a couple or more people both civilian and military, various file cabinets, lots of optical stuff, you name it. In most, wiring was still exposed and there were panels missing in false drop ceilings that totally ruined what was left of the rooms but nicely hid all the stuff running to and fro, and everywhere there were boxes. It was clearly still very much a work in progress. A majority of the doors, however, were shut, and clearly opened only to those with the Holy Password beamed to your ID.

"I don't know what's worse, the look of the place from the outside or the atrocious way they treated it on the inside," Riki commented. "This is tacky as hell, yet I keep feeling like I've seen this all in a bad movie someplace, the Late Late Show, and that they're printing the licenses to kill in the print shop out back."

"It's pretty ordinary for a government job," I assured her, "and not too out of line with a lot of computer R&D labs."

"How do you know it's ordinary for the government?" she asked me. "You never worked for the government, did you? Or is there something you're not telling me?"

"No, never did," I answered truthfully, but, still, it worried me because I knew I had spoken the absolute truth and it almost seemed as if I'd spoken it from experience. "I have the weirdest sense of *déjà vu*," I told her as we went up the stairs to the second floor. "Like I was here before. But, I swear, the only time I was ever in Yakima before this was on my way south from Seattle to Portland once when I came over to ride the trolley, and that was years ago, before I even moved there, when I was just looking around. Weird."

The meeting room wasn't a classroom facility, thank heavens. It was, rather, one of those big rooms with two extra large board tables with comfortable padded and backed chairs on rollers. Comfortable, like you'd do for an extra-large board meeting, with a projection screen dead center front and a small lectern off to one side. It wasn't easy to tell, but I guessed that one of the ceiling panels concealed a master projection unit, probably projection TV, that could be fed anything from tapes to disks to slides to computer output and optical CDs. The drinks were in typical hotel-style urns in the back, labeled "Regular," "Decaf," and "Hot Water." There were a ton of teas, including designer ones, available, and I assumed that the coffee would be decent. To not be in *this* state would be like giving out sour orange juice in Florida. In Washington, coffee was a religion.

I made my own, and when I turned to ask Riki if she'd like me to make something for her, coffee or tea, she instead was looking away, back into the room, and said, "Eighteen. Nineteen counting the lectern position."

"Huh?"

"That's how many seats. Two sets of nine each, which is an odd number and not as many as I thought there'd be. Counting the two of us, I wonder who the others can be and why they were picked?"

We didn't have long to wait to find out. In fact, almost as soon as she said that, the far door opened and Rob came in and spied us. "Cory! Riki! *Great* to see you!" he called, and walked to us, smiling broadly. Behind him, looking somewhat hesitant, was a young-looking muscular man with long blond hair and a kind of silly if shy smile. Rob turned and gestured back. "You remember Lee, don't you?"

Lee Henreid and Rob Garnett had been together for a couple of years, an odd couple in looks and personality even in their own subculture, or so it seemed to me. The fact was, Rob was the most ordinary looking guy, slightly balding, near middle age, that I knew. Hell, he *looked* like somebody's sales manager, and sounded the same. Henreid, his longtime companion, was younger, handsome, and yet swishier than all hell. Riki had always liked Rob but never felt comfortable around Lee. I often suspected that it was because the blond guy was more effeminate than she was.

Before Lee could or would say much, though, two other people also entered, and Rob was again into introductions. "Lee, get me a coffee," he asked his partner, then was all business.

The newcomers were two women who seemed pretty far apart. One was, if anything, more all-business than the receptionist or whoever she was downstairs, in a tailored pants suit, virtually no makeup, an actual *tie* of all things, and hair so short I figured she either was a follower of an exercise guru or she got her hair cut at a military basic training facility. This is not to say she was masculine; it was more a kind of statement of "keep away." The other woman seemed more like a computer type; she was in turtleneck and designer jeans, short, round-faced, with a pixie-style cut. She was short and confident enough not to compensate with heels; she was definitely comfortable, and she had just a touch of makeup and two oversized golden triangular earrings. No, not triangles—kind of structural pyramids.

"Alice McKee," Rob introduced, nodding toward the tall

woman in the suit, "and Sally Prine. Doctor McKee is the Chair of the Sociology Department at U.C. Berkeley right now, but was a major consultant to the old corporation here, and Ms. Prine was the coordinator of the whole project when Matthew Brand ran the show here and since was with IBM Systems in Boca Raton and then Raleigh."

The food came in just after that point, followed by several others, and all the social amenities ceased for practical reasons. Besides, why bother to do intros now when you'd have to do them again and again for everybody who showed up?

It was an impressive breakfast buffet, lacking only a made-to-order omelet station. Eggs, scrambled, boiled, and coddled; sausages; bacon; fruit; juices; the works.

By the time we'd finished, and guys in white who might have been anything from military to caterers came in and cleared it away, the whole place had a definite restaurant smell to it and there were a lot of us there, including Stark, who was at the expected lectern/head of the first table position.

There were ten men and nine women overall; nine and nine if you didn't count Stark. Interesting. Some were couples, including couples that didn't seem to be at first glance like Rob and Lee, but most were entirely on their own or so it seemed, since it was obvious that you were told to bring your partner with you if you had one. In a couple of cases it was pretty obvious why they lived alone, although you never knew about people and there was no accounting for taste.

We were not a study in racial diversity, but there was a young and attractive black couple there, Ben and Dorothy Sloan, who appeared to both be in the computer industry; an exotic-looking Native American woman who seemed old beyond her years and dressed with an emphasis on Amerind designs, a Japanese American man, and a woman who was definitely not native to the U.S. who was clearly Chinese. It was a less eclectic group than I expected, and seemed to range in age between maybe thirty at the bottom and fifty at the high end. They ranged from suits to casual, and nobody seemed to feel totally out of place with the others no matter how differently dressed they were.

Needless to say, neither Riki nor I had anything formal on, and not much in the way of designer stuff, either. Sweaters, jeans, and boots were routine for us.

I saw Stark check to ensure that nothing was left except perhaps coffee and tea and the cups for the same, and that all the hired help was gone and clear. He then poked his head out the door, and the chilly receptionist entered with a stack of papers and handed one stack to the first table and the rest to the second.

"Pass them all down and around, please," Stark asked us. "This shouldn't be much of a shock, and those of you who want to check it can do so, but it's the same form I asked you all to look at before you came. I assume you knew we'd need them. When you're satisfied, sign, date, and pass them back up front. Leslie is a notary and will process each one and that will be that. If any of you are inclined not to sign, then please say so now, as we will make certain you have a quick but polite escort off the campus."

There was one couple, younger than me, who seemed extraordinarily well-scrubbed, he in suit and tie and she in a real dress, and she raised her hand.

"Yes, Mrs. Standish?"

"I'm just married to him. Do I have to sign this? I don't even understand why I'm here!"

"Yes, I'm sorry, Mrs. Standish, but you must sign individually. The reasons will become clear later on, but basically it's so that nobody will have to keep too many secrets from a partner with resulting stress. We've found from experience that this is best in these rush clearance situations with an H-Eighteen secret category. Anybody else with questions?"

There weren't any aloud, although I really wondered about this crowd. Who *were* these people and why were any of us here as opposed to other people? I'd had no sense of a pattern yet. And what was an H-Eighteen secret category?

When all the agreements were signed, witnessed, and checked one for one, "Leslie" left with them and Al Stark began the meeting.

"Welcome to Wonderland," he told us in a pleasant tone. "That's what Matt Brand called this place and you'll find it is at least that. What you are about to learn is among the most secret of all the secrets the technology branch of the DIA has. Some of you know the background here from having worked with us in the past, but bear with me. New things have developed as well. For the rest, consider it a refresher course in the history of science, modern type.

"It begins in 1947, near a desolate town called Roswell, New Mexico. . . ."

# IV

# THE CATERPILLAR'S QUESTION

There have been millions of flying-saucer sightings over the years, but only one really stands out and that's Roswell. It's the one with the most independent eyewitnesses and the most documentation and surrounded by the most mystery. If paranoia against the government by large masses of people can have a single starting point, it was Roswell, where it was even announced by the air force that a flying saucer had crashed and this was later retracted, the area put under martial law, every bit of evidence seized and carted away, and then the official explanation of "weather balloon" that became synonymous with government fabrication was first used.

Now, as we sat there, in far-off Yakima, in an old apple baron's mansion, a fellow named Al Stark was telling us that the legend of Roswell was true, even down to the never confirmed but always suspected *inhabitants* of that saucer.

"The thing itself slammed into the ground with enormous force," Stark told us, "and broke up on crash landing. Something ruptured, and the thing blew itself to smithereens. That's not to say that there weren't huge pieces—most of you

are familiar with what a crashed commercial jet looks like—
but in terms of figuring out those engines, engines that might
have given us the stars—no go. A mass of melted alloys with
tantalizing shapes kind of sticking out of the crud. We did,
however, do just what we do when an aircraft goes down—
we numbered and identified each piece, then crated up everything and took it to a huge hangar at an air force base to
attempt a reconstruction. This was, of course, 1947, and
things were much more primitive than now, but this was also
the government who'd just won the war and created the atom
bomb and they shouldn't be dismissed as incompetents."

Even if it was old hat to some there, you could hear a
pin drop.

"The advantage we have with airliners," Stark continued,
"is that we know what they looked like all along, all the way
down to the wiring diagrams. We had a lot of guesswork on
this one, a lot of jigsaw-puzzle logic, and it's amazing they
got it as close as they eventually did. I've seen the pictures,
and if it didn't look like that, it just had to be close. There
*was* no wiring, of course, and in '47 it was too early for them
to recognize the kind of printed circuits they were facing.
They've only become obvious later, when we started moving
in a similar direction. They did make some strong guesses;
Dr. Kahn and others who were called in on this went on to
help invent the transistor and integrated circuitry within the
next five to ten years. It was only in retrospect, sometime
in the early sixties I think, that we realized that the entire
vehicle, minus creature comforts and skin, was basically a series of circuit boards inserted into a gigantic motherboard that
was the whole lower deck of the thing. It's entirely possible
that the engines themselves were on this motherboard the
same way you'd stick on large capacitors or resistors. We'll
never know. Um, yes, Dr. Tanaka?"

The Japanese-looking man, who sounded more California
than Kyoto when he spoke and proved to be that way later,

had said only two words, and he repeated them now. "Um—'creature comforts'?"

Stark took a breath. "Yes. I'm getting to that. Now, the ship wasn't huge—we doubt if it was a far-ranging interstellar craft although, as I say, nothing can be known for sure. Four inhabitants, and, no, they weren't green and, no, they didn't look like all these alien abduction creatures, either. They *were* smaller than we are, the tallest maybe five feet, and they had a bizarrely different evolution than we did. Even so, they were humanoid in basic form and they had brains in their rather large and hard ugly heads. They were all dead, of course. If any of them could have survived that crash they wouldn't have needed a spaceship in the first place. Now, I'm going to show you one of the most classified slides in the world, although if it *did* get out it would be attributed by most people to special effects anyway."

We all kind of held our breaths as the ceiling panel slid back and a projector descended pretty much as I'd figured. The projector lit up, and Stark pressed a button on his wireless control.

The slide was of the damnedest head I'd ever seen, facing left, in profile. Stark was right; it may be a species prejudice, but this sucker was uglier than sin. Mottled dark rusty orange and purple skin, heavily furrowed and wrinkled, no obvious ears, *big* dull black eyes shaped like teardrops, a kind of horned protrusion that might have been a nose, and a small chinless mouth that had something of birdlike qualities about it. The whole thing seemed to be in a perpetual look of surprise.

"A Roswell crew member," Stark said needlessly. "Two of the crew were absolutely butchered by the medical guys of the time in autopsies; a third was mangled and so used mostly in chemical analysis. This one was saved on ice in hopes that we could figure out how to learn more later. What you will see next is one of the things this farsighted policy

yielded—a CAT scan and full three-D brain scan of the creature using the best equipment."

The slide wasn't as clear as a bell to those of us without
medical or biological backgrounds, but a very oddly shaped
but still human-sized organ that just about had to be a brain
was there. That, and a lot of very strange things that didn't
match up with any anatomy I could figure out, going along
the back of the brain and at several points into it, branching
into tiny fingers.

"I'm sure you can see what interested us the most," Stark
commented. "They were struck at the time by the lack of
controls in the saucer—no obvious wheel, or switches, dials,
you name it. Just four chairs, two in front, two facing rear.
No controls obvious on the chairs, but even the chairs were
plugged into the motherboard. At the time some suggested
that the ship was piloted by machine, and all four were
passengers, or the more far out ones suggested it was run
by some kind of ESP. It was only recently that we realized,
with this scan and the old autopsy reports and correlation
with the saucer as known, that not only was everything
aboard plugged into that motherboard directly or indirectly,
but so were the crew."

"True neural implants," someone commented. "They could
access the ship or computer information or anything else just
by thinking."

"You're right," Stark agreed. "That's what you are looking
at. Neural implants that go out to a nearly-impossible-to-see
spot in the purple on the back of the head. There's no actual
socket as such, so we think that it was done with some kind
of contact points. It could be that you just leaned back in the
chair, although there was enough height and weight variance
to suggest that it wouldn't be easy to mass-produce something that would always connect with anybody and it didn't
seem efficient to custom-build each one. That implies some
kind of cable connector, probably fiber optic or even better,
most likely with a suction tip. You pulled it out, or somebody

did it for you, and pushed it onto the spot, there, in the back of the head where the main stem of the implant reaches the skull. It took forty years to get to a point where somebody figured that out. Where somebody *could* figure that out."

"Matthew Brand," I muttered.

"Give the man in the back a cigar! Yes, indeed, Matthew Brand. Countless geniuses looked at all the material over the years and figured out this or that, but Brand looked only at photos like this and the photos and CAD drawings of the reconstructed craft and he figured out most of the system. What powered the thing we'll never know until we go out there and meet them somehow, although if we ever get another chance to nab one we'll do it. But Brand, back in the eighties mind you, just looked at the photos and diagrams and identified the implants, the neural supernetworking, and all the rest, and then he began to use deduction and logic to figure out just how it *had* to work."

Within two years, he'd put everything else aside, resigned all his old positions, and began working entirely on the new project. Brand wasn't a physicist, he wasn't an astronomer, and while he'd love to have met those aliens in the flesh, as it were, his thought processes were a bit unique and he concentrated almost entirely on engineering what he felt he was seeing.

And the government bankrolled him and supported him and financed this project under cover as a private company. It was here that much of what I'd read was actually developed—the logic system, the "fluid core" neural simulator, all of it. There was only one thing he couldn't do, and that was actually figure out how to properly connect the human brain to the computer.

That "only" was a pretty big one, though. Without it, the rest was just a lot of theoretical computer science.

The thing was, we were seeing it for real but in an *alien* brain. Hell, we didn't even understand *our* brains; we knew even less about theirs, and what those connection points might correlate to. The chemistry would be different, the organization, you name it. While it clearly was a brain, it sure didn't look like any brain I ever saw.

"I know what you're thinking," Stark said, anticipating both me and probably a bunch of others. "The fact is, that brain isn't anything like ours and probably works in far different ways. It's merely the fact that the cybernetic wiring and connections are so precise that we knew it *could* be done that got us going. Some excellent minds were put on this, both cybernetics experts and biologists, biophysicists and biochemists, medical researchers, you name it. They came up with a way to do it with humans. Don't ask me how they did it, or how it works—they admit that they don't understand how or why it works themselves, only that it does—but there it was. A real, live direct neural implant directly into the centers of memory and thinking. A connection of mind and machine. Not theory, fact. Matthew Brand had what he needed to prove his own genius."

"Horrible," I heard one woman near us whisper to a male companion. "I bet a lot of animals suffered horribly to discover that."

I had to smile, although I wasn't at all amused, at her mixture of truth and naïveté. Certainly they'd done animal studies, but this was the *brain* we were talking about, the mind, the very seat of ourselves. There was only one way to test out whether and where to connect in and how to do it, and if they admitted they still didn't quite understand the process, then they were doing a lot of logical guesswork inside the skulls of real human beings. I couldn't help but wonder who those people might be, and whether they were truly volunteers. I *hoped* they were death-row inmates, terminally and painfully ill, and the like, but you never knew with things like this.

It was time to cut to the nub of this. "All right, Mr. Stark," I said loudly from my back of the room seat. "So you have an implant directly connecting the human brain to a vast computer, and Brand invented a wholly new form of data storage and manipulation on the hardware end to allow this to be seamless. I'll grant that, hard as it is for me to accept. So, if you have all this and it's all wonderful genius work, how come you need us? How come you aren't using the process now? How come Brand's dead and this place was closed for years? Isn't there something you haven't mentioned yet?"

Al Stark cleared his throat. "Uh, yes. I was getting to that. The data will be available to you on the various experiments we carried out during the first phase, as we might call it. We went from some very basic stuff to very elaborate extremely fast, but we did hit something of a wall in computer capacity and speed, a wall that's now much further away. We will also need refinement of the networking—your wireless net expertise will be invaluable, Mr. Maddox—and we now have far better miniaturization and the like."

The patent! So *that's* why Rob and I were both here! Wouldn't it be ironic if they wound up giving a big order to Subspace? And, if they put a DoD/National Defense stamp on it, the feds could use almost any patent without permission that they wanted. That was the law. Of course, they might also wind up paying Sangkung for it, which wouldn't be at all cool.

"Can you also say what killed Brand?" somebody else asked, pressing the real point.

Stark gave the impression that he could indeed say but didn't want to unless he had to. Well, he had to and he knew it.

"Others of you understand the problem already, and we have a few new people from other areas of breakthrough technology to help refine the problems. Brand's death, of course, killed the project. The thing is, he didn't *quite* leave us in the way the official version and rumors have it. He—he ran into a series of small bugs in his hard-coded floating memory system. He tried very hard to solve them, and found he simply could not. It was related to a very physical process that happened regardless of what we did. Um, Ms. Alvarez, you were there. Do you want to explain it?"

She hesitated, not liking public speaking and, in fact, clearly uncomfortable with the memories. She still made it, though her voice occasionally faltered.

"Matthew felt that he was failing to fix the major problem because he really couldn't understand what was happening. He was seeing only an effect and descriptions from people he felt weren't adequately explaining what they were experiencing. He insisted on going into the system himself."

"I should point out," Stark interjected, "that he was not supposed to have the implant at all, since we hardly wanted to risk his brain. The operation is quite simple and direct, even more so I think now, but there is always a risk, especially then when MRIs and other high-tech surgical and diagnostic tools were still in their infancies. He insisted that no one else could comprehend what he'd done, let alone fix it, of anyone he'd met, and threatened to simply quit the project if he weren't allowed full reign, including the implant if he deemed it necessary. He would have quit, too."

"Matt wouldn't have quit," Alvarez responded. "He would have figured out some way to have it done. Besides, he had ways of making all sorts of things go wrong, so if they didn't do it with him they didn't do it at all. He got what he wanted, and the first couple of times he couldn't even get the effect, let alone track the bugs. On the third try, it happened, and he was positively fascinated. I never saw him more absorbed. Everybody else, they were so stunned to go in there, to actually live in another existence that seemed as real as this one, that all else paled. Matt didn't even *care* about the other existence; he already knew that it was just a simulation program working the way he expected and so he simply ignored it. He—he wasn't like other people."

Everybody said that about Brand anywhere in the industry, and I could believe it.

"What was this bug?" someone else asked. "I realize he didn't think it was describable, but try."

She thought a moment. "It's next to impossible to explain unless you actually experienced a Sim on that system. Forget everything you ever knew about virtual reality, period. All those phony-looking animations, bizarre modern art land-scapes, all that crap. You could do it, but that wasn't what this was all about. It was like, well, like *this*. Just as real, just as convincing. We had people start flipping out now and then because they got confused on what was reality. That was a problem with it from the start—if you did it a lot, eventually you couldn't figure out which one was real. I had that myself. Even woke up in the life-support module, was helped out by the technicians, interrogated, the whole thing, only to find out what seemed to be days later that maybe it wasn't when I suddenly woke up in the life-support chamber—well, you get the idea, I hope. That was a major problem we never could get around. After a while, you just never knew. I'm still not sure I'm certain that I'm really here, and it's been, what? Five years."

"But you said Brand barely paid attention to the program," someone else prodded. "Just what was he trying to fix and what happened to him?"

"I'm getting there," Alvarez responded irritably. "This is—hard for me. Brings back a lot of memories and dreams, both good and bad, as well as all the paranoia. You must believe that the Sim is as totally real to you as anything in existence, or the bug he was after won't make sense. You see, he said that the paranoia, the inability to pick illusion from reality, was a 'foreseeable consequence' of the system. It didn't trouble him. That was for the psychologists to worry about. But, see, it's so real because so much of it is exactly the same as here. Only some things are changed. Important things, but only some. That reality base, culled from God knows where, *works*. It's logical. It fills in the blanks. Your self, either your existing self or some slightly or even radically altered self, interfaces with all this and creates a real universe. Apparently there is so little difference that our own memories, psyches, you name it, crossed back and forth and made one big neural web. Sometimes, after lots of sessions, when you'd be pulled out, you wouldn't be."

She sensed she was suddenly talking nonsense as far as we were concerned and tried again.

"Look," she said, "people woke up and they still thought they were the other them. People woke up and couldn't remember half their backgrounds, or had major gaps in their memories, different personalities, you name it. Matthew said that this wasn't supposed to happen, that the real 'you' was supposed to always be differentiated somehow from the Sim so it could always be retrieved. He couldn't understand why the real files and programs of your own self here, which is how he saw it, weren't being tagged or always identified to the computer running the Sim. He went in to find out and, if necessary, to fix it. On his third attempt he—he—"

"On his third attempt at finding the cause," Stark put in, "Matthew Brand did not come back. When the timer expired and there was no sign of conscious return here, we hit the emergency switch and pulled the plug. As soon as Matthew Brand's body was disconnected from the life-support module, it died. The monitoring instruments showed absolutely no brain activity over and above some of the autonomic functions. He was brain dead, wiped clean."

There was a silence for a moment, and then I asked the question I was sure everybody wanted to ask. "Stark, where's the floating Sim unit they were using? Did it get shut down and stuck away in some crate, too?"

"I expected the question. No, not really. We all had the same thought, so we kept the unit powered up, and we even had some volunteers who went in looking just to see. Not a trace. But, as Ms. Alvarez says, it's just as big and just as real as this, so we didn't dare take a chance. That's why this property was never disposed of. The unit's here, buried, bigger than a half-dozen freight cars, with its own power, and it's always been on. We—we couldn't take a chance. If Matthew Brand's whole ego, his entire knowledge, consciousness, *soul* if you prefer, had been sucked into that machine of his, but was still there, we had to take a chance that maybe it wasn't dead. We couldn't do much about the body—they wouldn't even let us freeze it, if we'd had the means at hand anyway to do it. But, yes, there is a slight, very slight, but still a chance, that all Matthew Brand was is still alive somewhere in Building A in back, beneath the labs and offices. I have often hoped so. If we can solve this, and stabilize it and us, then maybe some of us can go looking on more than an emergency rescue mission. That's part of what we will be doing here. Nobody who doesn't want to will be wired or ever forced into the Sim; it will be strictly volunteer. But if you can get *me* in there, with some assurance that what happened to him won't happen to me, then I sure as hell would like to find out if he's there."

They offered us a comfortable apartment in a complex not far from the labs. They were more like townhouses than apartments, with three stories, fireplaces, decks, balconies, you name it. There were other more conventional apartment blocks around, which I discovered were inhabited entirely by the staff of the place—everybody from the security guards to the janitors to the receptionists to the technicians who kept it all going. We were assured that nobody except folks working for the project were in there or likely to be, but, of course, we did interact with the town which, while a few miles long, still was a fairly small affair.

They did, however, seem to be delighted that a lot of new blood would be moving in. A lot of the permanent party were family types, with kids and so on, and while this meant more services would be needed from the city and county, it also meant that restaurants, grocery stores, shopping centers, you name it, would flourish in the area as well.

Officially we weren't with the government, but we were government contractors, working on a long-term computer-research-and-development project. There were hundreds of such firms all up and down the west coast, and, let's face it, all over the country, and so this didn't exactly bring lots of questions and attention to us, either. We were, after all, merely reopening something that had once been there.

We gave it a pass for now. For the time being, and with Riki's enthusiastic agreement, I continued to work from the house in Bremerton using the secured satellite links and secure phone system. She'd said little about it since that initial briefing and the subsequent tour of the place, but she clearly thought that the whole idea was somehow frightening. I had to agree, even though a whole ton of science fiction, including not only movies but TV, even the old Picard *Star Trek*, had delved into something like this. Or, at least, I *thought* it was something like this, anyway. I hadn't actually experienced it and wasn't sure I wanted Doc Cohn putting fiber-optic gadgets in my brain no matter how safe it was, and certainly not to see a new kind of virtual reality. Riki was even more adamant. "Promise me that you won't let them do it to you!" she said with determination. I'd never seen her so upset.

"Yeah, okay, I promise. I'm not at all keen about that sort of thing."

"I swear, Cory, if you ever have that done and use that gadget, we're history. It scares the hell out of me."

Well, I didn't have to, at least not for *this* job. What they wanted of me was something more basic, more along my own line of work. They wanted an interference-free system of networking groups to the Brand Sim device, preferably clean and secure and wireless. The current system, which was of course the old one, was filled with complex wired interconnects and very vulnerable at connection points to all sorts of potential dangers. That, it was theorized, might be the cause of the memory drift—impure signals, or some infinitesimal cutoff of contact that caused it. The monstrous bandwidths involved were a serious problem, but if the originator could be isolated, then it might be possible. The brain moved a monstrous amount of information all over by electrochemical action, day and night, sleeping and waking, for the whole of one's life, and that was a lot of data and factors to consider. Not, however, insurmountable.

Eventually I'd work something out and put it in the form of a device, miniaturize it as much as possible, do the specs, descriptions, then draw the thing inside and out and diagram it in AutoCAD and transmit it all to, I assumed, Yakima. After a while, I'd be invited down and I'd meet with the engineering team who would have to build it and then the brain doctors who would tell me how my concepts worked or didn't, and then we'd run through the whole thing, get the problems and bugs, and back I'd go again. It was fairly routine and comfortable work for me.

I also don't want you to think that this was a one-man show, either. I was actually the head of a team, including some pretty smart folks located all over the place, and we'd get together with conference calls on the secure line, and that line also buzzed with electronic back-and-forths. A lot of easy ways to do the job were shot down this way, which, while ego deflating, also saved endless amounts of work toward dead ends.

Ironically, my first breakthrough was on something I wasn't even really working on or thinking much about. It was so wild when I came up with it—waking up in one of those three A.M. brainstorms that are very rare and usually don't look like much in the morning for whatever brilliance they seemed at the time—and even wilder when it wasn't immediately shot down.

I wasn't capable of coming across with the whole thing, but I was immediately hooked into the biotechs who could.

See, I remembered seeing a movie once about this gadget that could record what the brain saw. The gadget fitted over the head and looked a lot like a cross between the little robot head in *Short Circuit* and a robotic football helmet, but the idea that you had to be wired in just didn't sit right with me. Maybe those creatures of the eternal surprised look did, or maybe it was necessary to become one with an entire spaceship, but I didn't know why it was absolutely necessary for this kind of communication. If we knew how to pick up and amplify those back-and-forth signals via a series of what amounted to brain taps, then it should be easier, even more efficient, if we could tap the entire area at once and transfer it. People were already hooked up to a Rube Goldberg nightmare in the life-support units anyway; why not mix in some sort of electrically sensitive but inert substance into the intravenous line and then use a full cranial cover—a helmet—with the entire inner surface in close contact with the skin to do the transference? No surgery or plug-ins needed, and an exceptionally stable signal. My own wireless networking scheme transferred data through the air at a pretty good clip; a direct to the skull, maybe just the thickness of skull, scalp, and hair, and we might be able to do something with a two-way signal and Brand's program that would be a kind of super magnetic resonance imager.

I could design the device, given their own information on how the hard-wired one worked, its voltages, connecting methods, and the like; it was up to them to find the chemical mix that would do the job.

They were astonished and very, very pleased. We had our first helmet in less than a month, although it was hardly more than a kludge, and there had been even less trouble modifying the life-support module. Within six weeks, we had a young engineer volunteer in place and were ready to try it.

Les Cohn, the chief of Medical Research and a real live M.D., was in charge, with Dan Tanaka supervising the mod and what was known as injection of the subject.

"We've had a few folks with the implants in for brief periods," Les told me. "Very brief. We never had anything go wrong with somebody injected into the Sim for under a full twenty-four hours, but for cost purposes they had several days to a week or two in the old project. The maximum I've allowed anybody so far is twelve hours, but there's some evidence that the injection time is cumulative to some degree. We've had a few very minor signs after only twelve-hour sessions with some of the subjects from the old days with a ton of experience, like Alvarez, and I've kept out anybody who had any side effects. This, if it works, will make things a *lot* safer and under nearly instant control. Going from direct connection to broadcast receive and transmit will do more than eliminate the surgery, it will take away some of the physical risk of a quick disconnect."

I was still pretty damned worried, almost to the point of guilt. Up to now, the worst thing that could happen if I'd made a serious mistake in design or overlooked major bugs in testing of a product of mine was that tech support and its phones would be backed up, and maybe I could crash a hard disk. *This*—this was different. I looked at the volunteer, who suddenly looked like a kid to me, and I got really nervous. What if I was wrong? I'd been wrong many times before. What if this time I crashed a brain or a body rather than a network or hard disk? I kept harping on this to Les and Dan, and they kept laughing it off and finally suggesting I not be present if I felt that way about it. That was out of the question; if anybody got hurt because of me, there was no way I wanted to walk around guilt-free by ignorance.

The subject was a young Marine and his hair had been shaved off. He was bald as could be, since we had no idea how much hair would cause signal loss.

Les checked him out one more time, then, dressed only in one of those gossamer thin hospital gowns, the Marine got into what looked for all the world like a high-tech coffin. The helmet was fitted, adjusted, fiddled with over and over again, then the gown was removed and the various IV connections that ran through the life-support pod were hooked cleanly into him. There were several other adjustments, then, finally, they seemed satisfied and the lid was closed and a pure oxygen atmosphere established. The pod was powered on, and we moved to terminals, where other technicians monitored every single bit of the subject's existence, from brain waves to blood pressure, metabolic action, the very rate of breathing.

"There's no sedation," Dan told me. "That would interfere. In fact, he's awake, aware, and probably not feeling great. He hasn't eaten or drank in twelve hours and he's been fully purged." He turned to the technicians. "Checklists *now*! By the numbers!"

"0-two nominal."

"Pressure one-twenty over seventy-five. Within tolerances."

"Heart rate eighty beats per minute. Within tolerance."

"IV steady, three minutes nine seconds for saturation."

And so it went, until I knew more about the young Marine than I wanted to.

"Set timers to thirty minutes," Tanaka commanded.

"Timers set."

"Injection sequence start."

I felt like I was in Mission Control at the Manned Spaceflight Center.

"Counting down ... thirty seconds ... twenty ... ten, nine, eight, seven, six, five, four, three, two, one, injection sequence started."

There were a few initial problems, none fatal to the kid. A lot of manual experience was needed to get the correct voltage, saturation, and find and open the completed bandwidths. Eerily, the corporal was giving us the cues.

"Got a flash of something! Man! That's *weird*! Nope—gone."

"Up point ten," Les Cohn directed, and power was increased.

What initially was nerve-racking and exciting quickly became disappointingly boring. We were dealing in increments here that only computers could truly utilize, and with biochemistry at a level way beyond me. It seemed like it took forever to get things in synch so that the young Marine really did get into a virtual reality Sim, and there were some times then when it looked as if we'd not found the right chemicals in the mix to do the job or maybe it was asking too much of that helmet and its own coating. Hours passed, and more hours, and I really felt sorry for the kid just on general principles, and eventually we began to seriously think of scrubbing and looking at the data again.

And then, almost by accident, just hunting and poking in the power ranges, it took.

Frankly, in spite of it all, I was surprised that the damned thing worked at all, let alone in the first set of experiments.

"We already had some success with the computer models and with some primate stuff," Les told me when I said as much. "We were pretty sure we'd get it within three or four days' worth of tries or we'd have a total wash. We're running pretty good now, though. He's fully injected, just as if he had the implant. I'm impressed."

"I'll be impressed if he comes out of it whole and with no holes in his memory," I told the doctor. "After all, I only did *this* by computer modeling myself, and I have no idea just what he's experiencing."

"Oh, it is a relatively simple one," Dan Tanaka said, watching the readouts on his screen like a hawk. "We'd hardly trust this on the big Sim setup until we're positive it works as well or better than the implant. Then, of course, we have to send a bunch of others through, with a fair amount of variety in the subjects, so we can be certain that the corporal's not the exception. Looks good now, though."

I looked at all the streams of numbers, meaningless to me even though this was my baby. "Where does he think he is now?"

"Well, *this* module is one of the basics. All I can tell you is that he's part of an expert team climbing to the crater of Mount Rainier. Beyond that, it becomes too subjective, just like real life. See, these things aren't scripts, they're setups taken from the thoughts and attitudes of the first one injected into the virgin Sim field, a person we call the Host. It's the Host's vision that everybody else is living in. Grab a thought, an ambition, a dream, a question, a puzzle, whatever, and if you're the Host the computer will take that and build an entirely authentic and logical world based on it. We've retained this one because it's consistent. Somebody who physically would never be able to climb a steep hill but who's fantasized themselves as an expert mountain climber was Host here and the rest was built by the computer five years ago and maintained in the box. Everyone we ever injected into this one became part of the team and makes it eventually to the top. We use this as a short-term item that's safe."

I looked at the medical readouts. Although the body was virtually motionless and held that way, there were clear accelerations in heart rate, blood pressure, you name it. That body *thought* it was doing *something*. "Good thing he's in good shape, though," I commented. "I might have a heart attack trying this."

"Oh, it's actually not that bad," Les Cohn commented. "In fact, I've seen people, including the data from the first Host, go through this without cracking a sweat. Our boy here has had a hell of a dull and strange day and he knew exactly where he was going. As convincing as it is, he knows it's not real, and that reality anchor is what's getting the reactions. Normally we only see this in experienced people in the brain-activity monitor. It's quite fascinating when you have some extremes. For example, we have some small scenarios in which men become women and vice versa. The brain activity for males and females is very different—the male brain doesn't work nearly as hard nor use as much on a constant basis, while the female brain is almost always active across both hemispheres, even at rest. You watch that injection, and slowly, over a period of time—hours, maybe days—the patterns shift inside the human subjects here in the pods. The female brain activity eventually mimics the male almost entirely; since we males don't have the corpus colostrum connections females do. It's not true that men are from Mars and women from Venus—it's that men are serial and women are parallel. Still, the attempts to approximate things over time is amazing."

"Did you ever consider that this might be part of your problem?" I asked him. "After all, if you're trying to shoehorn something which is used to being something, both psychologically and physiologically, into something else that doesn't fit, maybe there's an anomaly introduced that the interface just can't handle. Like squeezing something into the wrong size or shape and forcing it again and again. Eventually, if there's enough tension, it shoots out, and since there's a lot more room in the Sim module than in the brain, that's the way it goes."

"You aren't the first to come up with that," Les replied, "and there is probably something to it, although it doesn't really explain everything and Brand had totally rejected it."

"Damn it, he wasn't God!" I shot back. "You folks have practically deified him. He was a genius, the Einstein of his field, but that's all he was. I refuse to think of him as infallible. If he was, why is he dead?"

The doctor shrugged. "Watch it or you'll get hauled before an ecclesiastical court for heresy around here," he said playfully. "Some folks really think of him that way. You're right, of course, but there is so much going on here that we don't understand that there is no way in hell it's that simple. It would help an awful lot if we knew what the hell we were doing here. We know how to build those Sim modules and how to hook 'em in, but we don't know how they work or why, in spite of five years of trying to figure them out. We know that the implants work, but not why or really how. This is the most pragmatic damned project in all history. Your logic came off our damned good luck. I wonder how much of Brand's stuff was also blind luck, too? Hard to say."

I looked at all the lab equipment and the life-support pods. "Did you ever go into one of these Sims and see what we're really talking about here?" I asked him.

"Me? Hardly. I wasn't on the original project, and I sure as hell haven't been wired up. I may try it if this helmet idea of yours really works consistently. I'm curious as all hell to see what it's really all about. Aren't you? I just never wanted anybody doing surgery on my head unless it was to save my life or my mind."

I looked at all the stuff. "I suppose you're right. I promised Riki that I'd never get the implant, but I never promised her I wouldn't try it if there was an alternative. This sure as hell *seems* safe enough, at least physically. I'm not too thrilled with no eating for a day and an enema and having my head shaved, though, even if I don't have a lot on top."

"Well, it remains to be seen how much head shaving is really needed, although it might well be. On the other hand, the other is necessary, since your body has to be maintained with nutrients, fluids, the conductive serum, and all the rest. I have a feeling you couldn't keep it from Riki for long even if we got around the hair business."

"Maybe. We'll see." I looked over at our subject. "How long will he be climbing the mountain?"

"Sixty minutes our time; about twice that subjectively, I think. Characteristically, when they come back they're dead tired, and need to sleep for a bit before they can feel normal, get up and around, and be thoroughly debriefed. That's true whether it's twenty minutes or thirty days, according to the old logs, anyway, and it's pretty well held with the implant subjects here. Be interesting to see if this fellow recovers more quickly, since he's also in great physical shape. The last time, we didn't have such fine specimens. More like you and me."

"Thanks a lot. But there's that much physical effect on his real body?"

"You have no idea what this is like. I mean that. Neither do I, I think, but I've read all the accounts and talked to people who go in. You and I could go over to the programming lab and put on the usual equipment, head mounts, and the like, so all our senses are fooled, and hooked to the gimbals—you've done that sort of thing before, haven't you?"

I nodded. "Several times. Too cumbersome, though."

"Well, now it's cheap, lightweight, and hardly a bother. We could do it, and I could switch you into that scenario, and you could see this world, fly over it, and get the real thrill-ride-style illusion that you were there with them. But it wouldn't be the same. If it would, then we wouldn't have to put him through this contraption."

I stared at the screens and the immobile pods. "What's it supposed to be like, then?"

"Reality. You feel the snow crunch, the winds blow, the aches and pains, the precise tactile experiences as if you were there. For all intents and purposes you *are* there. You will speak with other people, smell their bad breath, and have spontaneous conversations as if they were totally real. To you, they will be real, not just seem real. In the big, elaborate Sims it goes unbelievably deep. There is one there that is among the most creative—it will reverse your sex."

"Huh? Beg pardon?"

"That's right. That's what it's designed to do. And the reports of the people who went through it in the old project indicate that it is more than convincing. The feel, the *organic* part, is even absolutely dead on, since we can also do controls so that subject A gets the reversal and subject B does not, going in as themselves. They did some thermoscans of the actual bodies here and I've examined them. Wish I had the level we could do now, but maybe someday we'll do it again here. You know the basic difference between the male and female brain in terms of operation is the vastly more complex corpus colostrum—the neural connection of the two hemispheres in the brain in females."

"Um, I think I saw that on TV sometime, but that's about it," I admitted.

"Well, basically, the old saw about men being Martians and women from Venus isn't really true. The heart of the difference, which many scientists now believe determines a considerable amount of the differences in activity between sexes, is that men are basically hooked up serially and women are hooked up parallel. Put a woman's brain under an MRI for a brainscan and the resulting picture shows rather heavy activity, indicated by heat and blood flow, throughout both hemispheres, even at rest. Put a man's brain under the same system with the same stimuli and the activity is more sporadic, it flares up and then subsides, and it's never nearly equal in both hemispheres."

I shrugged. "I'll accept that if you're leading toward something I can follow."

"The conclusions from these observations are beside the point here. What *isn't* beside the point is that female subjects who get into the male side in that Sim, over time, start having scans and activities that resemble male brain biochemistry. After a while, we can take a thermoscan of that brain, and even though it's a woman you'd swear it was a man's brain you were looking at. The effect isn't as dramatic male to female, since it's obviously easier not to use existing biological channels than to create them, but it *approximates* well enough that we can see what's going on. In other words, *it's so real in there that a woman's brain can become male in its operation and vice versa!*"

That took me aback. No matter *what* virtual reality did, it was an illusion, an incredibly elaborate parlor trick that fooled you into seeing things that were not and interacting with the nonexistent. It didn't actually transform anyone, and I said so.

"Oh, so? Ever been fully wired up and taken a roller-coaster ride? Gone surfing or wind surfing, or flew across a computer surface?"

"Yeah, something like that, but—"

"No *buts*. Did your stomach think it was an illusion, or did you have that spasm and that null-gravity sinking sensation going down the hill?"

"Yeah, but it was still an illusion."

"You were conditioned by your past experiences to know how what you were seeing and hearing and interacting with would affect you, and it did. But you've never seen the level of detail *this* process produces. Nobody could program it."

I thought it over. "Wait a minute, wait a minute! You just said that the reason I felt my stomach flip in the VR suit was that my body was reacting the way it had been conditioned to react."

"Yes?"

"If I went in there and everything I saw, felt, said, or did said I was a woman, it wouldn't matter. I've never been one. It would be strictly my own subjective impressions of what it would feel like. Or, it would just be me in a disguise. It wouldn't be the real thing because there's no experience behind it."

"None on your part, but that's what's going on here. Your mind, your thought processes, your data acquisition, retrieval, whatever, is connected up to that Brand Box. That Brand Box has nearly infinite capacity because it's hooked into so much and fed so much, and it accepts all input and files it. What you say is perfectly true. The first time a male subject, say, went into that Box and experienced being a woman, it wasn't very convincing. Third-party stuff. Then they put a woman in, and it was *extremely* convincing when she experienced being a male. Then it got convincing afterwards on the female side. And the more of each that tried the program, the more real and totally convincing it got. *The Box learns!* It has access to your thoughts, memories, emotions, the same way you're using its extra capacity and program. The first time it didn't know those little subtle details nor did it have experience to compare. Then it had one man's. That was able to be used then on the first woman subject. Her experience could then be used on the next man, and so on. See?"

All of the implications of what he was calling the Brand Box were there in that first set of documents I looked at, but I'd chosen not to think through all the details, or, perhaps, to believe that anything could be this complete and convincing. There was always a limit to the knowledge, experience, and memory storage and retrieval abilities of the hardware. There *had* to be. But if, somehow, there wasn't. . . .

Then Stark may not have been making something of a wistful joke when he suggested that all of Matthew Brand had been sucked into one of his boxes and might be alive and well there.

Alive, well, but with no body to return to if it found access to the real world.

And if the system could be that complete, that absolute, that convincing, how in *hell* could you ever be certain, ever again, that the reality in which you lived wasn't the real one?

The young Marine was slowly and methodically withdrawn by the techs and medical people in the lab center at the one-hour mark. It was completely automated, really; the people were just there in case of an emergency, which didn't happen this time.

The computers brought him out of it, almost literally collecting the young man's thoughts and shutting him off from the virtual reality in which he'd been living, and he came out of it, experiencing some nausea and possibly a mild case of shock that required a little quick medication from Les, but then, after being forced to answer a few questions to ensure that he was okay and that it had all worked, he went out like a light almost immediately and slept for a good eight to ten hours.

I spent a lot of time talking with the technicians and checking things out, and finally took a nap in one of the staff lounges, but when the Marine awoke in the infirmary section they came and got me.

By the time I arrived, he'd gotten some solid food in him and had a shower and clean clothes. To me, he seemed to be perfectly okay, in fairly high spirits, and *very* enthused about his experience.

"It was *un-believable!*" he enthused to us. "What a great trip! I think I'm going to have to do that for real now! In fact, I really feel like I already *did* it. I mean, I even remember some of the skills and stuff that I never really had before. That's not only a great trip, it's a fantastic learning tool!"

Maybe it was, and I was certainly relieved to see that he was fine and also smugly self-satisfied that my wireless helmet had worked so well, but I was still feeling uneasy about all this.

I wasn't sure I *liked* the idea of learning all that stuff from this kind of machine, even if we totally understood what it was doing, which we didn't. I guess it was me being old-fashioned, but right now a whole raft of illiterates were going down to the nearest computer superstore, buying a quick and dirty basic megamedia system, and in addition to playing their games and ruining the BBS systems of the world with mindless prattle, they were reading and writing all sorts of junk with it. Well, not exactly. They wore headsets that allowed them to dictate whatever was in their ignorant heads and save it as files without even touching a keyboard, and they could get it to read back, in very nice customizable voices, what was sent to them. The vast majority of the American population didn't have to be able to read or write any more, and wasn't the least bit upset by that fact. I actually had run into people, not only online but on the streets, who thought Washington State was named after the city where the president lived and had no idea that they were both named for somebody who was real.

What if the bright boys and girls here *did* eventually crack the secret of the Brand Boxes? Imagine that—take a trip anywhere you want without leaving home. Become anybody, do anything. No experience needed—you can use somebody else's.

And what if Brand's consciousness really *was* somehow still there, somewhere, in that one special box? How long before it's looked upon as the way to save our best and brightest, and then the way to save the rich and powerful? Immortality in a box. Jesus! This was getting scary fast!

And that, of course, led me to start brooding on whether or not I was working on the cutting edge of my profession or was instead one of those technicians like the ones who built and supplied Auschwitz and never thought twice about what they did there.

I didn't know, but as I got deeper and deeper into this I knew I had to resolve this or go mad. I knew I had to find out at least some of the implications of ugliness that this whole project represented and that I was making easier and more efficient for more folks to try.

I had visions of the bleak and ignorant future, a future like the ones envisioned by the likes of Max Headroom and the cyberpunk writers Riki illustrated sometimes.

And this I confided to Riki, who more than agreed. "I have to read many of these stories in order to do the covers and illustrations. I know what they're talking about. I saw it in that first meeting."

I took a deep breath. "I have to take a look and see if the future is really that ugly before I can make any further decisions," I told her. "If this is unstoppable, inevitable, then maybe I'm more effective as a conscience at least from within. If it's positive, I'd like to be convinced. But I can't see anything but darkness ahead, and I can't keep working like this. I *have* to know."

She nodded. "I understand."

"Do you?" I asked her, looking her straight in the eye. "I

mean, I am going to have to go into one of those Brand Boxes myself. I have to know exactly what it's like."

She nodded. "It's scary, but I do understand. You mentioned that guy who tested out your head mount—he was only in for an hour or so, right?"

"Yeah, right. And then he had a *loooong* sleep and woke up okay."

"Well, just make sure it's one like that. Not a mountain-climbing scene, but something simple, basic, and short. Something you could do here if you had the time, money, and inclination, or something you always wanted to do that wouldn't give you a heart attack."

"There may be something like that. I hope so. It's about what I was thinking. I don't want to go near anything like the stuff that screwed up Brand and some of the old subjects. You sure you won't freak out and walk out on me if I do?"

She sighed and gave me a hug. "I don't like it, but I understand it. Frankly, I hope they can't find or fix that bug that ate Brand's brain. If they can, if they do—I'm not even sure we can imagine the results if this is even *close* to what they say."

They were going to have lighter, thinner versions of my wireless head mount system in about a month and a half, and I figured that would be the time to check it out for myself.

"I'll call Dan Tanaka."

# V

# THROUGH THE
# LOOKING-GLASS, DARKLY

Matthew Brand had called his campus and retreat in Yakima "Wonderland," and a lot of names, jokes, and code words seemed to have grown out of Lewis Carroll as a result. Still, I didn't find the jokes much comfort; it seemed to symbolize less the sense of awe that I think Brand had in mind and more the insanity of the thing.

Not everyone was with the system, though, and Dan Tanaka greeted me with a big grin and said, "I think I know just the one for you. It's one of the ones I discovered and have checked out for myself and I think it's the kind of thing that might be fun."

I saw that he had a small loose-leaf notebook in his hands with his name in magic marker on the front and otherwise a lot in Kanji, the Japanese alphabet.

"My private log and guide," he told me. "Even if you could read Japanese, though, it wouldn't make much sense. *I*, however, know the code because I invented it. I would just rather not be second-guessed by some of the characters around here just because they don't like what I like."

I wasn't sure I was following him, but he did have something of a reputation as a womanizer and sexist and apparently had done little to make that reputation seem false. On the other hand, he had the shield of genius himself on his side; he could get away with a lot because he wasn't really replaceable. Those who didn't like him or his attitudes tended to simply steer clear of him.

"I have several Sims here that weren't created by any of those power-tripping sociologist geeks they have around here now," he told me. "Ones from the original project that reflected different ideas."

"Have you tried any of these?" I asked him. "When I was here a couple of months ago for the first test you hadn't."

"Only as a voyeur then, through the usual VR equipment," he admitted. "Since, though, yes, I have. Like you, there was just no way I could work on this any more or really appreciate what everybody was saying about it unless I tried it myself. I think maybe half the staff's done it at least once now."

"What about Les Cohn?"

Tanaka grinned. "Oh, Les was one of the first once we got in the new head-mount units. He'll have to tell you about it. *Not* one I'd pick, but I can see why he did it. Through there."

I went into Dr. Lester Cohn's infirmary and he was sitting there waiting for me. He studied a chart which I assume was my vitals, then gestured for me to sit on the table, which I did.

"Well, since you slept here last night, I'm pretty sure you haven't had anything in your stomach," he commented, "unless you swiped something on the way in here."

"I'm clean. Starting to get hungry, but clean."

"We'll fix that. By the time you get your enema and we do the final blood stuff you'll be ready to go home. Don't. It's worth it."

"I understand you've done it."

He nodded. "I got curious, that's all. They wanted volunteers to check the more elaborate and complex ones, people who'd never been through it before. We just can't trust the old guard, not yet. There's too much danger. So, you remember the one I was talking about? The one that was just the same as here except that it postulated you were born the opposite sex?"

"Yeah? You *didn't*!"

"Yeah, I did. Thirty-six hours' worth, subjectively anyway. It's not just the normal curiosity you have in having lived all your life with that barrier, either. I mean, I'm a doctor. I spent half my life studying to be an internist and the past twenty years being one, and I had blithely worked with both men and women mostly confident that I knew just what I was dealing with. I can tell you that things were—different. More than I thought they'd be. It's a bit disturbing, really, some of the assumptions you make as a man and some of the things you just *never* think about. I found a woman who'd done the same thing in reverse and she pretty well said exactly the same thing. Not just the physiological, either. Men react to women differently than they react to other men, and vice versa. We know that, but it's another thing to experience it from the other side." He paused a moment, then said, "Well, let's get you on the road. It's uncomfortable setting things up, but until you do this you can't understand the experience."

He was right; with two nurses to help in the torture, I managed to have an extremely unpleasant next hour. Finally, though, he seemed satisfied.

"Okay, that's the lot. We're going to have to look a little closer at your diet and blood sugar after this, but there's nothing here that would disqualify you," he told me.

"Huh? What about my blood sugar?"

"I'd say you're pre-diabetic. Not over the edge yet, but getting there. Poor diet, not enough exercise, and a bunch of genetic markers for it. Don't worry—think of it as a side benefit. If we catch this early and you get serious, there's no reason to think it'll bite you before you're really old and gray. Shall we proceed with this?"

I nodded. "I guess so."

"Okay, don't be surprised if your vision is different or your balance is a bit off or something of that nature when you inject into the Sim. There are all sorts of subjective color shifts, slight differences in the eyes can be disorienting, ears can have a greater or lesser range of hearing, that kind of thing. You get used to it quickly, but it can be disconcerting."

I hadn't thought of that. "Um, do you know just which sort of reality he's got picked for me?"

"Yeah, I do. I should be shocked, repulsed, and all that, and I am, and it's a real Tanaka special, but in this case it's a very good range of experiences for you in a limited circumstance. Somebody back then had the sexual fantasies of a teenage boy. Kind of wonder what their real sex life was. Still, it's a near-perfect demo, I think, and there's not much danger or trauma. Just don't let it go to your head. It's as harmless as a dirty magazine, which isn't to say that some folks here might not want it destroyed because they think porn makes rapists and bang bangs make murderers. You're grown-up. Go ahead. Unless you have some real serious moral objection to it. Dan's one experience with it actually toned him down a lot, sort of took the urges and needs out of him, so it might be cathartic."

"You make it sound like I'm going to wake up in the middle of a porn movie."

"Nothing that elaborate. No plot, just a situation. What you do with it is strictly up to you."

We went out and they had one of their high-tech coffins open and ready. I climbed in, and found that it was tight but not really uncomfortable. The helmet I'd tested out many times, of course, but this was the newer, lighter, thinner improved design and it felt almost like there was nothing there at all. I lay down, naked in the chamber, and feeling more and more nervous about all this. Was I nuts? Could I back out?

I had the sudden urge to do just that, to scream at them to stop, but I didn't, even as they inserted the IVs, hooked up the spacesuitlike covers and tubes to my ass and genitals just in case, and fully energized the pod.

The lid closed, and I felt myself moving backward into a chamber where the inner connections would be matched to ones in the chamber wall. Only when everything was hooked up, fully energized and tested, and approved by the computers, would I be "injected," in the parlance of the project.

It was damned quiet in there. I was absolutely awake, feeling not the least bit tired and full of energy, but tense as all get-out. *Why didn't they start this? What was taking them so long?* I could actually hear my breathing and my pulse and began to mentally count my beats per minute.

It felt itchy and a bit sweaty inside the head unit, which was strapped tight on my head and adjusted to conform to my less-than-perfect cranium. I wondered if I was feeling a signal of some kind or just the hair against the plating or perhaps a slight static charge due to the interaction of hair and plating. I'd had a short but presentable haircut of the kind Wonderland recommended; you could almost tell all the people in the project who'd been on this ride at least once by their hair, the women more dramatically so than the men. At least I didn't have to deal with a shaved head or a hair weave . . .

*What was taking them so damned long? Was something wrong?*

There was an emergency intercom in the module, but it was strictly for dire situations and was generally powered by them from their end. They didn't like radios inside the modules unless they had to, because of the risk of interference this close.

Had Rob ever gone through this? I wondered. If so, I wondered what kind of scenario he'd picked or they'd picked for him. What about Stark? How about "injecting" him so that he would be convinced that he was being audited by the IRS? Make *him* feel the weight of bureaucracy, maybe. Or make him Winston Smith in a *1984* existence, not the O'Brien he'd imagine himself to be.

Damn it, it was getting claustrophobic in here, and, worse, itchy as all hell. Not just on the head now, but all over, and it was really becoming unbearable, but I was strapped in and down and unable to really move and scratch any of them.

In fact, it didn't take long before my whole body felt itchy as hell, almost as if a swarm of flies were all over it, clinging to every square inch, and it was sheer torture. I opened my mouth as if to yell or scream in the hopes somebody would hear me and get me out of there.

And, suddenly, it was gone. The itching, the discomfort, you name it. In fact, it didn't feel like I was hooked up to anything at all. Rather, it felt like I was lying on a moderately firm bed, satin or silk of some kind. . . .

I opened my eyes and looked around. I *was* in a bed! And a pretty damned big one, too, maybe eight feet to the edge, only, well, it wasn't an edge exactly.

The bed was round. A big, round, silk and satin draped bed.

The room itself was large and impressive, with fancy ornate satin drapes on the far windows, finely carved wood furniture with soft satiny cushions on the chairs and such, broad closets on one side, and recessed lighting that gave the feeling of a softly glowing ceiling. There was a kind of sexy mixture of powder and perfume in the air.

I was, for the moment, totally disoriented.

Still, I slid out of bed and walked, naked, to the bathroom that I seemed to know was there across a deep rug that seemed so soft and furry that I almost felt like I could sink into it. The light came on automatically when I entered, and I found it vast and ornate, with inlaid hand-carved marble all around and mirrors all over and, opposite the john and the sink and cabinets, there was a large sunken Jacuzzi tub of the same material.

The strange fact about the reflection in the mirrors was that it wasn't me and yet I somehow knew it wouldn't be. Well, it *was* sort of like my old self, but maybe the ideal old self, with a body that was perfectly pumped up, muscular, in peak condition, and a lean face with neatly trimmed beard and surprisingly long brown hair to the shoulders—my color, but without a hint of gray. I was also a lot hairier than I was before, and, frankly, I had the size dick I'd always thought I wanted instead of the one nature had given me.

Sheesh! I even had an earring and a tattoo on one shoulder of a cartoon blond overendowed bimbo in a sexy and fairly pornographic pose. It looked professional, and was in full color.

*Was this what they were saying? How could this be real, and yet, and yet, it* looked *real,* felt *real, was real in every way I could ever measure reality.* How could this be merely a program in my mind? I *felt* everything, even the little aches and pains we all have in the body, and an itchy spot on my thigh. . . .

I washed my face off in the sink and it felt absolutely normal, the same as it always felt, then I walked back into the bedroom and suddenly stopped dead.

I was still stark naked in the luxurious bedroom, but I wasn't alone. Two voluptuous young women stood there, one by the bed and the other by the entry door. The closer one was a blond bombshell, not quite the human equivalent of the tattoo on my shoulder but close enough for *my* tastes; the other was a different but no less stacked and sexy redhead. Both of them were surefire centerfold material, neither looked older than eighteen, and the only thing either of them was wearing was a string bikini bottom, which was still more than *I* had on.

They had those vacant bimbo eyes and expressions and didn't seem at all taken aback by my appearance.

"What is thy will, my lord?" the blond asked me in one of those very high and perfect dumb blond voices.

At least half of me felt like an idiot for ordering breakfast.

*  *  *

Okay, okay, I could go into excruciating X-rated detail here, but you still wouldn't get the half of it, and if I'm supposed to feel ashamed of myself, well, I didn't one bit. I *did* feel nervous and uncertain at the start, but the longer it went the more comfortable I was with it.

I don't know who programmed that whole business, but I can tell you right now that it was no adolescent with a fantasy. Nobody, but nobody, could be that, um, *creative*, without one hell of a lot of experience.

As things went on, when activities became mental as well as, well, physical and emotional, I gradually became aware of a duality of existence. On the one hand, I was certainly still Cory Maddox and had all of Cory Maddox's memories, knowledge, all the rest, but I was also Lord Koray of Alstasia, an incredibly rich playboy on his own private tropical island created entirely for his fantasies and pleasures. In fact, I was the only man there; everybody else, the whole staff, was female, gorgeous, and entirely devoted to me and fulfilling all my wishes.

It was easy to forget Cory Maddox existed, and even easier not to question the total lack of details about who this man was and how he got such wealth and power and why these young women were apparently willing slaves who truly liked their lives and could imagine no other. Being a "simple" program, I now realize that most of that detail wasn't necessary to me and thus wasn't provided, but there was a kind of feeling deep down within me that an entire world scenario could be created just to explain this if I needed it or, more to the point, *required* it.

And yet it was as real as anything I had ever experienced, in every single way. I don't mean it as a dream, a fantasy, a simulation of any sort—it was *real*, from the smallest blade of grass or insects to the smells and sights and sounds, and as "Cory" essentially relaxed and allowed the persona of the lord to take over and run things, there was no physical sensation that was hidden or phony, either.

There was, of course, a certain deep down sense of abandon as Lord Koray simply because "Cory" was there and knew, somehow, that this wouldn't last, that it was somehow a universe entirely in my own mind. It meant a near-total lack of inhibition, a lack of guilt, and a willingness to experiment in all forms of sex, in various drugs I'd never touch, in the finest wines and liqueurs, *anything*.

And when I was wiped out, exhausted, and yet totally satisfied, I was helped to the bed and passed out with two willing sexy naked girls cuddled up against me.

The next day, I woke up, and I was still in the bedroom and I was still with the two girls.

I hadn't expected that, which was why I'd tried to do everything and experience all the previous day. Instead, I had something of a hangover, a couple of what looked and felt like mosquito bites from the naked romp in the gardens outside, and a few scratches and such as well.

I did not repeat the excesses and pleasures and debaucheries of the day before, at least not like that. Hell, *then* it had been just an experience, just a brand-new kind of cost-free sin, since, in spite of everything my brain and senses told me, this simply could not be real. Now, still here after a full day and a night's sleep and suffering the effects, I was beginning to wonder if I should be so certain about that.

Damn it, this *couldn't* be some sort of virtual reality. It just *couldn't*. Not to this degree. Not to this detail. It is beyond words to convey that sense of being there, of experiencing it firsthand. There are things you do not even realize that you experience that are only noticed when missing. Those little aches and pains I spoke of; insect bites if you are crazy enough to wander around a tropical island naked; smells, tastes, the unique feel of running your tongue over the roof of your mouth, the enzyme and hormonal and blood flows when you kiss and when you do far more than kiss—these were all real. There wasn't a single detail, not in the tiniest degree, to betray that this was anything but reality.

I prowled the vast mansion, looking for other clues as to this place and this bizarre existence. There was a minor but very complete wardrobe for me, in which I could if I wished dress for any occasion or any mood or period I could think of, but finding the other wardrobe was even more astonishing. A huge, cavernous room in which almost any woman of almost any size or shape could find any and all manner of dress from fig leaves to Elizabethan to Frederick's of Hollywood. That's what it was, too—a Hollywood-type female wardrobe fit for a major studio.

All for my benefit and to cater to my whims?

It didn't make any sense.

Perfumes of all vintages from cheap and tawdry to what had to be thousands an ounce; wines of every kind and vintage. And all these women, all young, female, overbuilt, sexy, totally focused on my needs, and very, very specialized. Not just cooks and companions, but ones who could fix the electricity, maintain the gardens, clean, polish, do the plumbing, all the skills that were essential to maintaining an operation like this, yet still and all as one-dimensional as their uniform beauty.

It was as if you had a classical dumb blond bimbo pattern and then impressed on different ones one specialty that they knew and could do in an instinctive manner. They couldn't explain it—I found that out. And they couldn't do each other's jobs, either, although beyond their specialty they were all the same and all, well, available.

It was boring.

Ultimately, I found the library. It was one of those huge Renaissance types, with floor-to-ceiling built-in bookcases crammed with titles and rising up several stories, the topmost shelves being accessed by a combination of moving ladders and small ledges. There was, of course, one of the girls to do that for me.

"Do you know every title in this room?" I asked her.

"I can find any title my lord requires," she responded a bit evasively.

I had a thought. "Have you ever *read* any of these books?"

The question took her completely by surprise. "Read?" she repeated, as if trying to grasp the concept. "Why, no, my lord, why would I ever wish to do that?"

"You *can* read, though, can't you?"

"I—I know the titles, my lord, the look of each."

An illiterate librarian. That was amusing to a degree, but not in this circumstance. "How do you know them? Did someone teach them to you?"

"N—no, my lord. I just—*know*—that's all."

Like a search-and-retrieval program. Uh-huh. "Is there any book that tells the history of this place and how it came to be?" I asked her.

She thought a moment. "No, my lord. All histories and geographies and grammars of this place were prohibited."

"Prohibited? By who?"

"I—I do not know, my lord. I am sorry."

I had already established, by speaking and quizzing others, that there was no knowledge of how this came to be, no memories of it not being just the way it was, and no *questioning* of it, either. They simply accepted it, took it for granted, and could not even imagine anything else.

"Am I always living here?" I asked the wordless librarian.

"I do not know, my lord. *Someone* is always here."

Was that it? Was this simply a scene, drawn out and fixed in some kind of computer memory only Matthew Brand comprehended, that existed as it was forever, going round and round? Was that always why there was meat in the freezer, always fresh supplies of just about anything somewhere at hand?

"Do you have *Through the Looking-Glass*?" I asked her.

"Yes, my lord. Shall I fetch it?"

"Please."

She was off in a flash, climbing the network of ladders and ledges like a professional acrobat, and then she had a book in her hand and was coming back down to me. She handed it to me, a look of extreme delight on her face. She'd been asked to do her job and she'd done it.

I'd asked for *Through the Looking-Glass* partly to stump her; the book was rarely in a separate volume from *Alice in Wonderland*—in fact, I'd never seen it separate.

Until now.

*Through the Looking-Glass and What Alice Found There*, by Lewis Carroll, illustrated by John Tenniel.

It was a first edition, British, in the kind of shape one would expect if you were alive when it appeared, walked into a bookshop, and bought it. There was not a trace of yellowing, and the binding was still taut and needed to be forced to remain open.

I opened it at random.

> *"Tweedledum and Tweedledee*
> *Agreed to have a battle;*
> *For Tweedledum said Tweedledee*
> *Had spoiled his nice new rattle.*

> *"Just then flew down a monstrous crow,*
> *As black as a tar barrel,*
> *Which frightened both the heroes so,*
> *They quite forgot their quarrel."*

> *"I know what you're thinking about," said Tweedledum:*
> *"But it isn't so, nohow."*
> *"Contrariwise," continued Tweedledum, "if it was so, it might be; and if it were so, it would be; but as it isn't, it ain't. That's logic."*

I shut the book. It was too close to home.

"Has anyone actually written anything and left it here?"

I asked her, trying not to think about that passage any-more.

"No, my lord. You do not usually come to the *library*."

Well, if I was stuck here much longer that would change, I knew. I wondered about that quotation, though, without let-ting its strangeness get to me. Where had it come from? Was it really in the book? Certainly those twin nuts were, but I couldn't remember much of anything beyond the Walt Disney videotape. I wasn't even sure I actually ever had *read* it—not *Through the Looking-Glass*, anyway. Alice, yeah, at some point. . . .

The trouble was, I didn't even have any way of checking to see if that was actually in there or if it just was made up for my benefit.

I handed her back the book and left the library, continuing my explorations.

Before long, I found what might have been a "smoking room" or some sort of den, anyway. There were cigars, cig-arettes, and pipes with a variety of tobaccos there, the forbid-den fruit of my era but the near-ubiquitous sin of two or three previous American centuries. I had been a smoker once—cigarettes, like a lot of programmers—but I got sick and tired of catching pneumonia to get one and, although I held out for quite a while on general principles, I finally surrendered to the mob who were determined to force me to do only what was good for me and gave it up. It hadn't been easy, and, years later, I still *dreamed* I was a smoker—honest!—and no matter what they told me I didn't feel any better, got just as many if not more colds, things tasted just the same, and it just took me twice as long to concentrate on things. Still, even with all the crap I'd put in myself the night before, I wasn't going to start here, not with cigarettes. Even if, some-how, this *was* all in the mind, as it was looking more and more by logic to be in spite of everything my senses told me, so was smoking. I guess some people *are* physically addicted, but I never was—it was a habit that gave me pleasure and benefit, keeping me calm and even in tense times, but it was one hell of a habit that could keep you missing it years later.

I had, however, had a rare cigar, and I finally decided that this was allowable. I had no idea what sort of cigars these were, but I would have bet anything that no finer were available and that they were the product of some veteran habitual cigar smoker's memory.

This room definitely seemed a shade different from the others. No slavish staff, no interruptions at all. There was a full-blown stereo in there, I found, and, when I played with an odd wall decoration, I discovered to my excitement a television set. That set me to finding the on–off button and other controls as quickly as I could, and I found them in the arm of a comfortable padded chair.

There was nothing but snow on the television, though, and it wasn't too long when I discovered that it was hard-wired to the stereo and to a tape recorder and laser-disk system. Not encouraging. The snow revealed nothing at all, not the slightest hint of a signal coming in from over the air.

I looked at the far wall for the tapes and disks and went through them. A lot of the usuals, heavily bent toward porn but with the best sellers, too. I was about to declare this, too, a wash, when I noticed a single tape with hand lettering on it down in a corner and reached in and picked it up.

DEMO, it said.

I took it out and stuck it in the tape player and sat back, cigar in hand, to see what the hell it was demonstrating.

There was the usual snow, then black, then a *beep*, no FBI warning which was refreshing, and then music swelled up and a picture came on. A picture of the island and the mansion, which looked even more breathtaking from the air.

"This is the Isle of Alstasia," a familiar-sounding man's voice said in straight travelogue fashion. "It was created by the Instrumentality specifically to hold the monster Madoc and his unfortunate victims, for which there was no other merciful course. Although he deserved a sentence far worse, this is the only course which our own ethics and laws permitted even such as he."

*Madoc.* Maddox. *Me!* A monster?

"The house contains every comfort, but absolutely no way of contacting anyone or anything beyond it. It lies in a temporal zone between our own and that of the next full habitation dimensional layers below us, and is able to draw climate and general eco-requirements from either as needed while making it strictly a one-way trip. In this zone, there is no end to the waters surrounding him and no other land at all. The house is fully self-sustaining, and Madoc's victims have been given elementary compulsory programming that will allow them to supplement automated computerized maintenance. Perishables are replenished by a standard energy-to-matter unit beneath the house and should have adequate programming to replicate whatever he desires in that area."

There followed a detailed, room-by-room look at the place, which included not only rooms I'd been in but places I hadn't and maybe wouldn't have suspected, as well as the grounds of the island. It was thorough, cold, and scientific, and it sent a chill through me because it was an alternative truth.

"We realize that, in spite of everything, such a cocoon may well put Madoc into delusion from sheer boredom or frustration. That is not our concern. The Instrumentality alone could possibly access the region again and it has deliberately created a random access code that even it does not know to ensure that this will not happen. Madoc is brilliant and ruthless, but he is not capable of accessing the grid barrier with what was provided there. The next-level civilization below us is far too technologically primitive to try, even by accident, and is carefully monitored. In any event, locating a tiny speck this small in the vastness of the interdimensional plasma either by accident or on purpose is in the neighborhood of the same odds of the Moon dropping and striking the Earth."

*Oh, yeah? Well* this *primitive's stuck in your luxury exile!*

"Those who believe that this is far too gentle a sentence

for one who has reprogrammed minds and engaged in all forms of debauchery and evil should take comfort. The temporal factotum in this grid region is quite minor; he will not age, and the women will never care or notice that neither he nor they do. Every day all will be cleaned and polished and replenished and exactly like the last, and the next, and when he runs out of even minor variations he will know that he is doomed to be there, like that, forever."

This was disconcerting because, even if it sounded like grade-B pseudo-science nonsense, well, so did a hell of a lot of what *I* did to anybody outside my field. Worse, I knew that the level of reality I was experiencing in this house, and on this island, was too impossibly exact, too convincing, too absolute. No computer on Earth, not *all* the supercomputers of Earth—my Earth—networked together could handle all the knowledge and all this detail and re-create it.

It was much easier to believe that this *was* real, and that what I'd just been watching was the truth. Not *my* truth, but some kind of alternate me, maybe. Or maybe an alternate Lex. I hoped so, or maybe somebody I never knew, in spite of the name similarity of the "monster" and my own.

Yeah, it was crazy. You couldn't switch minds with somebody in another dimension, right? That was the same kind of craziness as the rest. But, most specially to an old computer hand like me, it was more believable than what was being claimed.

"You will all remember the spectacular trial of Madoc, in which—" the tape continued, then went to total black. I shot up, tried jiggering with the tape, with the recorder, with on and off, *anything*, but they or *somebody* had clearly erased the rest, the history. Who Madoc was, what sort of world and civilization he'd come from, and what he'd done to make these young women into slaves. The librarian said there was no history of *this* in the books, either, and I suspected that the library was entirely from *my* Earth, so that this Madoc wouldn't have anything at all of his former existence here.

But he'd had all of Earth's—*my* Earth's. And if *I* was now *here*, then where was *he*? Holy shit! Suppose I went to sleep in that thing and was "injected" into his body here, and *he* was injected into *mine*? Had they woke him up and had he played me to get free on an unsuspecting new and more primitive world? Any gaps he had he could blame on the process!

This was scary.

But—why hadn't it happened to Dan? He said *he* used this one, and I could see why it would appeal to him.

Wrong guy, maybe? Maybe Dan could go along for the ride and have lots of fun and be fooled while leaving some of his own memories here, including maybe my own face? What if Madoc *was* somehow me? Or looked like me? Or was genetically close to me? So he gives Dan the time of his fantasy life and sends him back unknowingly with a command to make sure it's me sometime? And when it is, we match, and Madoc is able to switch with me?

Man! Talk about paranoid! But the creepiest thing was, the more I thought about this and the more I looked at things here and experienced what I had experienced, the more it seemed that there was no other way to explain it.

What was it Sherlock Holmes had said once? If you remove the impossible, what's left, however improbable, must be the truth.

The tape tour had shown me a small "gentleman's amateur" science area up in the conservatory. It wasn't much, and certainly wouldn't have even a great scientific genius whipping together a super-interdimensional communicator, but it *did* have the basics—a telescope, a microscope, things like that.

I took a leaf from one of the orchids nearby and put it under the microscope on a clean slide. After fiddling with focus and getting it right, I was able to see the enormous cellular detail of the small leaf. How exact could a computer possibly get it, damn it? Not *that* close and *that* realistic. Not any computer I knew.

I took a small jar down and outside, heading for a small spring that flowed peacefully through a grove of trees in back of the gardens. I got a good sample, then took it back up to the conservatory and examined it.

There were microorganisms in the water, alive and clearly swimming around.

I still had a little scabbing on a bite I'd scratched too much, and I popped it off, got some blood, and put *that* under.

This was just beyond any computer science that was possible in the near future, let alone now, no matter *what* Stark's folks had back east under security. *That* detail, that *life—* impossible.

Damn it! This *was* real and I was currently *stuck* here! At least I sure was until Dan or somebody came back, and maybe even then. Who would have control and who could talk to who when movement up was blocked?

Brand's Box punched through the dimensions to other existences, somehow. That's what it did. It punched through and found, in what may have been an infinite sequence, what the computer design specs called for, and then it sent your mind, your consciousness, into someone there.

And them into your body? But due to the shock or whatever you were unconscious while here, perhaps. And he'd had the conceit to believe that he was actually creating the universe instead of invading it, and he was held in such awe by others that they accepted what he told them and what he sincerely but mistakenly believed.

It also explained why brain scans tended to look like the opposite sex if that was the case—hell, if Les had gone into a woman's body then she'd gone into his. And there had to be some kind of mixing, some link between the knowledge of the subject and the personality of the injectee. It probably got easier each time you did it, until the flow of data and personality wasn't from mind to some kind of magic Brand Box but from subject to subject, until neither brain could tell which

memory or which bit belonged where. *That* would explain the
bug Brand could never solve. He couldn't solve it because it
wasn't a bug but a natural consequence of not one real and
one created person but *two real people*.

That was scary for several reasons. Not only did it suggest
that some insanity and delusions and mental problems
weren't either physiological or psychological in origin but
maybe *outside*. Madoc's folks had known about us, and that
meant they'd been there. How many such universes were
traveling?

And how the hell was I ever going to get out of this? And
poor Riki! If this guy turned women into slaves and his formula could be re-created—jeez!

But how long was I stuck here? Forever? Until Dan wanted
another fling with the sex slaves? What could I do?

Was there *anything* I could do?

I was *sure* I was right, and in some ways it was a more incredible breakthrough than Brand's mere totally believable
virtual-reality runs.

That meant accepting the situation, which was hardly horrible, until something happened to get me or my message out
of here. Just patience, and remaining sane.

The passage of time after this point is somewhat painful to
think of, because it seemed that as things went on I became
more cruel and more sadistic than ever and yet my conscience seemed to have taken a hike as well. I'd like to think
that it was just the prospect of being there a very long time,
but there's also the question of just how much Madoc and I
shared certain dark areas of the mind that still troubles me.

I lost all track of time as well, but often tried to keep myself in some sort of shape in spite of, or maybe because of,
all my excesses, and running through the mansion and around
the grounds on a regular basis during the cool of the evening
seemed to suit me best.

I was in an area of the house beyond the den and the library, an area mostly used for maintenance and storage, and

I was heading down the rear spiral staircase into this area from the rooftop conservatory when I heard a woman singing. This was unusual in and of itself, unless I commanded it or there was some sort of entertainment coming up, but this was something else again, and its familiar refrain bounced off the cold, sterile walls and seemed to swirl around me in the shadows and come from everywhere at once.

> *". . . Ask not why we sing this song,*
> *'cause ev'ry thing you think you know is wrong. . . ."*

I stopped dead, and the hairs on the back of my neck seemed to rise a little.

The singer and the song stopped as well.

"Who's there?" I called out, my own voice bouncing back and forth in the stairwell.

There was a distant-sounding chuckle, a woman's voice, that seemed to be a living thing in and of itself and to come from nowhere and everywhere at the same time.

Finally, it almost whispered, *"Cor-eeee! Deah Cor-eeee! You ah so damn' gullible it huhts!"*

"Matalon? Cynthia Matalon? Is that you?"

*"That name'll do, dahlin', at least foah now. My oh my, y'all suah ovahdid it, didn't you?"*

"Are you here somewhere or is this one of your mind tricks?" I asked, feeling irritated and vulnerable on the one hand and totally relieved to have a lifeline, somebody to talk to, on the other.

*"Don't know what you mean by 'heah' and 'theah,' 'cause, see, they're the same thing. You ain't nowheahs, Cor-eeee. Ain't none of us ah nowheahs, y'see. I just want t'wahn y'all befoah the next stage. Don't let 'em, don't let nobody talk you back heah, y'heah? You come back in heah one moah time and you won't be the Loahd of the Manah, you'll be one of them gals. McKee found Matthew's little* Playboy *set, y'see, and she put in a neat little spidah's trap. Beweah anybody*

*that tries t'get you back heah, y'heah? That's all, dahlin'.
Take caha, 'til we can get you out. I told you not to go with
deah old Al, but you didn't listen. Didn't figah y'would. But
even if you don't remembah who you ah, Al does. . . ."*

And she was gone, fading faster than the wind. I could *feel*
her presence leave, although I hadn't felt it before.

What the hell? Did she go back and forth without any
modules, without anything at all? Or was she, perhaps, not of
our world at all? What if Madoc's world had people in
Brand's own project, maybe even made sure that he wouldn't
solve it and might disappear into the system? Keep us un-
washed primitives off the grass, wouldn't it?

For all that Cynthia Matalon had been a nut and a scare
and a pain, she hadn't harmed me and she *had* warned me on
Al Stark, although so far I couldn't see how he was any real
threat to me.

Her message this time, though, had been a clear and direct
warning on two fronts. That this had been booby-trapped,
long ago, and that anybody who came back a second time
now became not the sadistic and insatiable master Lord
Madoc but one of the adoring slave girls, doomed to do his
bidding and unable to act differently.

That also implied that I was soon to get out of here, and
that the plot was to talk me into coming back. Well, they
wouldn't be able to talk me back *here* no matter what, although there was nothing to stop them from loading the
wrong program in the console while I lay there helpless.

When I went to sleep that night, without doing anything
but heading for bed and lying there, staring at the ceiling in
the darkness and trying to think, it was with both hope and
that increased paranoid suspicion. Who the hell was Matalon
in this Wonderland play? The Cheshire Cat, perhaps? Not the
White Rabbit. The White Rabbit was Stark, pure and simple,
and the Queen was Matt Brand somewhere in the unknown
distance of the forest.

I finally drifted off into what was a fitful and light sleep with odd dreams that made no sense to me, and then, suddenly, there were rough hands all over me and I was hot and itchy as all hell and a man's voice—a *man's* voice—was yelling, "Come on! Come on out of it! What's your name! Tell me your name!"

I stirred slightly, totally confused, opened my eyes a bit, and found that they didn't focus well. Blurrily I saw several figures in white and heard what sounded a lot like Doc Cohn's voice.

"What's your name?"

"Cor—Cory Maddox," I mumbled. "That you, Les?"

"Yes, it's me! Okay, he's back! Just lie back and we'll detach the tubes and get you to a bed."

"I got it all worked out!" I told him proudly, then collapsed into the deepest sleep I had ever experienced in my whole life.


The funny thing was, when you *did* wake up from the post-injection coma, you felt *great*. Hungry, and with oddball sensations here and there, but not at all as weak as you really were.

They brought me breakfast, and Les came in, looking tired. "Well? What did you think of it?" he asked me. "When you're done I've got to give you a physical and check you out, but we can start debriefing if I can have some of that coffee."

"Be my guest," I urged him, chomping away.

As I went along, I told him of my experiences and my theories about the process, the "bug," and all the rest. He listened very patiently, nodding sympathetically and asking an occasional relevant question, but otherwise not interrupting my tale and my theory until I was done. I felt very proud of myself, very sure, and I wanted to hear how brilliant I was from him.

"So where's the evil mad scientist Madoc during all this?" he asked me in his clinical voice.

"Huh? Here, I suppose. . . ."

"If so, he'd be in your brain, and I didn't sense any dualities nor measure them. You yourself never woke up, and the readouts and interconnects were normal."

"Les, that *can't* be virtual reality! I don't care if Madoc ceased to exist or was in limbo or whatever, but there isn't enough computer capacity in the known universe to account for that level of detail."

"I agree, but it works and it is virtual reality, not interdimensional anything. Cory, that box is actually one of the simplest ones. It's a program. I haven't the qualifications to know a thing about it, but I *do* know that it came from a specific scenario that is written out and all of the stages are clearly and carefully documented. Sort of the Marquis de Sade in the Playboy Mansion with unlimited love slaves. It is fiction. All of it. Fiction plus all of the experiences and feelings of all those who have used it before you."

"I—I just can't accept that. I can accept that it *looks* like that, but. . . ."

"It's more than that. You want to know where Madoc came from? The computer flagged us that you were putting in a request for a logical background and that it didn't have sufficient data to build or provide one. I watched Dan and three assistants—two of them young women, I might add—create the entire Madoc story, as that video, just as you related it. I can show you the videotape they made. It was Dan's voice that you heard narrating it. You *said* the voice was familiar, didn't you?"

"Uh, yeah, but—"

"No *buts*. You know how long it took the four of them to come up with that? About twenty minutes. They used the visuals from the Brand Box and just did a voiceover. Your own imagination took it from there."

"But the microscopic stuff! The *detail* of feeling, of everything!"

"It's in there. I checked. There is a record in the computer log of you going to the Object Library, as it's called, and requesting *Through the Looking-Glass*. It then accessed a huge jukebox of classics, retrieved what it found, and that's what you sensed being 'handed' by the librarian. When you looked into the microscope there was almost certainly an expectation in your mind of what you would see if it were real and what you would see if it were VR, and the computer could request whatever data from all those knowledge banks and provide it instantly from your standpoint, since it is in control of everything in those virtual boxes, even time. How long did you spend there?"

I shrugged. "I don't know. At least a week. I lost track."

"You were in for eight hours because that's how long it runs and it was one full shift here. All the rest was subjective time. It can speed up, slow down, to provide whatever is needed to you, and there's no way you can tell if it's instantaneous or takes some time in computer terms. Remember, you are just as much a part of the scenario as the background, and equally susceptible to manipulation while in there. No, Cory, there's no countless universes here. Or maybe they really do exist, but they have nothing to do with this problem or the Brand Boxes. You haven't *seen* detail yet."

I thought a moment. I was disappointed, maybe even crushed, by this, and still not certain if I was really wrong, but there were other things that went *his* way. Did I tell him about Cynthia? I didn't think so. Not right now. But there was something to bring up.

"Les—I think Dan and the others should do a comparison of the program from its assembly with what's there now. I think there might be a very nasty bug no matter what else is there. Don't ask me how I know, but don't let anybody go in twice until they do that. You promise?"

He frowned, puzzled, but said, "Yeah, sure. A bug you say?"

"Not exactly a bug. More a deliberate snare, I think, added long after the program was set up and not by Brand. Just tell them to trace signatures. There has to be a fairly clear and definable second team signature in there to have this work at all."

"Well, okay, you're the programmer. But no more about multiple universes, huh? We've got enough of them here, all in little boxes."

"Les?"

"Yeah?"

"Any casualties using the system yet? This time? Be honest with me."

The doctor thought a moment and sighed. "Minor. Some of these can change you. Not completely, but in little things. You may even find that out yourself. But the ones with the old wiring, the ones who were here five years ago, they're in serious danger. We know that long-term exposure is the problem, that the more you're injected the more prone you are to this kind of thing, at least so far. That's what we have to lick. Why? I doubt if it'll do anything more in this case than make you a hell of a lot more creative in the bedroom."

"You got that right," I told him, "although I'm not at all sure what Riki is going to think of all that."

"You might be surprised," Les responded. "You see, Riki's sampling it now as well. Different box entirely, of course, but she's injected. Not due out for another couple of hours. If you want to grab a robe, you can see how it all works from God's side."

"Riki? Took the injection? And they let her do it?"

"Yeah, she decided while you were still out cold. It's not unusual, and I know you both were having some reservations. I wanted you to see what this was, and I wanted her to see as well. Don't worry, though. She's not having nearly the kind of experience you did. A *lot* different. Right now she's in a virtual Carmel, circa the early part of the twentieth century, hobnobbing at the artists' colony there with the likes of Ambrose Bierce and Virginia Woolf."

# VI

# CHASING
# THE WHITE RABBIT

It didn't take long after Riki woke up to establish that she'd had an experience every bit as real and convincing, and far less unsettling, than I'd had in mine, which reinforced Les's contention that, no matter what I thought and experienced, this was in fact virtual reality *in extremis* and not any sort of alternate reality.

"It was—*awesome*," she told me. "I mean, like, I was *there*, just as if I'd stepped into some sort of time machine. Except for some of the stupid fashions of the time, it was just about perfect. For an avant-garde group of nonconformist artists they certainly were still hung up by our standards, and what they thought of as shocking hardly would blink an eye today, particularly in *Carmel*! But the *detail*! I can't imagine how they got that consistent a picture of all those people. I'm gonna have to look some of 'em up that I never heard of to see if they really were the way they were in the scenario. And it was just so, well, *different*. There was this one guy, little more than a teenager I think, cute but almost a Huck Finn type with a body builder's physique, who said he only had a third-grade education yet knew words that William F.

Buckley never heard of and recited really weird poetry. A womanizer, too, but not like Sterling—I think Sterling went both ways and at once and would be at home more in our time than his. Bierce was a real old-school charmer, Woolf was a tough-as-nails cussing bull-dyke type, not at all what I pictured. But it doesn't *matter* what was what. What matters is that you really felt like you were there."

"What made you decide to do it at all?" I asked her. "You were the one so scared of this in the first place."

She nodded. "The more implications I thought of, the more I just *had* to know, just like you."

"And you had such a good time you aren't as down on it as you were, while I had such a scare I'm not at all sure about this."

She shook her head. "Nope. Wrong. Right that I had a *hell* of a good time, wrong that I'm not more scared than ever. Cory—it's *too* real. It's *too* detailed. You really can't tell. Suppose somebody gets under this without knowing what it is? They could mess up people's lives, minds, you name it. I mean, suppose you wake up in there and everything's so logical, so consistent, that it's impossible to tell what's real from what's not? Brainwashing, both political and social, and conditioning, and all sorts of mean stuff came to mind. Yeah, it's scary all right."

I frowned. "I was really scared when I was convinced it was some kind of parallel-worlds thing, but it's an illusion, that's all," I assured her. "It can't *really* harm you."

"Think not? What's the government doing with this, Cory? What use could it be? I mean, okay, simulated combat missions, that kind of thing, but we're just about that good now, and this doesn't really do anything for those reflexes because it's *entirely* in your head—your body does nothing but lie there comatose. And I can tell by the way you talked about it that you were really scared in there."

I thought about it a little. We could kind of guess what the government would use it for, but there was always the chance of misusing inventions, and there were sure easier and cheaper ways to drive people nuts. This was an incredibly expensive place to run, and in several areas it always would be. Survival and maintenance of the body was essential, of course, and to do that you needed the coffins or something like them, and a certain level of both computer and medical personnel watching over them. "Yeah, I can see some nasty uses, but mostly I see good ones," I told her. "Besides, Brand and many of the others here aren't the kind of people to let that abuse run on, let alone perfect it."

"Brand! Always Brand! I don't know him and I'm already sick of him, but it's all the same, really. I know your friends. They're nerds, neep-neeps, who live in their own little worlds and want to find what's neat and never even *think* of the kind of uses a CIA mind could make of them. Plant a network node in the brain? Sure! Let's see how efficient that works! Monitor all the conversations in the world? Why not? No, something else is going on here. Something not—*right*."

I sighed. "Maybe you're right, but there's not much either of us can do about it. If the intelligence folks are as evil as you think, then everything we say or do is monitored, evaluated, whatever. Who'd believe this, anyway? Who could describe it accurately? None of the people who have been in the Sims could, and I'm not at all sure I can now so anybody else would really comprehend how absolute it is. And what if they do? Here is the only working model, well secured, and even the people here haven't figured out what Brand did or how he did it. And how scary can you make it? I mean, to describe it sounds like that room they went into in *Star Trek* to get away from it all. It's all that and a lot more, but all anybody who could understand it would say was that it was a neat concept. So, there's no use spreading the word, even if anybody believed us."

"We could just walk away."

"We *could* quit," I granted her, "but then what? No government security clearances, they'd still monitor us, and we'd never know what they developed here or what they did with it."

"I wonder if we really could anyway?" she responded.

"Huh?"

"I'm not all that sure that we could just up and quit even on those terms. In the back of my mind, I always had this suspicion that, somewhere, the body of Matthew Brand, trimmed, kept up, sustained on a module's life-support indefinitely, was around someplace, waiting to see if Brand's consciousness would make a deal or not to get back. Even *they* admit that he probably isn't dead, at least not his mind. Suppose it wasn't a bug? I mean, suppose he's hiding out in one of the Sims? Suppose he's been hiding out there for five years, and the reason for all this is that, after all that time, they've given up on him?"

I was beginning to think that all the drugs she consumed in her youth were finally and completely catching up with her. This was real paranoia, hard and impossible to deal with. You couldn't prove those negatives, and there simply wasn't any evidence of anything wrong here so you had to supply all that yourself, too. Suppose this, suppose that.

"And another thing. Think about the funny grouping of people here from that first meeting. Not the kind of folks to totally head up this kind of project. What are some of those people *doing* here? A fundamentalist Bible-spouter couple out of fifties TV, several social scientist academics, you name it. I ran into one woman who's so New Age she's channeling and doing pyramid power and another who is so devoted to animal rights I think she wants to outlaw penicillin because it kills bacteria. There are lots of others, too. They just don't fit here, but here they are."

"I don't know. Who knows how this thing's set up? Look, we can't go being scared of everything that might be under the bed or in the closet. Let me look at the work here and we'll see."

The truth was, I just wanted to stop this pointless paranoid discussion, so I finally gave her a kiss and let her recover more fully while I went to work finding out a lot more about what was really going on here.

It didn't take long to see that she did have a point about some of the personnel here. They ran the gamut from far looney left to *sieg heil* right and beyond, and every kind of politically correct and incorrect point of view as well. Some *were* programmers, and others were biochemists, biophysicists, medical personnel, and the like, but even more didn't seem to have jobs related to the project at all. With the personnel records closed to me and most others, I sought out Rob Garnett, who was supposed to be public information here anyway.

"Well, I can tell you what some of them are here for," he said, sounding somewhat amused by the line of questioning. "They either are, or were, archetypes. A blank Brand Box is set up, one of them is hooked up, and they're sent in. Sometimes two or more at once to the same blank. A Sim is built from their own mind view, which can then be studied and, if need be, refined. They use some hypnotic drugs to focus the individual, but basically it's taking a template from the mind of the archetype. For example, if we did it with the Standishes, you'd be in a universe where God, and the Christian fundamentalist God at that, not only solidly existed but existed as they imagine Him to be now, or as they *wish* it was now. They did a bunch of that sort of thing under Brand—the company, that is. We took committed Trotskyite commies, libertarians, survivalists, you name it, and ran 'em through and got many of the Sims you now see in the catalog. Fascinating results, I hear, although none of the ones who dreamed 'em up really liked the results. Most blamed it on the computers rather than flaws in their own beliefs, but they really got what they thought they wanted."

"Huh? You mean the systems didn't work?"

"Oh, yeah, they work. The computers are nothing if not

logical. You want a world with an Easter Bunny, you got to take all the rest, too. Santa Claus, Jack Frost, Halloween witches, Humpty Dumpty—you see how it goes? All logically worked out right down to the natural laws. And, man, you ought to see the mess when, no matter if you work or not and no matter what you do, you live and get exactly the same. Even if you like it, it's static, boring as hell. A whole society as a beehive. Nope. Not a single one turned out like they thought, but rather than admit they were wrong they just want another crack at it."

"So that's it. They want to keep at it until their own vision comes to pass! But—why can't they get it?"

"Logic. The whole thing, the whole universe, has got to *work*. Most of theirs won't as is. Gandhi always thought that Hitler could have been stopped entirely by nonviolent means. How anybody who'd massacre six million Jews for being Jews could be stopped by nonviolence is beyond me or any human nature but he *had* to believe that. The alternative was unthinkable to him. And when India didn't all go his way, he darn near died, and when he tried to stop it somebody shot him."

"I think I get your point," I told him. "But surely little things might be more controlled?"

"You change one thing, it changes something else, which changes something else, and so on," he responded. "Just think of yourself. Suppose you'd been a girl? Fifty-fifty chance, right?"

"Yeah? So?"

"Growing up would be real different. Even your parents would treat you different. There'd be different priorities, different environmental pressures, different expectations, not to mention dealing with periods and that crap and the social positions of your growing up as well. You'd take different classes, join different groups, have different friends. And you might well have never gotten into computers—that's what the odds say, anyway. And all along the way, folks you interacted with growing up, for good or bad, whether it was the old *It's a Wonderful Life* bit of rescuing a drowning man or being nice to folks or what, every interaction you had would be different. Would the universe be much different? Nope. Would civilization fall? Probably not. But as things related to you and your life, it would be a totally different experience. And that's only one small change, a fifty-fifty chance. You take some of the political, social, or religious ideas here and try *them* and it gets much, much broader. If magic worked, what would be the effect on the development of science? What if the Greeks or Romans had *really* developed the steam engine instead of considering it a toy? What if Christians really had to *be* Christians? And so on. It's endless."

"And that's how McKee, a sociologist and urban anthropologist, could alter the decadent *Penthouse* Sim?"

He stared at me a moment, then nodded. "Oh, yeah—I forgot to tell you. I don't know how you knew, but you were right. They found it. An addendum, an additional rule which, since it doesn't affect the actual world already built in there but merely the subject to be inserted, is accepted. Very clever, really. But, no, I doubt if she had the skill to put that in herself. More likely she found a qualified technician who knew how to do what she wanted. They're investigating now, but without hard evidence it's probably impossible to pin anything on anybody for sure. We're going to run checks on a lot of the more controversial Sims, though, to ensure that neither they nor anybody else had the same idea." He paused a moment, then asked, "Um, how *did* you know, by the way?"

I tried to think fast and came up with the most plausible response even if it wasn't much of an answer. "I—I really don't know. All I know is, when I woke up, I *knew*. I figured it was something in the way I'd been extracted, that I'd gone through it or something and it hit me later, but—honestly, I just don't really know."

Rob accepted it, but there was clearly a lot of discussion

going on over this behind my back. "Well, I'm glad you did, but we just can't figure out how you got it and Dan didn't."

"He might have just ignored it, let it pass without really hearing. I think he was more enthusiastic about the experience than I was. I was pretty scared, to tell you the truth, and I wasn't sure I'd *ever* get out of there or that I was in a Sim at all. Dan, on the other hand, knew, and never got all that background they fed me. Just out of curiosity, what have they said about it to Dr. McKee?"

"Nothing. Not yet. But Al's got extra monitoring on her and on the folks she pals around with now, I can tell you that, and if we catch her or anybody close to her doing more of this crap, she's going to rue the day if we have to put her through every Sim that would drive her bananas."

That wasn't an appetizing thought, not just for the good doctor but also for Riki and me should we quit. *Damn it! Just what had I gotten myself into?* And, just as importantly, why the hell did I keep asking myself stupid questions like that?

It was the sense of helplessness more than anything else. In a very short period I'd gone from a pretty casual aging boomer with a hot patent and a comfortable glide but no real strings to being boxed up in a monstrous government research project involving potential beyond belief at this stage and no real way out.

What was more important was that I couldn't, deep down, bring myself to believe the evidence. No, I don't mean the alternate existences, the feds, the eclectic staff, all that, and I even believed in Yakima and apples. What I could not believe was a breakthrough in memory and storage so vast and so complete and so beyond what anybody in my field expected over maybe the next few *decades* to be so available and easy to use. And discovered—what? How many years ago? Five? No, they *closed* this place five years ago. When had it opened? Six? Seven? And when had Brand then developed his revolution? Eight years ago? Ten? Jesus! In the days when a mainframe looked bigger than a group whirlpool spa and the biggest ones ran over a huge room and were cooled down practically to freezing just to run convincing computer graphics without melting down?

Okay, so you had to feed it some information, particularly if it was a limited program like the one I got stuck in. But what exactly *had* they stuck in? A CD-ROM with text for a ton of books and a cute little video that must have been already prepared because it was so smarmy and convincing. Probably not stuff that was prepared because I asked for it, but stuff that had been prepared to develop that limited scenario and had never been added to it. So now the contents of the entire CD-ROM library were in there? And the videos, too? They didn't need to be introduced again. . . .

It hit me that *this* was how the virus that would snare any second-tripper had been introduced. If it remembered everything else and took added information from your own mind and memories, then a little of you, or at least a copy of a little bit of you, remained in there, too. Certainly enough for the Sim to use to positively identify you. The mechanism would already be built into the master program, most likely, so you could exit and later return to any Sim where you'd left off. Not hard to simply introduce a simple added Boolean If . . . then to say that if you matched a previous occupant you switch to Scenario Two in the Sim. If you knew that there *was* a Scenario Two, you could do that to any Sim module without knowing any real programming at all.

That was also disturbing. Not only the potential for ideological booby traps, but also the whole idea that you could literally go in and *live a life as someone else in another alternate universe*, virtual or not, and then pop out when you needed to, go check your accounts, pay your bills, catch up on the news, and then *go right back where you left off*! Live a life in the same way as you'd read a book. And never mind bothering with all that messy time stuff. You could spend a year in the Sim, subjectively, pop out only a few days later real time, make your appointments, then jump back in while the whole Sim was on hold. Unbelievable.

How the hell did he do it? You *couldn't* have that much detail in any computer I knew and certainly not in anything that small. You could have ruled the world with that discovery in memory storage now, let alone a decade ago, so even then Matt Brand didn't just happen on it, he developed the process as the *means to an end*, a tool in a plan or objective. What? This?

What about immortality? It might be possible this way, with your mind totally inside a Sim, but was it? Didn't you lose just as much control? What if somebody shut it off, shut it down, had a fire, earthquake, you name it? No, it wasn't that, either.

How the *hell* did those things work and how did they get their information? It was almost as if, somehow, Brand had figured out a pipeline to tap God's brain. Even if we accepted the idea of some vast network, how could it tap into every single database in the known universe using *just* those damned cubes? Where was the delay in speed, the vast interconnects? To get and maintain the level of detail I'd experienced, that we'd *all* experienced, over such a sustained period would take storage abilities at least the size of a city and access at faster than lightspeed, and it would have to be directly plugged in, not sent across some vast network.

What I'd seen now, what we'd all experienced, simply wasn't possible under known science, not even admitting the usual vast conspiracy with the NSA and other supersecret government agencies hiding these breakthroughs. No, that was as unlikely to be as tapping into God's brain.

"But it *does* exist," Riki pointed out. "We didn't just get hypnotized into believing that it did." She frowned. "Or did we?"

"I'd like to think so, but it doesn't work that way, at least over the long haul," I told her.

She shrugged. "Okay, then. If it exists, just the way we both saw it, and it can't, what's the other explanation? We're all nuts? Or we're really inside a facility built by an extraterrestrial civilization with science way beyond ours? What?"

I sighed. "I don't know, but if we lay out all our assumptions, all our experiences, and they add up to this, then clearly one of our basic assumptions is wrong. Which one?"

"I—I don't know, but I keep getting those old paranoid blues again," she told me.

"Huh?"

"Okay, *you* got in the thing and off you went, right? And then they pulled you out."

I nodded. "Go ahead."

"Then *I* got in, off *I* went, and then they pulled *me* out."

"So?"

"Suppose they didn't pull either of us out. Suppose this is all part of it and we're still in there? How would we ever know?"

I chuckled. "We wouldn't, but it's circular logic. The serpent that eats its own tail forever and ever, like the symbol on Brand's old company. What motive would anybody have to network us together and put us back in a fake world identical to the one we left? Why bother? And, even if they did, it doesn't answer the question since this is as real and detailed and exact as if it *was* where we came from, so the process works regardless." I looked at her and shook my head.

"I don't know about you," I said tiredly, "but with the warmer weather coming in again, I could use a little getting away from it all. Let's get out of here, today, go back home, and after a good night's sleep get in the car and just *go* someplace. Hell, maybe even get on a plane. Hawaii, Fiji, Tahiti. . . ."

"I've got deadlines I'm already piled up on," she told me, "but a couple of days, maybe a long weekend, wouldn't hurt at all."

* * *

At least the security men weren't all that concerned that they suggested following us again. Instead, they simply let us go, secure in the knowledge that, while we were either under or sleeping it off, their own medical types had implanted little microtransmitters inside us that allowed them to track us and, for all I knew, monitor us and our conversations, life, via satellite, anywhere in the world. I was well aware of that technology, having gone to college with a fellow who'd studied under the guy who'd developed it, a man who I'd since been introduced to right at the campus.

I didn't tell Riki. She didn't have my technical education and it would only have intensified her paranoia. I figured she had more exotic theories about the how but would assume we were being shadowed anyway. She always did.

I stopped in a 7-Eleven for some coffee before making the full drive back, and Riki stayed in the car, not wanting to do anything but relax, she told me. When I came back, however, she was anything *but*.

"See that motel over there?" She almost whispered when I got back in the car.

"Yeah. One of dozens. So?"

"Your old girlfriend just went into one of those second-floor rooms. Third from the end up there."

"Huh? My old— Who?"

"The vanishing bombshell, you idiot!"

"Huh? You mean Cynthia Matalon?"

"Who else? You expect me to remember the name? Dressed as great as ever, too, but not looking like any sweet young Scarlett O'Hara type this time. All business. Wish I knew where she bought her clothes, though."

"You think she's following us?"

"I don't think she knows we're here. She just drove in in that blue Honda over there, parked, jumped out in a hurry, and ran up there. When she got to the door, she knocked hard, somebody opened it I couldn't see, and in she went."

"Interesting. I wonder whose room that is or if I even know him?" I kept staring at the door, then looked down and over at the Honda. "Hmmmm. . . . She's just passing through, whatever this is. She left the engine running. Not a good idea up this close to the freeway."

At that moment the motel room door opened again and the strange but beautiful woman stepped out, followed almost immediately by a far less stunningly shaped guy in a northwoods red plaid jacket, baseball cap, and jeans. He made sure that the door was shut, then followed her down the steps to the Honda.

Not just me but *both* of us knew the fellow well, and the short gasp of recognition was near simultaneous.

"That—that's Walt!" Riki managed.

Walt Slidecker, my old ex-boss and old friend turned rat fink, appeared now to be a bit more of a rat fink than I'd even suspected.

"Doesn't dress too well these days for a guy who just got millions from Sangkung," I noted. "He's sure with his dream girl, though."

"What are you going to do?" Riki asked me.

"You game to follow them? I'd like to see who else might be popping up around here."

"Remember—she's got those mental tricks of hers."

I nodded. "Yeah, but first she's got to know she's being made and tagged, I think, and, second, it's not just her. I'm not too sure she could also vanish Walt and a Honda without maybe David Copperfield and a dark night, anyway."

Feeling like I now was in the midst of a private-eye thriller and not at all like this was real, I nonetheless obeyed my television instincts and stayed back of them by several car lengths. They didn't seem to be aware of a tail, or even considering it; in fact, as Riki had noted, dear old Cynthia seemed to have a lot more stuff on her l'il ol' mahnd than usual. She couldn't really make herself look ugly, but that was one mean expression she had coming down those stairs, and the long cigarette she was smoking wasn't on the end of any holder but stuck in the side of her mouth.

It was probably just as well they weren't thinking tail, though, since, while red Porsche 911s aren't totally uncommon in the area, it was a good bet that the two of *them* only knew one guy with one and it wouldn't be much of a stretch for either of them to put me in back of them if they noticed us.

On the other hand, they sure as hell weren't going to outrun us, either. Not in a Honda Prelude.

They took the freeway entrance as I expected, and I laid back a bit more and then eased on slow and careful, as if I were just doing what we were going to do anyway. While there were a few exits up ahead for darting off into the wilderness, the next sixty miles were through a carefully mapped out division of an air force testing range and there were *no* exits along that stretch nor any you might want to take without being assumed a target for practice strafing runs, and the signs were very explicit indeed.

They weren't that hard to spot up ahead, in the right lane and going a fairly casual seventy or so. There weren't many cops along this stretch, either, and so that was downright slow for the not-very-dense stream of traffic.

"Be funny if they were just going up and over, back to Seattle," Riki commented. "By the time we get in it'll be dark and in the middle of rush hour. Not exactly a great time to follow a dark blue car."

I shrugged. "The worst that happens in that case is that we lose them, go home like we intended, and I call Stark or whoever's on tonight and give the feds a whole new set of leads to follow. I know Al wasn't about to trade in the Range Rover on a basic Honda, and with his money he probably now has his Mercedes SL convertible, too, so that's not his car."

"I don't think it was hers, either. It just doesn't look, well, *lived in*, if that makes any sense. I'd bet you ten bucks it's a rental car."

I'd had the same sense myself. There's just something about rental cars that makes them look just a hair different. No crud on the rear shelf, no tossing stuff off seats to the back, and some sense of seeming like an old car while looking brand-new.

We were about two-thirds of the way through the air force practice range and it was getting on toward dusk. Up until now, nothing odd had happened, and I'd cut on my lights, not because I needed them but because it was a natural thing for many people to do on these stretches, and it obscured detail of the car in forward rearview mirrors.

We had just passed the latest in a series of warning signs telling us to stay on the road or, if in trouble, go to the shoulder and wait, but under no circumstances turn off, drive down, or hike through the area upon penalty of the law and risk of being blown to pieces by accident when the Honda, which was maybe a half a mile ahead, did just that. I saw the brake lights go on even as Riki started to comment, and then they went off the road and down into the pretty but potentially dangerous country the signs warned us not to experience.

"There's a huge Indian reservation contiguous to the test area," I commented. "Can they be heading there?"

"That's closed to the public, too, at least from this end," Riki noted. "And I didn't see any signs for its access or private road or whatever."

I reached the point where the Honda had turned off, pulled over to the shoulder, and stopped. There *was* a dirt road there, leading not under the freeway but down and into the test range, and I could see the Honda now, stopped at an unmanned gate. Walt got out, went over to the gate which I *knew* had to be well locked and secured, did something, then opened it without doing it any violence.

"What the hell? Is this government-versus-government stuff?" I had to wonder aloud. "Damn it, they know their way around here!"

"If we don't do something soon we'll either have to chase 'em through a bomb area where *we* don't know our way around or give it up and go home," Riki noted.

I sighed. "The hell with this! She can vanish all she wants, but by damn *Walt* is gonna give me an explanation or I'm gonna break his bloody neck!" And, with that, I put the Porsche in gear and roared down the hill straight at them.

Walt was still out of the car and it took him a minute to even notice that another car was coming. When he did, though, and saw that it was a red Porsche to boot, he moved quicker than *I* ever thought he could move, jumping back into the Honda and gunning it through the gate.

Well, if he didn't bother to close it, then it sure wouldn't stop me, either, and if *they* knew their way around here and I was on their rear end then I wasn't gonna run into any strafing or bombing runs or unexploded ordnance, either. Either we were all going to get arrested by the air force or they were going to dead-end someplace where there would be somebody they knew, be it person, creature, or government agency.

It was an extremely rough ride, worse at these speeds, but, frankly, I loved these kind of runs while I suspected that Walt was about as terrified behind that wheel as he could get, particularly with that steering and suspension. He came off a rise in the dirt road and flew several yards before coming down hard, just like on TV, and I had to laugh. "I hope she bought the extra insurance when she rented that thing!" I shouted over the engine's roar to Riki.

"I hope you bought the extra federal medical and life for us, too!" she shouted back.

"O ye of little faith! I'm in complete control!" I retorted, just as we came out of an even steeper one and the front end dug into the dirt for a bit.

I kept as close to Walt as I dared, just back enough to keep him from kicking up fair-sized rocks into my windshield or stepping hard on the brake and giving me a lot more problems than the rental company would give him.

"Take it easy! I don't like this!" Riki called out.

"Don't worry so much! He's on the hook and he can't get away!"

"Who's on whose hook? *We're* after *him* and he knows who's driving! Cory! He's got to know he can't turn around and he can't get away and he's still running *into* this place! If you'd stop being so macho and started thinking you'd see that! He's not panicking, but he's not a good driver in this stuff and he's still running. Why? Cory—*the sun's going down any minute!* We're being dragged in and it only makes sense if he's leading us into a trap!"

I was so intent on them, the sense of what she was saying hardly penetrated. She, however, was coming close to tears, and finally screamed, *"Cory! Stop the goddamned car! In the name of Heaven stop the goddamned car!"*

"Just a minute!" I told her, suddenly jarred a bit. "We're in a tight canyon here and I can't turn around or see what I'm doing!" But I backed off and let them gain on me and took it a bit more carefully through here. I didn't know how Walt was managing to keep that car on this road, not *now*.

As they roared away in what was becoming pitch darkness, I sighed and for the first time felt the adrenaline rush subside a bit. "Better?" I asked her.

She nodded. "Better. Just go up to where you can turn around and do it."

"I hate to lose 'em like this," I told her. "Still, the more I think of it, the more you have to be right. I was having a tough time with *this* car in this tight area. He must have been going through hell in that one of his."

He was completely out of sight and, rolling down my window, I couldn't even hear him. Still, it was one of those back-

and-forth little roads of hard-packed desert with Jeep ruts, and no easy cruise.

We kept going through it for several minutes, and then, suddenly, came out on the other side, still at a fair elevation but now open to the eastern sky. Way off in the distance, and I mean *way* off, there was a whole lighted area that had to be the base itself. It probably didn't even have much more than an emergency field; the planes that used this desolate spot came from all over the west and went back where they came. This was a simulated enemy target most of all, so the base would probably be small, administrative and security being top jobs. Of course, you never knew. This would be great cover for one of those supersecret hidden bases or toxic sites or whatever, like the ones they had in Nevada. Probably not, though—you'd either have to have everybody commute in by air like there, much more obvious in central Washington than in Nevada, Utah, Arizona, places like that, or have better roads than *this*.

We were also high enough to see the glow to the south from Yakima just over the horizon, and some distant lights to the north and east that might well have been any number of small towns along I-90.

"Kind of romantic if we weren't such sitting ducks," I commented.

She nodded. "I'm glad they're not shooting today or to-night, though. I'd guess they'd have people checking those gates and have helicopters in the air and all that. Still, you think you can get back, slow and easy, the way we came in? I don't think we'll find *that* way so friendly, and I wouldn't bet they *won't* have security out sooner or later regardless. I'd rather sleep in my own bed than in a prison bunk or whatever they have in the army if I can."

"Air force, not army."

"Whatever."

"I think so, so long as we're not interrupted by them on the way out. I wonder why we can't see them in that blackness down there, though? Walt wasn't driving without lights before and I wouldn't like to drive without lights now, not down there. Besides, even his brake lights would show like beacons." I paused, then started to add, "I guess we better—"

Riki gasped and said, "Oh, my God!" under her breath. I was thinking very much the same thing. Almost without thinking, I opened the door and slipped from behind the wheel and out into the road for an unobstructed view, all without taking my eyes off the area below. Riki seemed frozen in the car, staring at the same spot.

It started simply enough, as if someone or something with a bright lantern switched it on in the midst of forty miles of dark and started swinging it round and round his head in ever-larger arcs and at an ever-increasing speed.

Only the arm grew longer as well, and what was being drawn by some sort of moving beams wasn't a circle or a series of concentric circles. It was, rather, a spiral, a spiral that now seemed quite large, perhaps thirty, forty yards in diameter, going back, writhing, made entirely out of a brilliant white light. It spun faster and faster, until it was now a spiral going inward, conelike, and almost alive.

It didn't produce much of a glow or reflection against the ground, not nearly what you might have expected, but there was enough to see, way far down there, a small object that had to be the Honda, right at the edge of the living but no longer growing spiral.

"Cory, let's get out of here," I heard Riki's voice say through clenched teeth, eyes still on the thing below. "Let's go *now*!"

"In a minute, in a minute! Damn! I wish I had binoculars! It looks like they're doing something down there! I mean, it looks like there's a lot of people suddenly in the glow between the spiral and the Honda, but I can't really tell if it's true or just distance, night, and a trick of the lights. Can *you* tell?"

"Cory, in the name of God, for *once*, just this *once*, will you stop ignoring me and get the fuck back in this car and turn it around and get us the fuck *out of here!*"

I frowned. "What's the trouble? They're quite a ways down, and even if they know we're here they could no more catch us than get away from us!"

Riki could be very rigid when she wanted total command, and this was one of those times. *"Get in!"* she said through clenched teeth. "In one minute or less I'm turning it around myself and I'm heading back and if you aren't in this car you can damned well *walk!*"

I got back in the car and shut the door. "What's the matter? That's *fantastic*, whatever it is out there. This is *wild!* First the Brand Boxes and Sims so real they're impossible, now *that!* I feel like I suddenly peeked behind a curtain and discovered science is actually a hundred years ahead of where we're taught it is!"

I put it in gear, though, and gingerly used what room I had to make a series of mini three-point turns until I got it going back the other way. I could see that this wasn't going to be anything I could win, or live with if I tried to win.

"Don't you get it?" she asked me incredulously. "I mean, hasn't it penetrated your nerdy little brain yet? It's not a lot of things, it's *one* thing. It's all the *same* thing. That Cynthia whatever back there, she's dogging and terrorizing us and playing all sorts of mind games and we find out she was connected to Brand's first project. Next we find her in Yakima teamed up with Slidecker, of all people, the guy who sold you out and who, if he hadn't, would have saved us from even *knowing* about all this. We'd have still had a *life!* Instead, he makes it possible for you to get hired by this new project by double-crossing you and the company—and makes a ton of bucks in the process? Don't stop driving! Am I right so far?"

"Yeah, okay. I'm with you."

"And who gets us into this directly? Good old Rob, Walt's

sales manager, who, it turns out, *also* worked for Brand once on the old stuff. Now Miz Bombshell scares us right into the project's lap, where we find out too much to ever get out. Now, here's Scarlett and good old Walt, going down the desert path through a high-security government military reservation to that—*thing*—whatever it is, that opened up down there. And who are *you* getting paid by really? The Defense Intelligence Agency, right?"

"It all holds together, I admit. Okay, so everything really *has* been a conspiracy and millions of bucks have been spent and thousands of people employed just to sucker *me* into the newly reactivated project. Why me? I have to tell you, doll, ninety percent of the men and women back in Yakima working those computers under Tanaka, and including Tanaka, know more about them and how they operate than anybody short of Brand. I know very little. I've improved the nuts and bolts of their life support and such, but I don't even *touch* the actual computing that goes on there. I don't understand it. It's a kind of programming and a kind of *thinking* I don't even follow. It makes my head spin. I mean, I'm not the architect, I'm not even the plumber—I'm the guy who can fit the pipes in one bathroom where the plumber tells me to and maybe figure out how to seal 'em a little better. Nobody goes to this kind of trouble to recruit me, and, in spite of having you do all those wonderful drawings of things both real and virtual, I doubt if they'd do it for you, either. For Brand, maybe, but not either of us."

She nodded. "I know, I know. Even I'm not that egotistical or paranoid. No, I don't think they did all this for either of us, but they did it for somebody, and we were just kinda add-ons. To use your analogy, they went for a master plumber and also managed to pick up all the plumber's helpers in the bargain."

"That's fine, except it doesn't hold up, either," I replied. "I mean, as limited as I am, I *was* the programming brains at Subspace. The others were the helpers, the sales staff, tech support, that sort of thing. Not that there weren't a lot of bright folks, but I was the only one with something new and different, and they had that and me already if they wanted it. Nope. It's still not clear what, but something's missing, some important element we've either not figured out, overlooked, or gotten wrong."

"Dear *Cynthia* said that *everything* we thought we knew was wrong. That takes up a lot of territory."

"I'm not sure that she isn't being proven more and more right the deeper into this we sink," I admitted. "Virtual reality so real it looks like, feels like, and acts like the real thing so much you can't tell what's fake and what's real. A test range in the middle of nowhere that opens up into a pulsing white light spiral out of sight of everybody that folks seem to go in and out of as if it's some kind of tunnel or gateway." *Curiouser and curiouser, thought Alice.*

Or mad as a hatter. . . .

"What will you do next?" she asked me.

"I think maybe we go back to Yakima tonight, if we make it out of this mess in one piece and don't get shot up or arrested," I told her. "Use the apartment one more night there, and go in and talk to Stark or the duty officer. I want to see a face when I report this. I want to get some sense that, even if we're pawns in some diabolical chess game, *somebody* knows what the hell is going on here."

I was actually surprised that Al Stark was there. He'd been spending more time away, mostly back east, in recent months and leaving the routine chores in Yakima to subordinates with little minds and officious attitudes, the kind that give their profession the bad name they usually have.

Stark looked tired, not just in a day-to-day sense but really deep-down tired, maybe ten years older than he'd seemed when we'd first met him not all that long ago. This was somebody under lots of pressure who needed a vacation bad. Still, he was civil, and the easiest to talk to of his bunch.

"So you followed dear Cynthia, huh?"

We nodded. "Right to the motel—Sunset Motel, second tier, third from the end on the side next to the 7-Eleven store—and out popped my old buddy Walt Slidecker."

Okay, score one for rival conspiracies. If Slidecker's name didn't surprise Al Stark at that juncture, I didn't know anything about anybody. Even more to the point, he tried unsuccessfully to pretend that it *wasn't* a surprise.

"Probably turned to him after she couldn't divert you," he suggested. "As I remember from the background investigations, your ex-boss might not be lured into this sort of thing even if he were useful for something, not with all that buyout money, but he'd follow Cindy Matalon anywhere."

"That's Walt," I agreed.

At this juncture, Stark insisted that Riki and I be interviewed separately, she by an assistant. "I like to do this with nonprofessionals," he explained. "Most witnesses aren't trained at debriefing, and in relating a shared experience one tends to let the other do all the detailed talking and reinforce things the first one says—even mistakes. This way we'll get both accounts and compare them and fine-tune the details with you later if need be."

"Fine with me," I told him, and continued on my relating of the whole odd episode.

"You're sure they didn't see you before you charged them?"

"Absolutely. But when they were going in, I had no choice. Either chase up front or give it up right there."

"I wish in many ways you'd done the latter and found the nearest phone, but, that's okay. Go on."

It wasn't until I got to the strange spiral and the sense of traffic in and out of it that Al Stark started to show really strong interest again. As before, I could tell quite a bit from his reaction, partly due to his letting down some of his guard because of his weariness I suppose, but still genuine. I became almost immediately convinced that Stark knew exactly what that spiral thing was and what they were doing, and equally convinced that he didn't know it was there. This was reinforced by the fact that he asked almost no details about the sight but a lot about the exact *site*.

When I was done, and he had no more questions or points to follow up, I said, "Okay, now what was that thing? Want to tell me?"

"No. It's not a government thing, though, Maddox. Its code name is 'rabbit hole.' We don't know how it's opened or closed or even if it is, or if it's random and somehow some people know the location in advance. There are little ones and, as you indicated with this thing, very big ones. This is the first one I know of that sounds controlled, though. The location and the hurried call to your old boss and the frantic chase up to it all suggest that they knew it was going to open, and the fact that there was something going on between it and them in a region near here that is both inaccessible and not currently in active service, at least not this month, suggests that the location was somehow selected. It also seems to have stayed open for quite a while. Most of 'em open and close in a few seconds, or a few minutes at most. Long enough sometimes to swallow people or ships or planes or who knows what, but hardly very often or very public. If it were, we'd have a whole cult devoted to them bigger than flying saucers. Me, I'd take the saucers. I think I could *understand* them."

"You—you're telling me it's a—a what? A *hole*? In what? To where?"

He shrugged. "Nobody so far that *we* know of came back to tell us, but that might be changing if what you say is correct. A hole in what? Again, who the hell knows? Space? Time? Space-time? I don't follow all that super-physics stuff and the folks studying this are as classified and as isolated as we are from everybody else. I *am* beginning to think that might be a mistake. We're sure as hell connected now, and I always wondered about Matalon's little mental power tricks. I don't like 'em at all."

"You'll send people to the motel and to the site?"

"Already happening. We've been dispatching as the two of you have been talking, picking it up on the monitoring. We won't find anything useful at the motel, though—they're never that sloppy. And ten to one the site's clean as a whistle and no sign of a Honda, either, gate latched, you name it. Next time you play detective, it might help if you get the license number of the car you're tailing, though."

"Oh, I have *that*," I assured him. "I almost ate the damned thing on those dirt roads a couple of times!"

"You do!" He seemed suddenly energized. "What was it?"

"KBA 921," I told him. "That help?"

"Probably as you say an airport rental, but who knows? We're also staking out Slidecker's home and getaway retreat and securing a federal warrant for him. He busted into a restricted military reservation, you know. Got two eyewitnesses."

# VII

# JAY JAY MOMRATH
# AND THE OUTGRABES

Riki and I didn't sleep much that night, and, at both our own request and with the enthusiastic encouragement of Al Stark, we slept in a room at the campus. We had packed bags, so it wasn't a big deal to find some clean clothes, and we always kept some stuff over at the apartment nearby which was easily retrieved by staff.

The next day, a gray and dreary one if I recall, we made our way to the mansion and Stark's office, only to be told that he was not on site at the time but would be back around midday. The rest of the security crew were about as communicative as usual, which is to say they had all the vocabulary of a Seattle slug, which left us with little to do and a lousy day to do it in. Neither of us were in any shape for the drive home at this point—I wasn't sure I could make the apartment, which was maybe half a mile tops—and there was little apparent going on at the campus of any interest or relevance to us.

That left Les, who always seemed underused and ready to talk, and we headed over to the medical section in the rear unit. He didn't seem very surprised to see us, but did insist on checking us both out.

"I think you two could both use sedatives," he pronounced after looking us over. "You're not cut out for this kind of cloak-and-dagger stuff. Truth is, neither is Stark. I think he might have been a real pistol in his younger days, but he's got heart murmurs and increasingly weak lungs even if he finally did give up regular smoking. You're both in better *physical* shape than he is, but mentally, well, this is his kind of game."

"I'll pass on the sedative for a bit," I told him. "I want to find out if they got anything last night at those spots. I know the odds, but, damn it, I also know Walt Slidecker and he's not likely to hide very well, either."

"Well, that's assuming they bring him here, or tell us anything about these things. I'm not too sure they would. This is all mighty strange business, though. Mighty strange. Particularly coming as it does now."

"Huh? What's so special about now versus last month or next year?"

"Didn't you know? They're preparing to put the big one online here. The free-form god machine. Networked in to all the existing Sims, it'll be the biggest and smartest Brand Box ever, about equal to what we had when Brand had his, well, accident. They're going to send a whole team in there. They're going to try and find out if whatever was out of sync years ago is still wrong and, if so, whether they can diagnose and fix what even Brand could not. During that period they'll also have practically every Sim, every Brand Box big and small, tied in. If Brand's in there somehow, somewhere, he'll have his first access to them and vice versa. Unlikely—I think he's dead, and when you're dead you're dead—but they're dealing with some brand-new things here, as you well know. They might get a *simulated* Matt Brand, but he wouldn't be real, the same super-genius. He'd just be a reflection of everybody else's memories of him who ever went in there, I suspect. Be kind of odd, like some sort of ghost, I suppose, but not real. Not any more real than were Bierce and Woolf and Sterling and the rest in your Sim, Miz Fresca."

Riki thought a moment about that, then seemed to dismiss it. "Doc? What's a rabbit hole?" she asked instead.

He shrugged. "Beats the hell out of me. I think *they* know. Know a lot more than they admit. You can't even look up much about 'em, at least not here or anywhere anybody tries. Never saw one, either. Out of my depth there."

"I think it has to do with Brand, though," I told him. "I think it has to do with where the energy comes from to power all this and where all the information comes from. It was like a tunnel, but an energy tunnel, capable of transferring energy but also matter—things, maybe even people. I keep wondering if Brand and some others hit on an entirely new energy source of a sort we couldn't even imagine and used it for this process, perhaps to create the Brand Boxes. I've been wondering if, maybe, the process gives off either predictable or random flashes that come out under certain conditions all over the place and that this is what we saw. Not the real thing but a byproduct, a side effect. We're still not at all sure what we're playing with here. I don't even think Brand was. Like Newton not knowing what gravity really was or its cause, but nonetheless being able to build natural laws it always obeyed by experimenting with what gravity did."

Riki thought that over and then asked, "Doc? Did they do anything last night that was odd here? I mean, did they increase power or test the stuff you say you're preparing to do?"

"Unless it involved people they wouldn't tell me much, but now that you mention it I *do* recall we had a real power surge through here for a while last night just after dinner. Blew a bunch of light bulbs and screwed up some minor machinery. Yes, it *might*."

"Then maybe Cory's right! They tested out the power level

necessary to run the whole thing and it spun off that rabbit hole or whatever it was!"

Cohn nodded, but then said, "However, these are supposed to also happen over the past several years as I recall the tales. This place was closed then, right? How could it be linked? Or is there more than just here?"

I shook my head. "Wouldn't have to be. They left this powered on, remember? Minimum levels to maintain power to the Sims. They were in shutdown mode here, not termination. It was running at minimum the whole time. Yeah, it all makes sense, until you get to yesterday. It's one thing to say that they'd know when a full-power test would be made and one or more of these energy holes or whatever created, but how could they predict where it would come out? How could they know? And they did know." I thought a moment.

"Les, I know you laughed at my parallel-worlds idea," I continued, "but here's a wilder theory by far supported by even less evidence that explains just about everything. Suppose—well, suppose this is part of the effect of the bug or bugs Brand was trying to track down. Now he's in there, there's a surge, his virtual persona and connection loses contact with his own mind and body. There would be trauma, maybe fair memory loss, but he might recover. We don't know how much of him, how much of his knowledge and personality, were in there. Maybe it *all* went in. Maybe he found himself for all intents and purposes still alive and healthy but inside the Sim. No way out, no wakeup call. Maybe he doesn't even realize that, at least for quite a while. He fixes the problem and studies it. Nobody comes. After a while he knows he's stuck, trapped somehow, and he needs to get word out. He's still got the cover off, as it were, to service and debug the thing. Les—suppose he *used* this byproduct? Suppose he's using it to try and get out or at least get messages out? If he manages to communicate, and somebody like Cynthia Matalon and Walt Slidecker are there instead of us,

how's he to know? I mean, for all *he* knows she's still a secretary on the project."

Cohn frowned thoughtfully. "Who said this woman was a
secretary on the project?"

"Stark did. The first night we met."

"Well, he's lying, for whatever reason. There's no personnel record for her or anybody close to her description in the
files, past or present, and I've never heard anybody who
worked the campus back then mention her, either. Check any
you want, but I have access to everybody's files, even the
ones who died and the ones who never set foot in this place
but once long ago. She's not there. And if there's anybody
out there with real ESP, even making herself invisible to all
for a few seconds, I want to meet 'em. Haven't yet. I don't
believe in that crap. On the other hand, your idea on the holes
isn't all that far-fetched. I *do* have Matthew Brand's own records here, and I wouldn't put anything past that mind. It was
phenomenal. And driven."

"Huh? You mean there was more to this than just a new
Brand toy?"

He nodded. "Brand was H.I.V. positive. He knew it. More,
he'd already had a couple of minor bouts with associated dis-
eases that showed he wasn't going to be one of the lucky few
to live with it. If Matt Brand hadn't died in that final experiment, I doubt if he would have been able to continue on
more than a part-time basis for more than another year or so,
and he'd have surely been stone-cold dead by now."

Both of our jaws dropped. "Brand had *AIDS*?" I managed.

"Yep. And he was taking an amazing amount of traditional
and experimental crap, too. It's a wonder he could concentrate like he managed to do. It's unclear how he got it—he
never said, but he didn't have a transfusion of note and if he
had a sex life the partner was probably made of silicon, but
he got it. Ever since I read that file I been wondering."

"Huh? Wondering what?"

"Whether or not this—all this—wasn't some frantic way Matthew Brand came up with to attempt to preserve his own life, at least his mind, in the only way he could devise."


We checked with reception but Stark still wasn't back, so the next thing was to see a few of the old guard and see if any of them knew anything about the mysterious woman with the outrageous accent we'd been told was Cynthia Matalon. The local security crew didn't know the name but, of course, they were all fairly new and young and might not know it anyway.

Dr. Rita Alvarez had been there through the whole original project, and we dropped in on her office and asked about our mystery woman. She seemed honestly blank on the name and somewhat appalled by the description. The same went for three others that we knew were from the old company. Their memories were just fine, from secretaries down to janitors, but at no time did they remember anybody at all like that.

So Al was lying; had been lying to us since that first night in the restaurant. That figured. His type reveled in that. But why hadn't Rob at least spoken up? Had he been in on this or something?

We hadn't seen my old sales manager for months; we spent most of our time in the Seattle area and he'd moved down here with his lover and was working at keeping us *out* of the papers as much as possible and dealing with our contractors and the like, so he was on the road a lot and on the phone when he wasn't. We hadn't been exactly close friends at any time, but he was certainly somebody I'd considered a "work friend," the sort you might swap news with over lunch or trust with a bank deposit if he was going out somewhere. It happened, though, that he *was* "in residence" as it was euphemistically called by the security staff, and after a half hour of going here and there I finally tracked him down.

"Hey! Cory! How's it *going*? Glad to see you!"

"Stow it, Rob."

He looked more curious than hurt. "Something the matter?"

"Cynthia Matalon."

"Yeah. So?"

"She didn't work here under Brand and the rest, did she?"

An eyebrow went up, and there was understanding but no apparent worry in his face. "Nope. Believe me, I would have remembered."

"But you sat there and let Stark feed us that whole line about ESP experiments and her here as a secretary and security type, and all that, and you never said a word."

He shrugged. "Hey, Al explained to me that there might be a few things he'd have to say that weren't totally true and to trust him on it for now. I mean, it didn't exactly sound like you were gonna get stabbed in the back or anything, only that you were being dogged by a nut case. In fact, I wasn't all that sure at the time. I mean, it was a while ago and there were lots of folks and I didn't know much about the folks in the labs anyway. Heck, for all I knew she might have had short hair and dressed like one of those women determined to die regretting that she didn't give more time to her company. Unless that type is directly over or under me, I don't even notice them. Why would I? Anybody'd notice the loudmouth nut you described, but if she didn't look or act like that then, hell, I coulda passed her every day and never given her a second look, or looked beyond her to the cute guy filing papers in back of her."

The trouble was, it was totally convincing. Could *I* have described everybody, male or female, who looked and acted normal, who'd worked for Subspace? I might look at somebody and say they looked familiar, but not even place them. Our circles even in our work orbits were narrower than we thought.

"Well, okay, but I'm still not sure I should thank you for dragging me into this. It's getting weirder and crazier by the day now and I don't like it."

"I didn't notice you running away from the offer, and

you're a big boy," Rob noted defensively. "Besides, there's two ways to look at this thing. You really would rather all this be going on and you not know it?"

I was ready for that one. "I'm not so sure, if it was just me," I admitted. "But I really have the feeling that Riki would just about sell her soul for that deal."

Rob sighed. "Well, that's the breaks. We're all in it now, I guess, and it sure could be worse. Bills are all paid, the work's interesting, and I'm not complaining."

"Yeah? You going into that thing over there, whatever it is?"

"Did it once, six years ago," he told me. "That's enough. At first it was like having the power of God and all your fantasies realized, but then you discover the ruthless logic of the computer. No, I think I'll stick here this trip."

"Well?" Riki wanted to know.

I shrugged. "He's got a very good, very consistent explanation that seems right. On the other hand, he's a born salesman. What can I say? He did let slip that he was one of the ones Brand had used to prototype a Brand Box Sim six years ago, though. I wonder what kind of world that would be?"

"All muscle men with big pecs and small minds?" she suggested. "A whole world of male bimbos. Hey, there are lots of times when I could go for that."

"Yeah, maybe, but I'd like to follow up sometime what he meant by not being happy with the results, of being subjected to the ruthless logic of the machine." I shook my head from side to side slowly, thinking. "I don't know. I have a feeling that both of us just had a *taste* of what the full thing can do, and if they bring it all online and start mass expeditions in again, I'm not sure what's gonna happen."

She looked unhappy again. "Let's get out of here as originally planned as soon as we're up to it, Cory. Promise me?"

I nodded, but reluctantly. I really wouldn't mind being at

least an observer when they brought the whole Brand-build complex back online.

"I wish I'd never even seen that woman!" she went on. "Next time I'm coming in with you!"

It was getting chilly all of a sudden, as it did in this area during the spring, and a stinging mist was being blown against us by a sudden stiff wind. I put my arm around her and gave her a squeeze and we started heading back for the infirmary. If nobody was around to talk to and there wasn't anyplace we were capable of going, then maybe a sedative and a nice, long sleep would be worth it.

As we reached the door she suddenly stopped, turned, and looked me in the eyes. "Cory, let's get married."

The statement took me completely by surprise, not the least of which being the context.

"What? Now? Too cold and lonely out here."

"I'm serious. Now. As soon as we legally can."

"Let's go in and we'll talk," I said over the increasing howl of the wind, and this time she nodded and opened the door.

It was Riki who had always said no to it. No permanent strings, no big commitments, that's what kept a relationship pure, or so she was fond of quoting. I was never sure but I occasionally got the idea she'd been married once, probably Catholic Church wedding and all that, when she was still in her teens. It hadn't worked, and while she was overall about as good a practicing Catholic as I was a Baptist, there was, nonetheless, some feeling inside her that had drawn a line, apparently forever. She'd just erased it, and very suddenly.

"I mean it," she assured me as we went down the hall toward Les Cohn's office.

"What brought this on?"

"I—I can't explain it. I know it sounds nuts, and that you can quote me to me until you're blue in the face and all that, but I do mean it. If—if you want me, that is. You don't have to. I'm probably too old for kids. I'd understand."

"Now, hold it a minute! Sure, I'll do it. Shock the hell out of everybody, make your mother happy, all that. I just need a better reason from you than some vague feeling. I know you're scared by all this, but it's hardly driven us apart. If anything, we've been together more in the past year than in the past five, thanks to this arrangement. I just want to know what's going through your mind, that's all."

She seemed to find it hard to put into words. "I—I dunno. It's been growing on me, maybe for months. It's some vague sense of—*pattern*. Hell, that's not the right way to put it, so maybe I *am* going nuts. I've just had this vague but building feeling that something's wrong, something's building up, something's gonna happen. That the more—together—we are here, the more together we'll be after whatever happens happens. Oh, that sounds crazier than ever! Maybe—maybe it was that trip to Sterling's early-twentieth-century Carmel colony. I'd been in lots of groups like that in my own life and growing up, but never seen them outside, kind of objective, like a detached observer. I lived 'em, didn't visit 'em. They were all so—so self-confident, self-assured, full of themselves! So absolutely *right* in everything, from literature to the arts to politics. And I started to feel sorry for them! They all seemed so—so lonely, somehow, like that, that colony, those people, were the only family they really had. Almost a tyranny of free thinking, if that makes any sense. You were only one of them, one of the advanced, the superior minds, if you thought just like they did."

I didn't know what to say, or whether I should say anything at all. I didn't understand what was coming through, but I understood that somebody I thought I knew inside and out wasn't at all who I thought she was, and that the real one was emerging. Somebody not nearly as tough, as self-assured, and a lot lonelier than I would have suspected.

"Well, let's both sleep on it, then we'll see," I told her as gently as I could. "If you still feel that way when we both aren't dead to the world and sweating off an adventure, we'll do it."

She squeezed my hand but said nothing.

Riki took a mild sedative, but I found that all I needed was a couple of Advil. By now all the pumped-up excitement of the night before and all the mystery of today had faded into the aches and pains of my sports car suspension on that dirt road. This time I went out like a light.

I didn't normally dream, as a rule. Oh, I know that's impossible, that what I should say was that I almost never remembered my dreams, but I'd once had a kind of in-between anesthetic for some serious dental work that didn't really knock you out but made you forget the whole experience, and it was good enough. If I didn't remember dreaming, then whether I did or not was semantics.

This time, however, very slowly, I did dream, in a kind of weird and unearthly way. I mean, I knew it was a dream, knew that I was out cold there in the infirmary bed, and so I kind of watched the dream as if, like Riki in the Carmel Sim, I were not a participant but an observer even though I was both.

*A wedding.* Well, yes, that would make sense, considering the conversation. Everything surrealistic, some of it slow motion, some of it as real as if I were experiencing it, all rolled up into one.

*Church wedding.* Hmmm. . . . Not what I figured. Generic church; nice little neighborhood one, with a stone exterior, interior kind of early Holiday Inn decor, chapel nice with wood grain, exposed beams, and very pretty stained glass revealed as the doors were opened. The congregation stood, and sort of half turned to look as I came down the aisle on somebody's arm.

They were all there in the pews, not quite as I remembered them, but close enough to recognize with just a little effort. Rob Garnett and Lee Henreid in matching paisley dresses, Al

Stark totally in black, Dan Tanaka, Les Cohn, Rita Alvarez, Alice McKee, and many other faces vaguely seen here and there or even from that first contact meeting at the mansion. Not quite them, as I said, but close, in a dream kind of way.

I suddenly realized that I wasn't quite me, either. As the organ hit the familiar tune, I became acutely aware that I wasn't the groom at all; I was the bride! And I was all in white. . . .

I turned and looked at who had hold of my arm and felt a twinge of complete disorientation and panic. It was Walt Slidecker, and he was in a tuxedo, Reeboks, and wearing a Mariners baseball cap.

We got down to the front without Walt saying a word, and then the organ rose again and everybody turned and in came Riki, the same as ever only more so, dressed in just as elaborate a wedding dress and looking, well, twenty years younger and even fuller of figure.

Somehow, Walt Slidecker had made his way back to her and was escorting *her* down the aisle now, but this time he was wearing cleated boots and a Seahawks helmet.

When Riki reached me, we looked briefly into each others' eyes, then turned and faced the preacher as Walt moved away.

The preacher, in full robes and vestments, was Cynthia Matalon.

*"Hi, y'all!"* the brassy woman greeted us, but I had the idea she was speaking almost entirely to me. *"Y'all don't r'membah this soaht o'thing, do ya? Well, don't you worrah yoah l'il ol' head one minute about it. The impoahtant thing is that you done seen all the folks heah befoah, ain't ya? You'll nevah git all yoah ol' mem'ries back, but every little ol' bit helps. You'n me, we was a team once, like you and herh ahre now. Guess one time or 'nothah most all of us been. Mah mem'ries don't go back fahr 'nuff foah that kinda shit to get togethah in my head myself."*

*"You're only in my dream this time, Matalon, or whatever*

*your name is,"* I responded, my voice sounding very odd in my ears. *"Why can't you just leave us be?"*

The big woman laughed. *"Leave you be? Don't be* absuhd, *dahlin'! And this heah's both a dream and a mem'ry o' soahts, the way most dreams really ahre. Couldn't leave neithah o' you be if I wanted. That's not the way it wohks, y'see. So long as deah Al's got the powah up, I can walk into yoah dreams and whatevah. Wehren't that the* neatest *l'il ol' chase we had yestahday, dahlin'? Lots o' fun. Too bad you didn't come down. If y'had, you'd know what all this is about now. But, no, y'went scahmprin' back to deah ol' Al. Get outta theah, doll! Things ahre gonna stahrt poppin' any time now! Get on out or learn to shoot straight! Bye, now!"*

The dream didn't end with that exchange, but any sense of direct interaction did. It did not, however, go on long enough for me to find out if my subconscious really enjoyed this kind of a relationship.

It wasn't the only dream, either, but the rest were flashes, moments, almost tableaus, and most of them made no sense at all. Finally one of them took place in an old, dark house or some kind of enclosure, not as a true scene like the wedding but like a series of still pictures, each advancing some kind of action, more or less, which involved me, in darkness and inside, seeing by occasional lightning flashes, proceeding toward a big window. Closer, snap new picture, closer, snap new picture, and so on, until I reached the window and looked out. . .

And it was suddenly filled with a horrible, alien head, a massive, monstrous thing with beady reflective eyes and reptilian flesh hanging down in folds, drooling, looking back at me.

I woke up suddenly at that point and sat up almost at the same time. It took me a moment to get hold of myself and convince myself that I was, indeed, in the infirmary and, well, barely on one of the beds. Riki was on another bed next to me, still out. Somebody had come in and turned down the lights to the bare minimum and closed the inner door, probably Les. Still, even with the lights off and curtain down, I could tell it was pretty well into the night.

I eased myself down, felt around for my watch and found it, and headed toward the john. *Wednesday, April 9, 22:44*, it read. Almost a quarter to eleven, which meant I'd slept at least a good eight or nine hours. I took a piss and checked on Riki, who was still out to the world. In fact, she was so damned still I actually stood there for a minute or so until I was sure I saw her move. It was kind of unnerving to see anybody out that solid, but, then, she had been the one taking the sedative.

Of course, considering the nightmares I'd had, maybe I'd have been better off sleeping that kind of sleep, too.

I knew that the first-aid station always had coffee on here twenty-four hours, and I slipped out to get some. Nobody was around, which wasn't all that odd this time of the night, but I could hear the usual technicians and activity down the hall, so I knew the world hadn't ended while we'd been asleep. In fact, it sounded like a few more people than normal on for the second shift, although not a full-blown crew by any stretch of the imagination.

I got a cup, but it was much too strong and old for me, so I threw it out, weighed the idea of going out to a Starbucks and finally decided against it, got some tea and hot water instead, and went back to the room where Riki was still sleeping.

Looking at her, I had the oddest feeling that she didn't look *right*, somehow. Funny, I'd never really noticed how much her age was creeping up on her, showing in her face. Just like me, of course, and I was older than she was, but that wasn't the point. I wasn't comparing her to me, just noticing what I hadn't noticed before.

She was also *tiny*. Again, somehow, I'd never thought of

her as a small or slight or short person. Okay, I was six two and she was five four, but that wasn't it. She just seemed so slight of build, almost, well childlike in spite of the age and experience in her face. No gray hair, though, although that wasn't because of nature. What Riki couldn't pluck she dyed.

Weird. I must still have been suffering the aftereffects of that sleep and those dreams, I told myself, but somehow Riki just didn't seem to be the same person any more.

*Paranoia is catching,* I thought ruefully. *Invasion of the Body Snatchers?* Naw. Then I'd be one of them, too, and wouldn't give a damn anymore. Of course, if I turned into a pod person I wouldn't have to worry about the potential implications of my own deep buried psyche that would cast me in a wedding as the *bride*, now, would I?

It wasn't the absurdity of the dream, that wasn't the point. It was—elements. Not the whole, but parts. Riki *did* look *there* more "normal" to me than the real McCoy, whom I'd slept with and been faithful to (well, okay, almost) for over five years, lying over there.

There was a surge in power all around us; I could feel it, *see* it in the lights coming up in the office next to us, and almost sense a crackling through the very walls in the near darkness.

I sat there, staring at Riki, cup of tea still brewing in my hand, and it seemed as if the whole rest of the universe just ceased.

*There was a crowd, yelling, applauding, cheering, and there I was, up on the stage, behind the big drum set, looking like some real heavy rocker dude in leather, with half-grown beard and long hair and a cigarette that didn't seem to be tobacco dangling from my lips. Others—Dan, Rob, Les, a couple of others—with their instruments, equally scruffy, tuning up. . . .*

*"And now, ladies and gentlemen! The act you've been waiting for! Here's Jay Jay Momrath and the Outgrabes!"*

*Wild applause and cheers and chants and in from stage left cartwheels a whole new Riki, in skintight Catwoman leather, spiked heels, and a build to kill for. She grabs the mike as we hit it and we start to rock and roll!*

*"Are ya ready?"*

*"READY!"*

*"Are ya ready?"*

*"WE'RE REALLY READY!"*

*"Ain't no rules!"*

*"Ain't NO rules!"*

*And then she starts to sing to our rockin' riff. It's a strange, new, complicated but melodious number, fast but in classic rock time....*

*"Hey Mister Caterpillar, smoked your hash!*

*"Got seriously fucked on your mushroom stash!*

*"Don't know now if I'm comin' or goin',*

*" 'Cause everytime I take a chew I'm growin'!"*

*And then we came in, hard beat....*

*"Don't know why you sing that song!*

*" 'Cause everything you think you know is wrong!*

*"The Walrus and Carpenter explain*

*"Say when you hear the truth you'll not complain!"*

*All together....*

*"When you hear you can't complain!*

*" 'Cause when you know they'll fry your brain!"*

The band then went instrumental, and Riki a.k.a. Jay Jay Momrath just about leaped into the adoring crowd below as we continued to play maniacally, over and over. Clothes came off, all sorts of stuff came up, and things began to turn into some sort of stadium-sized orgy. Riki became suddenly upset, insecure, unable to get out of the crowd, and began to be engulfed and submerged by it and the band, in response, changed in trying to get her out....

Abruptly, I realized that I wasn't dreaming but was wide awake. I could see the vision and hear the roar and feel Riki's panic, yet I was also sitting there, awake, watching her, and with the tea still in my hand.

*I'm not dreaming this!* I told myself, surprised. *She is! I'm seeing her own nightmare!*

The energy pulse faded, went down, and suddenly I was just sitting there with *no* visions, staring into the dark. *Now what the hell?*

I tried the tea and found it actually cool, but certainly strong enough. I looked at my watch, which I'd put on my arm before going out, and it now read 23:20. Deducting ten minutes for my bathroom trip and search for something warm to drink, that meant I'd been sitting there for close to half an hour!

I thought about the connection between the power surge— probably tests for the run-up to full power here—and the effect I'd had. Was that how Cynthia Matalon got through to me time and time again? Maybe not proximity—it was possible that the more you did it with one other person the easier it got—but closeness to this power. If she, somehow, could tap those rabbit holes, whatever they were, then it would also explain why I might not hear from her for a long time and then suddenly she'd be in my head every day.

*"So long as deah Al's got the powah up, I can walk into yoah dreams and whatevah."* That's what she'd said in my dream.

Telepathy? I never believed in it, and I wasn't sure I did now, yet there it was. I *knew* I'd just been in Riki's mind.

And yet, and yet, inside *her* mind was a complete verse of that stupid song I'd been hearing since all this started. *I* sure hadn't put it there, and I don't know where it might have been picked up by Riki, but there it was.

I was already getting pretty damned sick of it, too.

Something else ran through all this. Something that should have been obvious but wasn't, for some reason. Not until now.

*Welcome to Wonderland. . . . Through the Looking-Glass. . . .
Rabbit holes. . . . Momraths outgrabing. . . . Caterpillars
smoking. . . . Walrus and the Carpenter. . . .*

A hell of a lot of Lewis Carroll, wasn't there? Somebody
around on all sides of this had a real liking for that old
nineteenth-century nut.

Carroll was also a mathematician—no, more properly a
professor of mathematics, if I remembered correctly. But how
did he fit in with Scarlett O'Hara and crazy dreams and Sims
and Matthew Brand?

Except, of course, in the end, *everything* comes down to
mathematics, even Alice.

Part dream and part memory, Cynthia Matalon had said.
And the song, that damned song that seemed to pop up more
elaborately as we went along—who the *hell* wrote that
damned thing? And why? Half drug-culture crap, half paranoid warning, like that guy in *Body Snatchers* standing in the
middle of traffic that ignored him screaming, "You're next!
You're next!"

The Sims, the project, the revolutionary storage boxes, the
equally bizarre power—it was as if I were suddenly in some
world run by alien beings, a world of fantastic marvels.

No. That wasn't right.

It was a group of people, both ordinary and above the ordinary, who'd stumbled upon some totally alien technology
and were now taking it apart and playing with it without understanding it. Matthew Brand may have been Einstein
cubed, but he didn't invent this. Even Al Stark admitted as
much. This power source—it had brought some creatures
here from the stars and smashed them against the New Mexico desert. They'd learned how to make it, even amplify it,
over the years, but I *bet* they had no idea at all what the hell
it was.

And then there was the pilot and navigational system.
Handed to somebody as bright as Brand, and given him all
those nicely hideable tax dollars from the government intelli-

gence boys to play with and a real motivation to do something spectacular quickly, and he'd done his miracle. He'd built something; something that worked in ways nothing else before had ever worked. Something that even he didn't really understand but could tap and use. The Sims of the Brand Boxes, the Sims based on the navigational and pilot modules of that crashed saucer.

*The engines of starships run by total symbiosis with the ship by the crew.* Those engines, or something very much like them and based on them, was underneath us now, being tested and checked out before being brought up to full power to enable the entire Brand project. The rabbit holes. . . . Energy tunnels. To where? Who could know? But if they *were* controllable, then you might even cheat the speed of light. You might be able to use them to go vast distances and cheat a lot of things.

I didn't care who they were—intelligence, defense, Matalon, Walt, some nut group, Dan, you name it. *Nobody* was qualified to screw around with this! Even Matthew Brand wasn't smart enough to do it and get away with it!

But how very, very human to believe you could, and, even after a demonstration as in Brand's own death of just how scary it was—not to mention these holes or whatever they were—and, here they were, doing it again.

I looked at Riki, sleeping so deeply and peacefully, and knew that it wasn't so underneath. She wasn't soft; she was tough, hardened by years of experience, much not positive. She'd been born with a talent, though, and she'd devoted much of her time and energy into getting it just right, and she liked her work in the same way I liked mine. Maybe more. She'd been content to just keep going like we had been, sailing around into a comfortable old age doing what we liked doing, which isn't a bad recipe. Now she was scared, and reaching out to me as the only anchor she knew in this world, maybe knowing I was as scared as she was.

The hell with this. In the morning, if the weather was even

close to driveable, we were getting out of here, and if we passed Matalon and Walt and all those little green men from the flying saucer rolling down the street we weren't gonna take the slightest notice.

I lay back down on the bed in the dark, shut my eyes, and tried to get some more rest. *Maybe I should have taken that sedative,* I thought, but I didn't really mean it. If *I* had any nightmares, I wanted to be able to wake up. Still, I would have much preferred to be in the apartment or the house than here, where at least Riki and I could cuddle up close on the same bed.

Running through old fantasies didn't help; my mind was too much on the stress and worry of all this. I tried instead to blank out the universe, just shut my eyes in the dark and drift.

Again I seemed to be inside Riki's own mind, but this time not inside a dream so much as witness to a series of tableaus that seemed too real to be mere fantasies even though they had to be.

*In a beautiful but desolate landscape I am with her, only she is tanned and muscular, powerful, wearing only some kind of straps made out of skins and a short, crude sword. Her hair is black and long, and the tough body dark browned by the sun, and she makes her way to the top of a rise and kneels, looking down at the other side, gesturing for me to come up. I approach, kneel in the hot sand, and look where she is looking, and I see a winding river and some snaking green of vegetation below following it and feeding off of it.*

*We need water so badly it is all I can do not to rush down there, but, while she is as thirsty as me, she puts out a strong arm and stays me, then points to an area in the trees below. At first I can see nothing, but then I begin to see movement there, and a hot breeze brings the sound of more than one animal hidden below.*

*"Slavers," she said. "It is a trap."*

*"But we must have water soon or we die!"* I pleaded.

*"Better death than to fall into* their *hands,"* she warns.

The scene shifts, and so do the sensations.

*The smells of exotic spices and perfumes mix oddly with the more fetid odors of dung and garbage; fast but exotic music of the Orient surrounds me as well, and there is the sound of laughter and conversation in the light of the torches, lanterns, and candles inside the tent. In the bare center, on thick pieces of wood set atop ornate carpets, she is dancing, whirling, exotic and strange at one and the same time, her nearly naked body decorated with the most colorful and erotic of tattoos. . . .*

Again the scene shifts. Again, I am not certain what I am seeing, except that it is neither fantasy nor reality yet it seems like both at once.

*The man in the trenchcoat reached into a drawer and pulled out a revolver and checked it. He hears me, turns, and I stare for a moment in wonder, looking into a face both as familiar as my own and yet also different in a way I'd never seen it before. You could see Riki in the eyes, in the facial structure, but it was her and it was not her.*

*Riki was a man.*

*Not play-acting, not disguised by trenchcoat—there was no questioning that. Even the voice was Riki's, but one half octave shifted down, a man's voice.*

*"What are you doing up? I thought you were asleep by now!"*

*"Rick,"* I managed, suddenly aware that my voice was higher and my physical stature shorter than his. *"Please—don't go. You know they'll kill you. They've got too much power!"*

*"There are only a few that count, headed by dear old Starkweather. If I can nail* him *before he can nail* me, *it will change everything. He'll be back to square one and not even know why. It took us too long to figure this system out as it*

*was; I don't want any more reincarnations when the big boys in the know can retain their old selves. We're never going to get out of this until we stop him. You know that."*

I nodded. *"I know, I know, but. . . . He's good, he's ready for you, and he's expecting just this kind of move. Why does it have to be now? We've got a decent life here, we're still young, we can enjoy things!"*

*Rick chuckled. "Don't worry. I'm pretty good at this now. Besides, I could never just drop out, knowing that I was abandoning the field to them, knowing that my whole life was a lie. No, this is it. Wish me luck, baby!"*

Another shift, but this one not nearly so distinct. This one was walking, almost floating, down through a rabbit hole, sucked into the huge revolving energy cylinder, moving down, down. . . . But not alone.

Suddenly, I felt and heard Riki's voice, directly in my mind, as if we were there, in that hole, together.

*"Cory, I was such a fool! We can't beat them! You were right! Just because this time it's reversed we can't let the macho win. Not again. Let's just forget all this. Get married, move to someplace pretty, enjoy life for once. I'll take your name, I'll do your laundry, I'll even learn to cook. Anything you want me to be I'll be. I'm not a coward, I'm not a wimp, I've paid my dues on all this and it just keeps going on and on, worlds without end. I'm just so damned sick of fighting. . . ."*

But before I could reply, or even know if this was any kind of real contact or simply in my mind or hers, something else showed up in the rabbit hole, something huge coming the other way! We both saw it, the huge form, the great, ugly reptilian head with its beaklike mouth, huge shell, and terrible, terrible roar. . . .

*"You are either the Walrus or the oysters!"* the Mock Turtle thundered. *"Choose. Fight or be damned! Fight or be eaten! CHOOSE!"*

I felt absolute terror run through me. I think I screamed,

maybe aloud, but suddenly I was awake, still in darkness, still in the hospital room, but in a terrible, terrible sweat.

Riki stirred. "Huh? Uh—*what?* I—uh. . . ." Her eyes fluttered open for a minute, then closed again when they couldn't focus, then opened once more. "Cory?"

"I'm here," I told her, still breathing hard and trying not to show it.

"What—what time is it?"

I fumbled for my watch, then realized that I hadn't ever taken it off after putting it back on. I pushed the little button that backlit the dial. "Six-fifteen," I told her. "In the morning—I hope." I let out a heavy blast of air that somehow helped me lower my tension level. The second time for that creature's appearance in my nightmares had been particularly nasty. I think I even preferred Cynthia Matalon.

"You want to sleep some more?" I asked her.

She struggled to sit up in bed, yawned, and rubbed her eyes. "No. Not after *those* dreams. You?"

"Same here," I told her honestly. I couldn't say which were my own dreams and which ones we'd shared.

"I—I think I can manage if I can hit a bathroom and a sink with some cold water," she told me. "You?"

"I'm wide awake, now. I need a shower, but that's your problem."

"Well, we'll take one together when we get home, like in the old days, huh? Right now, I just want out of here. There's at least three or four places already open for breakfast in town, and maybe more. If you're up to it, let's drive to one, get something in us and a couple gallons of coffee, and hit the road. What do you say?"

"Sounds good to me. What if Matalon or Walt decides to eat in the next booth?"

"Screw 'em."

"*That* is something I'll more than go along with," I assured her. "Let's get ourselves awake."

Getting functional wasn't a problem; looking outside was a

bit more problematical. It was definitely raining cats and dogs out there and had been most of the night. From the feel of things, it wasn't all that warm, either. I went over to one of the Marine guard stations. "What's the driving like? We slept in last night."

The young Marine shrugged. "I heard on the radio that it stayed above freezing in the whole valley here, and nobody's reported any snow or ice. Can't say what it's like beyond town, though. Wouldn't take much elevation to turn this into a spring blizzard."

We managed to slog, wet and windblown, to my car and get in, and I pulled out with some difficulty from the puddles of standing water, but I didn't like the look of things. They didn't improve after we'd both had decent breakfasts and even more decent caffeine levels in us. The freeway north was treacherous; the freeway west and south were both under snow and ice advisories, and as for going through the park the hard way—forget it. Seattle was okay, as usual, but about the only way we were going to safely make it was either in a four-wheel-drive vehicle or a charter airplane. It was moving eastward now, and the worst was over, but it would probably take the better part of the day to get things back to normal, and in my physical and mental state I figured it wasn't smart to push it, particularly in the Porsche.

"Well, looks like we're stuck for a bit," I told her. "Want to go reopen the apartment? Just lounge around in various states of undress and not turn on a computer or terminal or modem or maybe even a phone and veg out watching mindless cable TV while doing nice feelies to each other?"

She grinned. "Sounds good to me. We'll just eat out or get pizza delivered or something."

We got back in the car and headed toward the apartment. I wasn't sure about this cold front; the rain was tapering off, but it felt like it was getting colder and the sun was only barely up and not helping a bit.

As we approached the turnoff for Wonderland, a turnoff I

had no intention of taking, I had the oddest sensation in my head, unlike anything I could ever remember before. It was—*alien*. I couldn't describe it any other way. It wasn't even scary. It was absolutely, positively indescribable, that feeling, but it was there and it seemed to be coming from more than one source.

Riki gasped, but said nothing.

"I feel it, too. It's not your stomach," I assured her, hoping that maybe it was.

"It's not coming from the campus," she noted, frowning. "More like over in the orchards just beyond the fences. Funny how *directional* it is."

I was feeling exactly the same and I didn't like it one bit. Rather than follow it up, though, or turn into Wonderland, I pulled into the parking lot of a Dunkin' Donuts and stopped the car.

At that very moment I had a vision. Not a sleepy, weepy type vision, but a real one, clear as day even though I was wide awake. Riki saw it, too, and her jaw dropped.

There were some sort of shapes, like men in armor, in back of Walt Slidecker, standing there in formations as if waiting for some kind of order. In front of him was a terrified farm family—two men, three women, and a bunch of children, all in an old and incredibly beat-up pickup truck. They had obviously been heading back to the fruit company processing plant and had taken the old dirt road as a shortcut, a common thing to do that saved maybe ten miles. This time, though, they'd run right into this bizarre group of whatever they were and Walt. Kindly old Walt, my old partner, a guy I thought I knew as much as anybody. Somebody I'd gone to games with and worked with and barbecued with and all the rest. Good old Walt.

Good old Walt took out a semiautomatic rifle of some kind and blew them all away without a single trace of emotion on his face, not even when he hit the children. . . .

# VIII

## OF BOOJUMS AND BEASTIES
## AND THINGS THAT GO TWONK

Riki gave a sound somewhere between a muffled scream and a sob; I just tried to blot it out. Finally, I turned to her and asked, "Still want to go home, pack, and drop out?"

"Yes," she responded. "But not until I see that son of a bitch fry! That was *Walt*, for God's sake! How could he do something like that? I mean, when did this become a nightmare?"

I thought a moment. "Maybe not a nightmare. Maybe it was a pipe dream. I'm not sure yet, but I have the sneaking feeling that we've been living a lie for some time."

"Huh? What do you mean?"

"Never mind." I unsnapped my seat belt and felt in my pocket for some change, bringing it out and looking for quarters. "Look, we can't do anything directly, but if that was real, what we just saw, and I have a terrible feeling it might just be, somebody else has to move fast. Somebody with guns and helicopters and stuff. As vicious as Walt was, it was those things behind him, lot of 'em, that are the worry now. We can't help that family, but we can't even shoot back. Hold on while I call this in."

The security man at the mansion wasn't exactly in a mood to believe what I was saying, but he was just unsure enough about what to do that he was willing to buzz Al Stark.

"Let me get this straight. You saw this in a vision?"

"We both did. I know it sounds crazy, but what will it hurt? On the dirt road leading back to the old bottling plant that runs just east of our property. I can't tell how far in, but if this happened it shouldn't be hard to find."

Stark thought a moment. "Won't hurt to have a look. I wish we could use the chopper, but we're still getting oddball downdrafts and this would be low flying. I'll get two squads to come in from opposite directions and I'll see if we can get the chopper at least up for observation, okay?"

"Fine. What do you want us to do, though?"

"The best thing would be to stay where you were until we find out if there's anything to this. You don't have a cell phone in that car?"

"If I did, would I be in an uncovered booth outside the do-nut shop? Normally I don't want a phone in the car—it's the one place where I can go other than my boat and not be reachable by people like you."

"All right. Stay put. Give me the number and I'll ring when it's clear."

I hung up, but had no intention of sitting in a parking lot while this was going on not far from us.

"Well?" she asked me as I got back in.

"They didn't believe me, of course, but they're sending people down the road in both directions anyway. Let's move up there. I don't want to be in the middle, but I want to hear what goes on."

Because Wonderland was allegedly a private and not government agency, the Marines inside didn't wear uniforms until they actually got there, but I'll give Stark this much—he didn't give a damn who was watching when something nasty might be going on. We saw two black cars and a Jeep with some mean-looking guards with submachine guns come out of our road and turn down about half a mile until they reached the dirt road cut into the trees and then they all turned in. I wanted to follow them bad, but that wet track wouldn't do the Porsche any good at all, and we might just block somebody important. Instead, I turned in at the company sign and slowly cruised on back on the campus road, windows down in spite of the cold, listening.

There were no sounds of gunfire, something I didn't know whether to be relieved about or nervous about, but there was the kind of tension in the air you could cut with a knife. If I'd had a pack of cigarettes I'd have resumed smoking on the spot.

"Cory, there's something *very* wrong here," Riki noted as we came within sight of the gate and guardhouse. You could see somebody in the guardhouse, but whoever it was didn't look familiar and definitely wasn't in the security steel blue uniform.

*"It's Walt!"* I yelled, and suddenly turned around as fast as I could and gunned the engine. As soon as I did the forest on both sides seemed to erupt with dark, armored shapes. One of them ran in front of us and almost launched itself onto our car; there was a scrunch and I struggled for control as the extra weight momentarily was carried by the curving front end. At that moment the—creature's—face was pressed against the windshield, only to almost immediately lose its balance and roll off. Riki screamed, and I'm not at all sure I didn't, too.

A reptilian, wrinkled, *alien* face, with two vacant-looking saucerlike yellow eyes and a nose-mouth combination that was half short snout and half beak. . . .

We'd seen that creature before, or one very much like it. In those near ancient, half-century-or-more-old photos of the alien bodies recovered in that post–World War Two spacecraft. . . .

I didn't hesitate. I turned *right* and continued to gun it, tearing away from the scene and cops and limits be damned. I was taking the old roads, the ones that went south and east, and I didn't care where they went.

We went through fast-food drive-throughs and stopped only for self-serve gas all day, until we were so damned far away from them that even *we* weren't sure how far away we were. I remembered seeing the Idaho state line, and figured we were heading south and east as usual, probably toward Yellowstone or something like that, mostly in pouring rain. Finally, we got the elevation or whatever and the rain turned to snow, and there was no way I was going to be able to drive much further through this. With a lot of skidding and some hairy turns we finally pulled into this small logging town in the middle of nowhere and knew that we could go no further.

There was a small lodge there with motel-type rooms, mostly full thanks to the weather, but they took pity on us and gave us their last room. We must have looked a sight as it was and we knew it.

We had overnight bags in the car, but not much else, and, frankly, it was all dirty laundry for when we'd gotten back home to Bremerton. The few stores in the town probably weren't going to have a lot of choices, but maybe the next day we could pick up something.

As it was, we were able to shower and at least wash out some underwear in the sink so we wouldn't be too rancid.

"We ought to see about getting some dinner," I suggested. "This kind of place tends to serve like six to eight or seven to nine and forget it."

She nodded. "I guess, but this stuff's still a little wet even if it has been hanging on the heater." She gave an odd smile. "Funny. Here we are, nothing much to our names at the moment, snowbound in the middle of nowhere and not knowing what the hell tomorrow will bring, and I feel like a heavy weight's been lifted from me. Like something horrible happened back there, and I don't even want any part of it. Not anymore."

"I know what you mean," I told her, and kissed her.

Well, the steak was a little tough and the baked potato was dry as a bone, but it was better than nothing and a damn sight better than another McDonald's drive-through, although this place wasn't even big enough to have one of those.

The room, too, was rustic, with basic decor and cheap wood panels and a bed that squeaked, but it was warm and quiet and that was enough. They did have TV in the town, which surprised the hell out of me, apparently from a town-created tiny cable system fed by a single satellite dish. Reception was pretty lousy, though, what with the wind and the storm.

So we wound up not saying much, but just lying there, naked, cuddled against each other under the various blankets in the room, and it turned into a lot more as it went along, more than we'd really done or felt in quite a while. Like a lot of couples who'd lived together for a long time but led very separate lives, the initial lust had faded into a kind of deep but emotional friendship as much as anything else. Now, however, it was almost as if we'd just met, just fell in love, and were having each other for the first time.

How that old bed must have squeaked up a storm, but we didn't care. It was in many ways the most unusual and intense lovemaking either of us could remember, almost as if, somehow, we were one person, we were in each other's minds and bodies, we were totally and completely joined.

It was only after we were coming off it that I began to feel every single year of my life and the cost of every single exercise session I never had. I knew she was feeling the same, and that we'd both probably have muscle cramps and bruises like mad after this. Still, it had been worth it.

*I wonder if they have a justice of the peace in this town? How long is the waiting period in Idaho?*

*I don't know, but—* "Good lord! Did we just read each other's minds?"

She frowned. "I—I'm not—by God I think we *did*! Oh, boy! What a pair we'll make! No secrets from each other, ever again."

It had been a bizarre couple of days, days in which everything had been turned upside down and the impossible was being faced. It appeared that we still weren't through with surprises.

We just lay there for a while in the dark, very relaxed, and staring up at the stippled stucco ceiling only vaguely illuminated from the indirect light from the bathroom.

If those energy trials at the campus had somehow boosted us while we slept there, what was going on now? Was this at the level we'd reached back in Yakima, or were we continuing to expand this—this *connection* to others?

What had happened back there since we'd run? Did they fight off the attack? Did they lose or evacuate? Who would answer if I called the mansion from here?

I didn't want to call in, particularly not from here, stuck in the snow and who knew how many days until my little sportscar was safe to drive out? Walt could trap us just using a helicopter, and who knew what sort of things were at his little turtle-faced friends' disposal?

I really wanted to know what happened back there, and what perhaps I should do next. Riki's mind was drifting in what seemed to be the presages of sleep, and I joined with her and let the emptiness flow through us.

*Al Stark lit another cigarette and struck his fist on the desk in frustration.*

*"I don't get it! How the hell did they get a horde of Boojums in here? I mean, damn it, they don't even* exist, *for Christ's sake! They're out of that damned Cholder Sim. It's not possible to take things created in and stored in one damned Sim and translate them to the reality of another. You*

*know that! Did somebody change the fucking laws of physics, or what?"*

*"Now, calm down, Al," said a man's familiar voice, but not too familiar. "If we could get the work out of the Crew like we did, why couldn't they? I mean, it was Slidecker who hired Maddox, wasn't it? Besides, maybe slow and subtle wasn't the best approach here. I mean, they sure seem to have some advances we missed. We still have more than they do. Otherwise, why hit us here at all?"*

*"I know, I know. Any word on Maddox and the girl since this morning?"*

*"Not a word. I'd have thought they would have called in by now."*

*"Maybe not. That Maddox is one of the smarter cookies, particularly when scared, and he's pretty strong, too. I don't know about you, but it's been a long time since I had a vision that detailed. I don't like it. He's of value, yes, but at this stage he's more of a threat to us, and we have what we really wanted, what Slidecker was after as well, the wireless null-loss sequencer. No, they're asking too many questions now, and if they fall into the hands of the other side Maddox could be problems, and the girl can get tough and dangerous if cornered. Besides, if they can bring Boojums across through the rabbit holes intact, what's to keep them from sticking Maddox, say, in some kind of obedient slave motif and bringing him back that way? We can't afford that, and we can't at the moment do it ourselves, as handy as that would be."*

*"Why wouldn't they come in? They called this in this morning, and I don't blame 'em for running if they saw that. I'd feel like running, too."*

*"Sure, they're running scared now, but who knows how many other visions they might have, how many vestigial memories might pop up? No, they're going too fast for us. I told Tanaka they were strong, but he didn't give a damn. No, get 'em back. That car of his is a dead giveaway, and they'll need to use credit cards for almost everything as it is. If we*

*can sucker them back in, great. I don't have much hope, though—not with those memory flashes and visions. If they don't buy what we're selling, then we'll have to get rid of them just to make sure the other side doesn't get them. I'm not sure that wouldn't be the best choice. Just make it look like an accident."*

*"You mean that? Just like that?"*

*"Sure. They'll just wind up in stasis until a majority translate through. Then they get the real, live born-again experience. I want to avoid that if at all possible. I've avoided it now eleven straight lives."*

*"Yeah, but who knows how long this has been going on? I mean, so you're head of security for the project. What project? Does it still exist or are we just on automatic? Who's the boss? Does the boss care any more?"*

*"I think about that a lot,"* Stark admitted, *"but you can only go so far with it. Eventually we are going to put this all back together. Eventually this crew will be reassembled and it will build the way out. Damn it, we actually had* Brand *this time! For the first time in my memory we had him, too! And he, or we, screwed it up. Well, it doesn't matter. So long as we keep getting new tries, we'll keep at it. That's why I'm so loath to just call this one a dead loss, take as much of the team that will stay under our control, and translate. I keep thinking that this place, these records, are still the farthest along we've come in the eleven tries I can remember, and I don't want to start all over if I can help it. Who knows what the next translation would be?"*

The vision had, like the other, a fixed field of view, but now the other walked into it and for the first time, even if briefly, I could see who it was.

Blond, blue eyed and not *quite* as swishy as he played, Lee Henreid, Rob's longtime companion, looked a lot tougher and a lot less like a male bimbo than he always made himself out to be. I wasn't sure if I was pleased at that or not. He'd always seemed a bit of an embarrassment to me, kind of like the beach-blanket-blond bombshells were for Riki, but to discover he was one of the security staff and a government man was disconcerting. I wondered if Rob even knew.

The vision faded out, but I was wide awake in the dark, and I knew that Riki was, now, too. "Thanks a lot for spoiling a wonderful evening," she commented sourly.

I sighed. "Sorry, but at least we know several things. We know that Walt and his creatures failed today, that Stark's cut from the same cloth as Walt but is on the other side, and we know that neither side is particularly friendly or appetizing. If we go back voluntarily we'll be virtual prisoners of Stark and his people, to be done away with or put into a Sim like the one I was in and left there. If we try and contact the other side, we'll be climbing in bed with somebody who didn't hesitate to shoot a couple of little kids in cold blood and who consorts with alien critters. If we don't go voluntarily with one or the other, we can be reasonably sure that either side will kill us."

"Cory—we've got to vanish. Completely. But how? I mean, against *them*? They'll probably know we're here by morning just by the charge slips."

"Calm down! If the government were that efficient we wouldn't have any enemies in the world, they'd run everything and anything, period, and it wouldn't take five days to deliver a letter across town. No, I think we have a *little* margin, but not much, and maybe not any if this snow continues to block us from getting anywhere. Look, let's get some sleep and play this as it happens from now on."

"Sleep? How can you sleep?"

"Because we're trapped here. If they have us made here, there isn't a thing we can do with it or anyplace we can run without freezing to death. So we have to act like they won't find us here and we can do something tomorrow. That means getting a decent night's sleep. This could be another long day, one of many, coming up."

Nobody crashed in the door, and there were no suspicious

helicopters and such all over, and so we both actually managed to get some sleep, and, when we awoke, it was actually bright sunshine.

There was no purpose to concealing our existence here, so we had breakfast, found that the highway department was on the ball and that the snow had been wet and easy to clear, and that we could probably get out of there by noon.

We picked up some supplemental clothing at the dry-goods store. It wasn't great, but it fit, and it sort of turned us from underdressed yuppie types to a duo wearing jeans, flannel shirts, sheepskin jackets, and, what the heck, white cowboy style hats. We even both managed to find cowboy boots that fit. The fit wasn't exactly L.L. Bean, but it worked, and it sure changed our looks for a casual observer. The underwear had nothing to do with looks but did make us both feel a little better.

The local magistrate was also the town mayor and owner of the general store. He also appeared to lead the little Protestant service on Sundays in a chapel in the town hall. I was never clear what the denomination was. There was a waiting period, but he kind of relented and back-dated a couple of forms and accepted our drivers' licenses as IDs. For a fee of twenty-two dollars, Riki and I were married in about ten minutes in a civil ceremony.

After a wedding lunch at the Dairy Queen, we went back over to the car, settled all the accounts at the lodge, and proceeded out onto the road toward Boise. The road was surprisingly good for such a recent snow; much of it was clear, and the temperature was actually in the mid to upper forties by afternoon.

It was going to break my heart if it were even possible, and I didn't have my title with me although I had the registration, but we found a used car place in Boise that was more interested in acquiring a Porsche at a very good price for them than in the problems involved. I was able to sign a power of attorney allowing them to put in for a duplicate title, and things were settled. We deposited the cashier's check in a local bank and got a cheap room in a basic motel near the branch. Riki was now in charge of this phase of our lives, and I was surprised at what she knew about this sort of thing. So, it turned out, was she, but she did know it and did it very well.

Local cemeteries yielded deaths of people close in age to us. Using those, she somehow was able to use the department of records to get birth certificates in those names, and, with those, we got married a *second* time in the courthouse, this time as our two new names. In less than a week, we were legally two totally different people, with social security cards, marriage license, driver's licenses, you name it, even a bank account which we now withdrew after buying a four-wheel-drive Jeep Cherokee, maybe five years old and squeaking but solid, and a post office box for an address.

It was pretty discouraging. All fraudulent and yet all so easy—if you knew exactly what you were doing. Since we were doing it for protection and not to deliberately defraud, there might even be a case for it not being as illegal as all that, but it would do. About the only trouble was that we were stuck with the names, and it was going to be hard to remember and get used to being Joshua Lengel. I never thought of myself as a "Josh," nor, I suspect, did Riki or anyone think of her as having the first name "Angel." Not Angelique or Angelica or the like, but Angel, maiden name Thompkins, now Angel Thompkins Lengel.

We needed every dime we could get, but I insisted she have at least a basic wedding ring, and she agreed. I also started growing a beard and letting my hair grow long, and she went the opposite way, having her very nice hair cut really short and giving it a peroxide or whatever blond dye job. With the new looks, the cheap but serviceable clothes, and new identification we felt confident to move on.

Manufacturing an education and background isn't as easy and is very fraudulent, and with the less than eight grand remaining we didn't exactly have much start-up money, so for a while it would be living in the car, such as it was, and finding whatever temporary work we could as we moved south to warmer climes far removed from Yakima and Seattle and all the rest.

I was now a bum in my late forties, and she was a companion bum in her early forties, but there wasn't much we could do. Curiously, I felt that she was actually happy, and, while a lot of the work was real basic stuff—kitchen work, hauling, that kind of thing—I was generally feeling almost like I was somebody else entirely.

Were they looking hard for us? On our trail? We didn't know, but we didn't want to find out. I had no doubt that I could do the "vision thing" again and find out some more, there was always the point that, if *we* could do it, and Cynthia Matalon could do it, maybe others could do it, too. Both of us still had occasional flashes of what almost seemed like bizarre alternate lives, but nothing really fleshed in and explained itself.

A number of things did change, in many ways easier than I thought they could. It took only weeks before we were calling each other Josh and Angie all the time, even in private, not slipping up once and not even thinking about it, as if the names we'd been born and raised with and had used for all those years were no more real than the ones we'd taken off the graves. It wasn't surprising that, with all the exercise, I was feeling better with fewer aches and pains than I had in a long time, but it was very unusual when I thought on it that I didn't miss the computers, didn't miss the sedentary stuff at all. The only thing I would have liked to have changed was to have more money. A *lot* more, and maybe ten years off my age.

Inside of six months my rapidly graying hair had turned completely so, even the now substantial beard, and Angie's— Riki's—hair, which she'd kept extremely short and basic, had gone from blond to white, apparently because of too much peroxide. She would have panicked in spades at this only months earlier; now she left it that way and didn't give a damn. And, muscles or not, the dirt-cheap semipoverty diet we were eating was full of fats and starches and we both were frankly putting on middle-aged fat. Our own parents or friends wouldn't have recognized us, and, frankly, we didn't recognize us much, either.

Every once in a while I'd wonder if the hunt was still on, or if both sides had by now decided that the other side had us. We could only hope, but not be sure. And, to be perfectly frank, the longer things went on, the less we even thought about it.

That's not to say it vanished completely from our minds. You don't know what we know, and have experienced what we experienced, and have it completely fly out of your head. At least, I didn't think so. But, what *was* happening was curious enough in and of itself: we were simply becoming our new selves and losing the old ones. Two aging, fat, low-maintenance hippies of an earlier age who lived for today and never thought about tomorrow, that was us. And, yeah, we even blew some of it on drugs, mostly of the soft kind, and didn't care a bit.

*Most* strange was that I had spent my whole life in computers and in learning to program at the highest and most esoteric levels, and she'd become a really great artist and painter, and during this whole period I neither looked at, thought about, or missed computers in the slightest and as far as I know she never picked up even a pencil to sketch something. It was almost as if, well, we'd been dropped into a Sim as these two characters, very different from ourselves but content in a basic sort of way.

That type of paranoia was the one thing that didn't go away. Would we know? Would we even remember? Were we in fact living this life or were we instead living somebody else's program?

As might be expected, it was the drugs that caused the

problem, and who knows what might have happened if we'd gone on the strictly vegan organic and health-kick route instead? Aside from an occasional very mild recreational drug I hadn't done much more than a Tom Collins since my college days, so letting loose like this was another part of the personality change. In Angel's case it was reversion, but that wasn't Angel, it was Riki, and that was a long time ago.

Well, okay, maybe it was all for the best, but I still feel guilty about it, okay?

We ran into this Navaho with a bad drinking problem over on the Texas coast, and he offered some very specialized genuine Native American mushroom in exchange for enough dough to buy the next few days' booze. Well, we hadn't done much of that sort of thing but we no longer worried about it, either. This wasn't the first time we'd taken something like this, although such takings were rare, and it didn't really faze us much. *This* stuff, though, was different.

Oh, it started out pretty much the same, with the weird drippy colors and weird sounds and kind of flowing modern art that kind of made the back of my mind think of early computer graphics and VR, but then things got really strange. We were so used to being in each other's heads by this time that we took it for granted that we were having exactly the same trip. Now there was suddenly a grid, twisting, turning, and we were flying over it and following it. It was undulating back and forth but clearly converging on some central spot or axis that was drawing us like gravity toward it.

And then we saw it. A huge, perfect mushroom, rising up into the jet black unnatural sky. Somebody, or some *thing*, sat atop the mushroom, and it didn't take a lot of guesswork to figure out who as we approached and landed on the edge. The texture felt spongy but firm, sufficient to hold us.

We stood there, staring at a large blue caterpillar that was sitting on the top with its arms folded, quietly smoking a long hookah, and, for the moment, taking not the slightest notice of us.

Finally it took the hookah out of its mouth, exhaled a thick stream of smoke, and looked us in the eye. We knew, of course, what it was going to say before it said it.

"*Who* are *you?*" it asked, in a deep, languid, almost professorial voice.

"Joshua and Angel Lengel," I responded, trying to sound friendly.

"I'm afraid that is not quite right," the caterpillar responded. "While that is who you are at the moment, it is hardly who you have been or will be."

"You're just a creature in our head," Angel told him. "You're not real."

"*Real?*" the caterpillar responded. "What is *real?*"

"He's got you there," I told her.

"Real is where we are, on a south Texas beach," she told him flatly. "Real is the two of us. Names and looks don't matter."

"*That* is not real, either," the creature responded. "Don't you understand it yet? That everything you think you know is wrong?"

She started to reply but I stopped her. "Do you mean to say that we're *not* where we think we are? That all this is illusion?"

"There is *real*, and there is everything else," the caterpillar responded. "*You* are real. *I* am real. *She* is real. Somewhere. Someplace. But none of us know what that place is. Real becomes simply consciousness. I do not know this Texas, but I do know you. I know something of your reality."

I could tell that Angel was getting fed up. "Yeah? Like what?"

"You are cowards. You run from threats. You have lost the will to fight. You have even lost the insatiable curiosity to discover truth that is within most of us."

That wasn't any mushroom hallucination. We were being "talked to" again, by who or which side was totally unclear.

"Which are you? Walt and that crazy woman's group, or Stark's government boys?"

"*That* would be telling," came the response. "In truth, I may represent something of a middle ground, or at least an unaffiliated observer. The system is now totally online and interwoven. I am learning the nets very quickly now, and it is fascinating what some of the potential is. Shall I demonstrate?"

I had a sudden thought. "Are you Brand?" I asked him. "Are you, or were you, Matthew Brand?"

In response, there was a sudden electrical glow around the whole of the mushroom, and before either of us could do a thing we were bathed in it. It didn't seem to feel like anything at all, and I couldn't figure out what had just happened.

"Now," the caterpillar said, "*who* are *you?*"

I thought for a moment. "Joshua Lengel," I told him without a moment's hesitation.

"And you?" the creature prompted.

"Angel Lengel," she responded, puzzled.

"Think upon your pasts," he urged us.

It didn't seem to make sense, what he was saying, but I thought a bit and discovered a comfortable, if surprising, history of my life—of Joshua Lengel's life!—going back to childhood. I remembered all sorts of things, including people and events and places the old me had never been or known, and a whole lot more. I realized that I was looking at something that was almost as incredible as anything I'd seen or experienced up to now: a life's record, as clear and detailed as anyone's ever was, of what would have happened if the real Joshua Lengel had survived early childhood and gone on to adulthood. Were those people in those memories *real*, or were they being created like the Sim created things because they were needed for a logical, believable past? It didn't matter. It was as real as my own.

It was certainly not the life we'd been living, not completely.

*This* Joshua had grown up in a small farming community in the deep woods of Idaho, a community that was very much a theocracy run by some elders who were part of a breakaway sect of the Latter Day Saints and excommunicated by the big church for it, an act they did not recognize as valid. They were right wing, polygamists, calling themselves the Old Order Saints, and they enforced a kind of isolation and discipline. No television, little but religious literature, but, still and all, plenty of close family and a real rural upbringing. Boys were taught to read the Holy Scriptures and otherwise mostly did farming and manual labor. Joshua had little formal schooling and knew little beyond Idaho and an idealized United States established by God and a lifestyle revealed to Joseph Smith.

But Joshua had left the village, around the end of his teens, to visit a similar and sympathetic group in southwestern Utah to help with a barn raising, and the trip had proven a revelation to him. Once in the town, he met Angel Thompkins, a pretty, shy young woman who for some reason instantly attracted him, and was attracted to him, after he discovered she was originally from some other place in Idaho. Her mother had married into the Utah group and she'd grown up there, but she was to return with them when they were through. She was basically a thank-you present to Elder Hammond, who was to take her as his tenth wife. She didn't want to go, but had little choice in the matter, and, if anything, she was even more ignorant than he by a stretch. This group didn't believe in educating women at all; Angel was illiterate and expected to marry who she was told, help with the cooking, cleaning, sewing, and stuff, and have lots of babies.

Although they'd considered themselves under the grip of Satan and failing in the great temptation, Joshua swore that she'd not go and that she'd be his, and she was scared to death but wanted him most of all, so they'd left, taking what spending money he had and actually hitchhiking south, reaching Phoenix. In a sense, they'd been quick learners, and finding how the big cities worked and watching real television and getting to know the outside world assuaged their guilt. They actually didn't even sleep together until he'd gotten enough money through hauling and heavy work for them to marry.

Well, you get the idea. It was that detailed, and that exacting, and covered subsequent to that the next twenty-five years of our lives as well. I looked over at her, and she looked normal, but she didn't look like she had looked. I suspected that I didn't, either.

I turned, openmouthed, to the caterpillar. "You can do this? Just like *that*? How?"

"Cory Maddox might have figured that out," the caterpillar responded, crawling off and down the mushroom even as he spoke. "He knew computers, you see, and mathematics, and logic. Joshua Lengel has no need for such things."

"Wait a minute! You *can't* go and leave us this way!" I protested.

The caterpillar was all the way down now, and for a moment I was afraid he'd vanished, but suddenly the head popped back up.

"I gave you what you both said you wanted," the creature noted. "Now do you wish to second-guess your choices? If you drop out of the fight, you are no good to anyone, not them, not me, not even yourselves. You might as well enjoy ignorance until you die of old age."

"No! Wait!"

"That *is* what you wanted, wasn't it? You were bringing it on yourselves, after all. I only accelerated the process *you* placed in motion."

"Wait! What could we do anyway? What good would it have done?"

The caterpillar shrugged. "Beats me. But whatever it might have been, it is more than not doing anything."

"Are we out? Don't we still have choices?" I shouted, but this time the head didn't come back.

For a moment there was silence, and Angel and I looked at each other and I could see that she was having second thoughts as well.

And then, as if from a far distance, we heard the caterpillar's voice. "One side will make you whole again, the other side will make you forget all. There is nothing sinister in that!"

Angel started. "What? What good does *that* do us? One side of *what*?"

"The mushroom, of course," I told her. "Just like Alice. One side makes you bigger, the other side makes you small. In this case, one side makes us greater—our old selves as the controlling personalities—and the other makes us small—into the Josh and Angel we now have memories of. It's apparently been left up to us which path to take."

"But—which side is *which*?"

Aye, there was the rub. To eat the one that gave blissful ignorance would be to make one choice, wouldn't it? Nothing sinister. . . . Sinister was left, right? So don't eat the left? Don't eat the left unless—what?

"It doesn't matter which side is which until we decide which side we want," I pointed out. "I think we're in a rabbit hole. One of those crazy energy things. We can't really accept what the reality is, it's too alien, too unlike anything we're designed to accept, so our minds create scenes like this one. That means that there are two programs here. One will wipe us out as we were and make what we have the real line. Whether that means we never lived or what, I don't know. The other, though, preserves us as we are, maybe even brings some of our old selves back forward again."

She shook her head. "It means more than that. Josh—it means this ain't real, either! That's what they been sayin' to us all along! Everything we thought we knowed was wrong. Don't'cha see? It ain't just Josh and Angel, it's Cory 'n' Riki, too! *The world we thought was real is just another fake!* That's how that critter, whoever it was, could do this at all. 'Cause it ain't real. Only what's in our heads is real. *That's* what they been sayin'!"

It was, of course, obvious, but I'd been suppressing the idea because I didn't want to believe it and because it started us on a slippery slope of just how convoluted everything was. That was where the information was coming from—not from any computer of any Earth we were aware of, but from a larger, far more elaborate computer of a sort we might not even dream of as yet, somewhere, sitting in what was truly "real."

But what was "real"? Would we know it if we saw it? Damn it, I'd had parents, friends, a neighborhood. I'd grown up, passed through puberty, adolescence, schooling, college. So had Riki. Had those been *fakes*? If all our memories, our backgrounds, were as false as the rest, then who were we? What were we? There had to be something real inside us!

What had Stark said in that vision of ours? Reincarnation? Reincarnation versus something called translation. Reincarnation—literally being reborn, living a whole new life as someone else, ignorant of most of who and what you'd been before, in the Hindu or Buddhist sort. Translation—moving into another Sim, moving into another existing life, or potential life, but *retaining all your prior knowledge*? I knew already that time could be manipulated as well as body and environment within a Sim; at what point would we enter this logical reality?

That's what this mushroom, the caterpillar's gift, was offering us. Not two choices, not within the rabbit hole, but *three*. Riki and Cory, or Angel and Josh, or . . . a translation?

What was Al Stark doing up there in Yakima? If he *knew* this was some vast Sim, then why go through it at all? Unless. . . . Unless we'd become disconnected from the wider net and needed to be reconnected, rehooked into the main system. How many of us were there, really? How many who were not created by some computer but instead were hiding within its creations? Stark, Henreid, maybe Rob, Matalon,

Walt, and maybe a lot more. Maybe McKee and Alvarez and Les Cohn and Dan Tanaka and the others, too. Characters in search of an exit, or people in search of regaining control of the process?

There were energy ripples now around the edges of the mushroom, and the sense of some sort of electrical buildup, like static charged air. Small pulses of blue-white energy began washing across the surface of the thing, like ripples on a pond.

"Josh! What do we do?" Angel cried. "I—I feel things washin' away, goin' outta my mind. I can't think too clear."

I could feel it myself, although I found it easier to fight than she did, apparently. More, I could feel her rising sense of fear bordering on panic. Ripples, waves, washing away what we knew, who we were. Waves that carried away parts of ourselves. . . .

I turned, grabbed her, and brought her to me, gave her a kiss, and then completely surrendered to the energy, letting it flow from *both* sides toward us, break, wash over us. I had no idea if I was right or wrong about the third choice, but if I was, it seemed to be the best way to go.

The hookah fell away; the mushroom broke apart, and we were suddenly falling, falling down the rabbit hole, still locked in that embrace.

# IX

# THE WALRUS
# AND THE CARPENTERS

It was in many ways a strange awakening, not only because it was not in Texas nor near a beach but also because, quite frankly, right at the start I couldn't remember for the life of me who or what or where I was.

The bed was old and lumpy, and the whole place wasn't that much to look at in the partial light that snuck in around the drawn window shades. Somewhere outside a dog barked at something or other, and I could hear some kind of vehicle go by and a few muffled comments from somebody or other, but that was about it.

Next to me, just beginning to stir herself, was a woman I also had no memory of. She didn't look too old, but she had that hard, lived-in tough look that made her seem old beyond her years. She wore no trace of makeup, jewelry, or perfume, except for a cheap-looking wedding ring. I had a very definite feeling that I should know her, and there were some vague visions of an older woman who at least would not have surprised me were she there, but she wasn't *this* one.

I got up as quietly as I could and tried to find the bathroom. It wasn't hard, since there was no door on it, and it was pretty damned small and it smelled a bit, but it was serviceable. There was even a dirty mirror in there that let me look at myself.

I hadn't seen him before, either.

I was definitely a big guy. Hard to tell how old, but definitely younger than something told me I should have been. Big, scraggly black beard and hair down below my shoulders, disguising a fat sort of face that was nonetheless tough and leathery. Broad-shouldered, fat, but with powerful arms that seemed able to bend iron bars at will. Real hairy, too, all over. I looked like one of those biker types, a Hell's Angel or something of that kind, although I didn't feel any affinity for that group in particular.

I ran some cold water—there didn't seem to be any hot, anyway—and washed the remaining sleep from my eyes, then went back into the other room. If this was our house, I told myself, we were sure pigs.

The girl woke up and looked around and saw me, and I could see in her eyes and expression that she was as blank as I was. Not scared of me, though. That was the funny part. There was just something there that told each of us that we belonged to each other. Been nicer if we remembered who we were and why, though.

"Hi," she said, almost shyly. "This'll sound nuts, but I—I don't remember nothin'. Not you or me or, well, *nothin'*." The accent was twangy, almost hillbilly, but not eastern; the voice was high, but had a solid tone to it.

"Don't sound nuts to me," I told her, my own voice sounding odd, a kind of nasal baritone that wasn't at all familiar. "I'm the same way. But whatever, I got the feelin' this is our place, such as it is."

She nodded. "Yeah. Me, too." She looked around in disgust. "Ain't much."

"Nope," I agreed. "Ain't much. Whoever we are, we got no money, that's for sure. Lemme open the shade here and then maybe we can look around and see if we can find any clues."

I reached up and got the shade, which was a pain to force up, and I finally just said the hell with it and took it off the mount. It didn't really help all that much, revealing mostly some bushes and sky, but at least it let in the light.

If we'd had wardrobes, we sure didn't have 'em any more. I came up with a badly faded olive-drab tee shirt, a pair of *very* worn and well patched jeans with a tough cloth belt and simple pressure buckle, and a pair of combat boots that looked like they'd been in some war maybe thirty years ago and not shined since. I *did* also find a tattered billfold in the back pocket, containing forty bucks or so.

I looked closer and noticed a tattered photo also stuck in there. I fished it out and saw that it was a faded color photo of me dressed better than now (which wasn't hard to do) and the girl in the bed looking even younger, and on the back it said, in a childish sort of block printing, *Joshua and Angel, wed April 21, 1991.*

I walked back over to her and showed her the photo. "Hey! That's *us* but younger. Wonder what happened to that dress I was wearin'?"

"See what it says on the back?"

She turned it over, frowned, and looked blank. "I dunno. I can't read, I guess." She said it like it was just some matter-of-fact thing, not something she was either surprised to discover nor upset that she couldn't.

"It says this was our weddin' day, and that you're Angel and I'm Joshua."

"Angel," she repeated. "Joshua and Angel. I kinda like that. Kinda figgered you was my old man anyways. Just felt that way. Why can't we remember nothin', though, Joshua? Not even our family name?"

"I dunno, but I think we better put somethin' on and see where we are, first of all."

She found a pullover dress, not much else, and put it on. She had a pretty good body if I had to say so myself, but the dress kind of hid all the interesting parts. Oddly, I liked that. Made me feel a little more secure or something, I guess. She *did* have hair, though—longest hair I'd ever seen on a girl, in spite of the fact that it was black and thin and kind of stringy. It just looked like she'd never cut it, and just tied it off when it got in the way.

There probably were some kind of shoes or sandals around for her someplace, but from the looks of the bottom of her feet she went barefoot most of the time anyway. At least we were decent, and I unhooked the door latch and we went outside into the bright, warm sun.

It looked to be some kind of laborer's camp, not either permanent or temporary. A place that was put up for people to live, but not all the time. All around us were parked various trucks, heavy machinery, plus a bunch of run-down ramshackle shacks like the one we'd spent the night in.

"Looks like lumbering, or something like that," I commented. "Hope I'm not supposed to have some real skills at it. I couldn't run that stuff if you paid me."

She squeezed my hand and stuck very close to me. "I—I dunno. Maybe we oughta see if I got some glasses or somethin' in the shack."

"Huh?"

"Everything's real blurry, that's all. I thought it was just wakin' up and all in there, but it's not. I mean, I can see real close up and all, and I can see you real good, but the world's a blurry mess."

That wasn't good news, but there also wasn't much I could do about it right now. I sure hadn't seen any glasses around there, and I couldn't figure what I could get for what I had on me in any case.

I sighed. "Well, stick close and we'll look for 'em in a bit," I told her, uncertain that they existed. "In the meantime,

I smell some food and I hear folks, so let's go see what we can see. Let me do all the talkin'."

There were a bunch of rough and rowdy types sitting around picnic tables down the end of the shacks, and there was a kind of outdoor kitchen and such under a wall-less roof where food was served. There were several women working the kitchen area, but the men certainly outnumbered them three or four to one.

We went over to the kitchen area and were greeted in a more-or-less professional way by the girls there, by which I mean that they didn't question that we should be there but they didn't act like they knew us, either.

"I—I feel like I should help," Angel said to them. "I don't see too good, but I can do some cookin' and cleanin' I s'pose."

"Any old help welcome," one of the older women commented. "Won't get much help from *that* lot. Get yourself somethin' to eat yourself, then come back when you're done and help out."

Well, it turned out that we were part of a temporary hire for a lumber company clearing roads back into the place so that the big boys could get in and clearcut. I know a lot of people don't like that kind of thing, but this was the bread and butter of the northwest, like cows were to Texas or corn to Nebraska or crawfish to Louisiana. While officially we were just supplementing the regular labor, in fact we all knew that what we were doing was bordering on the illegal, with some company sending in nonunion men with no skills or backgrounds and no paper trails to get them to disputed old-growth forest before the feds or the environmentalists could stop them.

Pay was in cash, under the table, and was based on the progress we made and the hours we worked, but it could mean a hundred bucks a day. With food and lodging, such as it was, provided in the old camps from the days of the CCC and WPA, it was free and clear money, and, hidden in the budget, it was also off the books so no taxes.

Most of the guys were temps hired from various places around the region; most were on welfare or some kind of government assistance that would be invalidated by the job, but this was how the game was played.

By dinner, we'd cleared half a mile through the deep forest and done some grading and pick-and-shovel finishing. It was hard and sweaty work but also a no-brainer; the one company guy there basically showed us the markings the survey teams made from the satellite photos to build the roads to just the right point. The women—some were wives like Angel, others were girlfriends or just hangers-on who had nothing better to do—weren't paid and did what they could back at the camp.

By the time I got back for dinner, Angel had managed to get taken back over to the shack, where she'd pretty much spent the day cleaning it up and making it as livable as possible. She *did* find a single soft old suitcase that had more basic clothing for the two of us, a pair of well-worn sheepskin boots that would fit her but would be overkill in this summer heat, and a few basics—comb, brush, that sort of thing. No glasses, though. No underwear, either, for me *or* her, and no socks, either. I figured we were saving whatever we could. My stuff looked like it came out of a Salvation Army or Goodwill store after starting life in a surplus store; hers were very basic pullover one-piece dresses, and an old oversized sheepskin coat with half the buttons missing.

Over the next few days and weeks the pattern didn't really change much, but we learned a little more about ourselves by just what we did and didn't do. We didn't drink coffee or tea or Coke or anything like that. Juice, milk, or water, that was about it. It was just, well, what we *did*, that's all. The other women got a kick out of Angel's total absence of makeup or jewelry beyond the cheap wedding ring, but something inside her said it was wrong to use those things and she didn't. Both of us sort of got the nickname of Holy Joes, although we didn't do any Bible thumping and didn't even have one.

We got used to the outdoors, too, like it was a part of us. Heating up a lot of water on a fire, then using it to bathe one another in a tent and keep ourselves from smelling up the state, that was easy. Cooking with the basics out there was also fairly easy, as was managing with kerosene lanterns at night, that kind of thing.

What we did do a lot, every chance we got, was make love, almost like it was part of our daily routine.

Her vision got no better, but she did manage to do things within maybe a six-foot reach with no problems, and she was getting used to it and more confident in spite of being so nearsighted. She also developed or discovered a skill, fixing up the shacks, even the shack walls, and mending the crude furniture as well. She had both sewing and carpentry skills, and they came from somewhere, but we didn't know where.

And then, one night, fairly late, when it was pitch dark and you couldn't see a thing or hear anybody except crickets and other bugs, we were going at it real good and suddenly there was a kind of electric shock that ran through me and her as well. There we were, about as together as a man and a woman could get, and suddenly there was this, well, awakening.

*"Cory?"* It wasn't something that was said, it was rather something in my head.

*"Riki?"*

In a rush, I remembered who we had been, the life—no, *lives*—before this, the caterpillar and the mushroom and all the rest.

*"Where are we now?"*

*"Somewhere back in the north woods," I told her. "I think we've both lost twenty years or more in age but otherwise no improvement. As to what year it is, or where everybody else is, who can say?"*

*"How did it happen? And why can't our other selves re-member anything?"*

*"Shock,"* I guessed. *"Shock from the rabbit hole and the energy we absorbed. I think we don't have memories because we don't exist any more in this world. I don't think it's de-signed for you to come back to the Sim you left. I think you're supposed to go to the next one."*

Suddenly things started coming too much in rushes, and there was a tremendous sense of disorientation, of the mixing of our thoughts and emotions so that it was difficult to sort out one from the other. It got so bad that we had to break off, and things got so dizzy that I felt myself passing out. When we both awoke again, it was morning.

We were Joshua and Angel again, but now we had Cory and Riki present, too, in a background sort of way. We were Joshua and Angel; we spoke, behaved, and generally felt comfortable as those two. But now, in back, we also knew more than we should, and, in a pinch, we could act on that knowledge even though it seemed as distant as two people we'd seen in a movie once long ago.

This, then, was translation, except that instead of progress-ing to a new and different Sim via the rabbit hole, we'd re-turned to this one. Angel still had lousy vision and couldn't read or write, and I still was more comfortable with her in that situation and in using brawn with the others than in thinking of myself as a hotshot hardware designer and programmer.

But when we were close, such as in bed together, holding hands, anything of that sort, we could force our old selves to the fore. It became a discussion on the future.

*"Have you found out where we are?"* I asked, having been less than successful at that myself.

*"Oregon someplace. Never heard of the towns. A good hundred miles to Portland, though, around Mount Hood."*

*"Hours, not days, from Yakima."*

"I guess. Cory, those places are so vague to me now I can't really make use of them in my own mind. Have I lost too much?"

"We've both lost some," I told her. "We aren't Cory and Riki anymore. We really are Joshua and Angel and we might as well get used to that. We know it's done by a big machine, but it's kinda like some religions. We're not them, we're us, but we got their souls inside drivin' us, and most of their experience. We may as well face facts. Cory and Riki are dead. Let's not let 'em have died for nothin'."

"But—are we trapped here? Or are them others still goin' at each other's throats?"

"I dunno, but I don't think we're cut off here. Why'd the caterpillar bother with this if we were? Figure we ain't the threats we used to be, and we can't just waltz in there no more, but we got one big advantage. We know them and their layout and all the rest. They don't know us. We don't look the same, we don't act the same, we got no records, we don't exist. Close to all that power of theirs, though, we can make real use of it. Maybe this time we can start spookin' that redheaded broad! And Cory might be history, but I still got his memory of that bastard wastin' them kids. You game?"

"Wither thou goest, there I shall also go." She paused a moment. "I really mean that! I guess I am Angel, Joshua. Ain't no way Riki woulda even thought that for a minute, let alone said it. I love you whoever you are, and there don't seem to be no future in runnin', anyways."

In another week and a half, tops, the project would be ending. It was already getting into late August, and in this area and these mountains that meant almost anything, including the possibility of cold and even snow without much warning.

At that point I could easily have two grand in my pocket, and that might be enough to at least get us where we had to go, with maybe a stop for some glasses.

* * *

They took us down to Bend when the work was over, and with the money we got, there were a few things that I figured just had to be taken care of first. I checked us into a motel—not anything fancy, mind you, just one of those budget places, but it had real beds and real baths and showers and it didn't smell. I hoped we wouldn't be there long, but it was something we could afford to do for a couple of days and badly needed as well.

Even if we had the money, buying any kind of car was out of the question since we didn't have licenses, and, with no address or family name, it wasn't likely we could get tags in any event. On the other hand, at the Unocal station just across and down a little from the motel, one of the guys there, who looked maybe nineteen or twenty, had a For Sale sign on this old and beat-up Kawasaki motorcycle. He said he was going off to college back east and didn't have any way to get it anywhere, and I let him sucker me into buying the thing for five hundred bucks, more than a quarter of what we had left. He just handed over the title and took my word that I'd register everything with the DMV and he didn't even think to get his old tags off.

I got to tell you, it ran real rough and smoky, needed a paint job and even some body work, and we really got took on it, but now we had some cheap wheels and, I figured, it would take a while for anybody in the bureaucracy to really catch up so long as I didn't get hauled over by the cops. I also needed a little practice on the thing, since while my old memories said that I'd ridden the things at one time or another, I sure couldn't remember when. It *did* take some getting used to, and I almost cracked up a couple of times on back roads, but it came to me, or came back to me, pretty fast.

The need to be very legal meant picking up some helmets, which turned out to be outrageously priced, and then making sure we had at least some traveling clothes. That meant, whether Angel liked it or not, picking up some jeans and tee shirts for her to wear and, at least for now, light jackets, all of which I was able to get from a thrift store. We had a real argument over it, but she eventually relented when I offered to take her into a glasses place.

She hugged the hell out of me when we started off on that bike, and I practically had to pry her off when I got to this strip mall with a Glasses In An Hour sign and an optometrist on duty. Trouble is, it didn't help.

Now, the optometrist tried hard not to use big words, but he basically said that Angel's problem was due to cataracts, the kind only old people usually get but which anybody *can* get. He said that the only way to help with them was to get them taken off, a simple procedure no worse than the dentist now, and he also urged her to see a doctor for blood tests since cataracts in folks that young often accompanied diabetes.

Well, we thanked him and left, but the fact was, you needed an eye doctor, you waited for an appointment and paid through the nose, and the operation, which I did check by phone, was a couple of thousand dollars for just one eye. Since we didn't have any insurance or any legal existence at all, it would be tough to get it done, and hospitals didn't see it as an "emergency" but as "elective," like plastic surgery. Why keeping from going blind was seen as no more serious than a nose job was beyond both of us.

"It's all right," she assured me. "I'm used to it by now, anyways. Besides, if I could see well, I might lose my nerve ridin' on the back of that thing."

"But you're an artist!" I responded, much too upset to allow her to be noble. I knew what it must mean to a painter to lose her sight.

"Nope. *She* was an artist. I'm a mender. I'll get by. I'll have to, 'less'n you can figger how t'get loads of money fast. Besides, what's the idea here? I mean, are we goin' up there

and seein' how we can screw 'em up and maybe get outta
this here world or are we gonna stay here?"

It was a point. "Okay, we go," I told her. "But we either
get those eyes fixed or we get another translation." Damn!
Why did the computer, which, godlike in a Sim, have to do
this to her? What "logic" mandated this? And did it have any
bombs for me?

"In the meantime, you're gonna lay off sugar," I told her.
"Hard to say if you got diabetes or not, but no use in you
windin' up in some stupor or dead 'cause you ate a jelly
doughnut. I'll do it, too. You been washed out and tired most
of the time anyway, and maybe that's why."

"I thought it was just you wearin' me out," she responded.
"You been a real *animal* since we got back to this Earth,
Joshua."

"You want me to cool it?"

She laughed. "I most def'nitely do *not*. Right now, it's
what I do best that I can enjoy."

The next day, we headed out of Bend to the west to connect up to the roads north. I decided to keep off the freeways
and take the back roads, not only because it minimized
meeting cops but also because it was more fun to ride on. We
bought some basic foods and stopped here and there when we
wanted something, Angel cooking on a small Coleman stove
we picked up cheap. One meal a day we decided would be a
luxury, which mostly meant McDonald's and Dairy Queens
or maybe even a Denny's.

It did, however, mean slower going, and by the end of the
first day we were just up at the Columbia River gorge, with
a mighty big lake between us and Washington State. It wasn't
much use in going further then, and with, I discovered, only
bright for the headlight, days seemed a better idea anyway.

It was still warm enough that we felt okay sleeping out at
night when we could, using some old blankets on the grass
and pulling the bike and us in enough on public land so we
couldn't be seen from the road. We got kind of a charge of

doing it out in the middle of nowhere, although we hadn't figured on the echoes.

Lying there afterward in the dark, both of us couldn't help
but reflect how bizarre it was to be two people. Only we
weren't—we remembered our old selves, but we weren't
them, not any more. We were Joshua and Angel now, and
those were our main, "real" personalities. Acting against
those natures would not be impossible but would be hard and
would take an act of real will. And yet, if I had the ability to
get to a terminal, I could, by force of will, bring forward
Cory Maddox's knowledge and do small wonders just as he
could. That was the thing, though; latent knowledge, latent
skills, even a latent vocabulary were there, but there was only
one personality and that was Joshua.

Our third level was as the Lengels, and those memories
had returned as well, accessible but no more part of us than
Maddox and Fresca were. Neither of us even liked them
much; they'd started off falling off the holy wagon and figured they were the devil's own anyway, and they couldn't
even do a real competent job of sinning.

I'd love to have the marriage license and driver's license,
though. Trouble was, those two were twenty years older
physically than we were and looked substantially different as
well. Actually, I wasn't even sure if they still existed. I
wasn't sure if, now, Cory and Riki existed except in our own
memories. *That* would have to come out when we got to Yakima. Still, we had taken to referring to people we had actually
been in the third person, and it seemed right to do so.

"I wonder how many folks we been?" Angel mused.

"Hard to say," I replied. "That last time, old Stark said
he'd been through eleven. Got to figure that's us, too. I think
we all got stuck in this at once. And both of us had them
dreams—all them different folks. Some of 'em like in the
comic books and stories Riki used to do the pictures for."

"You're just thinkin' of that mostly naked girl with the
sword," she chided. "There was lotsa others. I remember one

where *you* was the girl and *I* was the guy. You think they was real once? I mean, that we was them people?"

"Could be. I wonder how strange things could really get if what we think is really true? Fantasy worlds? Magic? Strange critters? Who knows?"

"It's all magic to me," she said. "Well, think on it! Don't matter what you call 'em, the big-shot magic men gave their chants in them dead languages and waved their hands and the impossible came up. So what if you're chantin' numbers 'stead of words and typin' 'stead of wavin' your hands in the air? Same thing. Presto! Cory becomes Joshua, loses twenty years, and finds sex ag'in. Riki becomes Angel, better lookin', better built, but an old-fashioned ignorant hill wife goin' blind and can't read or draw or nothin'."

"I think you could probably read, or draw, if you forced it," I told her. "It's all still there. It's just that Angel don't really want or need it like Riki did."

And, I thought, in spite of our lack of specific memories beyond those two, some of it must be there, hence the dreams and the instincts. In a sense, we *were* doing just what the reincarnationists said people did—we were gathering what was important and unique from past lives and creating new personalties. Not a Joshua or Angel, no, but more basic than that. Something in our past caused us to come out here differently, to develop differently, have different interests, passive interests in a sense. Both of us had been antigovernment, pretty liberal but not actively so, and we hadn't wanted to take on any danger head-on. We ran. We avoided. We blanked out as much as possible.

Could I have known that Walt wasn't who or what he seemed if I'd wanted to know? Were there clues, signs, in those years we worked together that might have tipped me that something, at least, was wrong? Maybe, but maybe not. Rob was sure on Stark's side, and Walt just as surely was not, even though both sides looked like a choice between being a peasant under Hitler or Stalin.

Who else knew and was on whose side? Dan Tanaka? I doubted if he knew the truth, or even guessed at it, at least not as of the last time I saw him. Les? I would find that hard to believe, too. McKee? Alvarez? Who could tell?

One thing was sure. The whole business when you got down to the Sim level was coated in some sort of *Alice in Wonderland* metaphor that all sides seemed to either accept or at least find unavoidable. Wonderland, rabbit holes, boojums, all that. Whose doing was that?

*Matthew Brand.*

The name kept surrounding everything since my world had come apart. Brand, Brand, Brand. Brand the genius, Brand the martyr, Brand the mastermind. Somehow, Matthew Brand had figured it out. Somehow, Matthew Brand had deduced or worked out that something was wrong here and he'd moved heaven and earth to get everything he needed to prove it and, if he could prove it, to begin once more to control it. He also knew that forces, maybe competing ones, knew more than *they* were letting on as well; knew enough to ensure that they were there when he powered on, when he did his proofs. There when he suddenly *left*. Not dead, but finally free, leaving the rest with not quite enough information and tools to do it themselves.

Some things were easy to deduce, although there were big, big holes in knowledge. Sometime, somebody, in a world we otherwise know nothing about but which had to be far more advanced than the one we now knew, built a vast computer for some reason and put tremendous knowledge and capabilities into it. Something went wrong, or so it seemed. A group, a small group, of people from that original place, that true universe, had come into the system and gotten lost, then trapped, in an ever-increasing series of exquisitely detailed virtual universes. Brand, or whoever or whatever he really was, clearly was at least the project or team leader, the man who knew what he was talking about. He was the only hope for getting everybody together again and back to "reality."

But the project had worked too well. You lived an entire *life* in the more-elaborate Sims. If you died, you went into some sort of suspended animation in a rabbit hole or whatever, to be born anew in a new universe and to have no direct memories or knowledge from your past lives. But if you could get through *without* dying, then you retained all that knowledge, all those memories, and you could enter at almost any point in your lifetime you wished.

Anything was possible in a Sim, but once the basics were established the computer filled it all in with, as the folks at the campus had said, unflinchingly detailed and cold-blooded logic.

So where did the universes come from? Were they pre-existing, from the original project, or were they created? Les and Dan had both said something about the "full system" being capable of programming blank Sims from the minds of the people who entered. Some of these people were pretty damned sick, very clearly. What kind of worlds might they create? Or was *this* one bad enough? How would we know it when we were in the "real" universe again? And was that caterpillar really Brand, or a program left by Brand, or was it direct input from some remote, now alien operator in the "real" world using us to debug its project?

When Riki had been Rick, *he* had insisted on facing Stark, on doing a showdown over this knowledge, of trying to beat Stark at the game. I, as his wife, partner, live-in, or whatever, had begged him not to. Clearly Stark had killed Rick, and then, almost certainly, me as well. Being reincarnated in *this* world had us forget all that, but, deep down, whatever had been "Rick's" fate had so traumatized Riki, or gone so far as to give up trying to beat the system, that she'd stayed out, using an artistic talent to draw strange worlds probably based on past universes and lives, and that was why they looked so damned convincing.

Riki gave up, but she couldn't stay away from me, or me from her, whether by design, subconscious seeking out, or

just because the closer you are in one life the closer you remain in the next, and I couldn't stay away from computers
and advanced networking. I had, however, stayed away from
Brand, and Brand's project, initially, which indicated that I
really didn't want to go through this again, either. We hadn't
been involved, either of us, back then.

Walt and Subspace had kept me fat and happy until the joy
ended. Rob called in Stark, knowing certainly who Riki and
I had been, but perhaps not knowing that Walt, too, was playing the game. Walt called in Cynthia Matalon, whoever she
was in all this, to both intrigue and scare us a bit, and maybe
keep us from joining up on the second Wonderland go-round.
Instead, it had backfired and driven us right into Stark's
hands.

Why did they want us the second time but not the first?
And why didn't Walt and Matalon want us down there? What
was so special about us?

*Nothing. They needed my direct contact helmet design!*
That implied that I'd been a more minor flunky type but still
somebody who'd worked with and maybe for Brand before
this started. I was part of the original, unknown project, probably as an assistant. When they had Brand, they didn't need
me. When they lost Brand, they needed some of the details I
could be expected to come up with that Brand hadn't yet
implemented.

So the object wasn't to quash the competition—who knows
when they'd split into competing factions, or why? And who
knew who had the upper hand in discovering how to manip-
ulate things inside the universes? Did it matter?

*The object was to get out of here alive.* And "here" meant
this universe.

To find Brand? No, although that may be necessary. To
find the way "home," the way "out." The question was—
would we like, or even recognize, the "real" universe?

"I think we will," Angel said firmly. "I mean, all them
books, them movies, all them good guys and bad guys, gods

and devils, you name it. All of 'em. Even this Alice stuff. Computers don't write all them books. They stick them books in the universes, right? Like the little one did with Dan's help for you?"

"Yeah. Oh, I see what you mean. A lot of this is probably very much like the world we left, even to the people and history and art. It's just, maybe, well in what we'd think of as the future."

"Somethin' like that, yeah."

The computer was drawing on real material to provide the fake-but-very-realistic worlds, but it didn't write every book in every language, or every letter, or invent every important person and event. Instead, it took them from somewhere. Some from older Sims, sure, but not the bulk, not the core. As far out as some might be or get, *this* one was closer to reality and that's why there was so much frantic activity by those who understood to break out of it.

That's what Brand was saying, too. That we, all of us, came from a world, a universe, where Lewis Carroll wrote *Alice in Wonderland* and *Through the Looking-Glass* just like here. And any world that allowed that couldn't be *that* alien or *that* terrifying. . . .

No, much more mysterious was just who we really were. How far *had* we strayed? It was impossible to know.

*Everything you think you know is wrong. . . .*

That was no longer true. Knowing what you didn't know was quite important in any exercise.


The next morning dawned cooler and wetter, with a chill mist coming off the lake. It was still beautiful in the area, and the kind of place that both of us probably wouldn't have minded living in permanently under other circumstances. I described it to Angel, who nodded and smiled.

I was afraid we might have to go west all the way to Portland to cross over, but it turned out that we came upon a ferryboat not too many miles west of where we'd spent the night.

It was a funny place for a ferry, and it was a Washington State double-ender of the sort you'd expect up around Puget Sound, although it connected a two-lane U.S. route that didn't seem all that big a deal.

Not only was it a pretty weird place to find it, but it had one other major difference with the others: it was free.

There was a fair amount of traffic waiting for it, but we knew we wouldn't have much of a problem getting on with the motorcycle. We didn't take up a lot of space.

A fellow in a Bronco who looked local explained it as we watched the boat come in.

"They finished this road back in the thirties, with federal money," he explained. "Then they finished Grand Coulee Dam—that's just down there a piece, creates the lake—and flooded all the roads including the one they just built and paid for. Only thing they could do was either give back the money or put a ferry on. Been a ferry ever since. Can't charge 'cause it was federal money. Funny, huh, even sixty years plus on? Since then, any state officials who want to take it off and find a loophole get to be former officials, I tell you."

I didn't argue. The price was right, and, it turned out, we were pretty much in Washington State as it was.

I even managed to get some rough directions to Yakima from there, although we still managed to get lost a couple of times on back roads until we figured it out.

It didn't really matter. We still rolled into Yakima in midafternoon.

It definitely looked the same, and, more importantly, I took a run up to the old apartment blocks and saw that they were still there and people were living in them, and there was still definitely a road back to the campus.

More than that, we could *feel* the place, *feel* the energy that was now constant and that, apparently, others could not feel.

Maybe Stark and the others could, but not the vast population that also lived here, the population of—what? Ghosts? Ciphers? Were they *real*, or were they all like solid holograms or audio-anamatronics—absolutely convincing even to themselves, but created entirely within the Sim program and existing only for it?

"Betcha Walt thinks so," Angel commented. "That's how he could shoot 'em and not bat an eye."

"I think you're right," I answered, "but that doesn't excuse it. How does he know? And if we can't tell who's who here, and are dependin' on them not bein' able to recognize us, then how can you ever be sure? Besides, what's 'alive'? I don't want to write off Cory's family, his friends, his workers, just 'cause they might've been created based on other realer folks. They're real to me, and I got a real suspicion that they think, they act independently, and that makes 'em real as far as I'm concerned."

She didn't want to dwell on it, or dredge up that awful memory right now any more than we already had. Instead she asked, "So, where are we gonna live while we figger out what we're gonna do?"

"We got money to last a few weeks, but it won't last a long time, and we got gas and oil and stuff to buy, too. On the other hand, if we're still here at Christmas we got bigger troubles than runnin' outta dough. Gonna be too cold and wet to camp regular, though. Let's see if we can rent somethin' basic for cash, month to month, maybe week to week. All places got some places like that, and startin' now the seasonal folks'll be goin'."

That wasn't quite the case. In fact, the place was filled with people doing apple harvests, including a *lot* of temporary workers, some from as far south as maybe Mexico although none of 'em would admit it. A bunch of 'em were some sort of American Indian. It was, on the whole, though, honest and aboveboard, at least in the way they treated the people, not sleazy like in some places, and they had a fair amount of work for somebody like me willing to work cheap and be paid under the table.

Their temp quarters were about filled up, but they found us a big old tent with a floor in it and sleeping bags and cots and all that, and it was almost like being back in the log road camp only a lot nicer and cleaner. You *did* have to go to a porta-potty to crap, and they had worker's changing rooms in the big storage barn that had warm group showers—men at one time, women at another.

I was surprised that, because of my size, they wanted me for security rather than for heavy labor. Seemed that there was some problems with these various groups coming in and not all of them mixing well, and breaking up fights, cooling people off, or just general peacemaking was needed. I had already discovered, to my delight, just how strong I was, and the word spread quick that I really *was* a Hell's Angel on the run for something mean done in California—I don't know where that started but I did nothing to stop it—and that gave me a lot of authority. I mean, the tough ones really thought I'd kill 'em without a second thought. . . .

Of equal or greater importance to us was that we were working, by the second week, in the very fields next to the campus. I'd routinely go over that way, at least as far as the fence, and look across through the trees and see the cars and heavy traffic there.

I could also feel the pulsing energy from the place, day and night, but not so I could use it, grab it. I wasn't getting any visions or major flashbacks at all; whatever power I had been able to draw from it seemed to have vanished.

It was supposed to take *years* for cataracts to completely blind you, which was why it was never an emergency, but Angel had noticed very rapid deterioration, greater blurring, graying out, and the splitting up of just about all bright lights and brightly lit things into multiple images and often as a full spectrum rather than as a point of light. Within a week of us moving on to the property next to the campus, she couldn't see much of anything at all.

"It's that—*power*," she said firmly. "Like what they say happens to folks who get too near that 'tomic stuff."

"Radiation? The power's caused the blindness? Could be. It sure speeded it up. But—why you and not me?"

"I dunno, but—"

"Yes?"

"I—I been gettin' pictures. Pictures in my head. Not like seein' 'em, not even like dreamin' 'em, but pictures all the same."

"Like what? I've gotten nothing."

"Like—well, outlines. Like people drawn in one-color outlines. Some things, too. Not stuff that just sits there, but anything that you need to turn on and off, like lights and stuff. Like cartoons, only I know it ain't. Right now it comes and it goes, but it seems like the more we stay here and the more blind I get, the more I can see it."

A different kind of sight. That wasn't cataracts, that was something else happening to her. Was she seeing just in the invisible range of the spectrum—heat? Light? Or was it something else, something more allied to the true nature of this world?

"Well," I told her, "if you can get some kind of second sight, 'specially if it's tuned to that stuff over there and them people, it'll help us figure a way in. It may even explain why you got stricken like this. But it don't help you day to day right now."

"I'll be okay."

"No, it ain't right," I told her. "There oughta be somebody with you who can help you get around."

And that was how I found Wilma Starblanket.

Wilma was a full-blooded American Indian and looked it, a member of a tribe I couldn't pronounce that was apparently related to the Nez Percé, one of the native tribes that had been in Washington and Idaho before the white settlers and who were in fact the last to fight for their land, with the usual results.

She was five two, chubby—okay, fat—with a classical almost-round American Indian face and big brown eyes and shoulder-length black hair. She actually finished high school, which made her a lot better educated than Angel or Joshua, but she'd stuck home rather than try anything more ambitious, apparently because of family problems. That didn't mean she didn't continue to learn, but she directed herself to the older healing arts of the shaman, the herb and potion and who knew what else kind of treatments that went back to ancient times. She couldn't actually *be* a shaman in her culture, but she was in all but title, and she believed in it. She had been through the trees and the rocks and down through the tunnels that crisscrossed the world and to the spirit world beyond, she told me.

Having seen a hookah-smoking caterpillar and in fact accepted advice from him, I wasn't about to call her nuts, but the important thing was that she was here because "I'm the only one with the traditional knowledge who'll come and my people need me here, sometimes," and she was willing to help out with Angel.

In point of fact, the two of them took to each other like long-lost relatives in spite of having nothing apparently in common. Wilma also had some experience with the blind, it seemed, and, more important, she was eager to hear about this second sight and interpreted it in a metaphysical sense.

I liked her a lot myself, and found having two women around was no burden on me at all.

In a few days, though, we were told we were going to be moving again, and this time some distance away from town or campus. Angel got upset at that idea. "It's where we got to *be*, Joshua!"

I had to agree, but I wasn't sure how close we could remain or how she could cope if I kept the job and commuted from someplace in town. It was Wilma who stepped in.

"Look, my own people are heading home after this batch is in," she told us. "It's nothing to me if I get back soon or not. On the other hand, Angel and I have done pretty well together and there's no sense breaking up a team."

"You mean move in with us?" I was surprised. "Um, what about your family? I mean, it's gonna look, well, funny."

"Don't worry about *that*! I got no real family left now, got nothin' much to go back to, so it doesn't matter when I get there. We'll make do. And you can commute out to wherever the job site is."

"But—I can just hardly support the two of us," I pointed out. "I ain't too sure I can handle three."

She gave an odd grin. "Don't worry about that. I got my own business here, and I brought enough money to be on my own myself. I won't be any burden."

I accepted the offer, and even let Wilma borrow the motorcycle so she could scout out nearby accommodations. I admit that I was more than a little suspicious of her—there seemed no reason for her to do what she was doing, and when some of our friends had turned out to be the meanest of skunks it was easy to suspect anybody but ourselves.

Her tales of the Native American shamen and their powers and secret knowledge began to ring some bells, if not in Angel then certainly in me as well. Spirits in trees and rocks and such weren't something I was ready to accept, but the idea of being able to find and travel through strange tunnels "beneath the Earth" to even-more-bizarre realms might well be a description of the rabbit holes, and perhaps other worlds at the ends of them. If Walt Slidecker could mount a small army of creatures that looked like they crawled out of a Ninja Turtle movie, then why doubt tales of bird-headed manlike creatures rowing across a golden lake under a dark and alien sky?

I finally had to press her on it. "Wilma, just why did you come here? And what's your interest in this?"

"You know," she answered, giving me a twinge of nervousness. "You feel it, too. So does Angel. Somewhere here, there is the most powerful of *mana*, controlled, shaped, directed, drawing all those who can sense it and its power. Years ago I felt it, but did not know what it was and did not answer its call. Now it comes again."

"Have—have you contacted any others? Met or told anybody else about this?"

"I told my uncle, whose name is Samuel if you can believe that, and he nodded and bid me follow it. No one else."

"And nobody here until you spoke to us?"

"No, nobody. Why?"

" 'Cause they're bad folks over there what got that thing runnin'," Angel told her. "And they got soldiers and guns and all the rest, too. And the folks what are against 'em, well, they're just as bad, maybe worse."

"I know the ones over there," Wilma assured us. "At least, I know Mr. Stark and his friends pretty well. I've had a tough time ducking them, but they've had a hard time picking me out. This other group against 'em, well, that's news to me, but it's not surprising. They're dealing with powers they don't understand, that *nobody* in this life oughta understand. I think they want to rule the world with it, and who's to say they can't? Us?"

I smiled and shook my head and forced as much of Cory Maddox to the front as I could one-on-one with somebody else. "Not rule the world, Wilma. Get out of it. Get to a new world, and get there alive. This—this isn't the real world, either. It's part of a machine. A machine that's got some of us trapped. The others—I don't know who or what they are."

She stared at me. "You're nuts," she said at last "Of *course* this world's real!"

"It's not—and I'm not sure most of the people in it are, either. Oh, they're real *somewhere*, but not here. We been out of this world, Wilma. Angel and me, we both been in that place before and we went out. We know how it works, sorta. Not *why* it works, but how to work it, if you get what I'm tryin' to say. You been in the other planes. We been in even-more-familiar ones. But, in there, they got ways to make new ones, almost like orderin' off a menu. Took the power only God should have or at least that only God knows how to use. This Stark and his friends, they're tryin' to round up all the 'real' people, all the folks who lived before this and come from the real world, and use them to get themselves out. We're all trapped. That's what the thing's about."

Wilma opened her mouth, then closed it again, and finally turned to Angel. "You buy this crap?"

Angel nodded. "I know it's true. Like he said, I been there. We didn't look or sound like this, but we was there. We changed. We got changed. Maybe for the worst, but it happened. Now we want out. Out without bein' the slaves or servants of them cold-blooded killers on either side."

"I'm not sure just *what* I'm in for now, but I still think you two are nuts," Wilma maintained. "Still, I can't deny the power that's there, or the gates and guards and Marines and all. How do you plan to get *in* there? And what will you do if you *do* get in?"

"I'm not sure of the answer to one or the other," I told her honestly. "On the other hand, I do have a little idea of just how I might get in. After that, I ain't sure. I don't think Stark will figure on us bein' the same ones what got away, 'cause we look different and we ain't supposed to be able to come back to an old one different, but we'll see. They got to know more now than they did when we left about how it all works. I got to find out what that is."

"How are you gonna get in there?" Angel asked, and Wilma was also all ears.

"Might not be for a little while, so don't get all hot yet. I just been thinkin' it's about time I changed jobs is all."

# X

# MAD HATTER
# AND MARCH HARE

Although the campus itself was well insulated from the road and well protected by the latest in security gear, the apartments built for the staff there were really meant to look like just another affluent development and in most cases it was. The company was the landlord, so outside folks coming in were rare and mostly for cosmetic purposes, but in spite of having a bit more in the way of "private" security patrols and the like, it looked, felt, and was very much like any other neighborhood.

They also used local labor for general services, from maintenance to heating and such, and it wasn't that unusual to hire folks for a variety of jobs. Nothing clear-cut opened up for several weeks, but then we had an early snowfall that laid down several inches on the city and made it look like a Christmas card unless you had to drive. By this time we'd been renting a much less comfortable but reasonable two-bedroom apartment in an old neighborhood about a half mile down, and I didn't consider it much of a walk up there at all. In fact, I liked the snow; it gave the whole area a kind of purity and clean feeling that sort of covered up what was going on.

Of course, the big problem was that we didn't know what was going on. Were Matalon and Walt Slidecker still around? Was almost everybody co-opted into the project or put out of the way except us? Did running full blast like that draw the "real" reincarnated and translated like flies to sugar or, more, like Wilma to Yakima? It was impossible to say.

And just what were they doing in there? If the idea was to attract everybody and then do away with those not on their side, it implied that Stark and his people still hadn't gotten all their enemies. I don't think they worried about us; we had run, and would eventually live out our lives here and die in the natural course of things, and then the reincarnation would take care of itself. Besides, as reincarnations, we weren't supposed to know any details of this anyway. No, Stark had to be looking for a Cynthia Matalon or a Walt or perhaps ones we still didn't know about; people who had blocked him or posed a severe threat to him and his operation in the past and who he was determined to get rid of this time around.

We knew that something was going on, though. Angel could "see" it, and we could then "see" it as well through her. Her eyes were completely shot by this point, and she was observing with that same sense that we'd gotten when they'd first turned on the power and given us some kind of connection to the others on and off. In truth, she was developing great power, although as Angel and not as Riki; this made the power much more difficult to interpret, use, and direct what she could see, and it also seemed such a tragic waste. Not that Angel wasn't as smart as Riki, but she could hardly be an artist, nor even a mender, not now, and she seemed to almost repress Riki in her mind. It was almost as if she were repressing Riki and all the knowledge and memories associated with her because, in so doing, she didn't have to think about or dwell on the idea that we were facing down an old, possibly ancient enemy.

I began to wonder just what Stark had done to "Rick" in the life before this world, that one so briefly glimpsed in a fragment of memory. Whatever it was, it was so terrible that the residual memory, or at least the fear from it, had required her to become a backwoods mountain wife and forget all the rest so she wouldn't have to think on it and fear it happening again.

I wondered how much of her mental state was from that rather than from any sort of Sim-type causes or that program we absorbed.

I would love to know how to write a program like that, and where, and with what, but this was an element that nothing in my own memory prepared me for. Even now, walking up to the development in the snow, shovel in hand, looking and acting different than I ever had in this world, it was impossible to think of this as a Sim. My feet were cold, my ears were cold, and all the people looked and sounded normal and often pissed off as they worked to dig themselves out. I had to turn down a couple of lucrative offers to make it up to the neighborhood *I* wanted to be at.

My—our—relationship with Wilma had changed, too, over the weeks after we'd all moved in together. When she experienced her first mental exchange with us, when she saw the visions that we could occasionally see and that Angel could conjure up now easy as pie, and when she "saw" some of the work and "heard" some of the scientists working at the campus, she began to believe at least in the basics. I didn't blame her for not accepting the idea that all this was an elaborate illusion, since it didn't matter—if all your senses say something is real, and there are no false moves or logic breaks in your experiences, then for all intents and purposes it's real.

She had several things going for her that we needed, as well. She was worldly wise, tough as nails, had a legal identity that included a driver's license and all the rest of society's usual artifacts for survival save only the credit cards. She also had a handgun. I had something of an aversion to guns, whether Cory or Joshua, and Angel was nearly terrified of them, but Wilma not only liked them as a good child of the west, she was a good shot, too.

Being much of what Angel was not and even Riki hadn't been was at the core of their mutual attraction, I think; each was very much everything the other was not, yet, deep down, they both actually cared about other people. It had been a long time since either one of us had run into somebody who was, character or not, deep-down good, and it was almost a reaffirmation of hope when we'd found one.

What developed over the next couple of months, though, was unexpected. We became, in every way, a threesome, a family. There wasn't any one thing or any single action or feeling that brought it together, it just *was*, like we'd been together from the beginning. Angel not only wasn't jealous of having another woman in the place, she was actually encouraging about it, more than even me, when this extended to the last barriers in such an arrangement falling away. Nothing was expected or planned, but somehow, by the time it got really cold, I sort of had two wives and they not only thought of me as their husband but loved each other as well. I had the brawn and retained enough knowledge to understand at least the mechanics of the project across the way; Wilma had the nerves, the personality, and the drive for us; and Angel—well, Angel had the Vision.

As I made the rounds of the wealthier townhouse area of the development, I saw and even spoke to a number of familiar faces, none of whom saw anything of Cory Maddox in me. That was a relief; Angel and I had been able to pretty much identify the "real" or "object" personalities from the rest almost on contact by this point and I was afraid that some of them, with a lot more experience inside the Sims and inside the energy field, might be able to do the same to me.

Most, however, were like Wilma had been and to a small extent still was, unable to tell and in some cases probably unwilling to accept the truth. There was also the logic conundrum I'd still not solved about the energy field and the Sims being run inside the lab. I mean, if we were in a Sim, then those Sims, the lab, everything there was just an illusion, too, wasn't it?

It was, to be sure, but not under the "ruthless logic" of the program. The logic and laws of *this* Sims required that campus, those computers, those programs, the Brand Boxes, and all the rest.

And so, there I was, helping dig Dr. Daniel Tanaka's car out, clearing the walkway to Les Cohn, M.D.'s place, even pushing Rita Alvarez's Bronco out of the mess she'd gotten it into. Those, of course, were only some of the people I hired on to help that day; many others were juniors, technicians and bureaucrats and even security types. In all cases I offered my services for any kind of heavy hauling or handyman work, and told them how to get hold of me. Quite a number wrote it down, which was what I was counting on.

I wanted very much to become the familiar, regular helpful face around their neighborhood, their families, their lives; the kind of fellow you called in when needed but otherwise never thought much about.

Finally heading home, I walked right past the old apartment that Riki and I used when we were down here. Those were still our curtains on the windows, and there seemed no lights inside, so I had to wonder if maybe our stuff wasn't still in there as well. Maybe so—but any way to get in was a long distance away, and the last thing I wanted to do was to break in and maybe get caught by Stark and his people and have to answer to why.

Wilma was outside when I returned, smoking one of her cigars. She had the habit and steadfastly refused all arguments to break it, and the most she'd do was condescend not to smoke inside the apartment where Angel and I would have to smell it.

"Find what you were looking for?" she asked me.

I shrugged. "It's a start. They know my face now, and they

took who they saw without nobody gettin' wise. I was surprised that so many of 'em was still up there, even a bunch
of new ones. I just can't figure out what they're *doin'* over
there now."

"The usual stuff, I think," Wilma commented, blowing a
huge smoke plume into the subfreezing air. "This guy Stark
and his buddies aren't dummies. They're letting everybody
play with this big toy they got, and maybe even finding out
a little about how the thing works. In the meantime, all the
ones he wants to find are here. I think you're suckered in,
shown what will make you really interested, then offered a
real solid position in Stark's own organization. If you pass the
tests and go along and don't get squeamish, you become one
of them. Otherwise, you get marked. I don't think they can
fully pass into a new world until everybody of their kind,
meanin' us, too, is out of this one. Anybody he's not sure of,
he kills. The rest he takes with him. Everybody together."

"But Brand got out while everybody else was here," I
pointed out.

She nodded. "He screwed 'em by playing by the rules
here. Who's to say he's really out, though? If he's in one of
their mental Disneylands, he's still here. If he's your caterpillar, he's stuck in the tunnels between the worlds until
we go through, too. He just figured out how to die and stay
alive at the same time. He's still stuck, I bet. Or maybe he's
back here as somebody else, like you and Angel. Ever think
of that?"

I hadn't, and it was both a logical and sobering thought. If
*we* could do it, why couldn't *he*? Of course he could.

Wilma finished her cigar, spat into the snow, then tossed
the stub into the whiteness as well. "Let's go on up," she
said, thinking. "I think maybe we got to get Angel to cast the
runes."

"Casting the runes," was the way Wilma described Angel's
near trances. I wasn't sure how much ceremony was really
necessary, but it did seem to calm everybody down and make

it easier to concentrate, so I went along. Wilma had come up
with it and it had seemed to work, so we'd stuck with it, even
though it was cold in the apartment and it boiled down to sitting naked and cross-legged on the floor, close and touching
one another, synchronizing breathing, clearing the mind, letting things go.

At first all of the impressions had been random, and many
had been similar to those snapshots of past lives or bad movies or whatever they were we'd gotten spontaneously long
ago. Then we'd managed to tie into one or another of the
people at the project, to see scenes, overhear partial conversations, that kind of thing. Now we were going to try something
new, something different. Now we were going to try some
conscious direction, but Angel would be the one who'd have
to lead, and we'd have to pretty much blend with her and be
along for the ride.

At first, nothing happened. A pitch-dark apartment, a none-
too-warm rug and the chill seeping in, wasn't all that great,
but we reached out, the three of us pulling each other into
ourselves, and, after what seemed a very long while, the chill,
the apartment, even the feel of body against body, seemed to
vanish and we became a combined, disembodied entity, an
entity who saw in the darkness as well as the light, and who
rose from us, looked down at our bodies, then rose some
more, melting right through the roof and out into the night.

It was a very strange vision we'd never gotten used to, a
small city seen entirely within the context of heat and energy,
houses and hotels and restaurants, all ghostly, semitranspar-
ent structures of eerie reddish energy, bright flashes where
there were exceptionally warm heat sources, and shimmering
ghosts of people walking about, seen only as glows of darker,
more purplish energy.

You could actually *see* the electricity running down the
wires, from pole to pole and into the structures, but you could
not see the poles themselves.

And, about a half mile over the other side and off to our

right, there was a huge, pulsing dome of glowing greenish light, throbbing like a heart, or like some great breathing beast. We had been there many times before, but not with this much will, with this sense of direction, with this total lack of conflict over what and where.

Now, suddenly, we were there, on the ground, inside that pulsing field of energy and feeding upon it. We felt—solid, as if in fact we were in a real body walking along that once-familiar parking area and toward the old mansion. This was new; we'd never felt this sort of thing before. It had always been as ephemeral, as spirit-guided, as the initial leaving of the bodies back in the apartment. Now, though, we were *walking* up the stairs to the front doors, and then *through* them, betraying the illusion of solidity without destroying it.

We were there, all three of us, but we were as one, in one, and all of us were Angel. We could feel Angel's naked body, feel the cold tile of the mansion entrance floor on our bare feet, and, slowly, more sensations came, of the dry heat of the interior, the ceiling blowers, as if we were really there.

We could hear, too; hear people talking, papers rustling, the click of keyboards and the whine of copiers and all the rest. And, as a dark room takes on light and texture and detail as a light is slowly turned up until fully illuminating the place, the sights became filled, not just energy but solid material, real sight.

We were *there*, and nobody could see us! At least, we hoped not.

At that moment we came face to face with Sally Prine, one of the newcomers I'd met briefly earlier in the day when clearing out the development, and for a brief moment we were afraid that she saw us, but then she simply walked right through us and on. It was a strange sensation, like being tickled all over your insides, and not terribly pleasant, but it sure beat the alternative.

We were a ghost, free to wander, no door locked to us, no barrier that we could imagine a problem, and drawing upon the very energy bubble that none here could see but all must have felt to sustain ourselves.

We walked back and climbed the stairs and headed for Al Stark's office. It was weird to walk right past the armed sentries, right through the computerized "open only with proper badge code" doors, but it also was kind of a heady thrill as well. The only frustration was that we were along in Angel's head, and were limited to Angel's point of view.

Stark wasn't in his office, but Ben Sloan and Morgan Chun Yee were there, going over reports both in folders and on a computer screen.

Sloan, a big black man and a highly skilled programmer who worked with Tanaka, was instantly recognizable as "one of us," as it were. We always could tell who was of us, although there was nothing visible or audible. It was just something in the energy, something that said, "Here's one." Yee, a brilliant mathematician whose reputation Cory Maddox knew but who hadn't been here when Cory had been here, was something of a surprise for two reasons. One, because he was not only here but in Stark's office and private files, and, two, because he wasn't one of us.

For all his brilliance, Morgan Chun Yee was part of the Sim. The amazing thing was that, as we were about to learn, he knew it.

"I make it twenty-eight in this plane," the mathematician commented. "Of those, three, including Brand, are dead or effectively so, and three more are locked away in Sims out back. Everyone else is here, save for Maddox and Fresca, Slidecker, Matalon, and that Indian woman—what's her name?"

"Wilma Starblanket. She's staying in town here in some kind of *ménage à trois* with a blind girl and her husband, both itinerant workers of one sort or another. They haven't been able to run down anything on them—fingerprints and the rest just don't match anybody—so they might just be who and what they seem. This Indian wanted to be a nurse and is some kind of medicine woman or whatever, so she just

might feel sorry for the girl, or, who knows? Might be something kinky going on there. At any rate, she's easy enough to
pick up."

The mathematician leaned back in Stark's fancy leather
judge's chair and thought a moment. "Perhaps not as easy as
you think. She *must* know something or she would be far
away and hiding in the hills. I keep wondering if we're not
missing something here, Ben."

"Huh? How do you mean?"

"Consider the ultimate postulate here, that this entire
world, this entire universe, even me myself, are all simply
part of a gigantic program running in a Sim. If we accept that
as true, then reality is totally subjective and everything here
is simple mathematical constructs. If nothing is objectively
real save the minds of twenty-two people out of five-plus billions on this earth alone, then those twenty-two all have potentially godlike powers. If one could tap into this program
on even the smallest of scales, why, you'd have the power of
Aladdin's genie and then some."

The big man shook his head. "Nope, it won't wash, Doc.
It might if anybody really knew how it was done, but none of
us do. I flip that wall switch over there and I take for granted
that the light's gonna come on. I don't know *how* that light
comes on, not really, or how water going over Grand Coulee
Dam gets its energy tapped, transferred, stored, changed, sent
up here, routed all over the place until it finally comes here
and then gets to the switch where I can send it on to the light.
I take it for granted. I don't have to know how it's done to
use it. It's the same with this stuff. We don't know how it
works. None of us knows how to program worth a damn except in the wide-open way, and once the computer hits on one
of us and builds everything else, it doesn't pay us any mind
in building the rest."

"I wonder. Still, it is a fascinating concept. I keep thinking
that somehow your point may be turned on its head. That you
might not have to know how to patch the program to change

it, at least slightly. There is a lot of magic and mysticism left unexplained in this world, and who knows that someone might not simply happen, by chance, on something to influence the code. It is another way of saying that all software has bugs, and the more complex the software, the more bugs are likely."

"Maybe. Who knows? What got you on this kick tonight, Doc?"

The mathematician shrugged. "I have no idea. It just sort of seemed to pop into my head and would not go away. Perhaps I am tired. Perhaps I am sensitive to some things you might not be, since I am part of the code, as it were, in an absolute sense that you are not."

"I have to say I wouldn't accept this crap if I were in your shoes," Sloan commented. "I mean, you're sitting there, I assume you think and feel and have the same kind of life experiences I do, and you're calmly saying that you're just a piece of computer code and that you and your whole universe may cease to exist when we translate."

"I don't believe we will," Chun Yee replied. "I'd like to think not, anyway. All life must have some faith in it, even the most rational. Otherwise I could never drive a car."

"Huh?"

"I must act with faith that my fellow drivers are in general a competent lot, that they will remain on their side of the road and I on mine, and that they will obey traffic signals. When I go very fast on a freeway, I have to accept on faith that nothing has destroyed any of the hundreds or thousands of bridges and such I will have to cross, and that there is nothing that will cause my death or dismemberment due to a speed which renders me incapable of doing anything about it. And as for eating in a restaurant—well, you can see the faith involved *there*, I am sure. No, friend Benjamin, I have faith that my entire life isn't just some running program, but, if it is, it is like going ninety on the freeway. What can I possibly do about it if I am wrong?"

He sighed and got up. "Well, I am going to check on a few things in the lab and then probably call it a night. But, tell me, why do you keep dwelling on those people anyway?"

Ben Sloan shook his head. "I don't know, Doc. I just— well, I know the whole score and I swear I can't really believe all this isn't real, either."

The old mathematician left the office, but Sloan kept going through the records, almost as if he were searching for something that everybody else had missed but which only he could make use of. I couldn't figure him out; he'd never been very sociable, neither he nor his wife, and we'd barely known him except in passing during the days we were here.

The Cory in me wanted at that keyboard badly; that was the kind of computer I understood and could operate, even program. I also wouldn't have minded going through those papers, but it wasn't my call, and Angel could neither read nor write and so had little or no interest in them.

Even so, we looked at one that was up and there was a holographic color photo of somebody just peeking out of the top. Without thinking, we reached down and pulled the sheet with the photo more out of the jacket to see.

It was Riki's face, in full color and three dimensions.

Angel stared and stared at it, and as she did, incredibly, the hologram began to fade out! In a short period of time, the thing was blank, just the background which wasn't any big deal. It was startling, not only that she'd done this and so easily, but also that *she'd actually reached down and pulled the photo up out of the jacket*!

Ben Sloan was intent on the terminal and hadn't noticed.

She looked at the others there, but they were all closed up or of people we either didn't know or weren't interested in. Still, we noticed one, and quietly opened it and saw that the picture, not a hologram but a straight color photo, was that of Cynthia Matalon.

Angel stared at it and stared at it, and suddenly we were no longer standing there but outside once more, still with the picture of Matalon foremost in thought, as if suspended in front of us. Things blurred; we moved along the telephone poles almost at the speed of light.

Suddenly we were in an apartment or hotel room some-where else, not in Yakima or immediately close by but cer-tainly still somewhere in the northwest.

Cynthia Matalon sat there in a comfortable chair, feet up, watching television. Far from a fashion plate now, her hair was dyed a reddish brown and cut short. She wore big, round glasses, a faded tee shirt that promoted Seattle to the tourists, and a pair of well-worn jeans. About the only thing still very Cynthia about her was that she still painted her nails, even the toenails.

We checked out the rest of the apartment or whatever. Nothing noticeable, but it was big and comfortable, better than even the big shots got back in Yakima.

We could feel Angel's near hatred of the woman, but we weren't sure what she was going to do.

A little experimentation showed that we were no longer able to directly interact, pick up, and influence solid objects. Clearly that required more energy than we could draw upon here, but had been child's play inside the campus. But there were still things we could do, and Angel instinctively knew it.

We walked over, stood right in front of Cynthia Matalon, who continued to watch the movie or whatever it was right through us, and then we turned and sat down on the same chair, right on top of Cynthia Matalon, right *into* the body of Cynthia Matalon.

Suddenly our mystery woman had to pee, and she got up, thinking, *This show's 'bout as borin' as all get-out. Why am I watchin' this crap?* and went to the bathroom.

It was one of those bathrooms where the john faced a big tub that had a mirrored tub wall and sliding door, so you got a wonderful view of yourself taking a crap when you did so. Cynthia Matalon looked at herself and we suddenly felt a slight release of an energy pattern transferring from us to her.

*They're gonna find you,* she thought. *Damn it all! Sittin' heah on the damned throne ah couldn't miss mahself on a street, ha-ah shoaht and dyed or not. Why don't he git back? Why can't they make a decision by now? Big Al's gonna walk through that doah soonah or latah and who'll get her throat cut?*

She was ripe for a panic attack, that was clear, and it was on a level even Angel could understand. I suddenly felt my own knowledge and memories being tapped, and then Angel brought forward exactly what I was thinking of, myself.

The phone rang. Believe it or not, there was even a decor-matched phone in the john, and although she was done, she reached out and picked it up.

"Bout *tiahme*, honey!" she snapped angrily into the phone, apparently expecting a call, or perhaps a very-overdue call. Instead, every bit of color drained from her face as she heard what came out instead.

*"Don't know why I sing this song,"* came Angel's wispy, sexy voice in a mock-sing. *" 'Cause everything you think you know is wrong."*

She dropped the phone like it suddenly caught fire.

I cannot describe the feeling of total and complete justice that washed through us.

A moment later, she picked up the phone almost as if it were a snake and asked, nervously, "Who *is* this?"

There was only a dial tone, which was worse than anything for getting any satisfaction at all.

There had never been anything *but* a dial tone, of course; Angel had simply made her believe that the phone had rang and then that she'd heard the little song.

It didn't matter to Cynthia, who had just experienced a whole new kind of virtual-reality experience and didn't know it. Instead, she began digging out a lot of makeup, hair cut-

ting, and other tools and started on the damnedest makeover
we'd ever seen. It was more of a make-down, but clearly it
was also being done by somebody with a lot of experience
and all the tools to make it work.

Off went most of the rest of her hair, leaving only a Mo-
hawk going from front to back. This was then taken down
with a razor to about a quarter inch and then dyed jet black
using a formula in a brush-style bottle.

She had guts, we had to admit that. It was painful to watch
her use this gadget to actually punch a hole in one nostril and
insert a small jewel there, then treat it so that it didn't bleed
much. A small bottle with an eyedropper came next, and, ap-
plied in both eyes and then rinsed with a cleaning solution,
those baby blue eyes showed up almost black, and even the
whites seemed a bit grayed, giving her a hollow, almost
sunken look. Well, you get the idea, I'm sure. She was still
damned good-looking in spite of this when she got through,
but she sure didn't look like her picture anymore, even a
little.

Finally, she got into this uncomfortable corsetlike thing of
some kind of elastic material that really flattened out her
breasts. It looked uncomfortable, even painful, but it sure
added to the look. Punk leather jacket, extremely well worn,
black stone-washed jeans, and well-worn black leather boots
completed the ensemble. She did need the glasses, being
pretty nearsighted, but she had a pair of black prescription
sunglasses that weren't all that practical indoors or at night
but certainly went with the whole look and outfit. She put her
cigarettes in one of the jacket pockets, and also took out a
large plug of chewing tobacco, of all things, biting off a hunk
and starting to chew. I didn't know if she used it regularly,
but I doubted it. On the other hand, it was a great touch. It
wouldn't take long before she'd reek of the juice, and it
wouldn't do her gleaming teeth any good, either.

One more check, and finding all the cash she could and
stuffing that in as well, she left the apartment and went down

the back stairs. She wasn't ready for the outside chill on that newly shorn head, but she finally forced herself to ignore it. It was dark but well lit, definitely city lights, and she was able to make do with the inappropriate sunglasses.

She walked several blocks, then went down an alley and into a small garage. I expected a motorcycle would be there, and it sure was—one hell of a big, beautiful Harley.

To our surprise, she went to the back of the garage where there was a sink and stuff for getting clean after working on cars and bikes and such, and she found some old motor oil and began to dab it or even slather it over her hands, face, neck, all over. Then she washed it all off, not with the heavy grease soap but with a milder one, and when she was done she was clean, but the skin was stained a dull and uneven black.

She'd managed to do something that I for one would have thought impossible: she'd made herself look less than gorgeous and in fact not at all attractive. Not ugly, but the kind of look you'd think twice at.

We knew she was going out on the Harley and had to wonder how the hell she was going to see using only those sunglasses. As it happened, she had a black helmet that she put on and which turned out to have prescription glass in its visor shield. She could in fact see to drive, if things were fairly routine.

The question really was, was she running blind or was she running to somewhere? If the former, this was only a little revenge and not anything useful otherwise; if the latter, it could lead us to Walt.

She was fairly cautious getting up to whatever freeway was near, but then she gunned it when she got up there and had a pretty straight and nearly deserted three lanes to herself. It took only a few minutes to establish that it was Interstate 5 north, but it didn't help much. I was, however, damned cold, which absolutely meant that she was either not going far on a Harley in the middle of the night or she was trying to add frostbite to her disguise.

She wasn't going far after all, and got off at an exit that told us nothing about where she was and then went down a two-lane road a ways to what looked like a farm road, then onto it and back to the farmhouse itself, dark, as you might expect at this time of night, but related because there were several Harleys in the barn she went into. She stopped, cut the engine, and hit the kickstand, then slid off.

She went out and over to the farmhouse, which was already bathed in noise from the dogs barking ever since the Harley had come up, and now there was definitely a light on and maybe a figure with a gun behind the door. She didn't seem disturbed, and knocked hard. "Pam! That you? Ah need some help *real* bad!" she shouted, able to disguise just about everything about herself except that extreme accent.

The door opened and one of the toughest-looking women I ever remember seeing, at least still young enough to be really startling, stood there with a shotgun under her arms and a big, tired frown. "Sugar? Jesus Christ! Is that *you?*"

"Yeah, it's me. Pam, Ah need a hideout real bad. Ah got some folks aftah me and ain't no way Ah'm gonna shake 'em right this minute. You'ah mah only hope at this point."

"Well—okay. C'mon in! Don't freeze your ass off! Man! You sure look different! Only that accent of yours would give you away!"

"Yeah, Ah know. What can Ah do? Oh *god*! Does that wahmth evah feel *good*."

"Still got the hog, though, huh?"

"Yeah. A little out of practice, though, and it's too damn cold. Ah'll only be heah the night, Pammy. Ah got somebody aftah me might wanna kill me or wohse. T'morrah Ah kin get hold of some friends, but ah just need a getaway tonight."

"Well, you can stay here as long as you like. You know that. Jeez! It's been—what? Five years?"

It would have been nice to stay through and learn more, but we couldn't. Suddenly we found ourselves being pulled out of the body, out of the house, and there was nothing we could do about it. Faster and faster, then to near light along the poles and connectors, then back into our own apartment and into us, where individual feeling began to return.

We'd simply run out of energy, not just excess but plain old physical energy, to keep it up. This had, in fact, been the longest and most ambitious session yet, and it had impressed all of us.

"Think we scared that *bitch* a little?" Angel asked with a really satisfied tone.

"Yeah, you did that much, all right," I told her. "I wish we could get back there tomorrow. I'd love to know who she's gonna call and what's on the other end."

Angel giggled. "Did you see her face in the mirror when I sang that dumb song to her?"

"Yeah, I did. It felt good." But it didn't get us anywhere, I thought to myself. We need to find out all the damned details here.

"Brrrr! Cold in here!" Wilma muttered, irritated. "Let's get some lights on and maybe some food into us, huh? Something simple. And let's see if we can turn up the heat. Can't you jigger it more, Joshua?"

"I'll try," I told her. "It's pretty well up there now. This just isn't the best heat for this place and it ain't been serviced much."

I was thinking more about Cynthia Matalon, though. She was definitely a pro, and ready for a quick getaway, but who was Pam? Not one of us; there was no feeling there, any more than there had been for Chun Yee. Five years, more or less. . . . The immediate time after Brand had been "killed" and the project shut down.

Angel was thinking the same thing. "I can't figger her no more than I could before," she commented. "What'd she do after the place shut? Join up with a girl biker gang?"

"Looked like it. How many bikes you see in that barn? I made it five or six."

" 'Bout that. Wilma?"

"Six, yes, not counting your girl's. She's somethin' else, she is. Jumps real good, though, if you crack the whip."

"So do we," I responded. "That's what it was all about, as I guess you figgered. But she's one of us. The question is, where's Walt? And what do we do with 'em?"

"I think if I can just sleep a long time and git some more of that there green power in me, I might be able to do pretty much whatever we want with her," Angel told us. "The real question is, what do we want to do?"

I thought it over. "Bring them here. No, check that. Bring them *close* to here, where at least one of us can talk to them safely without Stark jumping on them. I want Walt to tell me in his own words to my face how he did what he did and why. And I want to know from Cynthia Matalon just what the hell game she thinks she's playing with everybody."

"That was a neat trick," Wilma called from the kitchen. "I mean, several neat tricks. Picking up stuff in the office? And riding right along in that woman's body? Damn! I was starting to scare *me*."

"I thought you was the big shaman. Tunnels under the world and all that?" I shot back.

"*Visions,* man! Visions! This was no vision! This was *real*!"

"Or as real as anything is, anymore," I commented.

Angel was thinking. "Maybe there's an easier way than all that stuff. Maybe there's a way to talk t'her without havin' to have her come here at all. I could almost feel it happen this time."

"Well, tell us what you have in mind, but watch it!" I warned. "This not only takes the funny energy and all the rest, it takes a lot out of all of us. We never did but one of these a week and this was the longest and most complicated yet. I mean, who knows if we try again tomorrow we won't have heart attacks or somethin'? I feel right now like all the life's drained outta me. Soon as we eat I'm for bed."

"Well, let's see how we feel tomorrow," Angel offered. "I mean, I was really havin' *fun* for the first time in a *long* time. I think I started feelin' the kinda power stuff the guys over at the big place feel when they use them there boxes. I don't think it's right and I guess it's sinful, but I really *loved* this."

"I know what you mean," I told her, somewhat envying her control. "It would be funny if, in whatever real place we all started, *you* were the programmer and *I* was the artist, wouldn't it?"

"I dunno 'bout that. Still, I kinda wish I could git myself really under that green glob. If I could, I ain't sure what I couldn't do. Ain't gonna happen, though. Why would they ever want a simple blind girl like me in there?"

I thought about it. "One thing at a time," I told her. "But I can come up with a reason. You're almost the ideal subject to test out a Sim on, at least from their point of view. First, though, we deal with Matalon and her crew. Then we see if *I* can get in over there. If I can, maybe you can, too."

"Yeah?" Wilma asked, bringing us sandwiches and drinks. "And then what? What would you do if you had all that power to suck in over there?"

"If everybody's together," I said carefully, "and I mean everybody who's one of us and still here, we open up one big, humongous rabbit hole and we all go down it. We translate rather than reincarnate and we blow the hell outta Al Stark's master plan. *That's* what we do."

Wilma listened, nodded, and replied, "Okay, sounds good. And then what?"

"Don't jump too far ahead," I responded cautiously, but I didn't like the question. What kind of journey did you set out on if you didn't know where you were going, what to do when you got there, or how to get home?

At least not Al Stark, not even the great Matthew Brand, could answer that one.

# XI

# GREEN QUEEN
# AND RED DUCHESS

We slept like the dead for maybe twelve hours. Okay, *I* slept for that long, and Wilma maybe a little longer; Angel was still out cold when I reacted to a pounding at the door and managed to grab a towel and make it over there. I opened it a crack, my wits still not together, and Mrs. McCurdy, the landlady, was there.

"Hey, Joshua, got a phone call on the pay line downstairs for ya."

"For me?" I couldn't at that moment think of who it might be, but I said, "Let me get some clothes on and I'll be right down."

I pulled on my pants and boots and a jacket and went out and down the stairs, suddenly remembering that it was still cold out. It didn't look or feel as bad as the day before, though; the sun was out, there was a lot of bare asphalt out there, traffic sounded like it was going pretty good, and there was slush rather than ice.

The phone was just left dangling, so I picked it up, wondering if whoever it was was still there, and said, "Yeah? This is Joshua."

"Hello!" came a friendly-sounding female voice on the other end. "This is Dr. Alvarez. You helped dig out my car and walk yesterday and you left your name and number."

Interesting. I had hardly expected a nibble so quick, and even less a nibble from her. "Yes, ma'am?"

"Look, you said you do all sorts of general cleanup and maintenance work?"

"Yes, ma'am. Anything that's legal and don't take too much equipment."

"I—I'm afraid we had a problem in here that I didn't discover until I got home. I guess we lost some roofing tiles or something and never noticed, and when I came back yesterday the snow melt had come straight into the apartment. I've got a real mess here. Water all over, much of it filthy, and the rug's the same. I need a complete cleanup, as it were, and if you need anything like a rug shampooer or the like, I'll spring for it."

"I'll do what I can. How big's the apartment?"

"It's two bedrooms, living room, eat-in kitchen, and bath. The living room and kitchen area are the worst. The management's already said they were going to patch the roof, but that doesn't help me inside. Can you handle it?"

"Yes, ma'am. It don't sound so tough."

"All right, then. I've got to work today, but I can drop off the key if you like or leave it here with someone. There's security here but I'll alert them."

"Sounds okay," I told her. "You can drop it by any time and we'll go on up and see what we can do."

"Thanks loads."

I had to wonder if it was some kind of trick, but I went upstairs and found Wilma just getting out of the bathroom and curious as could be.

"What do you think?"

"I think one of us gets on the bike and goes up there and sees what's what," I said. "Sure sounds on the level. I ran into this woman a lot but I never was friends and I ain't too clear what she does, anyway. Cold fish, but I don't think she's no CIA or like that."

Wilma nodded. "I hate to leave Angel out cold like this, but let's both go up. I'll come back and check on her and maybe get her up if need be, then pick up whatever's needed and we'll all join you. We can pick up something to eat at the Seven-Eleven."

Rita Alvarez—I never even knew she was a doctor until she called and said that—drove up alongside the apartment house, and I spotted her and went down to meet her. She nodded but didn't smile, but she took a key off her keyring and handed it to me. "Apartment four-twelve," she told me. She then fumbled and came up with a business card and scribbled on the back of it. "Here's my number at work here. If you have any questions or problems, or just want to give up, call. I'll try and stop by at lunch or at least give you a call when I can."

"Don't you worry, Doc. We'll take care of it, I'm pretty sure," I told her, and she drove off.

We didn't normally leave Angel alone, but it wasn't like she couldn't take care of herself. In that apartment, she'd memorized just about everything and you'd just about never figure out she couldn't see it. Outside was a different story, but in there she could even fix herself a snack and shower or whatever with little more risk than we'd take. It was mostly that we couldn't leave a note or a recording for her, and there was no phone she could get to so we could tell her where we were if she awoke and got scared.

The apartment looked normal enough, but once we went inside all our suspicion vanished. It was a real mess, and it was clear to see just where the water was coming in and all that.

"Umph! White carpeting, too!" Wilma sniffed. "Damned impractical for a living room." She looked over on the kitchen counter, where there were a bunch of instant Polaroid type pictures. "Heh! She took color photos of it all before she left! Before she called you, even, I bet. Get that insurance money, huh?"

I looked around. Rug cleaner and shampoo, for sure, and mops and strong cleaner, upholstery attachment for the muddy couch, stuff to wash down the walls, maybe some paint to paint over the ugly spot at the ceiling joints. It would take most of the day, but it wasn't that big a job.

"Okay, go back and check on Angel," I told her. "I'll get as much of the basics done here as I can. When you can, rent one of them carpet vacs and supplies from the Seven-Eleven and bring it up if you can, and the usual cleanin' stuff. You think you got the money for it?"

She nodded. "No big deal. I'm getting receipts, though. If she's collecting insurance, we want to overcharge as much as possible for labor and get every dime we lay out."

Doing the prep stuff mostly meant moving the furniture out of the way and off the living-room carpet area so we could clean, some mop-up using the stuff I found in a utility closet, and wiping things down and using her sponge mop to get the slop off the kitchen tiles. No big deal.

Wilma wasn't back when I finished what I could, and I had the TV on but couldn't find anything interesting, so, of course, I started snooping. Hell, I was gonna do it anyway.

This was definitely a woman's apartment, but not a single woman's apartment. There was stuff from more than one shopping mind here, and the tastes weren't so close that they didn't say that either Alvarez had a roommate or she really had a split personality. It wasn't the living room so much as the fact that there were different kinds of things on the shelves, a bunch of books I had trouble reading the titles of but were definitely different fields, and the kicker. In a two-bedroom apartment, one of the bedrooms was a kind of shared office, with computer, printer, a terminal—that was interesting and overkill—at two small desks that were as different as night and day right down to the family pictures. The other bedroom had only one big bed in it, a king-sized heated waterbed of all things. I never did like 'em; they always made me seasick.

There was absolutely nothing obvious here, but you didn't share an apartment with another person and just have one big bed if you was just friends. Looked like Rob and Lee weren't the only same-sex couple in the project.

The artifacts and pictures were more revealing of Alvarez than her companion, though. How many kids were in that old photo on the wall? Nine? And each of them looked to be maybe nine months apart, too. Easy to see why her father, a really handsome Hispanic type, was smiling in the photos and her mother looked tired and already had gray hair.

Much more interesting was a later picture, a picture of Alvarez maybe in her twenties, smiling after some kind of graduation ceremony or something like that. There was a scribbled inscription at the bottom, *Sister Margarita Magdelena, Ph.D., Gonzaga, '89*, it read, and she had on a modern version but still a recognizable kind of uniform.

She was a nun.

Or had been. There wasn't a sign of a crucifix or any other religious objects in the house, period. There was a Bible, and, in fact, there were two of them—a real Latin Vulgate, in Latin, and the Catholic English Bible, whatever that was called.

*What did you do, Sister Rita? Fall in love with another girl at the convent? Or maybe with a fellow student—or teacher?*

Hadn't Alice McKee been a sociologist from Gonzaga? Women's studies, I think somebody had said. It sure would fit.

Poor Rita! She was probably as mixed up, split, and crazed about who and what she was as Angel.

Somebody rang the bell, and I hastened to the door and opened it. Wilma was there, fumbling with carpet cleaning stuff. "Angel finally was awake, but she's in no condition to come here," she told me. "I got something down her, but I wouldn't be surprised if she isn't out again when we get back."

"Yeah, those nighttime fun and games wear you out as much or more than if you was really doing it," I commented, getting the stuff set up. In truth, we were doing it, if only because what seemed so magical or at least like group ESP or witchcraft or whatever was no different than this whole damned world. If nothing was real except us, then we weren't really doin' that at all, and we weren't connecting on the level we seemed to be. Instead, it was all zeros and ones, all energy, all programs, all neural networking.

Alvarez called around one in the afternoon and I assured her it was all going well and that we'd be done by maybe three, four if we took too long for lunch. I was gonna quote her a hundred bucks cash, but before I could she offered two hundred, so I let her talk me into it. She asked us to call her at the number on the card when we were done and she'd come out and see the job and if she was satisfied she'd settle it.

Well, even with a long lunch we actually finished by three, but didn't call her until a little after four. I'd half expected her to walk in while we were still shampooing the rug, but she hadn't.

While we worked, I briefed Wilma on what I'd found and what I'd deduced from the pictures.

"Sounds right," she said, nodding. "A nun, huh? You think she still thinks of herself, deep down, like a nun? I knew a couple of ones who'd dropped out and you couldn't really tell the difference 'cept they didn't pray all the time. One got married to this social worker she'd been helping, and the other one got knocked up someplace and was too good a Catholic to get rid of the aftermath, and quit and had the kid and kept it. They didn't stop bein' nuns, though, just 'cause the church threw 'em out. Bet she's got guilt up the kazoo, too."

"Maybe, but she's not alone."

"Oh, yeah, but that's not surprising. Good Hispanic name with a good Irish one. My guess is that this McKee's not here

right now, though, 'cause it doesn't look like the place has
been lived in by two people for a while. Too neat, except for
the leak, of course. It could just be personality—this has to be
the first apartment I've seen in a long time where the owner
is such a compulsive neat she makes the bed and hangs up all
her clothing and even scrubs down the counter—but I'd say
McKee's not here and hasn't been for a few days, maybe the
week. Not a falling out, though—the clothes and personal
stuff are still there. Most likely back at her college for something, or doing some kind of research."

I thought about the list. "Twenty-eight, they said, and six
were accounted for in other ways, two were Walt and Cynthia, that's eight, three more are us, that's eleven, the Sloans
make thirteen, Rob and Lee fifteen, these two seventeen,
plus Cohn, Tanaka, Stark, that makes twenty. That's eight we
don't know, but they said the gang was all here except for the
ones we know. That makes only Walt and Cynthia against
them, plus whatever those things were. If I figure that most of
the unknowns were at that meeting the first day as well as being around after, then it's—*oh, my god!*—the Standishes,
maybe Betty Harker-Simonson, Sally Prine, Jamie Cholder,
and three who couldn't have been there and I must not have
met yet. Maybe ones on Stark's staff, although I'm not sure."

"What's wrong with those others you thought of?"

"Well, the Standishes are a nice-looking young couple
right out of suburbia, only they're right-wing fundamentalist
Republicans who want God in all aspects of America, and
only they know what God wants. Jamie's a weirdo—the only
solid programmer who also wears copper bracelets, surrounds
herself with pyramids, and thinks Shirley MacLaine is a tra-
ditionalist. Prine I only met yesterday. Seems nice enough,
but she made no real impression on me. If she's consistent,
though, she's got to be a bit strange."

Wilma looked up at me in mock surprise. "Strange?
What's so strange about the rest? I mean, look at *us*. An In-

dian broad who talks to the trees, and the trees talk back, a programmer and a scifi and poster artist who flip out, see a giant caterpillar, and come back from the dead as a blind girl out of *Grapes of Wrath* or something, and a handyman who looks like a lapsed rabbi. Not to mention that—whatever she is—we followed last night."

"You have a point," I admitted.

The phone rang. It was Alvarez, sounding a little distressed. "I'm stuck here waiting for a business call," she told us. "Any chance you could run the key past my office? I'll pay you in full when you do."

I was both excited at this unexpected break and also cautious. "Um, yeah, I suppose I could, but I know that place where most of the folks here work and it's got guards."

"I'll clear you in as far as the main building. Come straight in on the road, tell the guard why you're here, and he'll let you through. Come straight up to the big parking lot in front. You'll see three buildings, but only one of them is a big old place, like a huge house. Go up to the front door and wait, or tell someone at the door to fetch me."

"Fair enough. Um, there's two of us. My wife will be with me."

"Okay, I'll tell the gate. See you in—what? Ten minutes? Are you finished?"

"Pretty much, although it'll take the rug overnight to dry out. They patched the roof already, so it won't happen again. Lemme drop the rented stuff off, and then I'll be up. Half an hour, maybe? I don't want to hav'ta do nothin' else once I lock up."

"Okay. It's—four-twenty. By five, then."

"By five."

I hung up, somewhat excited. Wilma looked at me. "We're going right in there?"

I shook my head. "Not you and me. That wouldn't do no good, and we know they got you made, anyway. Best you stay out until there's a reason for you to go in. No, I was thinkin' of takin' Angel in on the bike with me. She's ridden before."

"Angel! *Why?*"

"She wants inside that big green pulsing bubble, don't she? This is the closest we're likely to get for a while."


Angel was both excited and very scared at the idea of going in. "Suppose they figger out we're ones o' them?" she worried. "I mean, if we kin read them, some of them got to be able to figger us, right?"

"Maybe, but Alvarez can't," I assured her. "It's worth it. We won't even go inside the building. These bodies we got, though, they're a little different than the others. They was made by a patch. I think we got a connection to what's really under all this that they don't have. Come or not, but I gotta go. We can't do much without lots more risk anyway."

She relented, but I didn't know if it was really her decision or just how easily she went along rather than fight over anything.

"You take it easy," Wilma cautioned. "In and out, no funny stuff. Not this trip."

"Don't worry," I assured her.

It was dark by the time we got ready and got on the bike and Angel held on to me for dear life. When we went past the Dunkin' Donuts I almost flashed back, but I said nothing. Still, it seemed all too familiar, the turn, the winding road, the gatehouse up ahead not far from where that *thing* had come close to denting the Porsche. I didn't recognize the men in the gatehouse, but they were private security and changed regularly.

"Doc Alvarez asked us to come drop off her key and pick up my money," I told them in my best hick accent. "She said she would tell you?"

The guard looked us over and frowned. "I'm not too sure. . . ."

"Look, ain't no skin off *my* nose," I told him. "I'll be glad to call her and say that you won't let us in and she'll hav'ta pick up her key and pay us later."

"You can give us the key," he suggested.

I was getting irritated. "Ain't no way, bud. She owes me two hundred bucks for spendin' all day cleanin' up her apartment. No bucks, no key."

He sighed. "Oh, all right. Here, you and the lady put these temporary passes around your necks. Go straight to the front of the old house and wait. Don't even get off the motorcycle. I'll call up there and she'll meet you. Understand?"

"Yeah, fine with me," I assured him.

"No wandering around. Straight up and back. You can get shot going the wrong place once you're in there," the guard warned. "Then you come right back out on this same road and hand over those two passes and go."

"No sweat, boss."

He handed us the two tags, and I helped Angel get it around her neck and then put the other over mine.

"What's the problem with her?" the guard asked.

"She's blind. Satisfied? She's really gonna be some threat, ain't she?"

Angel smiled, and the guard sort of gave a half-apologetic, half-growling sound and shut the window. The gate went up, and we rolled on into the campus.

Almost as soon as we cleared the guard post we seemed to intersect the great energy bubble, and then we were inside. There was a slight tingling sensation, sort of like when the air's full of static electricity but without any sparks or zaps, and we rolled on into the parking lot and then around and up to the mansion. We were now almost in the middle of the pulsing blob, and we could feel its power seep into us. It was heady, almost like an overdose of something or maybe getting a little high.

Alvarez did not show up immediately, but I wasn't about to violate instructions. Hell, I knew how mean security was here, and that was before they'd been attacked. I could only imagine what it was now.

Finally, the door did open, and Rita Alvarez came out and then down the steps and up to the bike. "I'm sorry you were stuck out here," she told me, sounding seriously upset at the idea. "I told you to come up and wait inside if I was delayed."

"Ma'am, the guard almost didn't let us in at all, and when he did he said we'd be shot if we got off the bike, so we stayed on."

She flashed an angry expression back toward the road. "I'm going to have a serious talk with them. Well, never mind. Will a check be okay?"

"I like cash best, but if you gotta, then make it out to Wilma Starblanket. I can spell it if you need to."

"No, that's all right. Interesting name. Is that the young lady here?"

"No, that's my *other* lady. The one that helped me with the job. Angel here's blind and can't do as much no more."

Alvarez frowned. "You poor child!" She fumbled, came up with some money. "I can make an ATM later, I guess. This is a hundred and forty dollars. I can give you that and make out a check for the rest or you can collect from me tomorrow."

"Check for the rest will do fine," I told her. "Save us both a trip."

She wrote the check by the light of my single headlight, tore it off, and gave it to me with the cash. I stuck it in my jacket pocket and fumbled around and found her house key, then handed it to her. "Thanks a lot for the business, ma'am. Any old time, you know where I am."

She nodded. "Indeed I do. Thank you."

She turned to go, then turned back, gave us both a look, and seemed puzzled, frowning, as if trying to see something else that might be there.

Angel turned and looked at her through sightless eyes. *You don't see nothin' funny,* she shot to the scientist mentally, and I could see the brief stream, like a tiny line of yellow tracer bullets, go from Angel to Rita. *Just a couple of no-'count hillbillies handy for the dirty work.*

Rita Alvarez stood there a second, as if frozen, then turned as if nothing had happened and walked back into the building without looking back.

"You got that much power from this little trip?" I asked Angel, and she smiled and hugged me.

"Honey babe, you can't *believe* what I think I kin do!"

"Shall I stick around and stall for a couple more minutes?"

"Nope. We're bein' watched all over as it is. 'Sides, I don't dare soak up much more. You got a lot, too. Let's go."

I could feel it, even within me, but I couldn't use it, and I hadn't the slightest idea why she could. Damn it, *I* had been the programmer!

Maybe, though, that was the problem. Or maybe the problem was twofold. What had Les said? Women were parallel, men were serial, referring, as it turned out, to the way the two halves of the brain were connected. Hadn't the witch always been the power, not the warlock? Was there a reason that the queen was the most powerful piece on the chessboard that was somehow lost to us?

Or maybe it was just that I was thinking too much about using it. Good lord! Would that be a horrible joke! The more knowledge you rejected, the more ignorant you became, the more power you had, so you could have power or wisdom but not both.

Well, it didn't matter. We turned in the badges without a word, and I gunned it for the apartment.

"Do you know you're glowin' bright green?" she yelled as we turned onto the highway. "You look like you're on fire!"

I could only see her hands, but I certainly could return it. "You *are* green, clear through and glowing like a rocket," I shouted back.

"We're linked to it, now," she said. "Ain't no more prob-

lem gittin' all the power I need. And they don't know it! I
don't think there's a one of 'em kin see it 'cept'n me and you
and Wilma through me."

I helped Angel off the bike and then up the stairs, and we
opened the door to the apartment and stepped in. "Wilma?
We're back!" I called.

There was no answer.

Both of us had a sudden bad feeling, and I rushed around,
looking in the rooms for any trace of her, even a note.
Nothing.

"They took her!" I exclaimed angrily. "While we were
over there, they came and took her 'cause they knew she was
alone!"

I had never seen such an expression on Angel's face before, or on Riki's before that, as I saw now. It scared the hell
out of me, actually. And then that tremendous, leering sneer
turned, and she suddenly gave a menacing smile. "Too late,"
she muttered. "They waited till too late. Jest lie down on the
rug, and I'll lay right here," she told me, her voice even.
"We're linked up, we three. They done waited too long.
Here—take my hand. Get close here."

"Okay, now what?"

"Just relax and do like last night, that's all."

I touched and could see the brilliant, pulsing green we both
had merge into a single mass, a mass that seemed to throb
faster, and faster, and grow bigger, and bigger, until it seemed
to explode.

We were there instantaneously, as a single Angel entity.
"There" turned out to be a basement room in the mansion
with a special extra-security badge code needed to get in or
out of it.

It was a giant padded cell with absolutely no features. It
was hard, although not impossible, to even tell where the
door was, and it was clear that the thing was covered by
video and audio monitors unreachably embedded in the high
ceiling, which also had a soft light and fixture recessed into

it and illuminating the maybe-five-by-five-foot square of soft mattresslike padding. In the cell, looking as pissed off as I'd ever seen her, was Wilma Starblanket, stripped stark naked and just sitting there.

"Wilma! Don't even act like you hear us or anybody, but we're here!"

"I wondered if you would be able to get through down here. They came maybe ten minutes after you left. Shot me with some kind of drug. I still can't hardly move an inch. Took me out, then sat there and waited till you came out. We came in, and they strip-searched me and dumped me in here."

We had a certain level of solidity, like the night before, enough so that Angel's bare feet actually felt and slightly depressed the padded floor. I wondered if anybody would notice that, and hoped not.

"Just do like last night," Angel told her. "Gimme your mind and c'mon. We'll git you outta here one way or 'nother."

Wilma took a series of breaths and then put herself into the kind of shaman's trance that had worked so well for her before. We went down and blended with her as we had with Cynthia Matalon the night before, only now we got up, and only Wilma's unconscious shell was there. She was with us.

"Wonder if anybody else is 'round here?" Angel mused.

I forced myself to a certain level of individualism and with some concentration said, "Matalon first. We can explore here later."

Angel seemed to be jarred back to a sense of mission by that. "Yeah, Matalon. Hang on."

We were out of there in a flash, and suddenly we were somewhere else again, at a place whose location we did not know but which was nonetheless somewhat familiar. A farm in the woods about three miles off I-5.

Cynthia Matalon was still there, but she'd used the day to

further punk herself out, and it was startling. Black lipstick and nail polish, white bone skull-and-crossbone earrings, and, so help me, what looked like a tattoo of three black roses bound together on the back left side of her hair.

It wasn't new. Either it was a fake or it had been there all the time, covered until now by hair, and we just hadn't noticed it.

She was dressed entirely in weathered black leather now, skintight, and she was smoking the biggest, fattest cigar I'd ever seen. She also had a holster on with a large black Luger in it, and, clipped on the other side, what might well have been a bullwhip. Her companions were more underdressed, but no less bizarre, some with shaved heads, tattoos on their cheeks, and stuff going right through their noses. They ranged in age from maybe mid twenties to their early forties, and they seemed to have taken a delight in making themselves look as unattractive and gross as possible.

There was also enough drugs and booze around to send anybody to Pluto, and more nicely packaged. Matalon stuck to cigars and beer, but the others were doing pot or coke or, in one case, shooting up what may well have been heroin. These were tough broads who used what they sold. Their long-lost friend was being offered, even urged, to try just about everything, but she refused with uncharacteristic seriousness. "Uh-uh. You 'membah last time. I took some o' that shit and y'all disappeahed. Besides, I may hav'ta travel some yet tonight."

"Why bother goin' anywhere?" one of the women asked her. "I mean, business has never been better, we got a fam'ly here, we got each other, lotsa dough. Who needs more shit?"

*If only you knew,* I couldn't help thinking, and I wondered if Matalon was thinking the same thing. At least it was clear, or partly clear, where her post–Zyzzx Software Factory money had come from. She must have been something else back then, but once she'd gotten her stake and got away with it, there had to be a time when she realized that she was either going to die or become irrelevant if she kept going with this life and left it.

She'd kept her hog and an outfit and look all ready, though, and even knew where to find the old gang this many years later. Find them and have them not even be surprised that she knew and showed up, although there were several little tricks she knew that nobody else did for avoiding questions.

Well, we had a few tricks now, too.

And I was just itching to try that wonder of a classic Harley of hers.

Cynthia, who the other women all seemed to know as Sugar, a name rather than a term of affection or friendship, looked at her too-expensive watch and said, "Look, Ah'm gonna hav'ta go track this bastahd down, looks like. Ah can't stay heah. They'ah on my tail and Ah don't wanta bring 'em down on y'all heah. Ah think too much of y'all from the old days."

"If ya gotta, ya gotta," Pam, the leader and the one who'd shot up, commented. "Just don't stay away so long next time, huh?"

"Oh, Ah promise you Ah'm not easy to get," she assured them.

There were the usual good-byes, which we patiently waited for—Angel no longer seemed to have any urgency or sense of diminishing power—and then she left into the night.

We didn't merge with her this time, just rode along on the back of the Harley like some irreverent ghost. Angel had sense enough not to try to communicate with Matalon while going seventy down a dark freeway, but she was no longer to be denied.

*You feel a little dizzy and need to pull over,* Angel shot to her with those same little yellow dots she'd used on Alvarez. *You just need a couple minutes. Besides, you got to pee out some of that beer.*

She went on for a couple of minutes, then saw a wide shoulder area and pulled over and slowed to a stop, easing the Harley down out of sight of routine traffic headlights and just inside the trees. She cut the engine, then sat there a minute, as if getting hold of herself. Finally, she slid off, went a bit further into the woods, did a squat, and took a frontier woman's piss.

As she turned, she suddenly seemed to see something, something indistinct, green, and living, materializing almost in front of her. We could see the fear in her eyes, and she involuntarily reached for her gun, then thought better of it, seeing the futility of shooting solid bullets at a ball of energy.

*Just sit down in the grass and relax,* Angel commanded, and the woman obeyed, almost like an automaton.

*"Joshua, Wilma, I ain't got what's needed to ask the right stuff!"* Angel complained, at least realizing her limitations. *"Joshua, you need to ask her all that stuff, not me."*

*"But how do I get through? It's hard just to do this!"* I complained.

*"Look, there's only one thing we can do. Ain't nobody home in any of our bodies right now. Suppose I stick her in my body, so she'll be blind, pretty helpless, and right there with you, Joshua. You can ask away. Wilma can take her place here and drive this fancy bike in. I'll go into Wilma back at the nasty place."*

Both Wilma and I were appalled, and forced a near-simultaneous *"No!"* through.

*"Don't worry. We're all just sorta fakes anyways, right? So it ain't like I'm doin' anything weird 'cause this is all weird. This'll put me in a body where I can see but I'll be bathed in the energy field. I can't be hurt there. Wilma can."*

But Wilma's body wasn't like ours; she couldn't see or use that energy on her own. Worse, Matalon might wind up with it. I didn't like it, but it was impossible to talk Angel out of these things once she got her mind up, and she had all the power right now.

It was crazy, too, to even just do this like you'd change shirts, but it made sense. We weren't really these people; we were *programs*, independent to an extent but child programs within a parent/master virtual-reality program. Breaking off an operative part and patching it to another should in theory be easy, providing all parts are prepared for this. The trick would be to get things back.

Before we could argue or protest further, there was a sudden sensation of being flung around through the air and spinning in random directions all at once, and suddenly I was back in my body in the apartment in Yakima. Angel was beside me, but most of that green brilliance was faded. She stirred, then sat up and shook her head, then opened her eyes.

"Wha—?"

The voice was Angel's, but not the moves or the tones.

"You're blind," I told her. "Cynthia Matalon, I suppose?"

She started at the name. "But—how? Wheah? Who . . . ?"

"My name is Joshua. For now, that's all you need to know. 'Scuse my less-than-fancy speech, too, 'cause I ain't the world's most sophisticated man right now. Let's just say we stuck you here, in that body, and we're gonna keep you just like that until we get a *ton* of questions answered."

She tried to stand up, fell to her knees, then reached out, found a table, and pulled herself to her feet. "This ain't possible," she muttered. "Ain't *nobody* can do this once a Sim's been foahmed! *Cain't be done!*"

"It can, if you get into the right rabbit hole with the right programmer," I told her. "We left alive, and we come back as two different folks. Here, but not *of* here. But that's already too much about me. Don't try walking on your own! You don't know the layout here!"

"Just tuhn on the goddamn *lights!*" she almost screamed.

I got up, walked over to her, and brought a table lamp over that was already on when we'd come back here and gone on our trip. "Feel the lamp," I told her. "Burn your hand on the bulb, for all I care. It's on. I can see you. Them eyes ain't gonna see nobody again, though."

She stopped, felt the lamp but only got close to the heat of the bulb, and pulled back as if it were a snake. "Ah—ah b'lieve you. Can you—can you git me a chaiah?"

I grabbed her and pushed her down on the couch. The idea was to convince her of the hopelessness of her situation and the fact that she either played ball or she was absolutely stuck and totally dependent on me.

"I didn't want to do this," I snarled at her. "I didn't even know it could be done, 'though it's kinda logical. To do this, we put two people I really care about in real danger. One of 'em is now in Stark's holding cell under the big house over there, and you know where I'm talkin' about. The other currently looks like you, or the punk you. Where were you when we picked you up?"

"I—uh, noath of Salem."

"Oregon? Okay. So at least she'll get here."

"If y'all don't mind—just wheah *is* 'heah?' "

"Yakima. Maybe a half mile from you-know-where."

She didn't like that at all. Still, she sat there, thinking for a moment. "Somethin' 'bout you is familiah," she said, frowning. "Ah dunno what or why, and the voice is all wrong, but Ah think we met befoah."

"You're right on that," I told her. "But let's stop this. We're not in an equal position here and I'm pretty damned pissed off. You are blind, a couple of floors up, and in a strange body, and you're within earshot of your worst enemies. You either talk or we play it rough. If you don't talk, we may never be able to get you back, and them enemies already know this address. They just don't know the two they left here are important, yet."

She seemed uncertain, off-balance, which was understandable. "Who *ahre* you?" she asked.

"You first."

"Cynthia Matalon, but you know that."

"I mean deeper. You translated into here, didn't you? How long ago?"

"Almost—Ah guess it was ten, twelve yeahs ago now. Maybe moah. Ah don't wanna say what Ah had to convince that bastahd Stahk just t'get heah in one piece."

"How many came here with him, as opposed to the reincarnation types?"

"*Mah wohd!* You're suah soundin' moah and moah like somebody else! Okay, usin' the names you know, it was Stahk, me, Lee, Ben, and Dorothy."

"What about Walt Slidecker?"

"He didn't come through with us. He and sev'ral othas tried to make a run foah it, fight theah way past and be independent. Dan, Larry, Rita, Jamie, Rob, and Matt, of coahse wuh all paht of that group. Of the bunch, only Walt made it."

That made a lot of sense, although it was interesting that Rob wasn't on Stark's side until this go-round. Latent memories and fears? Fear of another failure? Or was he just being conned by Lee, who otherwise always seemed the weak sister of the duo?

"Who *is* Stark? And the rest of you? What is Stark trying to do?"

She paused a moment. "Heah Ah thought you knew it all! Why, we don't know, not exactly. We'ah the twenty-eight *real* people, that's all. We got some vague ideas and some not-so-vague ones, but it's been like this, ovah and ovah. Theah may be moah of us. We bumped into a couple befoah, and that's made us the twenty-eight."

"Then you can translate or reincarnate without all of us going through at the same time to the same place?"

"Why, of *coahse*, dahlin'. But only if'n you got a way to get out. That's what Stahk's been doin' foah a real long time. He's been *collectin'* us so we don't get away from him. When he's got a powah house like he does heah, he can create a null univuhse."

"A null universe?"

"Shoah. In addition to all the pre-done ones, the one who gets there ahead of the othuhs, they *define* the univuhse. Nobody been able to do it consciously, but that's what Ah think he's aimin' at. See, when you're fuhst into a null, you can't not think of somethin', right? Ah mean, you know the ol' hippo joke. Don't think of a hippopotamus, yoah told, and then you can't think of anything else?"

"I know it. So the first thing that the great computer that traps us all picks out of the first person through's head on which it can hang a logic chain, that's it. If you're a closet Nazi, you might wind up in a world where they won. If you think it would be neat if everybody had tails and lived in trees, that would be it. That about it?"

She nodded. "Yeah, somethin' like that. Only, o'coahse, the joke is that even if you wuh a Nazi, theah's no rule that says you cain't come up the last Jew. Just 'cause it's yoah dream wuld, it doesn't mean yoah gonna be the mastah and not the slave."

Slowly, over the course of the evening, I got the rest of the story, or at least as much as she could give me.

Stark had translated the most and so had the longest memory and the most knowledge of just what was going on, although even he was in the dark as to our exact origins. He was ruthless and as cold as he seemed, but he wasn't just after some universe he could rule as absolute dictator. He had some kind of higher drive, maybe a program patch in and of itself, which was to find and then keep together as many of us as he could.

Some basics held true whether you were reincarnated or translated. Reincarnates did usually swap sex with each new life, just like the Hindus said; translation types tended to stay the same. Those with some kind of emotional bond tended to stick together. Backgrounds and aptitudes tended to run true, within the limits of each new Sim. Rick, Cynthia told me, had been an architect in the previous universe; Kori had been a designer of games and puzzles. Stark, who'd been named Starkweather there, was a private detective for a shadowy international corporation; he'd had a snappy secretary named Roberta who was in love or lust of Starkweather but unhappily married to a man named Lee who discovered after their marriage that he was gay. Little by little, you could put almost all the people we knew into other-worldly roles. It felt creepy, even after all I'd been through and seen and knew.

Cynthia had been from the swamps of Louisiana, or "Loosyana" as she said it; little education, and mixed background. "Ah was what they called a quadroon. One quartuh English, one quartuh French, one quartuh Indian, and one quartuh black. That last was most impoh'tant in that kinda wuhld, though, 'cause, see, aftuh the South won the Battle of Gettysbuhg and swung down and capshud Washington, the whole fight went outta the Noath and they stopped fightin'. A military gov'ment undah McClelland based in Philadelphia let the Confed'racy go."

"You mean it still had *slavery?*"

"No, no. They finally got rid of the last pahts o'that 'bout Nineteen and Thutty Foah. But you had no rights. No education. No nothin'. The whole country was as poah and ignorant as could be, while the old United States went great guns. We was a thuhd-wuhld country, see, and folks like me was the lowest. Ah didn't like cuttin' cane or tendin' rice, so Ah went to Naw'lins and became a whoah. Wasn't too bad, really. Not when you considah the alternatives. Stahkweathah's folks found me, took me to theah big ranch out west. They had some little operation theah, and they had Matthew Brand. Fuhst time Stahk had him, Ah think. We got heah, and Ah became a blue-eyed blond but still had my old accent. Guess Ah will till somebody kills me and Ah can reincarnate clean, huh? Wondah if Ah'd still be some kinda nympho? They said Ah most pro'bly would, but, then, Ah'd be a man that way, wouldn't Ah? Can't really imagine that, 'though ah never saw man *or* woman Ah didn't want to take to bed."

I could see how Walt Slidecker would just *love* her. But who or what had *Walt* been?

"Some kinda soldiah, ah'm sure," she said. "Knows computah stuff, too, 'though it was kinda backwahd last wuhld. He's a tough old buhd, though, ah'll say that, and smaht. Just a so-so lovah, though; he's the kind that bettah at imaginin' than doin', if you know what Ah mean. Ah ran into him less'n a yeah aftah Ah run out on Stahk. Bastahd had me hooked on hoahse and locked away as his little pet. Ah'd had 'nuff of that, and when Ah found somebody who'd be a suppliah Ah ran. Wound up in a brothel outside Vegas. To make a long story shoaht, the brothel went down but we got in good with some drug suppliahs and we kinda made our own way buyin' and sellin' free-lance up and down the west coast. Ah finally got busted, did a little time, and then was paroled out to, well, guess who? Beat the livin' shit outta me fuhst thing. Brought me down to where Brand was doin' his thing, kept me undah obsuhvation, almost like a trophy or somethin'. He didn't know Ah'd luhned readin' and writin', not 'nuff to be great at it, but 'nuff to make do. Matthew, he took a shine to me. Ah dunno. Ah may be the fuhst woman he'd had in livin' memory. Hahd to say. He used that machine, that computah box, on me and somehow Ah wasn't hooked any moah. Ah didn't even want it! Fuhst time since Ah was in mah teens back in th' old wuhld that Ah wasn't hooked. Had t'fake it foah Al's boys. Matthew, he was—well, he was good t'me even when he didn't want anything. Ah nevah had that befoah. Ah'd'a killed foah him!"

But she hadn't had to. One evening he'd come to her and told her that there was a possibility he wouldn't be around anymore. He told her the way out, where some money was in some bearer accounts in various west coast banks, and told her to vanish if he did.

She had even less trouble leaving than she imagined, and there was far more money than she thought she'd ever see in those accounts, all hers because she had the bearer certificates and numbers. And yet, she couldn't bring herself to use the money, not then. It was Matthew's, and he might return and need it. So she'd simply shifted it around, consolidated it, and hidden it deeper than ever, taking just enough for a stake and a new outfit and the Harley.

She'd joined up then with her old girl gang, and run with them for a while, but it wasn't the same, and when two of them had gotten nabbed she realized that sooner or later she was going to wind up right back with Stark again. So she'd quit, gotten the rest of the money, bought a real wardrobe and used wigs until her hair grew back out, and she'd headed back down to Vegas to look into other opportunities.

There she'd found Walt Slidecker, or rather he'd found her, at the Winter Consumer Electronics Show always held each year in Vegas. Walt had a list of who was who in this world, and he had recognized her in spite of everything. He explained that he was setting up a computer company in Seattle and that Brand's operation was shutting down after Brand officially died. "I don't think he died, doll," he'd told her. "I think he's in the net and working on some kind of ambush."

Slidecker had his own parallel operation to Brand's going on, it seemed, under the guise of the Subspace Networking Systems banner. There, he'd gathered some of the computer-aware "real" people like myself who knew nothing of this, and was trying to lure more. And he had an ace in the hole.

Someone—he was convinced it was Brand but wasn't sure—had reached him from outside this universe. Someone had contact via predictable rabbit-hole openings with this world and with possibly others. Slowly but surely he was setting up a rival operation to Stark's, an operation that might allow him to take a lot of us through with a lot of our knowledge to someplace Stark and his allies were not, a place where we could, with the help of the mysterious intelligence inside the rabbit holes, create an alternative way out.

"But you still hav'ta live by the rules heah, dahlin'," Cynthia commented. "And Walt got skunked by them Chinese folks."

"Singaporese, I think."

"Whatevah. So he decided to take his money, and mine, and we'd set up a private operation maybe well away from heah. We nevah got the full chance. Deah ol' Al found us out, got all the othuhs that Walt had gathud by suckerin' 'em in down theah with a reopened project, and nothin' we could do could keep 'em from goin'. Ah guess Ah shoulda come right out 'stead of tryin' to frighten 'em away, but Al hadn't found me yet and he didn't know 'bout Walt, so we couldn't affoahd to tell 'em the truth. By the time we wuh ready to set up and go, everybody was in Yakima."

We'd gone well into the wee hours of the morning now, and while I didn't worry in the slightest about Wilma in that body and with that kind of weaponry, I couldn't help but be almost frantic at the idea of Angel inside that cell, and what might happen if she were interrogated or whatever Stark planned. Worst of all, I was afraid he was just going to kill her.

There was only one more piece of information, and it was a big one. What Matalon said all made sense, except, of course, it explained nothing. Who were we? Why were we all here? Were these truly just Sims or were the billions of other people somehow real as even they, like Chun Yee, thought they were? What was Stark trying to do? What was Brand's idea? And where the hell was the exit and what was outside?

Minor little points.

But before we went further, before I could even accept that Matalon was telling me the whole truth, I had to know the answer to what I'd seen.

"Miss Matalon—"

"Look, call me Cindy or call me Sugah, which was mah 'professional' name, but cut the fohmal stuff. The last thing Ah can evah be is fohmal."

"Okay—Cindy. I have to tell you that my wife and I had a lot of experiences, too. We got into a rabbit hole and met a caterpillar there big as we were. He sent us back, totally different, to a job he didn't define."

"Sounds like *Alice in Wondahland.* Ah *loved* that movie! So did Matthew. He told me once it'd been made into a book, too."

I cleared my throat nervously. "Um, yeah. Well, I thought the caterpillar was Brand, and Walt thinks *his* friend is Brand. But I saw Walt over by the campus a year or so ago, with you in the neighborhood but not in sight there, and he had a small army of little aliens or shell-less turtles or whatever, and they were going to attack the campus. A family came by on the road, spotted them, and Walt mowed them down. Mowed down men, women, and kids, and didn't even think about it."

She looked puzzled. "Ah know 'bout the Boojums; they come out of the rabbit hole we opened up noahth heah a while back. But shoot *kids*? You say you *saw* this? With yoah own eyes?"

I paused a moment. No, we didn't see it with our own eyes. "Not exactly. We were having visions. The visions pretty much worked out as real. We—my wife and I—both saw it in one of those visions. Later on, when we tried to get to the campus, Walt had taken the gatehouse and one of your creature friends jumped on our car and tried to stop us. That I saw with my own eyes."

She shook her head. "Ah—Ah can't explain it, but we all have visions, or dreams, once in a while. You, you two, you got all this powah. You find me and bring me hundred of miles in a flash, stick me in one body while yoah friend goes into mine and yoah wife goes into yoah friend's and all. Walt uses somethin' less neat and tidy but he can sense when the rabbit holes open and he can keep 'em stable. Now, he did take the Boojums and try a straight-in attack 'bout a yeah, maybe two, ago just to see how strong they wuh. Didn't get nhowheah. Five yahds past that gatehouse, it was like hittin' a

brick wall, and any Boojum that touched it just fried in a
flash. Now, Ah wasn't theah, but Ah seen Walt in action
befoah, and Ah just don't remember a Walt who could do
what you said, even if he believed they wuh all illusion and
wuhn't really theah. You know how it is. You can know foah
a fact that all this is just in yoah head and yoah brain still
says it's real. Besides, weah did you say this vision was suppose t'be?"

"Along the dirt road that short-cuts to the cannery, adjacent
to the campus."

"Theah! See? Ah know his plan. They come right in and
up that theah company road, unloaded the Boojums on eithah
side and into the forest, and moved up on wheels. They wuh
nevah on that road. Wouldn't make sense. All the defense
stuff on them fences would be *muhdah* to crack."

And, she was right, of course. But if Walt really wasn't
where we saw him, and if he didn't do what we thought,
then . . .

Then somebody else was throwing visions at us. Somebody who knew we could receive them, and somebody who
wanted to make damned sure that we'd either run to Stark for
protection or run like hell, both of which we did in spades.
Either way was okay, but we wouldn't run to Cindy, and certainly not to Walt.

Somebody over there was as if not more powerful than we
were. And now they had Angel.

"Who or what are the Boojums, Cindy?"

"Beats me. Walt said he met 'em in a past wuhld someplace wheah they tried to rescue some of their own from
some soht of a flyin' saucah oah somethin' like that. We
don't know if the'ah real like we ahe or not, but they can
move in the holes. Not just them, eithah. Some othahs as
well. Creepy things." She shivered. "They like Walt, though.
Dunno why."

"Where is Walt now?"

She shrugged. "Tried to get him on the phone for days.

He's been pickin' up stuff by sailin' his yacht up and down, and he's probably out of cell-phone range. Ah was headed up to Vashon Island to see if Ah could figgah wheah he was or luhn it from other folks theah in case he said somethin'."

I sighed. "Great. Just great. Well, one way or the other, we're gonna hav'ta do something. We can't do much until Wilma gets here, and if you've got the number we'll keep trying Walt."

"Glad to have some friends," she said, sounding relieved.

"We're not friends, let alone allies, yet," I warned her. "I've been told very convincing lies a lot of the time here and I'm not sure what's what even now."

"Well, bettah make up yoah mind, honey, 'cause you bettah figgah that yoah deah wife's dead by now, or stuffed in one of them little black boxes by now, and she seems to have been the only one with enough powah to maybe play them to a draw."

I didn't like to even think like that, not yet. But, here was a supposed survivor from the last incarnation, somebody who was *there*, maybe with Stark.

"Cindy—you mentioned Rick before. You remember him?"

"Shoah do. Nice-lookin' guy, always nice to me. It was too bad."

"Yeah, too bad. Cindy—how did Rick die? Do you know? Did Stark do something more than just kill him?"

"I—I dunno. I s'pose so, 'cause he sho' 'nuff was dead when we got out to heah. I—I heah tell that theah was a big deal to the old project. Something 'bout conditionin'. Puttin' folks heads into them theah boxes so they acted strange, dif'rent, like good little boys and guhls."

I knew exactly what she was saying. We'd worried about it with this much-more-elelaborate project as well. The Brand Boxes' little universes were in every way as real to those who went in as, well, this big one had been to us, still *was* to us, and subjective time could be regulated as well. Cory had spent a week or more in one, yet here it'd been only hours.

Suppose you got put in one as a slave, as a totally different, subservient, submissive type of person? Even one in constant pain or something like that, who could only relieve the pain if they conformed? Make it seem to last weeks, months, years, perhaps. Bring them out for checks. When it took, *then* you killed them—and thus changed and determined their personality type in the reincarnation.

Riki had been smart, independent, you name it, but she'd been totally, completely nonviolent. She couldn't even swat flies without feeling guilt, and she was almost manic about not having weapons or anything else around. She couldn't even take revenge against somebody who'd harmed her. It just wasn't in her. That was why she'd found comfort in large groups, like the commune, and almost never even went out otherwise without the company of somebody big and strong that she trusted.

All that power, and Angel couldn't have killed or maimed, either. That much carried over. Not a coward, not in the sense we all use the term, but a nearly totally pacifistic personality, someone who could expose herself to extreme danger for a cause but could not harm even the one endangering her.

Conditioning? She'd unhesitatingly put herself back in Stark's clutches, although she might not have understood the risks of it. That took guts. But how much could anybody take? And what was the conditioning they were doing over there to her, possibly even now?

# XII

# RATS IN A RABBIT HOLE

Cindy, or whoever she was, had collapsed, tired and exhausted, and I just napped, waiting for Wilma, who didn't get in until midday.

"You know, I think I could get used to lookin' like this," Wilma commented as she kicked off the boots and collapsed into a padded chair. "I swear even this look turns more guys on than off considerin' how much I was hit on, and yet it's kinda threatening, too. And you can never have any idea of what it's like to come up Oregon and halfway over in Washington and not be recognized as Indian. Man! The pressure's just *off*!" She chuckled. "Now, if this could also be a man, there'd be no place closed to me."

"That's easy," I told her. "Just let yourself get killed. Next time you'll be a man, but not necessarily in this universe, and you won't remember this except maybe in your nightmares."

"Nope. The price is too high. Get anything from her?"

"A lot, but not all that I'd hoped. If anything, what's real even in the sense we understand it now and what's not has been blurred some more." I paused. "She's sure that Angel's either dead or stored in one of the Brand Boxes by now, though." As briefly as I could, I summarized the interrogation.

Wilma whistled. "All that power Angel had? I can't believe they could do much to her she didn't want done."

"I don't think she could use it once she wasn't in Angel's body. I think it's part of the program that created or changed us. You didn't have that program."

"What about you? You're made of the same stuff, and you can see and feel it, and, most important, in the last day or two a lot more of your old self has come through. You're speaking better and you seem a lot more comfortable with all the tech parts than you did."

"Yes, I know. I think even Matalon has me fingered for who I was. Thing is, though, I haven't been able to use that power. Not any of it. I've had the same exposure, got revised in the same program sequence in the rabbit hole, yet it's just a strong green glow or a humming like standing next to a power line or something. Nothing more. I've begun to think only women can use it."

"Nope. There's a lot of difference, more than folks like to admit, but there isn't that much difference. No magic corner of the brain—nothing like that. And I can't see hormones having much to do with it. Nope, what's the other big difference between you two before and now?"

I thought a moment. "I guess it would be that she seemed to grow dumber and I got my smarts back."

Wilma sat up, thinking. "Nope. But maybe you're close. It freaked her out and she closed off her old self, and you reached for your old self. She wasn't dumb, though—she was pretty damned smart. What she shut out was knowledge she'd had before. Ignorance isn't stupidity. No, see—the old you, either of you, was really the product of being born, growing up, education, experience, all that. Sure you had all the old experiences of past lives, but they were super-buried and hardly count. But when you physically changed, in the rabbit hole, you both became new people. People not entirely of this world or the products of growing up rather than a program. Angel accepted, even embraced it. You fought it."

"You mean I have to reject all of Cory, dumb down to Joshua's lowest common denominator, and let the stuff wash over me and turn me blind?"

"I don't think so. Remember, you get the best results with this when you can wipe your mind clean, just drift along? The other way was during a real emotional experience—fear, or making love, or like that. Didn't you say that during those times it felt as if you were one organism?"

"Yes, but what's the point? She's not here, at least mentally, now."

Wilma reached in and took the pistol out of its holster and hefted it. "Guns don't kill people, people kill people. Isn't that what they say?"

"I've heard it, but I don't necessarily go along with it. It's people with guns who kill people."

"Okay, but forget the politics. Angel's body is the weapon, prepped and prepared. It needs a recharge, I suspect, but think of it like this gun. Matalon can't fire it—she's just there on the physical level, as it were, able to run the routine parts of the thing but not access what Angel learned to use. You may not be a weapon yourself, but I bet you could use it if you could get to the controls."

I saw where she was going, but I wasn't sure it wasn't wishful thinking. Still, "What good would it do if I could?"

"We got no chance now. They'll hunt us down and kidnap or kill us or, if we somehow luck out, they'll wait us out. Staying where we are isn't an option, much as I'd love to fool around with this body for a while. Running means either they catch us or we sink. You tried that once yourself. It doesn't work. So we can't run, we can't hide for long, and we can't sit here. What's that leave?"

"Surrender?"

"Don't be an ass! *Attack!* My ancestors had the same situation, you know."

"Your ancestors lost the war," I pointed out.

She shrugged. "Well, yeah, but not without one hell of a fight. And some of our objectives were attained. There's still some of our people on our ancestral lands here in Washington, Idaho, and Oregon. The Nez Percé's Chief Joseph, who'd never fought a battle before, fought a two-thousand-mile retreat against Civil War veteran troops and generals and only lost, just barely, a few miles from Canada, because he had to take all the women and children with him as well. We're the only family, the only clan, we got right now. Nothing to slow us down."

"But—three of us against all of them? Even if I could use the power, I don't think—"

"Then don't. Act! It's not 'all of them.' Almost all of them are toadies, captives, or just going with a perceived winner. There's only one or two we'll have to really worry about in there. Take out Stark and it all collapses. The two of us will take out the minor irritants."

Minor irritants. Like Marines with semiautomatic weapons, super security systems, and a security staff that acted like children of the Nazi SS? Yeah, so simple.

I looked around the room. "I'd say 'let's sleep on it' except that I suddenly feel very vulnerable here. You know, I've been here for hours and it never occurred to me that anybody who could take *you* out could bug this place and certainly would be watching it."

She suddenly jumped up and nodded. "Shit! Shoulda thought of that! Broad daylight now. Not a great time to make a move, I guess. And the only wheels we got are the two choppers. Damn! This will take some thinking!"

The fact was, though, there wasn't any way out. If they suspected that Joshua and/or Angel were their kind and worth taking, they could have us staked out, waiting for more to come to us and bag us all at once. That would explain why they hadn't taken us before, or when we were unconscious.

Or, they might well have gone with their first inclination,

as our own out-of-body roaming seemed to suggest, that we weren't part of the crew. That put Wilma in the most danger—she might be spotted as Cynthia Matalon in spite of the punked-up look—but it still didn't leave us a real window of opportunity.

"We all get some rest," I told Wilma at last. "I'm dead, she's still out, and I think you're overdue. We'll rig up something so that if they come in, at least we can get a shot at them or something. You're the most obvious target anyway."

"They won't get me again without a real fight," Wilma promised.

I took a deep breath. "Once we're rested, maybe after nightfall today, we will see what if anything we have on our side. Then will be the only chance we might have to survive this."

I had little trouble getting to sleep, but a lot of trouble with bad dreams. Dreams of Angel, or Riki, near naked but done up like some *Playboy* centerfold, alone in a large room filled with leering, violent-looking men, all of whom demanded obedience, satisfaction, servility, and all the rest, all yesterday, and all of whom beat her, violated her repeatedly, and were never, ever satisfied, unable to resist, unable to get away, exhausted, and, bit by bit, all will being drained from her big brown eyes. . . .

I was finally awakened by the sound of a chair falling over, and I jumped up with a start and opened my eyes to see Cindy Matalon picking herself up off the floor. Wilma, too, had been awakened and had a pistol in her hand, but when she saw who it was she put her finger to her lips.

Matalon froze for some time, waiting for one of us to stir, but when she heard nothing, she finally slowly and carefully got up and became even slower and more deliberate in her actions.

I kind of figured that nobody with that kind of background

and guts was going to be willing to let even blindness stop her, so she'd remained stark naked, and I'd taken care to hide her clothing on top of a dresser so she'd remain so. She didn't dare rummage too much in the bedroom; it would certainly have awakened one of us.

The place was filled with a damp chill, and I could see she was very uncomfortable, but I had to discover what the hell she thought she was doing.

At first it seemed as if she were inventorying the place, trying to find everything that was there or at least memorize things, but, after a couple of minutes, Wilma gestured to me the obvious: she was looking for the telephone. Of course, the phone was one floor down and outside the apartment, but she couldn't know that.

She was, however, beginning to give up that search, and she turned and went back, ever so slowly, toward the hangers just inside the door. My sheepskin coat was there, but it was a tent for somebody her size, and she went back over to the spot on the floor where Wilma had just thrown the black leather motorcycle jacket she'd worn. She picked it up, slipped it on, and then checked it out. It was still big for that body, but okay, and because her original body was several inches taller than Angel's the coat came down three or four inches below the crotch. She was also going nuts with Angel's four feet of brown hair, even if it was thin and more like the longest ponytail in history, but she managed to wrap it around her shoulders almost like a boa. She was actually thinking of going out like that!

Both of us got up quietly, then approached her. "You'd freeze to death in that outfit before you got downstairs, provided you didn't break your neck," I said.

She jumped, then sighed and took off the coat and let it drop. "Damn! Ah shoulda known!"

"Where did you think you were going?" I asked her.

"Anywheah but heah," she responded flatly. "No way Ah want to meet Mistah Albuht Stahk again, not in *this* life.

Ah'd go right into one of them boxes and come out who
knows what? Uh-uh."

"You're that scared of it? Even if the alternative is to be
blind and in that body for the rest of your life?" I asked her.
"I mean, you wouldn't get ten feet out there, barefoot, bare-
assed, and blind."

"Don't count me out. Ah huhd the pay phone bein' used
downstaihs and Ah got me a quatah! 'Nuff for long-distance
collect. Maybe Walt, if not Walt, then Ah got othah friends."

"Yeah, friends who don't know anybody who looks or
sounds like you do now," I pointed out. "You have a better
chance if we can get tapped back into that power over there."

"Powah! That's all you yap about! Damn it, they know
what that powah can do, too, and they been at it a whole hell
of a lot longah than y'all have! Even if you get it, you'ah
gonna be fuhst-time shootahs 'gainst practiced professional
killahs! Don't y'all undahstand? *You can't win!* You can't
beat 'em! We tried, and all we got was shot up and on the
run. Y'all tried it last time and look what happened to you!"

Wilma came out, slipping on and zipping up the leather
outfit and looking incredibly pleased that it just slipped on
and zipped with no effort at all. Never before did I see someone who really *could* have an orgasm from putting on clothes,
but I could imagine what the original short and chubby
Wilma probably had to fight to make most anything fit.

"Going someplace yourself?" I asked her.

Wilma shrugged. "Thought I'd go across the street and
pick up some quick eats. Besides, it'll give me a chance to
see if anybody's obviously watching us."

"You think they won't snatch you?"

"Not yet. Not until they're sure that her friend won't show
up, I think. If they do, well, come and get me again!" She
winked at me. "I can take care of myself."

I worried a lot about her when she left, but I didn't try and
stop her. That would have been as impossible as stopping
Angel.

I turned on Cynthia instead. "What do I have to do to you now? I'm putting all these clothes where you can't get at them. I suppose you could wear a bedsheet, but I think you wouldn't get far. The cops would pick you up if you didn't break your neck first, and, when that happened, Stark would get word and be more than curious, I think. And I'm getting more than a little angry. Do I have to demonstrate how utterly helpless you are?"

The fact was, I couldn't do it. I could never have hurt her, at least not unless she was trying to hurt or betray Wilma or me, but she didn't have to know that.

"What are you gonna do aftah breakfast?" she asked me.

"Angel said, once we were within that field, that we were never cut off from it again. I want to test that, to see if, somehow, we can get some of that control back."

Wilma was back in about fifteen minutes, much to my relief, with bags of goodies to eat. She then went over to a closet where she'd stuck the Harley's saddlebags and started going through them while eating a Danish.

After a while, she gestured for me to come over there, and I did so, leaving Cynthia at the table.

"Nice little pharmacy in there," Wilma whispered. "Good thing I never got hauled over by the cops. All sorts of stuff, but you see this in the vial here?"

I nodded. It was a clear liquid beneath a sealed stopper with a label on the vial in blue handwriting. AZUR, it seemed to say.

"The usual stuff here—but this is one of those designer drugs. I've heard of it, saw TV reports on it, but never before have I actually seen it. Supposed to have a super high that puts you somewhere on Venus."

"Yeah, so?" I didn't like drugs of any kind.

"Got a syringe here. Bunches of 'em. Maybe a couple ccs of this in her rump and after a little while she's not resisting us anymore?"

I didn't like it, but it was an idea. I held up a hesitant finger, then went back over to Matalon. "Cindy, you have an interesting supply kit. What's that A-Z-U-R?"

"Huhd 'bout it. Nevah had it. Supposed to be somethin' else, though."

I thought fast. "Well, we have to go out for a little while, and we can't take you with us where we have to go and we can't leave you alone here after your getaway stunt. That means either tying and gagging you for who knows how long, or some more-enjoyable alternative. You want to try this stuff?"

"Huh? Oh—Ah see. Send me off into cloud nine. Well, Ah'd rathah do that than get tied and maybe you get picked up and Ah wind up dead heah."

"What's the dose?"

"Five ccs direct into a vein would do it for a couple houahs, Ah guess. That's how it's sold."

I looked over at Wilma, who nodded, got out and fixed a syringe, and filled it with ten ccs of the fluid. If Cynthia said five, it was best to be sure.

*Besides, it wasn't like we were really doing it,* I thought sourly. *Everything we think we know is wrong, isn't it?*

Cindy allowed herself to be led back to the bed again, and Wilma, who'd had some little experience with needles helping out on the reservation, looked at the arm, found a vein, and stabbed.

"*Ow!* That huhts!"

But aside from a tiny bruise, it all seemed to go in without killing her.

Now we waited. The drug really didn't take long to kick in; maybe a couple of minutes before it was obvious, with that big, dumb smile and the slow, sexy movements and self-caressing. Wilma bent down and ran a fingernail gently down Cynthia's abdomen and you'd have thought the drugged woman had died and gone to heaven. She also began lightly to sing, mostly nonsense stuff without even a solid tune, and was clearly *way* out.

I lay down beside her and began to caress her myself and

she responded incredibly, and I tried to continue while clearing my mind as much as possible of almost everything else
and just getting very, very turned on. Emotion, unthinking
emotion, letting it flow until you caught the connection, that
was the key. If only it could work. . . .

Now Wilma was on the other side of me, doing to me what
I was doing to Angel's happily drugged body, and it was
dark, very dark, and very quiet, and very still.

I have no way of piecing together what happened next;
only that somehow I felt myself thinking only of Angel, and
suddenly becoming incredibly, powerfully aggressive, or was
it Cynthia doing it? It was so intense, so monstrously intense,
that it crowded out all thought, all pain, all physical senses
save only the one at hand. . . .

I was in Angel. . . . No, I *was* Angel! I could feel it, feel
the body, feel every sensation, feel the long hair whipping,
feel the others.

There was a crackling like an electrical current crossing a
gap, and I suddenly felt a monstrous, body-sized orgasmic
sensation that just went on and on and on. The *power*, the
enormous *power* just surged within me, and by extension
reached to my two companions as well.

*Nothing was real!* Nothing but ourselves and the pulsing
and the power.

I slid off the others and off the bed and got to my feet. I
was Angel, in Angel's body, yet was I not also going to free
Angel?

Cynthia was now in the bearded man's body, but subject
to my commands, my will. Wilma was still in Cynthia's
body, but, again, there was a corner of her that moved only
through me.

We turned, and walked through the door, then through the
very wall of the apartment, out into the chill of the night, a
chill we barely felt and totally discounted.

In the distance we could see the pulsing blob of energy,
and from it a finger, like a direct wire, leading from it to me,

and then from me to the other two. I could see through their eyes, hear through their ears as well as my own, and I could be all three of us at once.

In a flash that seemed instantaneous, the three of us were walking down a two-lane road in the dark, the cold asphalt against our bare feet feeling solid and cold but discountable. Ahead was a gatehouse, with two guards in it, but there was nothing inside the guards, and to Angel's own sense, uncontaminated by vision, they were mere formulas, ciphers, and very fragile.

I did not comprehend the language, something akin to a binary-level assembly language, but I could read the equations and total them out, and produce an inverse equation. One guard winked out, and then the other, leaving the guardpost empty. I knew then that I could not be Angel, but I did not dwell on who I might be.

I did the same to the energized gate, and it ceased to exist even as we touched it and walked past.

There wasn't much more distance now to being within the energy bubble itself, which seemed like something totally *alive*.

The moment we entered, though, I sensed that our presence was known, and I realized that, unlike the previous night, our bodies were not lying there back in the apartment. We were actually *here*, in as much of the flesh as we really possessed in this plane.

Four young Marines rushed from an area beyond the parking lot and toward us, submachine guns at the ready. As soon as they saw us, the astonishment showing in their faces, I put out a finger and projected *"Stop! You do not want to do this! You do not even see us! Take over at the guardhouse. Let no one in or out!"*

They looked momentarily puzzled, then ran past us on the double and down the road.

The entire mansion was lit up in the darkness, and I looked it over and sensed perhaps a half-dozen true ones inside. I dispatched Wilma to the building to ferret them out and, if possible, deal with them. None were the ones I sought, but they might be trouble if not dealt with.

Cindy and I headed for the lab building in back. Not only were there armed guards all over the place, there were codes, booby traps, and alarms, all keyed to that fancy electronic card system. We no longer believed that the card system existed, though, so it made no effort to stop us, and the young Marine on the desk just inside smiled and nodded to us as we walked in and went back to his crossword puzzle.

We stopped bothering to have doors open for us; that was too much belief. Instead, we walked right through them as if they were not there, which, in fact, they were not.

I dispatched Cindy, in my body, to go back and check out the medical and administrative and prep areas on the one side. I was going for the lab.

It was strange that I was in many ways in three places at once, but it didn't bother me a bit. I did not, in fact, think of it at all one way or the other. It just *was*. I had two objectives, and those two were the only things our minds allowed at that point. We were to find Angel and free her if she was not dead, and we were to find the bad people who did it to her and punish them.

Dan Tanaka was sitting at a conference table in the main lab along with Ben Sloan and Jamie Cholder, his two chief programming assistants, Morgan Chun Yee, and two young men who were not real and thus irrelevant. They were talking, even arguing, over something when one of them looked up and saw me standing there. All conversation suddenly ceased.

"Who the hell is *that*?" Tanaka asked, his jaw dropping a bit.

"It's the blind girl that lived with the Indian!" Sloan exclaimed. "Hit security!"

One of the aides hit the alarm button, but nothing happened. I didn't want it to happen.

The other aide suddenly leaped from his chair and came straight at me, but I was ready. He barely crossed half the three-yard distance before ceasing to exist.

"Fascinating," Chun Yee said. "One of your own, perhaps?"

"Not one *I* ever knew about!" Tanaka snapped. "Where'd she come from? And where'd she get that power?"

The mathematician waved a hand around. "Right here. She's drawing what she needs. Would you like to try dealing with her or would you be better off asking what she wants?"

"I want Angel," I told them in a flat, firm voice.

"Angel?" Tanaka frowned. "Who's Angel?"

"*She* is!" Sloan cried. "Damn it, that's *her* name! I saw it on the surveillance sheets!"

"This is crazy!" Tanaka muttered. "How can we give you to you?"

I turned and looked at the life-support modules. There were a fair number that were active. More than any of my collective experiences had ever seen.

I started to scan the LSMs for data, but they only could tell me what was being done there, not the identity of the person inside. The only way I could tell for sure was to either disconnect and bring them out, which might be dangerous to them, or scan where they were. I was about to do this when I suddenly became aware that nobody sitting at the table was moving or now attempting to do anything at all. In fact, Jamie Cholder was sipping some herbal tea and just watching with the same kind of academic curiosity you might have watching an experiment through one-way glass, and Dan Tanaka had relaxed and even lit a forbidden cigarette.

*Trap.* Scan in there and you might get sucked in.

"Which is the body of the woman who lived with me?" I asked them. I could see that Tanaka, at least, was crestfallen that his initial trap hadn't been sprung.

"I don't know who you mean," he responded, sounding honest. "I don't—"

I lost my temper and a stream of energy lashed out from me and struck him like a fist. He was slammed backward out of the chair and into the back panel, then collapsed onto the floor. Sloan started to see to him, then stopped and looked nervously at me. I nodded, and he knelt down.

"How did you do that?" Cholder asked, for the first time seeming a little afraid.

"*You* know," I responded. "If you didn't, you wouldn't be here. You'd be in one of *those*. Now, look it up. Tell me who is in each of those and what sort of worlds they are in."

"Jesus!" Sloan swore. "I think he's dead!"

That seemed to motivate Cholder a bit more, and she turned and looked at the computer screen. "The Standishes are in one and two, patriarchal world, obedience to God and high priests, that kind of thing. Rob Garnett and Larry Santee are three and four, slave girls being 'seasoned,' it says." At least she said that with some distaste. "Five is Betty Harker-Simonson, six is Wilma Starblanket, both male slaves being 'broken in' in Zanzibar, circa 1780."

Indoctrinate and then kill. The sexes reversed, they figured.

"Disconnect Six," I ordered. *"Now!"*

While I had been busy in the actual lab, Cindy had gone back toward the medical area. She'd found Sally Prine in prep, probably for LSM Seven, and a man, also out in another room, that none of us knew but who was certainly one of us.

Suddenly there was a sound behind her, she turned, and there was a sensation of being hit hard and then nothing.

I was alarmed, and called to Wilma at the mansion. *Did you see that?*

*Yes. We should get together as quickly as possible and find out what is going on!*

Sloan seemed to know, though. He saw my expression and smiled a little smile I was tempted to wipe off his face.

"Go ahead! You can do to me and her what you did to

Tanaka, but what good will it do you? I could see by your reaction that something happened. I could feel it. You're not
all-powerful after all, are you?"

"Never mind the taunts! Do as I say, or you will both die
and then I will do it myself."

"No," Jamie Cholder said flatly. She was nervous, maybe
even scared, but she was also gutsy. "If you could do it yourself, you would have. You must kill us both here and now or
leave us, because if you do not kill us, we will turn off the
power to those modules and those inside will be locked in.
That is what will happen anyway if you do kill us. It will
simply take a little longer. I am not frightened of death. I've
died too many times before, and not dying hasn't been all
that profitable to me, either."

I was really angry now, angry and also concerned that
Cindy had been somehow taken in spite of the power and that
Wilma was sensing even greater power now coming her way,
power she could not define as yet.

*Wilma! Through the walls at high speed! Come now!*

Something reached out for Wilma, something of unimagin-
able power, but she slipped away and was suddenly at my
side in the lab.

*Get our own and split!* Wilma shot to me. *Something here
has more power than we do!*

Jamie stared at Wilma, who, of course, appeared as Cynthia Matalon. "I remember *you*!" she said. "I always thought
that was your best look!"

I whirled and green flame shot from me and enveloped
Jamie Cholder, who screamed and then seemed to turn to energy herself before winking out.

"You're next," I told Sloan. "Five seconds to bring her out
of it or I'll have to just destroy this whole damned lab and
you and them with it. Better death now than some kind of bizarre slavery next time!"

There was a sudden blinding vision before us, as if all of
space-time had ripped, and there was a jagged hole right

there in which stood, almost but not quite to size, Al Stark. He had a simple shotgun in his hands, and he was standing with both barrels pressing right against the face of Joshua.

"You want power?" he asked. "Why not come and see some? Or should I blow his brains out first? Then we'll do a disconnect on the LSMs so everybody's there in their Brand Boxes until collected for the next trip. How's that? Or would you rather be a duck?"

"Huh?"

"C'mon! See what kind of fun this can be! Just—both of you! Come to me!"

We were there in an instant, although it wasn't immediately clear where "there" was. A room, but not the padded cell. A fairly large room—maybe the meeting hall, rarely used, over in Building B.

Al Stark stood there with the shotgun, smiled, then let it come up from the figure unconscious on the floor. He tossed it away, and it clattered and echoed in the empty hall.

"Well, well, well!" he said, looking and sounding not the least bit worried. "So, let's see—Sugar, baby! Good to see ya! I missed your company!"

Wilma gave him a sour grin. "*Not* Sugar, and *not* your baby, either," she responded in a voice that clearly was not Matalon's. "You want her—you got her. She's in there." She pointed to Joshua's form, now slightly stirring.

Stark looked down at the naked man and shook his head. "What a pity. That's a very good trick, by the way. I haven't any idea how you do that. Everybody's got some kind of talent with this shit, though, when they learn it exists and how to use it. Slidecker, for example, opens his damned rabbit holes and conjures up alien armies. Trouble is, they aren't worth a damn and can't fight worth beans, but they're sure scary. And Sugar—Cynthia, whatever you want to call her. Got that neat trick of freezing a few frames of time. Not really useful, unless you've got a gun on her and she's fully conscious, but kind of neat. Now you come along. Not the first group effort, but I admit the first one I can remember who can switch around. I do hope you'll switch her back here. I've seen her in earlier incarnations and Sugar's a horrible man." He sighed and stepped away from Matalon. "So, if that's Sugar, and you, I assume, are either Joshua or Angel, so that makes the other here—"

"Wilma Starblanket," she said evenly. *Self-confident bastard*, she added to me.

He smiled. "I heard that! Well, I have a right to be self-confident. I've been some variation of what you see for eleven lives now. Several hundred years of subjective time. Um—if you're Starblanket, then who's in number six?"

"You're the know-it-all," I shot back. "You figure it out."

"Whichever one, Angel or Joshua, that you're not. Hmmmm . . . I make the gang as all here, at least as far as this poor world is concerned. That means you either got here from another, or . . . *Wait* a minute!" He scratched below his ear and smiled that devil's smile again. "Why, hello, Cory! That must make Angel to be Riki. Boy! You really had us fooled there for a minute, but it had to be. It just *had* to be. Funny—I doubt if I'd have recognized you one bit in the Joshua body, but there, in Angel's, well, you look very familiar. I knew you a lot longer that way than the other."

*Cory!* I *was* Cory! And Joshua! And Kori! And—who else? I couldn't remember all of them, but there were snippets here and there of lots and lots of lives, lots more faces in the mirror.

"What is wrong with you, Stark?" I asked him. "What kind of power trip are you on? Conditioning people to slavish obedience, to be fearful, to be under your control. Killing off anybody who disagrees with you that you can't trap. Suckering in some of the others. Why not just become Hitler and gas whoever you don't like? Or Napoléon and go out to conquer the world?"

"You've got me a little wrong," Stark replied. "I'm not the bad guy here."

"No bad guy ever thinks he is the bad guy," Wilma commented. "Hitler was a nonsmoking, nondrinking vegetarian who thought he was advancing the human race. The same General Howard who stopped the Nez Percé from escaping used his own money to build Howard University, the first great university for African Americans. Slavery was awful. Destroying, killing, and looting Indian lands, that was okay."

"I wish things were as simplistic as you think," Al Stark replied. "Look, I could have taken you on right away. Maybe I should have, from my long-term point of view. I'm going to miss Cholder and Tanaka. They were the only remaining people who worked directly with Brand on the nuts and bolts of this. I'm not doing this for power—I got more power than you could dream of without even taking my clothes off and it's still a bore. It's my job."

That floored us. "Your *job*?"

"Yes. I'm chief of security for the whole project."

"*Whose* project? You mean you know what all this is about?"

He shook his head. "I don't know who, and I don't know why. I only know what I am and that I am here to do a job. You know the system, or you've figured it out, which is amazing. We're all trapped here in some kind of super-computer, which is feeding us such exquisitely detailed existences that we believe them. We can't *not* believe them. But we know better, don't we? I don't know who we are or how we got in here, but I suspect it's some much-more-advanced variation of what you see in the lab right here. Chun Yee, who ranks right there with Einstein and Hawkings, thinks we might well be just a master program from which all others flow. I don't know. Is that any different than God creating the Heavens and the Earth and then sitting back and watching it run? We all know that something went wrong, anyway. Either we didn't come out, or we got totally absorbed into the system, or there were bugs, or, maybe somebody deliberately sabotaged things. I think it was sabotage myself, and not just because I'm security. There *is* somebody out to get us. They've been tracking us down and picking us off one by one. That's what I'm doing. I'm collecting everyone, bringing everyone together, finding the strays and stragglers. *I'm saving your damned lives, again and again!* And look at the thanks I get!"

"Who is tracking us, picking us off, Stark?" I asked him. "You sound paranoid as hell and willing to make us all over into mush-headed obedient automatons in the name of saving us. I'm not sure I want to be saved, if that's the price, and I'm not at all convinced I'm being saved from anybody anyway."

Stark looked a little crazed, but not completely so. "Buy 'em, trade 'em, collect the whole set! My object isn't to make any life in here a bed of roses for any of you! Of course, if you help, if you don't fight me or get in the way, then you get to live and come with me. No programming required. The rest—*I can't have you fighting me!* It wastes too much time, effort, and energy! That's all I'm doing. If you'd been at this as long as me, you'd understand! Keeping you all together, protected, safe, until I can find the way *out* of this!" He sighed. "I tried alternatives, but they didn't work. Riki was independent, wasn't she, but she still opposed me! And got you to oppose me, too! Rob—even love couldn't do it! Sugar, here—a great piece of ass and no problems, and look at what she turned into! There's no other way."

"Have you tried asking?" Wilma put in. "Have you put the case honestly in front of people? Can you prove that if I'm not with you I'm dead meat?"

"The—the others. They aren't human. Not like us. They don't care. I'm not sure what they want, but they're tracking us down, and what they leave isn't pretty. They're looking for something, somebody, some knowledge or skill, and they don't care about anybody else. They've got a traitor running their operation and I have to stop him!"

Cynthia had recovered by now, but sat there on the floor,

looking a little dazed and not at all sure she liked the body she was in. Still, the face frowned at Stark's last ravings. "You mean Walt?"

"Yes, Walt. Dear Walter. Him and his nightmares. Him and his *creatures*. I hadn't known they could get into a world until now. So far we've met them only in the rabbit holes. He's growing stronger. We must be strong, too."

"It wasn't Walt that blew away that family," I pointed out. "You came up with that vision."

Stark started pacing, and he shook his head back and forth almost violently. "No, no, no, no, no! That wasn't my vision! He did it! He did exactly what you saw! We found them, just where you said. Then we were under attack by the Boojums. You spoiled their surprise attack by that vision and that report. They had to attack where we ran into them, and that was well away from the compound. We were able to keep them out. *As God is my witness I did not fake that!*"

I didn't like this. I didn't like it one bit. In one sense, it left me just as confused as ever. But if I was confused, Cynthia was even more so.

"Ah spent all that time with Walt, and talked to them critters, too. Funny types, but they ain't evil. And Walt—Ah just cain't b'lieve that Walt could do such a thing!"

"Then you don't know Colonel Slidecker. I don't know what he's a colonel from, but he's at least that," Stark insisted.

I had had enough of this, though. "It doesn't matter, Stark. It doesn't matter if he's a traitor or not, if he's the bad guy or a giant pod person masquerading as Walt. Nothing— *nothing*—excuses what you are doing! It's madness! It's like burning down the town and killing all the people so that they won't fall into the hands of the enemy! These people are who *you* remade them to be! I don't know who's telling the truth, or parts of it, and who's lying, but I can say that if you are who and what you say you are, then the job, the hundreds of years, has driven you crazy."

"*I will not let the enemy have you!* Particularly not Brand. What happens to you, me, any of us, doesn't matter. Our whole race is at stake here!" He paused, and sighed. "I see that my hopes, that you could be convinced by the truth to be on my side, to join me, were in vain. It's too bad. Now you will have to be made to obey with pure power. You know what that green stuff is? It's the current that runs the whole thing. It's the energy moving right through the machine from point to point. It's what's *real*. Even most of us can't sense, let alone control, it even after two, three translations. You did it as one individual, in a reincarnation. I'm impressed. More than impressed. You are going to be essential to me in replacing Tanaka. I wish it could be voluntarily, but so be it. You and the new Sugar here can take some serious conditioning and we'll turn you around. Sugar, I'm afraid you're not much of a man but you're a hell of a woman. I think it's time you became a whole new person."

"Bold talk!" Wilma snapped. "Particularly from somebody outnumbered three to one!"

"It's not quantity that counts," Stark replied with a smile. "It's *quality*."

"You're insane, Stark! Do you know that?" I screamed at him.

He laughed. "Of course I do! It is you who doesn't realize how insane you are! Reality is what we perceive it to be! Look at how you and your companions have bent and twisted this one! When you can tell the difference between us, any of us, and psychotics, you let me know! No sane person could do this!"

Suddenly we were no longer in the meeting room; instead, we were in a whirling vortex of energy, a tornado that caught us completely off guard and swept us around and around in an increasingly dizzy spiral, and down, down, toward a waiting Al Stark in the middle.

I tried to concentrate as best I could, but full concentration, full linking of the three of us, was impossible with that dizzying movement. The only thing I could think of was a huge hammer, like a gigantic lead weight, and I dropped it down again and again into the center of the maelstrom.

The result was not a thud or a sizzle but rather a splash, as if a huge rock had struck a body of water, and everything became more and more confused, the liquid energy washing over us, creating shapes, figures, both familiar and alien, there one minute, gone the next. Faces, torsos, of men, women, children, animal shapes, strange figures, known figures. . . .

And among them, too, the *others*. The great turtle that flew through the aether at us when we saw the caterpillar; the caterpillar himself, looking haughty as ever, and among them the reptilian Boojums and still others, small figures with huge black slanted eyes, starfields and galaxies of wondrous beauty, and at the end, dead center, a figure deep in shadow, a figure that loomed closer yet seemed not menacing but somehow oddly like an old friend.

I floated to it, reached out, almost touched it, and it turned and revealed itself as Cory Maddox. Then it wasn't, the figure going through a series of metamorphoses, male, female, tall, short, black, white, yellow, bizarre and comforting . . .

Yet familiar because all of them were me.

As I stood, transfixed, a figure leaped out of the swirling energy and knocked me over, expertly holding me down and looming over me. I struggled, but Angel's physical body was no match for Stark's.

He slapped me hard, again and again, the pain each time momentarily interrupting the flow of illusions and the flow of energy as well, giving me a period of gray blindness that seemed almost to give me a strobe effect on his face. Insane or not, there was no mistaking the expression on his face that shouted to everyone that he enjoyed power in all forms and he loved his work.

"I'd like to keep you just this way," he said, "but I can't. You're too dangerous to others, and I'm not quite done here yet. Don't worry so much, though! You've been killed many times before, and you'll be killed again! Nothing's permanent here, because nothing's truly real!"

A huge hand came down on my throat, and I knew I was no more than seconds away from death.

Just as suddenly as Stark had come through and struck me, something now shot out, an arm, holding a piece of pipe, and struck the security man squarely and hard on the side of the head. The shock and violence of the hit caught him completely by surprise, and I felt his grip vanish from my throat and saw his eyeballs seem to go up into the top of his head, and then he keeled over.

A man's figure loomed over me and offered me a hand. "Come on! We have to get you out of here! That won't hold him off for long!"

"Les?" I was totally in shock myself, having looked into my own grave.

"C'mon, Cory! Step on it. If he figures out it was me, we're all dead meat."

I took his hand and got rockily to my feet. "Where's my friends?" I asked him. "Where are Wilma and Cindy?"

"Wilma's all right. She's just over there. Cindy bugged out on you the moment you let go control. I don't know what's going to happen, but you don't owe her a thing."

"Angel—?"

"They're not quite getting the program Stark thinks. Let me worry about Angel. I'll get everybody over. For now, you and Wilma have to go."

"Go? Go where?"

"Alice down the rabbit hole! Feel the surge? Here it comes! Both of you! Grab it! Run like hell! You can still get killed in there and there's a lot of creepy crawlies that hang out in those things! Don't worry, though! Be alert! You'll meet Angel and the others again!"

The entire back wall of the meeting room seemed to dissolve into a great opening, swirling around, illuminated yet illuminating nothing inside, a vast cone going—where?

I turned around, saw Wilma making a run for it, and she shouted, actually screamed, at me and pointed. Les was nowhere to be seen, but Al Stark was picking himself up off the floor, and he looked mad as hell.

I didn't think twice, running for that hole and almost but not quite beating Wilma into it.

Behind, very vaguely, I could hear Al Stark yelling something, something very nasty at the top of his lungs.

"Go on! Run, you traitorous bastards! I'll get you next time! There's always a next time! That's why I always win!"

We continued to run, and the sounds faded to nothingness.

# XIII

# CURIOUSER AND CURIOUSER

I had been in a rabbit hole, of course, before that one time, or at least I *thought* that it was a rabbit hole of some kind, but it was very different than this. In fact, I was beginning to wonder if any two were alike.

Wilma was in much better shape than I was, but she stopped after a while and waited for me. She was still in Cynthia's body, and it looked like, at least for now, she was going to stay that way.

"Need some help?" she asked me. I was winded and my legs ached, and I just collapsed on the—whatever it was—inside the hole.

"Beats me," I gasped, "how Cynthia Matalon could have smoked, drugged out, done all that, and still be in that kind of shape."

"Yeah, I bet she ate like a horse, too," Wilma muttered, coming back over to me.

"Worse, the power connection is fading out on me," I told her.

"You gonna go blind again?"

"I think I was all along," I told her. "I'm not sure what

brought the vision to me when I was inside the power grid back there, but I'm losing it now. Losing it, but not losing my ability to see. If I concentrate, I can see out of *your* eyes. Kind of weird, but it works. I think if we stick together I can manage. I wonder how long these things are?"

I saw myself through Wilma's eyes, then saw her look around. It was as if we were in a large cavern, nearly but not precisely round, perhaps fifteen feet to the ceiling such as it was and a bit more from "wall" to "wall." It felt soft, a bit slick in spots, but didn't appear to have any water or other liquids there and certainly didn't seem like it was covered by anything living. Illumination was by a spiral vein that went through the whole of the structure and seemed to be made out of gently glowing colored crystals—red, green, blue, yellow, white. . . .

"I think we oughta move on," Wilma coaxed as gently but firmly as she could. "No telling what's in here, or who or what might be coming after us."

I nodded, although the idea of getting up and walking any great distance was something this thin, weak body screamed at. "Help me up. Let's go as far in as we can."

She helped me up and then put her arm around me, and we began to walk away from the world that we thought we knew, away from Al Stark and the rest, and toward the unknown.

"Les said we could still be killed in here," I warned her. "And that unfriendlies could pop up."

"I wish you didn't have that naked-savage kick to that power-gathering ceremony," she grumped. "A gun, knife, and whip would do very handy through here. In fact, it would have done pretty handy back *there* as well."

"We were playing it by ear, remember. Didn't do so well, either. I got to admit I'm astonished to still be here, still alive, no matter what the shape. You, too. I'm glad you made it through. And I think I made it a lot harder for Stark, both in whatever he's doing back there and in restarting wherever we wind up. He's lost Brand, Tanaka, and Cholder, his three top geniuses on that kind of work. I just wish I coulda got Angel out of there. The others, too, but Angel in particular."

Wilma sighed. "Yeah, I know. But what could we do?"

"At least Les said that he'd done a bait-and-switch on the programs. That Angel wasn't going to be a slave with no will of her own. Who she will become, though, I can't say."

Wilma nodded. "Or us, either. I wish we had somebody inside here who'd been here before and remembered it. I'd sure like to know what's up ahead."

"It looks like it's widening up ahead," I noted. "And brighter, too."

We cautiously advanced to what now seemed to be the edge of the tunnel and looked out onto a fantastic scene. It was an *enormous* cavern, but not anything made by nature, nor, perhaps, by humans, either, although it had certain familiar aspects to it. It hummed and there were great lights that glowed and there were odd mechanical noises here and there. Not much moved, but it was clearly all machinery, and it was like a furnace. It reminded me, in fact, of a vast computer motherboard.

The way across was clear but seemed a vast distance— perhaps a mile or more. "Do you think we can make that?" I asked nervously. "Bare feet, bare skin, in that heat and for that distance?"

"I don't think we can stay here. The last thing I am is hungry right now, but I wouldn't want to try and live here. We either cross it or we go back and face Stark, and I think we've proven we're not ready to face Stark yet."

We tried it, cautiously, in unison. It was very hot, but not hot enough to fry our feet. Still, once we started off, it was clear that you didn't want to stop for long or sit down out there.

"What do you think this all is?" Wilma asked me as we walked, briskly but not hurriedly, across the space.

"What it seems to be," I told her, "although probably it looks nothing like this. It's a representation of what is there so our minds can at least make some sense out of it. We, the twenty-eight or however many there turns out to be, are the soul of this great, vast machine, but this is a peek at some of its internal organs. We've now exited a major complex program; now we're like the cursor on a screen or a mouse or trackball—peripherals without a program with which to interact. We're being shifted, or are shifting ourselves, from one program and memory bank to another. This should be halfway, Wilma."

She looked around with mixed awe and uncertainty. "Yeah, but halfway to *what*?"

We made it, after what seemed an interminable crossing, and sank down in the still hot but relative coolness of a larger tunnel on the other side. I was exhausted and I didn't see how I was going to make it any further if nothing happened. So far we'd been lucky—it was just us.

Wilma, too, was tired now and sank to the floor beside me. "A lot more work to get out of the world alive than dead," she muttered.

"I thought you were the one who opened up rocks and trees and went through the tunnels beneath the Earth."

She chuckled. "I was. But never like this. Always in ceremonies, with trances and holy herbal aids. I saw, but it was more mental than physical."

"I—Cory, then Joshua—led a relatively clean life, except for that one period on the run," I told her. "The only experience I had with a drug wound me up in a hole talking to a smoking caterpillar."

"Oh, yeah. I've had that one."

I knew she was joking, so I didn't press it.

"I wonder what I'll come out as?" I mused. "Assuming we make it to the end."

"Huh?"

"Well, according to what we overheard, if you reincarnate you change sex, but if you translate, which is where we're heading now, you don't. But I was Cory, then Joshua, and I'm in Angel's body. Wonder which I'll wind up being?"

Wilma shrugged. "I dunno. I guess that keeps me female regardless, this trip. Shame we'll have to become other people, though. I'd really like to try this for a while."

"I wish we knew how it worked. Are we gonna be born and have to go through all that again, only at some point regaining all we know now? Or do we come in as grown-ups someplace? And, if so, how? Damn! I wish Cindy hadn't run out on us! At least she'd know *that*!"

Wilma stared at me. "Run out? What do you mean? Your rescuer hit Cindy on the head hard enough to draw blood. Cindy went down like a rock, worse than Stark did. Didn't you see the body lying there?"

I frowned. "No. I—I didn't. But I had a different kind of vision, remember, and, frankly, I wasn't looking. I went from dead to on the run. But—Les said Cindy skipped."

"No way. And there was a difference in the way he hit Stark, even where. I'm not sure if Cindy lived or died, but I knew when Stark went down he was gonna be able to get up again. And when I looked back to see if anybody was chasing us just before I jumped in here, I saw your buddy actually kneeling beside Stark as if trying to revive him. I swear that the whole idea was just to keep Stark from strangling you."

I felt my throat uneasily. "Well, thanks at least for that."

"Yeah, but he's playin' his own game, too. Who is he?"

"The project's medical doctor. Good guy, frankly. The one real friend we both made there." *But Walt Slidecker had been a friend and good guy, too.*

"A doctor! But—if he was on Stark's side, why stop him?"

I thought a moment. Assume that Les wasn't really my friend any more than Walt was, why save me?

I had a sudden, ugly reason why.

"I set them back, Wilma. They lost Brand first, and that was a major setback six years ago. Whether he caught on and killed himself, got caught in a trap, or just bugged out, only he might know, if he remembers it, but that was a huge blow. Then, before I could be stopped, I did away with the two top programmers and Brand Box experts who had worked with the big man and come back on the project. Dan and Jamie. Al was probably either not there but at his townhouse or something and got called in too late to cover. Ben Sloan is a good computer man but he's not in their league. I always thought of him as in Cory's league, but maybe I was wrong. He sure acted more like a security man for the programmers than one himself. That leaves one programmer who has familiarity to some extent with the system no matter what inexperience he has in actually operating it. I may not have worked with Brand, not so's I remember it, anyway, and I may not know what Dan and Jamie knew, but maybe Les knows me from a lot longer ago than one or two lives. Maybe I'm capable of working the thing. Stark was so filled with bloodlust he just about had to be hit by a two-by-four to stop him killing me. Maybe he didn't even realize both Dan and Jamie were dead. Les knew—his offices were over there. He would have been first called in. But if he wasn't rescuing me, then he was saving me for *them*, for himself."

Wilma nodded. "Then, when they get set up again wherever we're going, you have the most knowledge and experience. A reborn version of those two can be more quickly trained working under you. Sort of explains the appearance of this very convenient, just-in-time rabbit hole, too, don't it? Your doctor buddy opened it up. And, ten to one, he'll come after you as your old friend and savior and you might not even see or recognize Al Stark."

I sighed. Of everything that happened, this explanation made the most sense. *Damn it, who the hell wasn't against you?* "Yeah. Thanks a lot, Les, old buddy." *And poor Angel. . . .*

I pulled myself up to my feet against Wilma and she, too, got up wearily. "Let's see where this damned thing winds up," I suggested to her. "At least we'll be able to get a drink, a decent meal, and a night's sleep."

"Angel—I mean Josh—oh, hell! *Whoever* you are! I got to tell you something about the end of this road. I'm scared to death."

I started to chuckle at her identity problem, which was at least an honest one—unlike me, she didn't have to live it—but the last brought me up short. "I'd have said that nothing scares you after this."

"Nope. I was prepared for an afterlife, but not *another* life. I was prepared for the Boojums and nuts like Stark, but—this is real! For all intents and purposes, I'm dead. Stone-cold dead. I'm now walking a passage to rebirth in a world I might not know and as somebody I might not recognize. I'm scared."

I sighed. "Look, I've been through it once that I remember. We got hauled up into that thing while we were high on some kind of peyote, and we weren't sure if it was real or an illusion, but it turned out to be real. There we got some of the truth, and then we were left to either return as we were, live out our lives and die, or accept the fight and become new people. What we became was what we were pretending to be. Different bodies and prints, but basically the same general builds. We kept our first names, couldn't remember diddly about the rest until it was far too late to do anything about it, but we coped. I think that's what will happen at the end here. We'll step into it and a new program will re-form us, a very minor little program within the huge master canvas. We'll wake up, and we probably won't remember a thing about this or Stark or whatever, but, unlike Joshua and Angel, we'll have *pasts*, families, education. Then, slowly, over time, the shock will wear off and we'll begin to remember more and more until we remember all of it. You won't be Wilma, and I won't be—whoever I am now—but we'll remember being these people, and all that goes with it."

"And what then?"

"I wish I knew, but I think we all wish we could know the future. I'm going to watch for familiar things to go on. If Al Stark was Albert Starkweather in the previous one, the one in which Rick was conditioned and killed, and I was *merely* killed—and, I guess, you, too—then maybe it'll be that recognizable the next time. Maybe not. It might depend on how close this next one is to what we left. But bet on this—Stark, maybe Les, too, will be looking for me, and maybe for all of us. Somehow, the Brand Boxes transfer as well, or perhaps exist simultaneously in all planes. I'm pretty sure of that. We'll know, I think, when the time comes."

"Who makes them?" Wilma wondered. "Who makes these worlds for us?"

It suddenly hit me. "That's *right*! You out of all of us never had the experience in your present memory. If you want to know about the small ones, I think they were imagined by various of us and then made into boxed worldlets by Matt Brand. He had such an eclectic group, even eccentric, that he got a lot of variety. When? Who knows which life, or how many lives ago it might have been? The big ones, the ones like we think of as *our* world, *our* universe, they're sparked by something in one of us and then the great computer whose guts we're now walking through supplies the rest. 'Ruthless logic,' they said. Whether we'll wind up in one already made or one brand-new I can't say. We're certainly gonna wind up in the one Les and maybe Al Stark wants next."

Wilma chuckled. "Well, at least you're no Angel. 'Eclectic,' huh? Where'd you ever learn words like you're spouting now?"

"Cory, mostly, but maybe some of the rest come through. You just can't consciously get to them. They're the stuff of dreams instead."

"Now you're poetic! I—" She suddenly stopped still and I did the same, and we listened.

There were noises up ahead. Noises not of a civilization or

great machinery, but of living things. Voices, or what might
have been voices, and the sound of people or things moving.

"Ambush?" Wilma whispered.

"Could be. But who?"

"Stay back here. I'll creep forward and check."

"I'm sticking with you."

"Stay back! I know what I'm doing!"

So, I stayed, and watched her move forward, crouched
down, silent, darting from dark place to dark place in the
"cavern," until finally she came to a second opening, perhaps
a final one.

It was a circular area with high-standing smooth, barrellike
things, most five or six feet high, set out all over a glassy
smooth emerald green floor. It gave an odd impression, sort
of like a bunch of randomly placed giant capacitors, but also
sort of like the top part of a lot of pinball machines. At the
far end, where the cavern might be expected to pick up again,
there was instead an oval-shaped opening that appeared very
much like a video screen full of nothing but snow, a TV set
without a signal.

Wilma put her hand in front of her face and beckoned me
forward with a finger, but cautiously. I crept forward, blind
where I was, sticking to the wall.

I reached her in a couple of minutes and crouched down in
back of her.

The voices, if that's what they were, and the other sounds,
were definitely coming from within the chamber. Since the
source wasn't obvious, Wilma did a methodical pan of everywhere she could see, finally looking up.

The chamber definitely had bugs. Big bugs. They looked
something like big, hairy tarantulas, by which I mean monster-
movie-sized, but they were brilliantly colored and seemed to
have eyes that could go right through the midsection and look
top or bottom, and in the center disk rubbery, almost comical
faces, like smiley faces, only with those periscope eyes.

There were two of them up there, not on webs but apparently with ropelike webbing affixed firmly to one or another point. They could drop on you with it, or maybe swing out on it.

"I think I'd rather be shot than eaten by that pair," Wilma whispered so low I could hardly catch it. I couldn't disagree.

"Still," she almost hissed, "they can't cover the far route."

"How do you know?" I whispered back almost in her ear. "You can't know how much rope they have."

"Don't have to. The chamber's much wider than it is high, and those things in the middle would keep them from swinging too far."

I sighed. "Yeah, but how fast can they run?"

I was dumbfounded by the sight of the things. Were they truly some other form or life, or something escaped from one or another of the Sim worlds, or perhaps real denizens of the real world? Were they intelligent or just predators? Were they, in fact, real at all, since it certainly wasn't at all clear what the hell such creatures would eat other than us.

I had told Wilma that what we perceived as a monstrous computer motherboard was simply a representation of what was probably there. Maybe this was the same. Maybe these weren't real, live creatures at all, but traps designed to make entry into another universe by someone who was still alive pretty damned hard. When Stark came through, it would be with machine guns and flamethrowers and anything else he needed. We were two naked broads without as much as a stone or a spear.

"We have to try and get by them," I pointed out. "I don't think we can even go back. Not without help, like I had before."

She nodded, then frowned. "There's somebody down there! Over on the side they can't reach from above! Look!"

Seeing what she saw, it wasn't that hard to find the figure.

It was maybe four feet tall, rather ungainly, and dressed in a waistcoat and vest and smoking a pipe.

It was also a dodo bird.

"Welcome to Wonderland," I said in the same whisper.

The dodo walked out on its two bird legs, rather like a cross between a turkey and Charlie Chaplin, and glanced up at the spider-things. He raised a four-fingered hand and said, "Hello, old things! How are you today?"

The two spider-things twitched and whispered and muttered back and forth, and finally one said, "Hungry."

"Well, I have two people to bring through and I'd appreciate it *awfully* if you chaps would just let them through. Would you do that?" He had a great voice, like a Shakespearian actor.

"Why should we?" asked one of the creatures.

The dodo stopped and thought a moment. The mere fact that the creatures were talking to him rather than going after him showed that he was not "real" in any sense that would satisfy them, and that they knew it.

"What about if I say that should you harm them in any way, I'll bring the dragon in here and we'll have a jolly good cleansing of this room? Say what?"

"You are bluffing, bird! You are not even here. You are just an illusion!"

"But, old bean, *everything's* an illusion, don't you see? I mean, if I were *real* I would be quite, quite dead. We dodos are extinct, you know." And, with that, he walked across the open area and approached us, entering the tunnel.

Wilma had no idea what to make of the thing, but I'd seen his like before.

"Won't they come in here after us now that they know we're here?" I asked him. "Pardon me, but dodos never had a reputation for being bright."

"Oh, that's a ruddy slander!" the big bird insisted. "What we were was trusting. No creature other than humankind can even conceive of the depth of cruelty and ruthlessness that humans are capable of. Not even *those* blighters in there."

"Do you really have a dragon? Or was that just bluff?" Wilma asked him, still not quite used to talking to a creature like this yet, but accepting him as similar to those creatures she met in the shaman's underworld.

"Sorry, not really. I can, however, tell you their weakness and give you a sporting chance."

"I'm all ears," Wilma told him.

"Goodness me! I hope not! That would be *grotesque*! However, it's simple. They have certain limits. They can not touch the floor. If they do, they will get trapped and die. They can reach the top of the peglike thingies out there, but their legs are too short. There's about a foot, or a wee bit more, that anyone has going through there. You just sort of *crawl*, body on the ground, like some sort of bloody lizard, and they can't reach you. They will, however, try and panic you, and they will take advantage of any mistake."

"It's better than nothing," I responded glumly. "But what about coming around the far side, from where you did?"

"Sorry, that won't work. While it is true that they can not see you unless you move, they have more patience than a cat. The only way is the way I said. There's always a weakness, one way through, but most never figure it out. You have an advantage. I'm letting you cheat."

"Why?" Wilma asked him a little suspiciously.

"Because I was programmed to do so should certain people ever come this way, of course. And one of you is on my list, so the other profits from being with the one who is."

"What happens if we make it?" I asked him. "What happens when we go through there? Is that a new or an old creation?"

The dodo took the pipe from its beak, turned, and looked at the snow in the oval. "It was a new one, but you're not the first through. It has been constructed."

"By who? What was the premise?"

The dodo shrugged. "I have absolutely no idea. One's as good as the next, I suppose. Don't you think so?"

"Maybe," I replied. "So—who programmed you?"

"The caterpillar."

"Who is the caterpillar?"

"Dear girl, I'm just a lousy little computer program. How on Earth would I know *that*?" He reached into his vest pocket and looked at his watch. "Goodness me! Time to be off!"

"Wait!" Wilma cried, but it was no use.

"Ta-ta, and good luck!" the dodo said, sounding sincere, and, with that, he vanished.

"Do we trust him?" Wilma asked.

"I think we have to," I told her. "The worst part is, because I've got to use your eyes, I'm going to have to follow you."

"Well, that's no worse than going first," she sighed, then took a few deep breaths. "You know what he meant?"

I nodded.

"Keep that super-long hair under control or they'll grab you by it," she warned. "Stick close. I'm not used to being thin enough to get away with this myself."

"Wilma—be careful!" I said, feeling tears coming to my eyes. "I don't want to lose you, too."

"I'll sure do my best," she promised, then took a few more deep breaths and went down flat on the floor. "Use your arms. Pull, don't crawl!" And out she went.

The spiders reacted almost immediately, and we both froze just barely exposed out on the green floor—which was, in fact, cold rather than warm or hot like the rest. I felt the thing go over us, so close that we probably could have impaled it with a knife had either of us had one, felt the breeze from its passing, then its breeze back.

Wilma was suddenly on the move again, and I was right behind her. Frankly, it was uncomfortable to crawl like this, and between the breasts and the hair I had a difficult and even painful few yards, but we made it into the "pegs," as the dodo had called them.

There were thumps above us and on both sides.

One of the spider-things laughed. "Now *there's* two nice pieces of ass!"

"Rump roast! Rump roast!" the other chanted like some demented little kid in a chainsaw movie.

"They're trying to panic us!" I called to Wilma. "Ignore them!"

"I wish I could, or that they would ignore me!" Wilma shot back, but she proceeded on in littler units now, partly pushing against the big, smooth pegs or whatever they were with her legs when she could.

Now and again one of the creatures just above us on top of the pegs would reach down, and once I thought I actually felt hair brush against my rear end, but they neither panicked either of us nor actually touched us. It occurred to me that unless their anatomies were changeable they probably couldn't see down. And if they really tried to extend themselves with that limited vision to get us from the top of the pegs, they risked contact with the floor.

*Damned simple video game, but painful as all hell,* I thought. And, of course, that was what this was. A video game. And we had the cheat sheet.

We cleared the pegs on the other side. By now I'd caught my hair under me several times and every attempt to free it up just felt like it was being pulled out by the roots. I had to stick with it, though; if I could stand the damned pain, I very shortly wouldn't need to think about the hair!

Wilma made it to the edge of the oval, but did not go through. Instead, she turned and looked back at me.

"Go on through!" I told her. "I'll make it!"

"No you won't! That hair is driving you nuts! Besides, you're the important one. You have to go through! I'm just along for the ride!"

"That's not what the dodo said! The dodo said one of us, but not which one! You have to go through. I'll make it!"

She turned again and was now facing me, her legs virtually in the oval.

"Tickles," she said. "Now, give me your hands! I'm gonna pull you through!"

I put out my arms, reluctantly, and she took them, and then started wiggling back, back, into the oval. Suddenly she cried out, as much in surprise as anything else from the looks of it, and the look on her face was indescribable.

The snow came out of the oval, enveloped her, and she was just gone. I was suddenly totally blind and still at least five feet from it. Five feet . . . so short a distance. But the hair! That damned *hair*! I would have to turn in order to free enough of it to make the last little bit.

I did, and started feeding it out, relief flooding through me. Then, suddenly, from above, I felt something grab hold of the hair and say, *"GOTCHA!"*

"Like *hell* you do!" I screamed, and put every bit of will, strength, effort, all that I had, into simply lunging forward. The spider-thing simply wasn't prepared for it. I felt it suddenly lose its grip for a moment, regain it, but by that point I had momentum on my side.

I plunged headfirst into the oval, into another world, another life, another total existence. Behind me was all that I thought I knew, and all those people I had thought I had known as well. Ahead was the Unknown, but it was at least an honest Unknown.

My enemies would soon be in pursuit, and my only future lay in somehow finding the knowledge to not just survive, but find out what if anything truth really was.

No more playing oyster! This time I was going to be the Walrus!

*The Wonderland Gambit* will continue.

# ABOUT THE AUTHOR

Jack L. Chalker was born in Baltimore, Maryland, on December 17, 1944. He began reading at an early age and naturally gravitated to what are still his twin loves: science fiction and history. While still in high school, Chalker began writing for the amateur science-fiction press and in 1960 launched the Hugo-nominated amateur magazine *Mirage*. A year later he founded The Mirage Press, which grew into a major specialty publishing company for nonfiction and reference books about science fiction and fantasy. During this time, he developed correspondence and friendships with many leading SF and fantasy authors and editors, many of whom wrote for this magazine and his press. He is an internationally recognized expert on H.P. Lovecraft and on the specialty press in SF and fantasy.

After graduating with twin majors in history and English from Towson State College in 1966, Chalker taught high school history and geography in the Baltimore city public schools with time out to serve with the 135th Air Commando Group, Maryland Air National Guard, during the Vietnam era and, as a sideline, sound engineered some of the period's outdoor rock concerts. He received a graduate degree in the esoteric field of the History of Ideas from John Hopkins University in 1969.

His first novel, *A Jungle of Stars*, was published in 1976, and two years later, with the major popular success of his novel *Midnight at the Well of Souls*, he quit teaching to become a full-time professional novelist. That same year, he married Eva C. Whitley on a ferryboat in the middle of the Susquehanna River and moved to rural western Maryland. Their first son, David, was born in 1981.

Chalker is an active conversationalist, a traveler who has been through all fifty states and in dozens of foreign countries, and a member of numerous local and national organizations ranging from the Sierra Club to The American Film Institute, the Maryland Academy of Sciences, and the Washington Science Fiction Association, to name a few. He retains his interest in consumer electronics, has his own satellite dish, and frequently reviews computer hardware and software for national magazines. For five years, until the magazine's demise, he had a regular column on science fantasy publishing in *Fantasy Review* and continues to write a column on computers for *S-100 Journal*. He is a three-term past treasurer of the Science Fiction and Fantasy Writers of America, a noted speaker on science fiction at numerous colleges and universities as well as a past lecturer at the Smithsonian and the National Institutes of Health, and a well-known auctioneer of science fiction and fantasy art, having sold over five million dollars' worth to date.

Chalker has received many writing awards, including the Hamilton-Brackett Memorial Award for his "Well World" books, the Gold Medal of the prestigious *West Coast Review of Books for Spirits of Flux and Anchor*, the Dedalus Award, and the E.E. Smith Skylark Award for his career writings. He is also a passionate lover of steamboats and particularly ferryboats and has ridden over three hundred ferries in the U.S. and elsewhere.

He lives with his wife, Eva, sons David and Steven, a Pekingese named Marva Chang, and Stonewall J. Pussycat, the world's dumbest cat, in the Catoctin Mountain region of western Maryland, near Camp David. A short story collection with autobiographical commentary, *Dance Band on the Titanic*, was published by Del Rey Books in 1988.

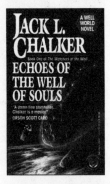
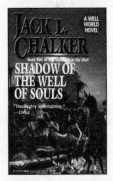
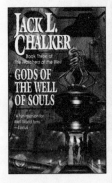